MATTHEW PLAMPIN

The Devil's Acre

HARPER

Harper
An imprint of HarperCollins*Publishers*
77–85 Fulham Palace Road,
Hammersmith, London W6 8JB

www.harpercollins.co.uk

This paperback edition 2010
1

First published in Great Britain by
HarperCollins*Publishers* 2010

Previously published in hardback as *The Gun-Maker's Gift*

Matthew Plampin asserts the moral right to
be identified as the author of this work

Map © MAPCO 2010

A catalogue record for this book
is available from the British Library

ISBN: 978 0 00 727397 3

Set in Meridien by Palimpsest Book Production Ltd,
Grangemouth, Stirlingshire

Printed and bound in Great Britain by
Clays Ltd, St Ives plc

Mixed Sources

Product group from well-managed
forests and other controlled sources
www.fsc.org Cert no. SW-COC-001806
© 1996 Forest Stewardship Council

FSC is a non-profit international organisation established
to promote the responsible management of the world's forests.
Products carrying the FSC label are independently certified
to assure consumers that they come from forests that are managed
to meet the social, economic and ecological needs
of present and future generations.

Find out more about HarperCollins and the environment at
www.harpercollins.co.uk/green

For Sarah

'People may differ about matters of opinion, or even about religion; but how can they differ about right and wrong? Right is right; and wrong is wrong; and if a man cannot distinguish them properly, he is either a fool or a rascal: that's all.'

George Bernard Shaw, *Major Barbara*, Act I

'I will tell nobody what I supply my arms for. If you want to buy, and say you will buy ten thousand of them, and will give me a fair price, you can have them today.'

Samuel Colt, from the minutes of the Select Committee on Small Arms

PART ONE

Bessborough Place

1

Colonel Colt was on his feet a good five seconds before the carriage had come to a halt, pulling open the door and leaping outside. A brisk spring wind was sucked into the vehicle like a mouthful of cold water, rushing underneath the seats, swirling through the hat-racks and almost scattering Edward's sheaf of Colt documents across the floor. He tightened his grip on it, coolly shuffling the pile back into shape, and conducted a quick inventory. Something critical was missing. Looking around, he saw a finely made wooden case, slim and about fifteen inches long, resting upon the narrow shelf directly above where Colt had been sitting. He tucked it under his arm and followed his new employer down into the street.

Colt was issuing orders to the coachman while straightening his broad-brimmed Yankee hat. Behind him towered a mighty rank of Italianate façades, among the grandest in all London, belonging to a variety of venerable clubs, learned institutions and government offices. Edward could not help but be impressed. I've harnessed myself to a real rocket here, he thought; Pall Mall, the seat of power, on my very first morning! This post in the Colt Company was his great chance – an opportunity of a kind granted only to a few. To prove your worth to a man such as Colonel Colt was to set yourself upon a sure path to advancement. He checked his necktie (his best, claret silk, knotted with special care) and caught sight of his reflection in a panel of the Colonel's mustard-yellow barouche. Possibly the largest private carriage Edward

3

had ever ridden in, it stood out among the clattering cabs of London like a great lacquered beetle in a parade of ants. Upon its glossy surface he was reduced to a near silhouette, a smart, anonymous professional gentleman in a black frock-coat and top hat, his face obscured by shadow.

The Colonel glanced over at him. 'Right here, Mr Lowry – the Board of Ordnance,' he said, nodding curtly towards one of buildings. Then he bounded up the flight of stone steps before it, surprisingly swiftly for someone of his size, and shoved his way through a set of tall double doors.

Edward went after him, feeling both admiration and a little amusement. The American entrepreneur went about his business with a single-minded vigour far beyond anything he'd seen during his six years in the banks and trading houses of the City. This promised to be interesting indeed.

The hallway beyond the doors was every bit as magnificent as the building's exterior, its floors covered with thick carpets, its walls lined with marble columns and its lofty ceiling positively groaning with gilded plasterwork. Portraits of British generals hung wherever one cared to look, their grizzled faces arranged into expressions of proud confidence as they stood to attention or leaned against cannon, conquered enemy citadels burning behind them. Pervading this sumptuous environment was an official hush so deep and still that it was almost accusatory. This is a place of the very highest importance, it seemed to say, where decisions are made that affect nothing less than the future of Great Britain; what the deuce are *you* doing here?

Entirely indifferent to this oppressive atmosphere, Colonel Colt strode up to the main desk and bade the smart clerk behind it good morning. The stare that met this salutation told Edward at once that they were not expected; no appointment had been made, and the clerk's stance in such situations was abundantly clear. Unabashed, Colt went on to ask if he might drop in on Tom Hastings, an old friend of his who he believed was currently the Storekeeper of the Ordnance. He was informed that *Sir Thomas* was fully engaged that morning, and would not receive visitors without prior arrangement in any case.

'So he's in the building, at least,' the Colonel interrupted with a hard smile. 'Will you be so kind as to tell him that Sam Colt is at his door, and wishes to have a word? He'll be interested, I guarantee it.'

The clerk would not cooperate, though, not even after Colt had introduced the possibility of a five-shilling note being left right there on his counter, to find whatever owner pleased God. So this is it, Edward thought. We are to fall at the first hurdle. It wasn't quite the result he'd expected. The Colonel looked down at the carpet for a full minute, still smiling but growing red in the cheek. Suddenly, he barked out an impatient curse and lurched away to the right, cutting across the hall to a stairwell and sprinting straight up it.

Instinctively, Edward fell in behind him, ignoring the clerk's protestations and the heavy footfalls that were soon gathering at his heels. Together they dashed through the corridors of the Board of Ordnance, skidding around corners and thundering down flights of stairs. Colt threw open doors at random, demanding directions to Hastings's office from the startled scriveners within – a good many of whom, Edward noticed, were occupied with newspapers and novels rather than government business. In the end, as the crowd of their pursuers grew in both numbers and proximity, Colt simply bellowed out the name of his contact as he ran in the vain hope that this might draw him forth.

They were finally cornered in a remote lobby. A part of Edward was convinced that the police would now be fetched and they'd be led from that place in chains; but he also found that he had an unaccountable faith in Colonel Colt's ability to rescue them from difficulty. Sure enough, instead of arrest, their detainment was followed by a brief and intense negotiation, during which the Colonel imparted his expectations with considerable forcefulness. A more senior figure was summoned, who in turn sent off messengers to several different regions of the building; and soon afterwards Colt was told that an audience had been granted with Lord Clarence Paget, Secretary to the Master-General of Ordnance, in a mere twenty minutes' time. They were then taken to a vestibule on the second floor and left to wait.

There was a row of chairs against one wall, but as Colonel Colt showed no inclination to sit Edward felt it best that he remain on his feet as well. The two men removed their hats, and for the first time that day Edward was able to take a proper look at his employer. The Colonel must have been about forty, fifteen years older than Edward himself. He stood in the centre of the vestibule with his feet placed apart like a Yankee Henry VIII; he also shared the famous king's imposing, barrel-chested build, and had the same small, sharp features set into a broad expanse of face. This was combined in Colt with the mottled, scarlet-shot complexion of the serious drinker, a reddish, close-trimmed beard and a head of dense brown curls which a generous lashing of hair oil had done little to order. His clothes were all the very best, and new. The bottle-green coat he wore was square-cut at the bottom in the American fashion, and had a lining of thick black fur which evoked something of his enormous, untamed homeland; of bears and buffalo, of great snow-capped mountains and rolling plains, of gold-panning and Red Indians; a place of fortune-seeking and wild adventure, very far indeed from the mud and grit of grey London.

Colt started to shake his head slowly, his mouth forming the beginnings of a scowl. They had done astonishingly well, in Edward's opinion, but the Colonel was clearly far from pleased. Adjusting the case beneath his arm – it was rather heavy, in truth – he asked if anything was amiss. The gun-maker took what appeared to be a twist of tarred rope from his coat pocket, along with a small clasp-knife. Opening the blade, he cut off a piece about the size of a thumbnail and pushed it inside his lower lip. It was chewing tobacco, Edward realised, the great Yankee vice.

'I know Paget of old, Mr Lowry,' he muttered, his jaw working away ill-temperedly. 'This'll come to nothing.'

Lord Clarence Paget was in the later part of middle age, long-limbed and plainly dressed with a large, squareish forehead. He was seated behind a desk, finishing off a letter with a fastidious air. His office had two wide windows that looked out over the treetops of the Mall and St James's Park; the branches, bare a fortnight earlier, were now dusted with budding leaves. The room was sparsely furnished – just a white marble fireplace, a couple of chairs and some mahogany bookcases – but it was packed with evidence of the work conducted within it. Framed prints of artillery pieces lined the walls, mechanisms from a multiplicity of firearms were arranged along the mantelpiece and the bookshelves, and scale models of cannon stood upon the desk, weighting down piles of official-looking documents and incomprehensible technical sketches.

Paget did not stop writing as they entered. 'You have forced this conference upon me, Colonel, so you must forgive my ignorance of what brings you here today. I don't claim to know how things are conducted in America, but in Great Britain it is customary to write first and arrange a meeting time that is convenient for both parties.'

'Guns, Paget.' Colt drawled out the name, biting off its end – *Paa-jit* – a pronunciation that had a distinctly belittling effect. The man's high birth clearly meant nothing to him at all. 'That's what brings me here. What else could it be?' He took a seat without waiting to be offered it, indicating that Edward should sit in the chair beside his. Then he extended a hand for the case, waving it over with a twitch of his fingers. 'This here's Mr Edward Lowry, my London secretary.'

Paget put a flourishing signature on his letter, scattered some sand on the ink and then laid down his pen, finally giving them his full attention. 'Your *London* secretary, Colonel?' he asked pointedly.

Colt did not answer. Instead, he flipped the catch on the front of the case and opened it up. He paused for a moment, an expert, showman-like touch; Edward caught a glimpse of mulberry velvet inside, fitted around a piece of polished walnut. Almost reverentially, the American gun-maker lifted out a revolving pistol, raising it before him for Paget to inspect.

Edward shifted slightly, feeling his pulse quicken. This was the closest he had yet come to one of the Colonel's creations. It was a fine thing indeed, beautiful even, over a foot long with a sleek shape very different from the artless contraptions that cluttered Paget's shelves. Some parts around the trigger had been cast in bright brass, but the main body of the weapon was steel, finished to a hard, lustrous blue so full and dark that it was close to black. An intricate pattern of leaves and vines had been pressed along the barrel, curling onwards into the corners of the frame; and a line of ships, sails full, cruised in formation around the cylinder.

'The Navy,' declared Colt with great satisfaction. 'Named for the Texas Navy, my very first customers of any note, who used my guns to crush the Mexicans at Campeche. This here's the third model, and the best by some distance. Thirty-six calibre – it'll punch a hole clean through a door at five hundred yards.'

Paget regarded the gun for a moment or two and then looked back to his letter. Edward could scarcely believe it: he was unimpressed. 'The British Government is perfectly aware of your revolvers, Colonel. I fail to see why this warranted my attention so urgently.'

The Colonel took this in his stride. 'I'm showing you this particular piece, Mr Paget,' he replied with heavy emphasis, 'as it will serve as the mainstay of my Pimlico factory.'

This regained the official's interest. His eyes flickered back up to his visitors. 'I beg your pardon?'

'What you see here is a Connecticut gun,' Colt enlarged, chewing on his plug of tobacco, 'hence these bits of brass, which I know John Bull has no taste for. Within the month, though, my premises down by the Thames will be turning out *London* Colts – pistols made by English hands, and from English materials. The machinery employed is of my own invention, and fully patented; the system of labour is entirely unique; and the combination of the two will lead to a gun factory without equal in the civilised world. Certainly nothing this country has at present comes close. It'll be able to produce hundreds upon hundreds of these peerless arms,' here he raised up the Navy once again, rotating his thick wrist to give a complete view, 'in the blink of an eye – fast enough to meet any order your Queen might see fit to place. And you can be sure that my prices

8

will reflect this ease of production.' Colt sat back, adding carelessly, 'Bessborough Place is the address.'

Edward had seen this factory. It had been the site of his first meeting with the Colonel, in fact, when he'd won his position with some assured talk of past dealings with the steel-men of Sheffield – and a spot of bluster about how deeply impressed he'd been by the Colt stand in the Great Exhibition two years before. His enduring memory of the pistol works itself was of the machine floor, a large, open area occupied by Colonel Colt's renowned devices, smelling strongly of grease and raw, unfinished metal. These machines had a functional ugliness; spindly limbs, drill-bits and elaborate clamps were mounted upon frames in arrangements of mystifying, asymmetrical complexity. Everywhere, laid out across the floor like giant tendons, were the canvas belts that would eventually link the machines to the factory's engine, via the long brass cylinder that hung in the centre of the machine-room's ceiling. A handful of engineers had been attempting to connect one of these belts to the cylinder, cursing as it slipped free and fell away. Edward had overheard enough of their conversation to realise that they were encountering some serious problems in setting up the works. Colt's sweeping claims to Paget were therefore largely false – but the secretary nodded in support of them nonetheless.

Once again, however, Paget would not supply the desired reaction. He was neither intrigued nor delighted to hear of Colt's bold endeavours; if anything he looked annoyed. 'Perhaps, Colonel, you would be so good as to tell me why Her Majesty's armed forces might possibly require your blessed pistols in such absurd numbers.'

At this, Colt's easy charm grew strained. 'My guns are in great demand throughout the American states,' he purred through gritted teeth. 'Countless military trials have demonstrated their superiority over the weapons of my competitors. They are credited by many veterans with securing our recent victory over Mexico. But what might interest you particularly, as a representative of Great Britain, is their effectiveness in battle against savage tribes – against the infernal red men with which my country is plagued.

I witnessed it for myself against the Seminoles down in Florida, and the Comanche have been put down quite soundly around the borders of Texas. Small parties of cavalry have seen off many times their number. And this is to name but two theatres. There are dozens more.'

Images of slaughter came unbidden into Edward's mind. He suppressed them immediately. You are a gun merchant now, he told himself. Such claims are your stock in trade.

Paget was looking back at the Colonel in utter puzzlement, not understanding the connection he was attempting to make. 'What the devil does this have to do with –'

'I'm telling you all of this because of your country's current travails in Africa, at the Cape,' Colt clarified, a little sharply. 'Your unfortunate war against the rebellious Kaffirs. The savage, for all his lack of Christian feeling and mental sophistication, has learned one important thing – our rifles fire *but once*. This is how their tactics against us have developed. They feint, and we shoot; and then, while we scrabble to reload, their main force charges at us from the opposite direction, gutting our helpless soldiers with their spears, or dragging them off into the bush to meet horrible fates in some bloody pagan ritual.'

Edward found that he had something to add here – something that would aid their argument. 'Excuse me, my lord,' he said with careful courtesy, 'but my cousin is serving in Africa with the 73rd. He has written to me at length of the terrors of Watercloof Ridge, and the sore need for repeating arms. He believes that they would force an unconditional surrender.'

Colonel Colt leaned forward. 'There we have it, Paget, straight from a soldier on the front lines. The tomahawking red men, seeing a company of Texas rangers firing at them not once but *six times*, break in crazy panic.' He slapped a hand against his thigh. 'Your Kaffirs could be made to do the same!'

Paget was sitting quite still. He remained unpersuaded. 'Regardless of the experiences of your secretary's cousin,' he began sardonically, 'it is generally understood that the Kaffir war is coming to a close. Both the tribes and the rebels have been dispersed, and the violated land has been reclaimed for the Crown. There is no need for revolving pistols or any other nonsense.'

This threw Colt for a fraction of a second; then he began shaking his head irritably. 'Wars against savages are never finished so easily, Paget – trust me on this. They've chosen to leave off for now but they'll be back. True victory lies only in the complete extermination of the aggressors. You'll have to hunt 'em down, and the revolver is the finest tool for that piece of work. An army supplied with revolvers, with six-shooting *Colt* revolvers, is the only way it's to be done.'

The noble official chose to respond only with resolute, uncooperative silence. This silence lengthened, growing decidedly tense. Edward glanced at his employer. The Colonel was staring at the mantelpiece. Without speaking, he handed the Navy and its case back to the secretary and got to his feet. Rising to his full height, the gun-maker seemed to expand, to fill the office, his wild curly head brushing the brass chandelier and his back pressing against the book-shelves behind him. He crossed over to the fireplace in two crashing steps and scooped something up, a black frown on his face.

Edward twisted in his chair; the Colonel was holding another revolver, hefting its weight with a critical snort. The secretary saw immediately that this second pistol was no Colt. There were only five chambers in the cylinder, for a start, and it was the colour of old iron. It had the look of a mere instrument, rough, angular and artless, wholly lacking the craftsmanship of the Colonel's six-shooting Navy. Also, even to Edward's inexpert gaze, it was clear that the mechanism was different. There was no hammer – this pistol did not need to be cocked before it could fire.

Colt returned his gaze. 'This here, Mr Lowry,' he said, 'is the latest revolver of my chief English rival, Mr Adams of London Bridge. And it is an inferior device in every respect.' He turned to the nobleman behind the desk. 'It pains me to discover such a thing in your ownership, Paget. It seems to suggest that agreements have already been reached, and government contracts drawn up for our Mr Adams – that I may be wasting my breath talking with you right now.' Angling his head, the Colonel spat his plug into the grate; it made a flat chiming sound as it hit the iron. Then he raised the Adams pistol, pointing it towards the nearest window as if aiming up a shot.

'Colonel Colt,' said Paget, rather more quickly than usual, 'I must ask you to put down that weapon, this instant. It is still –'

'I invented the revolving pistol, Paget,' the Colonel interrupted. 'I *invented* it. Even you must accept that this Adams here is little better than a goddamn forgery, and a second-rate one at that. We went over this in fifty-one, during my last sojourn in London – must we go over it again?'

Paget opened his mouth to make an acerbic riposte; but before he could speak, Colt rocked back on his heel, swinging the Adams's hexagonal barrel about so that it was directed straight at the centre of the official's chest. Edward gave a start, nearly dropping the Navy to the floor. This was a clear step up from bloodthirsty banter. He looked from one man to other, wondering what was to happen next.

The Secretary to the Master-General of Ordnance leapt up from his chair with a shocked exclamation, moving around the side of the desk. All colour was struck from his pinched face. Calmly, the Colonel followed his progress with the Adams, keeping him before it.

'The main spring in these double-action models is just too damn *tight*, y'see,' the gun-maker went on, his manner aggressively conversational. 'It requires such pressure to be applied to the trigger that a fellow's aim is thrown off completely. Now, watch the barrel, Paget, and watch it closely – you too, Mr Lowry.'

The ordnance official lifted up his hands. 'Colonel Colt, please –'

Colt pulled the trigger. There was a shallow click; and sure enough, as the cylinder rotated, the Adams's barrel jerked down by perhaps an inch. To stress his point, the Colonel repeated the action, with the same result. 'You both see that?'

Paget staggered, almost as if he had actually been shot, leaning against his desk for support. 'It is *loaded*, by God!' he blurted. 'One of the – the chambers is still loaded after a demonstration earlier in the week. I was waiting for a sergeant-at-arms to come up and empty it for me. Put it down, sir, I *beg* you!'

Colonel Colt, magnificently unperturbed by this revelation, examined the pistol's cylinder for a moment before knocking out a ball and an issue of black powder into the palm of his hand. 'Hell's bells, Paget,' he growled, 'are you such a fairy prince that you're unable to remove the charge from a goddamn revolver?'

Edward exhaled, the blood humming through his trembling fingertips, trying to work out if the Colonel had known for certain which chamber the bullet had been in. Surely he must have done. He was sauntering back across the room, continuing to act as if nothing whatsoever was wrong – as if he was, and always had been, the master of the situation.

'My point is made, I think,' Colt pronounced. 'If you honestly wish to equip Her Majesty's troops with such an unsound weapon – troops who are battling savage Negroes to the death even as we speak – well, Paget my friend, that mistake is yours to make.'

The gun-maker poured the powder and bullet onto the desk, the tiny lead ball bouncing twice against the wood before disappearing onto the carpet. Laying the Adams revolver stock-first before the still-petrified Paget, he looked at Edward and then nodded towards the door. Their audience was over.

The Colt carriage was waiting for them on Pall Mall. Edward climbed inside and recoiled with an oath, almost losing his balance. A man was tucked in the far corner, dozing away peacefully with his hands folded over his chest; woken by Edward's entrance, he stirred and let out a massive yawn. Completely unconcerned to have been so discovered, this intruder then heaved himself up, bending back an arm until he elicited a loud crack from one of his shoulder joints. In his mid-thirties, he had a long, horse-like face, a Roman nose and languid, greyish eyes. His clothes were fine but worn, and looked as if they had been slept in the night before. There was an air of gentlemanly entitlement about him, despite the clear signs of dissipation and financial hardship. He looked over at Edward and smiled sleepily.

'You must be the new secretary,' he said. A good deal of the polish had been scraped from his voice, but it was still plainly that of a well-born Englishman. 'So pleased to make your acquaintance.'

Before Edward could demand to know who this character was and what the devil he was doing in the Colt carriage, the Colonel climbed in, having given the coachman his directions. 'Alfie, you goddamn wastrel,' he muttered to the man by way of greeting, sitting down opposite him, 'I was wondering if you'd honour us with your company today.' He took off his hat, setting it upon his knee. 'Mr Lowry, this here's Mr Richards, my London press agent. He was supposed to accompany us in to the Board of Ordnance this morning, but clearly did not deem it worth his precious time.'

Edward sat next to the Colonel. There was an old familiarity between his employer and Mr Richards. This was an unwelcome development.

'My apologies, Samuel,' said Richards with a shrug, settling on the carriage's full cushions and refolding his hands. 'My schedule simply would not permit it.'

Colt looked at him disbelievingly, pulled off one of his calfskin gloves and then laid his naked hand against his brow. 'By Christ, my *head*,' he grumbled. 'I could surely use an eye-opener about now.'

Immediately, Richards produced a slim bottle from his frock-coat and tossed it across the carriage – no mean feat as they were moving by now, cutting back out into the traffic. Colt caught it with similar dexterity, gratefully tugging out the stopper and taking a long drink. This simple but well-practised exchange laid bare the nature of their relationship. Both were devoted to drink, and had no doubt shared a series of adventures about the city during the Colonel's previous visits. Richards had thus managed to earn the Colonel's indulgence, if not his trust.

14

'You still have today's pistol, I see.'

'I was disinclined to make a gift of it on this occasion.' Colt took another slug of liquor, sucking it through his teeth. 'We saw Paget.'

Richards was aghast; he too clearly knew Lord Paget. 'Was no one else available? What of old Tom Hastings?'

Colt shook his head, saying that it had been Paget or nothing. He gave a brief summary of the meeting, failing to mention his practical experiment with the Adams revolver but admitting freely that the door had been pretty much slammed in their faces.

'Mr Lowry here fought his corner, though,' he added. 'A cousin soldiering in Africa, saying my guns would force the savage foe to surrender! Why, he came at it like a seasoned operator. Nothing of the greenhorn about our Mr Lowry! Potential there, Alfie, real potential – like I told you.'

Edward grinned, well pleased by the gun-maker's praise. Colt plainly thought that he'd invented the cousin at the Cape to help win over Paget. This he most definitely hadn't – Sergeant-Major Arthur Lowry was very real, although in truth the half-dozen letters Edward had received from him contained only a single passing reference to revolving pistols and gave no indication of Arthur's opinion of their merits. He decided to keep all this to himself. Why risk spoiling the Colonel's contentment?

Richards was looking at the new secretary again. There was laughter in his eyes, and a certain opposition too. He sees me just as I see him, Edward thought: as a potential competitor, an adversary within the Colt Company. Edward found that he was unworried by this. Let the dishevelled fool try to knock me down, he thought, and see where it gets him.

The press agent stretched out luxuriantly, placing his muddy boots on the seat beside Edward, just a touch too close to the edge of the secretary's coat. 'He certainly seems like a sound fellow – a good London lad.' Richards paused to pick something from between his large, stained teeth. 'Not actually a *cockney*, I hope?'

Edward met this with careful good humour. 'No, sir, I hail

from the village of Dulwich. My father was a schoolmaster there.'

Richards inclined his head, accepting the bottle back from Colt. 'So you are seeking to rise above this rather humble background – to improve your lot under the guidance of the good Colonel. No doubt you expect that before too long you'll be at the head of one of his factories.' He took a lingering drink. 'A Colt manager or somesuch.'

This was exactly the future that Edward had predicted for himself a couple of nights before, while out celebrating his appointment with his friends; he'd declared it nothing less than a blasted *certainty*, in fact, standing up on a tavern stool, liquor spilling from his raised glass and running down inside his sleeve. The secretary looked over at his employer. Colt was staring out of the window at the elegant townhouses of St James Square, oblivious to their exchange.

'I have my professional goals, Mr Richards, of course,' he replied, 'but my only concern at present is to serve the Colonel's interests to the best of my abilities.' He cleared his throat. 'I have long been a sincere admirer of both the Colonel's inventions and the dedicated manner in which he conducts his business.'

One of Richards's eyebrows rose by a caustic quarter-inch. 'And how did you come to hear of the position? It was not widely advertised.'

'Through an interested friend,' Edward answered lightly, 'that's all. No mystery there, Mr Richards.'

The secretary thought of Saul Graff, the fellow who'd passed on the tip to him. Graff was like a voracious, information-seeking weed, his tendrils forever breaking out across fresh territories; God alone knew how he'd found out about this particular vacancy, but his timing had been faultless. He was owed a slap-up dinner at the very least – although he doubtlessly had his own reasons for wanting Edward Lowry placed with Colt.

'An *interested friend*. How very deuced fortunate for you, Mr Lowry.' Richards held the bottle up to the window, trying to ascertain how much spirit was left inside. 'Sam tells me that you know a thing or two about the buying and selling of steel.'

'I do, at a clerical level at any rate. I was in the City – the trading house of Carver & Weight's, to be exact.'

This jerked the Colonel from his reverie. 'Goddamn City men!' he snapped. 'Scoundrelly rogues, the lot of 'em. I do believe that I've saved you from a truly ignominious existence there, Mr Lowry.' He gave his secretary a grave, forbidding look. 'A life lived among stocks and shares, generating money for its own sake alone – why, you'd better blow out your brains at once and manure some honest man's ground with your carcass than hang your ambition on so low a peg. You get hold of some steel for me, boy, and we'll damn well do something with it, not just sell it on for a few measly dollars of profit.'

It gladdened Edward to hear this. While at Carver & Weight's he'd grown tired of the abstractions of the trading floor and had felt a growing hunger for what he came to think of as *real business*, where manufacturers innovated and improved, and communicated directly with their customers – where things were accomplished beyond speculation and self-enrichment. He was fast reaching the conclusion that Colonel Colt, with his masterful inventions and determination to win the custom not only of men but of entire nations, was the best employer he could have wished for.

The gun-maker cut himself a fresh wad of tobacco, effectively closing the topic of his secretary's regrettable early life and moving them on to other matters. He'd resolved to send off a letter to Ned Dickerson, his patent lawyer in America, concerning Robert Adams, and began to dictate in an oddly direct style, delivering his words as if Dickerson was seated before him – telling him angrily that the 'John Bull diddler' would not make another cent from his goddamn forgeries, not if there was a single earthy thing that they could do about it. As he took all this down, Edward got the sense that the campaign against Adams had already been a long and bitter one, with no resolution in sight. Alfred Richards, meanwhile, devoted his attentions to what remained of the bottle.

Some minutes passed, Colt's language becoming bafflingly technical as he detailed the precise matters of engineering

17

that the lawyer was to direct his attention towards; then he stopped speaking mid-sentence. Edward looked up to discover that they were on Regent Street; a long row of shining, plate-glass shop windows offered disjointed reflections of their mustard-coloured vehicle as it swept around the majestic, stuccoed arc of the Quadrant. After only a few moments they turned again, heading off towards Savile Row. Colonel Colt was putting on his hat, preparing to disembark; and seconds later the carriage drew up before the frontage of one of London's very smartest tailors.

'New waistcoats,' said Colt by way of explanation. 'I'm out in society a good deal in the coming weeks, and thought it a prudent investment. You two gentlemen remain here. I shan't be very long.'

The press agent's grey eyes followed the Colonel all the way to the tailor's counter. Edward watched him closely, certain that battle was about to begin. It was only when Colt's arms were outstretched and a tape-measure was being run across his back that Richards finally spoke.

'So how large *exactly*,' he asked, 'were the perimeters of the explosion?'

This was not what Edward had been expecting. He begged Richards's pardon, pleading ignorance of any such blast.

The press agent responded with a small, whinnying laugh. 'Why, Mr Lowry, I refer of course to the explosion of our beloved master when Paget first mentioned the name of Robert Adams!'

Somewhat patronisingly, Richards revealed that throughout the Colonel's previous sojourn in London at the time of the Great Exhibition in 1851, when he had made an initial, more modest attempt to establish a European outpost, Clarence Paget had been an energetic partisan for the cause of their chief English rival. He had (they suspected) encouraged opposition to Colt at every level within the British Government, rigged various official tests and leaked negative reports on the American's weapons to the press.

'Since returning, the good Colonel has not so much as mentioned Adams revolvers before today; but after an unplanned meeting with Paget he's sending vehement missives on the subject straight back to his legal mastiff in America. It don't take a detective genius to piece it together, Mr Lowry.'

Edward put away the unfinished letter. 'The subject was raised, certainly.'

'And what, pray, was said?'

Realising that Richards would learn about the incident sooner or later anyway, Edward related what had happened up in Paget's office as neutrally as he could manage.

The press secretary was heaving with mirth long before he'd finished. 'Well, Mr Lowry,' he wheezed at the tale's conclusion, 'that's our Colonel, right there. His defence of his interests is quite unflagging. You'd better get used to such forcible tactics, old chum, if you are to stand at his side.' Richards wiped his eyes; something in his manner told Edward that a card was about to be played. 'The Colt family has an impulsive streak in it so broad that it borders on madness. I'm sure you'll know to what I am alluding.'

And there it was, a veritable classic: the dark secret, casually touched upon to unnerve the callow recruit, to fill him with doubt and prompt a confused re-evaluation of his position. Edward found that he was smiling at this unsubtle piece of manipulation. 'Mr Richards, I assure you that I do not.'

Richards feigned surprise. 'You mean that you haven't heard of John Colt, the axe-murderer of New York?'

The smile slipped a little. 'I – I beg your pardon?'

Richards dug a bent cigar end out of a coat pocket and made a great show of getting it alight. 'Killed a fellow with a hatchet back in forty-two, in Manhattanville,' he said as he struggled with a match. 'There was a disagreement over money, apparently. They were in business together, you understand – and as you've seen already, a Colt will really go the distance when business is involved. Victim's name was Adams, coincidentally enough.'

'Good Lord.'

'And that's not all. Dearest brother John went on to *chop the body up*, if you can imagine such a thing. The mad blighter then stuffed the parts into a packing-case and sent it by steamer to New Orleans.' Richards sucked on the cigar, quickly filling the carriage with smoke. 'But the case started to pong halfway down the Mississippi. It was an unusually hot summer, I'm told, and the killer had scrimped somewhat on the salt. The gruesome contents of the case were duly discovered, and traced back to John within the week.' Richards stopped his tale here, deliberately savouring his bent cigar.

He has me, Edward thought with mild aggravation; I must ask. It seems that I might have underestimated the Colonel's press agent. 'What happened to him? Did he hang?'

Drawing in his long legs, Richards grinned around his cigar in wolfish victory. 'Ah, well, that's where it gets really good. On the eve of his execution, as they were putting up the gallows in the prison yard, he stabbed himself through the heart. It is said that our own dear Colonel, eager to spare the family the shame of a public hanging – and thus protect his own emergent business interests – both brought him the knife and talked him into this last desperate act.' He took the cigar from his lips. 'These Colts are a ruthless lot, Mr Lowry – as merciless with each other as they are with the world at large.'

Down in the street, a door opened; Richards looked towards the tailor's shop and then quickly opened the window on the carriage's other side, tossing out his cigar. Colonel Colt was coming back.

The yard of the Colt factory was a narrow, cobbled valley between two block-like buildings. A week earlier, during Edward's first visit, it had been almost deserted; but now it positively thronged with people, as many as three hundred of them by his estimation, replacing the empty silence with an incessant, excited chatter. They stood in a ragged line that stretched along the flank of the right-hand building and ran all the way back to the main gate on Ponsonby Street. Of both sexes and all ages, this multitude formed a great specimen box of the London poor, ranging from well-washed working folk keen for honest labour, through the dry drunkard and the hard-up gambler, to various incarnations of beggary. Edward realised that Colt's London machine operatives were to be drawn from this unpromising pool.

Even the best among them seemed a long distance from the skilled artisans traditionally charged with the manufacture of firearms. This, he saw, was the principal secret of the Colonel's revolutionary method of production: his patented pistol-making machines needed only the most ignorant and inexpensive of workers to run them.

The Colt carriage halted next to the stone water trough that stood in the centre of the yard, the Colonel jumping out in what the secretary was coming to realise was his customary fashion. He followed as quickly as he was able; Richards, who had somehow contrived to fall asleep once more during the twenty-minute journey from Savile Row, showed no sign of waking.

Down on the cobblestones, Edward took in the factory for a second time. It was an unlovely place, to be sure, given over completely to the efficient fulfilment of its function. The two buildings – the manufactory itself on the right, where the engine and the machines were housed, and the as-yet vacant warehouse opposite – were entirely undecorated, the walls blank brick, the windows small and grimy, the many chimneys nothing but crude stacks. Yet the enterprise had a sense of scale about it, of sheer purpose, that was unmatched by the other factories that clustered around the reeking thoroughfare of the Thames. Turning to face the gates, Edward looked across the river to the collection of potteries and breweries scattered along the southern bank. These squat brown structures seemed little better than shacks, at once ancient and impermanent, fashioned from the muck of the shore. The premises of the Colt Company, by comparison, seemed a site for truly modern industry – the kernel of a mighty endeavour.

Beside him, the two chestnut mares who were pulling the Colt carriage snorted impatiently, eager to be unharnessed so that they could drink at the trough. Edward noticed that a dozen or so of the American staff Colt had brought with him were standing by the large sliding door that opened onto the forge, surveying the line of potential recruits. Dressed in corduroys, flannel waistcoats and squat, round-topped hats, and liberally smeared with engine grease, they appeared less than impressed by the noisy English crowd hoping to join their revolver factory. The Colonel was going over to them, walking rapidly as if keen for the company of his countrymen after a half-day spent with Edward and Alfred Richards.

A whisper of recognition went up from the queue of applicants as Colonel Colt strode over the yard. All rowdy conversation stopped; every head turned towards the famous Yankee gun-maker. Hats were doffed and curtseys dropped, as if in the presence of a great lord or clergyman. A handful of the bravest bade the Colonel a very humble good afternoon.

Colt ignored them. Reaching the forge door, he beckoned to a huge brute of a man, larger even than he was, with the blunted, leathery face of a prize-fighter; Edward recognised him as Gage Stickney, the factory foreman. A good-natured exchange began, the Colonel asking for details of the morning's enrolment. Soon all the Americans were shaking with hard, masculine laughter. Looking on, Edward became rather conscious of the smart Englishman's top hat and frock-coat that set him apart from both the pack of chortling Yankees and the shuffling mass of aspirant Colt operatives. The pistol case was still under his arm. He wondered what on earth he was to do with it.

There was a colourful curse behind him, the 'r' of 'bugger' slightly slurred; Richards, in descending from the carriage, had caught a button on the door handle, one side of his coat lifting up from his gangling frame like a fawn-coloured bat wing. In a doomed attempt to pull it free, the press agent ripped the button away completely. He grunted with satisfaction, as if this had been his aim.

'Don't know what they're looking so deuced pleased about,' he declared, nodding towards the Americans. 'The last I heard our engine was barely strong enough to animate a sideshow automaton, let alone a sufficient quantity of machinery to occupy this blasted rabble.'

Edward considered the press agent for a moment, thinking with some distaste that this wretched fellow was actually the closest thing he had to an ally at the Colt Company. 'I'm

22

sure that the Colonel is not given to displays of undue confidence, Mr Richards.'

Richards showed no sign of having heard him. 'You see that Yankee over there,' he murmured archly, angling himself away from the Americans, 'standing a little apart from the rest?'

It was immediately obvious to whom he was referring. The man was smaller and leaner than the others, and the oldest of the group by a clear decade, his skin scored with scar-like lines that bisected his hollow cheeks and spanned his brow in tight, straight rows. He was dressed in a dark blue cap and tunic, creating a distinctly military effect that was augmented by the high shine of his boots and the precise cut of his greying beard. While his companions laughed with the Colonel he continued to regard the ragged assembly of applicants with the fierce focus of a terrier.

'Mr Noone,' Edward replied. 'The factory's watchman, I believe.'

'And a chap with the very blackest of reputations. I've heard it said that the Colonel risked losing several of his most trusted people back in Connecticut when he took the villain on – threatened to walk right out, they did, so low is the regard in which our Mr Noone is held among certain of his countrymen. But the Colonel wanted him – said he was right for the post, a fellow who could be counted on to defend one's interests at all costs.' Richards paused significantly. 'At all costs, Mr Lowry.'

Edward fixed the press agent with a probing look. The scoundrel wants me to beg for more information again, he thought, as I did with the Colonel's axe-murdering brother. Well, I shan't; I won't hear any more of his plaguing stories. He stated that he was going to take the pistol case back up to the factory office, walking past Richards towards the tall sliding door that served as the main entrance to the factory block. Before he'd taken more than a couple more steps, however, there was a flurry of rough shouts from inside the building. Three men, Scots from the sound of it, marched out to the centre of the yard, bawling curses against Colonel Colt and his Yankee contraptions. All three were drunk, and from what they were yelling had just been turned away by those enlisting the factory's personnel. Seconds later Mr Noone, the watchman, was upon them, backed by a couple of other Americans. They collared the malcontents and hurried them over to Ponsonby Street, administering hard kicks to their behinds as they reached the gate.

This spectacle was greeted with laughter from the line; as more people turned to take it in, Edward noticed a lively-looking young woman in the plain yet respectable clothing of a domestic servant away from her place of employment, waiting in the queue with several others in similar dress. She was smiling wickedly at a remark made by one of her companions – a smile that made him smile as well to behold it. In the middle of her left cheek were two small but distinctive marks, side by side and oddly even. As she turned back towards the factory door, her smile fading, their eyes met. For a single clear moment they both stood in place, contemplating each other.

Then Colonel Colt called out his name, clapping his hands together as he headed back to the carriage. Edward smoothed down a twisted lapel and went over to join him.

2

Sam took the steps of the American embassy three at a time. Ignoring the grand brass knocker, he hammered on the door with his fist. It opened just an inch or two, as if in caution, so he gave it a hearty push, causing it to connect violently with the forehead of the unfortunate footman on the other side and send him staggering back into a floral arrangement.

'Ice, right now,' Sam instructed as he strode past, flicking a shilling at his victim. 'That'll see you right.'

The servants were coming at him, taking little bows, their eyebrows raised all the way up in that queer English manner, but he would have none of it. Deftly, he weaved around them and loped up the main staircase, arriving in an emerald green hall with the doors to the main reception room directly ahead. It was an apartment designed to make a man not born to splendour feel small and worthless: columns, chandeliers, fancy pictures, gold leaf by the yard. Nonplussed, thinking that the effect was rather aristocratic and decidedly un-American, Sam turned his attention to the other guests. His mood improved immediately. The crowd was a grey one, and sombre-looking. This, he knew well, tended to denote the presence of some serious political authority. He also registered a handful of smart naval coats and crimson jackets, adorned with medals and sashes of various hues. Generals, admirals and politicians, rounded up in one place: prime hunting ground for a sharp gun-maker.

A voice bleated at his shoulder. Irritably, Sam turned to

see a persistent flunky asking for his surtout, his hat and his name; he supplied them, not bothering to disguise his impatience. He was announced to the company, and met their attention with a scowl.

'Take it in, you blasted Bulls,' he muttered under his breath as he attempted to flatten his curls. 'I shall have you yet.'

Mr Buchanan, the newly appointed American minister in whose honour the reception was being held, approached to welcome him, looking pretty damn distinguished with his neat white hair and high starched collar. 'It pleases me greatly,' he declared, 'that such a singular personage as Colonel Samuel Colt, perhaps the most famous American presently in London, can find the time to attend this modest gathering.'

Sam knew Jim Buchanan a little from Washington and their handshake was cordial enough. The minister was no businessman, though, and could not disguise his personal feelings. That oblong face with its prominent chin and small, mild eyes was easy to read: he considers me vulgar, Sam thought with some amusement, and is concerned that I might put lordly noses out of joint with my brash manners. They exchanged a few words about Buchanan's new post.

'I was on good terms with Mr Lawrence, your predecessor,' Sam said. 'He was a man prepared to extend whatever help he could to an honest American trying to achieve something in this damnably slow-paced country.'

'Indeed,' Buchanan replied carefully.

Sam saw at once that the fellow didn't want to give any sense of an understanding between them – to put himself in a position where he might be asked to overstep some invisible barrier of diplomatic protocol. This was a predictable attitude. The new minister was renowned for his aversion to risk, to anything that might attract critical attention; a general habit of life that had been fostered (or so it was rumoured) by his secret preference for male companionship in the bedchamber.

Taking Sam's arm, Buchanan guided him over to a large group of men and women whose colourful dress and openness of manner marked them as Americans. There was a round of introductions, and not a single name Sam recognised.

26

Binding them all was the false sense of familiarity that one so often encountered among countrymen brought together abroad. Their conversation was concerned entirely with Franklin Pierce, the new president, and the tragic accident which had befallen his family between the election and his inauguration; they were relating the details, Sam couldn't help but think, with a certain ghoulish pleasure.

'Crushed to death, the boy was, within the president's sight!' one lady pronounced, her eyes open wide. 'The railway carriage rolled over onto its side, you see, and the child had been leaning from the window – oh, I can't bear to think of it!'

'Pierce is a broken man, they say,' opined the fellow next to her. 'Barely made it through his oath. Sits in the Oval Office all day long with the curtains drawn, paralysed with grief for his lost son.'

Sam quickly concluded that none of these blabbering fools was of any use to him. He looked over at the silver-bearded John Bulls conferring in other parts of the room and prepared to break away.

Another of the ladies, moved almost to tears by Pierce's tale, intercepted him. 'How can a man recover from such a blow, Colonel Colt? Can he at all?'

His departure checked for a moment, Sam paused in thought. 'Of matters concerning dead children, ma'am, I really cannot say,' he answered. 'But it's going to be a tough time indeed for those of us that might have been intending to do business with our government. That's one reason why you find me here in London, setting up a new factory. Speaking frankly, though, my hopes for a Pierce presidency were always low. I've known the fellow for a number of years, from his army days. Far too fond of the bottle – and I reckon he's reaching for it now, with a new dedication, in order to take the edge off his sorrow.'

Buchanan, a close ally of the Pierce administration, pursed his lips in disapproval, and tried to jog the startled group on to a fresh subject – some vacuous fixture of the London social season about which he'd developed a sudden fascination. Sam took this opportunity to move off. Refusing a flute of

27

champagne – the stuff played merry havoc with his gut – he sauntered to the centre of the reception room.

The gun-maker had made ample preparation for occasions such as this. Just before leaving Connecticut he'd furnished himself with a folio of portrait engravings of the foremost British politicians. On the voyage over, with time on his hands, he'd memorised the various configurations of thinning pates, furrowed brows, bushy white chops and belligerent jowls; and by the time he landed in Liverpool he could put a name and role to every aged face. It had irked him to discover that they had all switched their posts about since his last visit. Lord John Russell, scourge of the Catholics, was no longer Prime Minister, but Leader of the House, whatever that meant; disappointingly, Lord Palmerston, a man about whom Sam had heard many good things, had lost the Foreign Office and was now Home Secretary. The Earl of Aberdeen was currently at the helm, and a dull dog he appeared. Sam got the sense that the present British Government was an uneasy coalition of men who would trample each other down in a flash if the chance arose. It hurt his head to think about this for too long, though, and he wished that these scheming nobles would just stay put for a while and see if their achievements didn't rise accordingly.

For perhaps half a minute he saw no one of consequence. Then it struck out at him – one of the first half-dozen portraits from his folio, coloured and brought to life. A sober-looking fellow, bald as a knee but oddly childlike about the face: it was Lord Clarendon, Palmerston's replacement as Foreign Secretary. And by God, the person beside him, fat-cheeked and jovial, was none other than Lord Newcastle, the Secretary of State for War. These were the very men he needed. Sam was considering how best to introduce himself when they shifted about, in response to the arrival of someone else behind them; and there was his friend Tom Hastings, the elusive Keeper of the Ordnance, addressing Clarendon with obvious familiarity. Sam's blood stirred; his nostrils flared. This was a proper piece of good fortune, and he would seize it with both hands.

28

Hastings, a stooped old turtle decked out in a naval uniform, saw him approach and smiled warmly. Sam noticed for the first time that he had the most enormous ears, from which greyish hair sprouted in bunches. There was little in his thoughtful face that hinted at his distinguished naval past; Commodore Hastings had served under Nelson, had taken Bonaparte into his last exile, and had been single-handedly responsible for every major scientific advance in British naval cannonry since. Sam didn't know too much about any of this. It was enough for him that the aged Commodore had influence, a passion for all things gun-related and a demonstrable predisposition for Colt.

'My dear Colonel, what is this I hear about you and Clarence Paget?' Hastings whispered discreetly, moving away from his companions to greet Sam. 'You pointed a *pistol* at him, in his own rooms? Can this be true?'

They shook hands. Hastings was plainly delighted to think of Paget being threatened with a gun; the two men were fierce rivals of long standing.

'Not exactly, Tom,' he replied. 'We disagreed, is all.'

Hastings grinned. 'A subject best saved for another time, perhaps.' He directed Sam towards the ministers. 'Here, come and meet these fine gentlemen.'

Clarendon and Newcastle were somewhat reserved, as might have been expected, but they proved open enough to Sam's conversation and soon became curious to learn more of the revolver factory at Bessborough Place and its many innovations. Sam invited both to take a tour, thinking that he would send them each a pair of the finest engraved Navys that same night. It was looking good, in short, very good indeed; then an English lady, clad in black silk and lace, appeared between the ministers.

'Excuse me, Lord Clarendon – Lord Newcastle – Commodore Hastings,' she said with an incline of her head, her voice surprisingly deep and full of confidence.

Sam was immediately vexed. Could she not see that business was underway? Was such a thing beyond her cosseted mind to perceive? He almost ordered her to leave them alone, to get back to her gossiping, but managed to restrain himself and turn towards her with terse civility. This lady was perhaps fifty and more heavy-featured than he usually cared for, but not without allure. There was an appealing energy there; was she a widow, he wondered, who had devoted herself to charitable works? She was looking back at him coldly. Although she had not yet said his name, it was plainly him that she had come over to speak with.

'Lady Wardell,' said Newcastle with a bow.

'Cecilia,' murmured Clarendon. 'How very nice to see you.'

There was definite apprehension in the Foreign Secretary's tone. At once, Sam knew that this Lady Wardell was the campaigning sort. She was there to confront him.

'And you, sir,' she announced sternly, 'must be the American gentleman who plans to flood the streets of London with repeating pistols.'

The skin around Sam's right eye tightened with irritation. These people were always so goddamn self-important; every one of them seemed to believe that he'd never heard their particular line of garbage before. 'I am Colonel Colt, ma'am, certainly,' he said. 'What is it that you have to say to me?'

The woman lifted her nose in the air; as with so many of these rich Bulls, haughtiness came to her as naturally as drawing breath. 'Only, sir, that you are quite unquestionably *a merchant of death*!'

This remark was made bluntly and bitterly, less as an accusation than a statement of fact, and it killed all other conversation within a wide radius. Newcastle and Clarendon glanced about in furtive embarrassment, as if they'd been caught smoking cigars without their host's permission and were looking for somewhere quietly to dispose of their butts.

Sam, however, was a picture of unconcern. 'Only that, ma'am?'

Her lips formed a resolute line. This was a veteran, a sturdy old cruiser with a long record of skirmishes behind her, and she would not be easily vanquished. 'Your dastardly wares are designed to kill, and to kill in greater numbers than ever before. This cannot be denied. How can you

30

possibly reconcile this with your Christian conscience, sir? How can you bear to profit from such copious bloodshed?'

'Ma'am,' said Sam with a sigh, readying his standard defence, 'I think we can agree that the people of this world are very far from being satisfied with one another. I call my guns peacemakers: yes, *peacemakers*. They are tools expressly designed for preserving the peace. If every man had a revolver on his belt, who on earth would dare draw one?'

Hastings, God save him, made a low sound indicating concurrence; the ministers, however, were drifting off like untethered barges on a canal, slowly distancing themselves from the gun-maker and the attention he was attracting.

The fractious noblewoman was unconvinced by Sam's solid reasoning. 'You cannot honestly believe that, Colonel. Surely you must understand that firearms generate violence in the exact way that liquor generates drunkenness. Put a revolver in a man's grasp and he will long to use it at the very first opportunity!'

There was no curtailing her now. On and on she went, enlarging on her theories about Sam and his business with furious vigour. Growing more angry, he considered mentioning the Kaffir War, and how much easier it might have been on the British Army if they'd had his revolvers; or perhaps the efficacy of the Colt six-shooter in the ongoing American struggle against the barbarian red men. He thought better of this, though. It was pretty certain that the self-righteous drab before him would not be won over by talk of proficient savage-killing.

'You must agree, somewhere within you,' she was saying now, almost imploringly, 'that it is the religious duty of men of ingenuity and engineering skill – men such as yourself, Colonel Colt – to *aid* the peoples of the world, not provide the means for them to destroy one another.'

The ministers were gone now, swallowed up by the company; Sam's speedy path to the higher levels of government, such an unlikely stroke of goddamn luck, had closed. Hastings had stuck loyally by the gun-maker's side, but was entirely cowed by this lady and therefore useless. Colt's tolerance for his aristocratic adversary, this creature of England's grandest houses and rolling private parks, suddenly left him.

'Unfortunately, precious few of the world's troubles will find a solution in these fine sentiments alone,' he declared with an air of curt finality. 'As I've said, ma'am, my revolvers are tools, that's all, designed and manufactured to the best of my ability, and intended to help disputing parties reach a condition of peace as quickly as possible.'

The woman stared back at him in horror; Sam thought for a second that she was about to strike him with her fan. 'The only peace to be attained by revolvers will be due to one of the parties being *dead*!' she spluttered. 'How on earth can you stand here and –'

'It's all very well and good for you to take issue with me,' Sam interrupted again, sticking his thumbs in his waistcoat pockets, 'but I'll wager that you ain't never had to really struggle for anything. You've never reached your end through sheer perseverance, have you, ma'am, or earned your due through honest goddamn effort? I am a businessman, and guns are my business. And that's all there is to be said.'

The lady had nothing with which to counter this thumping rebuttal, her pale, wide-set eyes registering her defeat. She was clearly not used to being addressed with such simple honesty. Sam felt a certain shortness of breath, and hotness around his ears. He noticed the bank of staring faces behind her, every one slack-jawed with shock, and realised that he might have been shouting. That milksop Buchanan was drawing near, no doubt to rush in and mollify the blasted woman – to apologise for the unspeakable rudeness of Colonel Colt. Sam decided that he wouldn't stay to witness this. He wouldn't be made to feel shame for defending himself.

Hastings was standing very quietly at his elbow.

'Enough of this, Tom,' he said, turning away. 'I'm leaving.'

The gun-maker's exit from the reception room and descent down to the entrance hall passed in a wrathful blur. Only the form of a short, blond, neat-looking Englishman, inserted directly in his path at the base of the stairs, prevented him from storming straight out into the night. Sam drew up, taking in the fellow irascibly. He was no servant, but no lord either. Was he a lackey of one of the ministers, come to upbraid him – or an embassy man, laden with the Ambassador's chidings? Not caring to hear either, Sam made to push past, bellowing for his surtout and hat, wishing to God that he had some whiskey.

'That should not have been permitted, Colonel,' this blond man said, 'the way you were treated up there. Lady Wardell should not have been allowed to have been so impertinent towards a businessman of your standing. Mr Buchanan really should have intervened.'

This won him another moment of Sam's time. He stood, wordlessly challenging the man to hold his interest.

'She is something of a fanatic,' he continued dryly, 'always toiling in the service of some great cause or other – and only content when raising funds for the religious education of the poor, or the dispatching of missionaries to distant cannibal isles. You are most fortunate, as an American, that she did not also take you to task over the dreadful unwholesomeness of slavery.' His eyes narrowed. 'I cannot help but suspect, in fact, that she only came here tonight in search of trouble.'

'Yes, well, some women ain't all maple sugar,' Sam answered warily. 'What the devil d'you want?'

The blond man made no reaction to this hostile tone. 'My name is Lawrence Street, Colonel, and I am a long-standing admirer of your inventions. I was deeply impressed by the pistols included in the display of the Great Exhibition, and have followed your fortunes closely ever since.'

Sam's surtout and hat arrived. He put them on, thanking this Mr Street for his kind remarks, genuinely welcoming the approbation after his mauling by Lady Wardell.

'I wished to say, also, that you must not fret over the loss of your chance with Clarendon and Newcastle,' Street went on. 'You must realise that our government, like your own, is rather out of sorts at present. The Earl of Aberdeen, although a fine man by all accounts, is a most unsatisfactory Prime Minister, and he has staffed his cabinet with men

33

as ill-suited to their posts as he is to his. Not, of course, that those two upstairs would be particularly suited to *any*; but they certainly have no notion whatsoever of the pressures of the international stage, or of the changing nature of modern conflict. Many feel that when a war of any magnitude arrives – and the sense among us is very much that it will, before too long – Great Britain will be found sorely lacking, thanks largely to the glaring inefficacy of our Lords Clarendon and Newcastle.'

This speech was delivered swiftly and softly, and heard only by Sam; Street had made it inaudible even to the servants standing directly behind them. It had the clear ring of expertise. This was an operator of the smartest variety. Sam regarded his companion anew. Mr Street was about his age, with cold, rather inexpressive eyes and a head of the most astonishing white-blond hair. There was something jerky and puppet-like about him, which his small stature served only to accentuate; he was plainly a political, desky type who'd spent his years within the cramped confines of the city, well away from wood, field and stream. But his calm, calculating face, framed by the full whiskers of an intellectual Englishman, told Sam that Lawrence Street was also someone with whom he could talk seriously – and who might well prove useful.

They walked together towards the embassy doors. Sam's mind was occupied now by a vision of a vast marching army, of two or three marching armies in fact, thousands upon thousands of men, each and every one of them wearing a new Colt Navy upon his belt.

'Mr Street, did I hear you say that there is to be war in Europe?'

Street nodded. 'It is believed so; in Europe or on her fringes. And Great Britain will not be ready. We need your guns, Colonel, and soon. Yet you have just seen for yourself how lightly our ministers wear their duty – and how easily they are distracted from it.'

'I'll regain their interest soon enough.'

They went outside. Sam welcomed the evening's chill; it felt like fresh freedom after the stifling ordeals of the embassy.

He left the surtout unbuttoned as he descended to the pavement of Grosvenor Square.

Street had stopped at the top of the steps. He was shaking his head. 'Forgive me, Colonel, but I must say that such a course would be a poor use of your time. There are others of equal standing and influence who have a true interest in your endeavours. They see the potential of your factory and your weapons, and the advantages they offer over anything already produced in this country – over the pistols of Mr Adams, say. They would have you *succeed here*, supplying our forces with all the revolvers you could manufacture. Don't take any further trouble with Clarendon and his ilk.'

Sam realised then that Street was at the ambassadorial residence that evening with the express purpose of meeting with him and having this talk. He was a proxy, most likely; a plan of some sort was being put into motion. 'By thunder, Mr Street, who are these people?' he exclaimed. 'And how do they propose that this is to be achieved?'

A faint shadow of amusement passed over Street's features. 'First of all, we need your factory to work properly. The main engine, I hear, is underpowered, and causing the machinery to drag most terribly.'

Sam frowned. His orders were that no one outside the Colt Company was to be told of the factory's troubles, but word had obviously leaked out. He opened his mouth to dispute Street's confident assessment, but said nothing. The man was utterly sure of his information – and furthermore, it was correct. This is a devious critter indeed, the gun-maker thought. He's trying to unbalance me, to set me on the back foot so that I will fall more easily into his wider scheme.

'Once the factory is running your friends can help you,' Street continued. 'Commodore Hastings upstairs, for instance, and also those to whom I have already alluded. All will be in a better position to make your case, and at the very highest levels.'

'Who the devil are these men, these mysterious *friends* of mine?' Sam demanded. 'This cloak-and-dagger horseshit don't butter no parsnips with me, Mr Street! I will *know*, damn it, or I will forget we've ever met!'

The little blond fellow crossed his arms, taking in the dark square, unmoved by Sam's show of anger. 'May I ask you a question, Colonel?'

Sam glanced up at the embassy windows. Someone was looking out at them; they pulled back abruptly. He gestured his assent.

'Why did you decide to establish your factory in London? Why not Paris, or Berlin, or Amsterdam?'

Rather impatiently, Sam began to reel off the list of reasons for his choice – the reputation he had acquired at the Great Exhibition, the frequent steamers crossing between New York and Liverpool, the common tongue that meant his engineers could quickly train up new operatives – when Street stopped him.

'Was it not because of the bond that you feel between my country and your own? The powerful sense that we are brethren, sprung from the same Anglo-Saxon stock, not only speaking the same language, as you say, but possessing the same enlightened feelings – the same civilising impulse? Did you not wish specifically to endow Great Britain's armed forces with the spectacular advantage of your revolver?'

Colt considered this for a moment. He could see the angle, and it was a damn sharp one. 'I . . . was conscious of such a bond, yes – an *Anglo-Saxon* bond, exactly as you describe it.' He felt himself warming to the theme. 'The Colt Company is in the process of taking on English hands as we speak. It has always been my goal, Mr Street, to give this venture of mine a transatlantic character. Why, two of my closest London employees, my personal secretary and my press agent, are Englishmen, taken on for their knowledge of how things are over here.'

Street seemed to approve of all this. 'You must repeat these sentiments often, Colonel, and loudly. It will detract from those who cite your nationality as the primary reason to reject your inventions – and they will remain our most tenacious opponents, I promise you.'

This unaccountable man then looked back briefly at the embassy doors, which were being held ajar for him; he'd got what he wanted from Sam and was about to go back

36

inside. He came halfway down the steps, jerking along in that peculiar way of his, and extended his hand. Sam went back up to meet him and they shook firmly.

'Know that you have your London allies,' Street said, producing a card and laying it across Sam's palm. 'We shall speak again when your cause is more advanced. Good night to you, Colonel.'

The doors shut solidly behind him. Sam muttered in bemusement, pulling on fine calfskin gloves as he turned towards the square. Carriages lined the black oval of lawn in its centre, their lamps out, waiting for the reception's end. He spotted his own quickly enough, despite the sooty gloom; its superiority was apparent even among the conveyances of Buchanan's noble guests. His coachman was not expecting to be called for at least another hour, and would probably be dozing on his box.

The gun-maker took out a screw of Old Red and cut a generous plug. As he ground it between his teeth, feeling the rich tobacco set his mind afire and his fingers tingling inside his gloves, he ran through what had just transpired on the embassy steps. Something satisfactory had been achieved, of that he was certain; although now he thought hard about it he couldn't say exactly what it might be. It had to be admitted, also, that he'd allowed himself to be put off the scent. Street had sidestepped his demands for information with professional efficiency. The identity of the Colt Company's unseen supporters, of these men who supposedly watched his progress with such close interest, remained unknown.

Starting over to his carriage, Sam paused beneath a street lamp and flipped over the card. *Hon. Lawrence Street, MP*, it read; *Lord Commissioner of the Treasury, Whitehall.*

3

Bolted down in its brick cradle, the engine was like a captive whale exhausted after a long struggle with the harpoon, emitting great sighs of white steam and the occasional high-pitched ping. It had been idling for the past two hours, but was still scalding hot; Martin heard Mr Quill curse as he brushed against the shining side of its copper boiler. The time was almost upon them. He looked over at Pat, Jack and the rest. They were hefting their shovels, ready to work. The warmth and closeness of that engine room was something devilish, and it was filthy too, grease, sweat and coal-dust mingling on every face and pair of arms to form a slick second skin. Darkness had fallen outside, and the factory lamps were lit. To Martin's right, through the short passageway that led from the engine room to the forging shop, he could see a shadowy row of drop-hammers, standing before their clay ovens like so many giant corkscrews. The mass of operatives had been gone now for over an hour, and away from the wheezes of the engine the building was quiet. Martin had stayed on, as he did every night. Mr Quill welcomed this diligence, and he was pledged to do whatever was necessary to secure the chief engineer's trust.

This campaign, in truth, was already pretty well advanced. Martin had been appointed as Mr Quill's assistant on the basis of his easy aptitude with the drop-hammer – something that had taken him quite by surprise, as he'd never so much as touched a forging machine before being taken on at Colt. Quill had told him that he had a natural knack for machine-work, and would not hear his protestations of ignorance.

'Learning is over-rated, Mart,' he'd said in his Yankee burr. 'Diligence is what's required, in the first instance – diligence in the service of a willing spirit. We'll soon have you up to speed.'

The foremost task before them was the engine, and it was a pressing one. Colonel Colt himself would come by regularly to see how they were progressing, and remind Mr Quill in strikingly straightforward language that the whole London enterprise was dependent upon his success. The engineer had talked Martin through the contraption's main fault: the stroke was wrong for the diameter of the driving cylinder, he'd explained, which set the pulleys out of true and prevented the machinery from working anywhere close to as well as it could. Remarkably, Martin found that he could not only follow what he was being told, but apply it usefully to his labours. Mr Quill soon pronounced him invaluable, and took to asking his opinion as well as issuing instructions. They'd worked on the engine side by side, cursing the inept English makers who'd put the damned thing together.

A critical point had been reached, and Mr Quill had asked him to form a team of stout-hearted bravoes who would stay on after hours with them to help with some final modifications. Martin had promptly nominated the half-dozen of his bonded brothers who'd secured themselves a place in the American factory. At first, Pat Slattery hadn't been best pleased. His view of their task at Colt was a determinedly simple one.

'Why the hell,' he'd spat, 'should I give one o' these Yankee bastards a second's more dominion over me than he already damn well has?'

But Martin had reasoned with him, arguing that the more they learnt about the place, and the more trust they could earn from the Yankees, the better their chances would be. Eventually, even Pat had to admit the sense in this. The Irishmen had stepped forward as one, and started tightening pistons and adjusting valves under Mr Quill's kindly, un-suspecting direction.

The chief engineer emerged from behind the engine, a large wrench in his hands. He was grinning fiercely, his hair sticking up like a crazy pagan crown, his leather apron stretched tight over his round belly. The black grease on his forearms almost obscured the chequered snakes that had been tattooed there, twisting down from his elbows. After giving Martin an assured wink, he turned towards Mr Stickney, the giant of a foreman, who lingered out in the foundry passage.

'We're just about ready here, Gage,' he boomed. 'Are the machines prepared?'

'Sure are, Ben,' Stickney replied. 'Set your micks to work. I'll head upstairs.'

Mr Quill gave Stickney a cheerful salute and opened the boiler hatch. Taking up his own shovel, he joined Martin and the others beside the fuel bin. Together they stoked the engine, the coal hissing off their shovels onto the wallowing fire within. Once it was up and roaring again, Mr Quill slammed the hatch shut and turned his attention to the engine's valves. Slowly, the pistons stirred, gears and pulleys started to move, and the revolver factory creaked into life around them. Straight away Martin noticed that there was a new pace to the engine, a regular smoothness that had not been there that afternoon. The engineer and his assist-ant smiled at each other. The labour of the past week was paying off.

'Sounds pretty goddamn good, don't she,' cried Mr Quill.

Soon the engine was really pounding along, the driving cylinder above them humming as it spun. For a minute or two the men took their ease, lulled into a strange kind of peace by the engine's thunder; then Mr Stickney reappeared, lumbering through the shadowy forging shop. There was a part in his hand, a pistol frame from the looks of it. Mr Quill went forth to meet him, and a detailed examination began. Both men had been with Colonel Colt for many years, and knew his arms inside out. Their verdict was a good one.

'By God, Gage,' exclaimed Mr Quill, holding the part up, 'this is damn near perfect. You couldn't hope for a cleaner bit of shaping than that – the drag is quite gone. I do believe that this here frame is ready to be jointed. The Colonel'll be cock-a-hoop when he hears.' He looked around. 'Christ Almighty, I've half a mind to fetch him here *right now*!'

With sudden boyish excitement, Colt's chief engineer rushed back past the boiler and clanged his wrench repeatedly against one of the engine's sturdy wrought-iron supports, letting out a triumphant huzzah. The Irishmen joined in, taking off their grubby cloth caps and tossing them upwards so that they slapped against the chamber's low ceiling.

Pat Slattery, however, did not cheer. He sought out Martin's eye and held it, his thoughts stamped clearly on his thin, hawkish face. The Irish in that room were all brothers, united by a sacred oath; and Slattery, the closest they had to a leader, never lost sight of their purpose. This was a moment for their mistress and namesake – the maiden Molly Maguire. Who she was, or who she had once been, no one could say for certain, but it didn't matter. Molly was their mothers and daughters, and everyone else they'd lost in the Hunger; the blighted fields and the famished animals; the dismal workhouses and the mass graves. She was the Holy Virgin's dark-hearted sister, watching over them always with her teeth bared.

Back in Roscommon, it was their pledge to Molly Maguire that had sent them out against the landlords and land-agents and bailiffs, fighting those who sought to evict them from their homes and starve their families, *her* families, from existence. It was Molly who'd set them rioting in streets from Boyle to Tipperary, smashing windows, breaking limbs, burning barns and worse besides. The others spoke of her often, of their loyalty to her; she was as real to them as the saints and angels, and every bit as beloved. For Martin, though, it went beyond this. He didn't know if it was lunacy or some form of sickness in his soul, but from time to time – when his heart beat fast and thick and his brain ached – Molly Maguire would come to call on him. He could see her right then, in fact, moving through the Colt engine room, slipping in among the men gathered there like a current of cold air. She was holding aloft loose handfuls of her dusty copper locks, singing one of the old songs in that scratched whistle of a voice; he saw the awful whiteness of her skin, and the way that tattered gown allowed a glimpse of the ribs standing out so painfully beneath.

The first of these visitations had occurred in the spring of 1847, just after he'd collected his youngest sister's body from the Athlone workhouse. As he'd sat slumped beneath a tree, half-mad from the poteen he'd drunk, Molly had slid across the borders of his vision like a figure from a dark, dreaming vale, beyond all wakeful reason; yet even through his stupor he'd known at once that she was there to protect and encourage him. From then on, when he was out doing her work with his brothers, he would sometimes sense her flitting around nearby, and hear her voice whispering in his ear. On the night when they'd broken into the manor house of Major Denis Mahon, who Slattery had proceeded to beat to death with a threshing flail, she'd laughed and trilled with joyful approval. This act, the righteous slaying of the worst of their oppressors, had been celebrated throughout Catholic Roscommon – but it had forced all suspected Molly Maguires to flee the county or risk the gallows.

Martin, Slattery, their friend Jack Coffee and a couple of others had travelled to London, trying to fashion new lives for themselves among the impossible numbers of Irish who'd also been forced to start over in the heaving rookeries of the city. The Mollys had thus established an outpost of sorts in Westminster, in the dank lanes of the Devil's Acre. A series of cockeyed plans had been devised, spoiled and abandoned. Years had passed. Molly Maguire herself had stayed well away, and Martin had started to think that she was done with him. He'd begun portering at Covent Garden; he'd even found a wife. Then Colonel Colt had settled just up the river in Pimlico, and back Molly came, rising once again to the shallows of Martin's mind. As always, she wanted vengeance for the suffering of Ireland; and now, at last, there was a way for her faithful lads to get it for her.

'Lord John,' Slattery had declared on that first night, after they'd all made it through the Yankees' quizzing and were employees of the Colt Company. 'Lord John Russell. He's our mark, brothers. He's the one what must die at the first bleedin' opportunity. There are others, o' course there are. Clarendon, that was viceroy; that damned Labouchere as well. But it's the Prime Minister, him that was in charge, who must fall ahead o' the rest.' He'd struck his callused fist against the tavern table. 'It's Lord John that would not give sufficient aid to a famine-stricken people, for fear that it might prove a burden to England. That stopped the public works, the railways and suchlike, which would have given many thousands o' Irishmen an honest living wage, and presented them instead with a charity soup so thin it wouldn't sustain a bleedin' farm cat.' His voice had begun to buckle, his rage twisting him up into a bitter ball. 'That could not overcome his bigot's hatred of the Catholic Irish even as he was given the power of life and death over us – that chose to let us die!'

The Molly Maguires had nodded, a couple growling their agreement.

'I've a name for you, brothers,' Slattery had continued. 'Daniel M'Naghten. Ten years ago this brave Celt went after Sir Robert Peel with a pair of flintlock pistols. He chose poorly – the man he shot was only Peel's private secretary, and he was brought down by the crushers before he could load another bullet. Well, thanks to the Yankee Colt, this sad result can be avoided by us. We'll be sure of our man – sure of his much-deserved death. And we'll fight our way out as well. All we need are a couple o' dozen of these repeating arms.'

Now, just over a fortnight later, the Mollys were gathered in Colonel Colt's engine room, being led by Mr Quill in a second cheer, and a third, as he kept on banging away with his wrench. After a minute or so of this, Stickney intervened. Martin thought him a bad-tempered bastard, and a bully as well; he frowned a little at the sound of the foreman's voice.

'Calm yourself, Ben, for God's sake,' he shouted over the engine, stopping Quill's arm as it was being raised for yet another blow. 'We're still some distance from our best. We could be getting thirty-five horses from this thing, and it's giving us eighteen at the very most.'

Mr Quill, red-cheeked and exuberant, regarded the foreman with something close to pity. 'Gage, if there were another seasoned Colt engineer within a thousand miles of where we're standing then, yes, I confess that it might be possible to wring some more life out of this here contraption. But look around you, friend! The London factory is working! We can *make a goddamn gun*!'

'Full production's a good way off,' Stickney countered. 'A distant prospect.'

Mr Quill would hear no more. 'The Colonel wants a London revolver, as soon as it can be made, and we've put this within reach. Sure, our work ain't done, Gage, but when is it ever?'

Having said this, the chief engineer threw open the valves, releasing a deafening flood of steam from the charging engine. With Martin's help he set about disengaging the pulleys from the cylinder. Once this was complete and the engine had finished its steady, rhythmic deceleration, he proposed that the company head off for a celebratory drink in the Eagle. The sulking Mr Stickney declined, saying he had letters to write and stalking away into the factory. The Mollys agreed readily enough, though, Pat included. Together, they headed for the washroom, recently established in the warehouse across the yard.

Mr Noone was standing outside the factory's sliding door, smoking a cigar. He looked at first glance like a soldier, a grizzled cove with a private, unfriendly air about him. Mr Quill, open-hearted as always, invited the watchman to come along with them, but after taking a glance at the engineer's companions he refused. This was to be expected. Whereas most of the American mechanics and overseers viewed the London recruits with varying degrees of contempt or indifference, Noone saw them as nothing less than the enemy, seeming to believe that the single greatest threat to the factory under his guard came from within. Martin thought this uncommonly quick. He was pretty certain that Noone had nothing on him and his brothers, but he'd spread the word that the watchman was someone the Mollys should keep a close eye on.

Mr Quill continued on towards the warehouse, peeling off his filthy apron. 'Another time, p'raps,' he muttered.

The Spread Eagle stood not twenty yards from the river's edge, on one of the few stretches of solid embankment that the City Corporation had seen fit to construct. It was a working man's tavern, drawing custom from the Colt factory, the Pimlico gasworks and every other site of industry along the Lambeth Reach. However, the main body of regulars came from one place only: the vast construction yard of Thomas Cubitt, the man who was building up Pimlico from nothing, street by street and square by square. These masons, labourers and joiners had put up the Eagle itself not two years previously. Now they stood about the bar and slouched in the booths, smoking, joking and arguing as they took their refreshment. This tavern was very different to the flash houses and tumbledown gambling dens that the Mollys frequented back in the Devil's Acre, and Martin liked it all the more for this. He savoured the newness of the place, the evenness of its construction, from the gleaming brass of the pumps and fittings to the smooth, level surface of the bar. As yet it was untouched by the London rot that crawled out of the Thames and seeped slowly into everything. You could still smell the river, of course – a window had not been made that could shut that out – but amid the welcome odours of tobacco, honest sweat and fresh beer, it was easily endured.

His brothers didn't agree, and drifted away after only a drink or two, to Mr Quill's very vocal disappointment. Martin remained, though, thinking that his being on the right side of the chief engineer could well prove a boon to Molly's cause. Amy wouldn't like this one bit – she'd be worn out and cross, the babies would be screaming, and strife would surely be waiting for him when he returned to the Devil's Acre – but for now, Molly Maguire had to come first. He stayed where he was, leaning across the bar to order another pot of dog's-nose for him and Mr Quill. The two men drank deep, shivering a little at the keen edge the gin gave the beer, and refilled their pipes.

'You'll do well at Colt, Mart,' said Mr Quill wisely, putting a match to his bowl and then passing it to Martin. 'I feel it – Christ, I *guarantee* it.'

This was said at least once a day, and often more. Martin assumed a humble smile. 'Ah, I'm nothin' much.'

Mr Quill shook his head, puffing out smoke. 'You have a fine mind – an engineering mind. I see it. The Colonel sees it.' He took the pipe from his mouth and pointed at Martin with its well-chewed stem. 'Many of those let in through Colt's doors in the past weeks will be with us for a few months only. But you're with us for the duration, Mart. I can tell.'

Turning around, Martin swallowed more of his drink and took a hard drag on his pipe. 'I do feel my confidence growing some, Mr Quill, I will admit.'

Quill raised his arm, the sleeve of his canvas jacket pulling back; for an instant Martin could see the diamond-shaped head of a serpent etched on the underside of the engineer's wrist, its forked tongue licking at his palm. Then he brought his hand down emphatically against the bar's top.

'*Exactly*,' he declared. 'That's it exactly. Confidence. All else will follow, Mart. Take my case. I started out in the engine room of a Collins steamer, criss-crossing the goddamn Atlantic three times a month. Now I'm one of Colonel Colt's senior engineers, making upwards of five dollars a day. This is what an ordinary fellow can achieve if he puts his mind to it.'

Martin nodded. 'Aye, I see it, Mr Quill, honest I do. This post I have with you, well . . .' He let his voice trail off. 'It is far beyond anything else that a Roscommon lad such as meself might hope for in this wretched Saxon city.'

There was sympathy in Quill's round, ruddy face as he sucked reflectively on his pipe. 'Well, Mart, there are no such barriers in America. None of these stale old hatreds. It's a land where a man can live without fear of intrusion or interference. It's the place for men like us, and by God, once the government of this mouldy old country has finally seen sense and made us both rich, I shall show it to you.'

He grinned, slapped Martin on the shoulder and then drank down a good deal of his dog's-nose in one pull.

Martin smiled as well. This here was a decent man. It made him regret the deception he was working, but he knew that there was no other way. He had to do right by Molly Maguire. He had to get her some justice.

There was a loud peal of laughter from around the corner of the Eagle's L-shaped saloon, followed by a burst of song. Martin looked over; squeezed into a snug at the tavern's rear was a large group of factory workers, men and women, several of whom he recognised from the Colt works.

'You're certain that we'll succeed here in London then, Mr Quill?' he asked.

The chief engineer put his empty tankard on the bar indicating to the pot-boy that he would have it refilled. 'Sam Colt has been plying his trade for a good long while, Mart. He has the greatest bodies in Washington tame as little white mice. Government men, soldiers, lawyers even – he conquers 'em all in the end. He can't fail here. These Bulls that seek to compete with him, or to confound his purposes, are in for an unpleasant surprise.' Quill sized up his new measure of dog's-nose and took another mighty gulp; he drinks harder than a bloody Irishman, Martin thought. 'Did I ever tell you how he broke the back of Eli Whitney?'

Martin had heard this tale before, twice in fact. It was one of Mr Quill's favourites. He shook his head, though, and settled down to listen to how the Colonel, after years of savage rivalry and manoeuvring, drove the Massachusetts Arms Company (of which poor Eli was the proprietor) out of the revolver business altogether. Long before the story's dramatic courtroom conclusion, however, someone called his name. He recognised the voice; it was Caroline, Amy's younger sister. She was walking towards them from the snug. Martin noticed that she was wearing the plain garments of a factory operative. The last he'd heard she was a chambermaid in a smart house in Islington, the residence of an important gent in the City. Something had changed.

Martin and Caroline had never been particularly friendly. He knew that she didn't much like her sister being married to an Irishman, and living off in the Devil's Acre. Amy and her had been close when they were small, there only being a year between them. The two girls looked alike, it had to be said, sharing the same broad cheekbones and pretty, slightly crooked mouth. Amy's hair was darker, though, and her eyes larger, and her thoughtful manner was replaced in Caroline by an argumentative, trouble-making curiosity that Martin found difficult to warm to. He asked her what she was doing in the Eagle, keeping his tone pleasant, knowing as he spoke what her answer would be.

'Why, Mart, I am an employee of Colonel Colt,' she replied, flashing Mr Quill a bright, saucy smile. 'I daresay I've been under his roof for almost as long as you have, though of course I ain't yet reached the same level of favour. I'm in here now with some of my new pals from the machine floor, enlarging our acquaintance, as they say.'

Somewhat reluctantly, Martin introduced her to Mr Quill, explaining their connection. He beamed back at her, utterly charmed. She already knew exactly who the chief engineer was, and had a series of questions lined up about her employer which it pleased him enormously to answer. After a minute, he turned to the bar to buy them all new drinks.

'Will you have some dog's-nose, Caroline?'

'Just gin for me, sir, if you please,' she said with a mock-curtsey. 'You may leave out the ale.'

Martin felt a pang of irritation. 'How did you know of the factory, then?' he asked. 'How did you know that the Colonel was hiring?'

She moved in a little closer, angling her hip towards Mr Quill as she took her glass of gin from his hand; the two moles on her cheek, distinct marks a neat inch apart, stood out like an adder-bite against the liquor-flushed skin. 'My sister told me that you were thinking of joining, Martin.' She hesitated. 'Along with some of your friends, them coves what was in here earlier, Pat Slattery and the rest. I'd just lost my position – through no fault of my own, Mr Quill, I assure you – so I thought I'd try gun-making for myself. I find that I rather like it.'

'It's fine work indeed for a strong, smart girl,' said Mr Quill approvingly, 'until a good husband comes along, at least.' He removed his worn sailor's cap, exposing his unruly thatch of hair. 'Don't suppose you'd consider the chief engineer, Caroline, scoundrelly old wretch tho' he be?'

Martin made a show of joining in their free, boozy laughter, just managing to hide his annoyance at the thought of this infernally nosy girl having placed herself within the gun factory. Molly's work could still be done, of course, but his sister-in-law's presence was something else he'd now have to take into consideration.

Caroline knew not to outstay her welcome. After exchanging a couple more playful remarks with Mr Quill, she polished off her gin, bade them a good night and went back to the snug. The engineer watched her go before drinking down his dog's-nose and ordering them both another.

'So,' he said when the drinks had arrived, 'you're married to an Englishwoman.'

Martin's self-control left him. He would not be rebuked or teased for this now, and certainly not by Ben Quill – a Yankee, for Christ's sake. 'Mother o' God,' he snapped, 'can a man control the workings of his heart? He cannot, Mr Quill – he *cannot*.' Surprised by this outburst, by the honesty in his voice, he quickly lifted up his pot again, hiding himself behind it as he took a long swallow.

There was a pause; then Mr Quill, with a sad shake of his head, knocked his pot solemnly against Martin's. 'By Heavens, Mart,' he murmured, 'I'll surely drink to *that*.'

The Eagle closed its doors at twelve. Martin and Mr Quill, both well-oiled, started wandering up the Belgrave Road, through the eerie silence of Pimlico's southern end. It was a warm night, a taste of the approaching summer; the two men puffed on their pipes, ambling along with no particular purpose in mind. Caroline had departed the tavern some time before. Thankfully, Mr Quill's interest in her had shown itself to have been light-hearted and of the moment only. After she'd left them, in fact, the engineer had seemed to forget her existence altogether. He was now engaged in some slurred philosophising, rambling on about the role of the machine in what he termed 'manifest destiny'. Martin wasn't really listening.

After a while, they left the main avenue, lurching onto a side-street. Identical apartment-houses, four storeys tall, built with red brick and fringed with stucco, loomed on either side of them in two long lines. Only recently completed by Cubitt's men and still unoccupied, the windows of these houses were as dark and smooth as tar pools. The sounds of London – the yelping of dogs, the rumble of coach-wheels over on the Vauxhall Bridge Road – were but faint ghosts of themselves, banished to the distant background. The street was as clean as it was quiet. Not a trace of mud or dung could be seen on the cobblestones, their fish-scale pattern catching the dull moonlight; and even the stench of the river was masked by the mineral smell of fresh cement and stone.

They reached the end of a row. The next block along was still under construction, swathed in scaffolding, the shadowy road before it piled with whatever materials Cubitt's foremen had judged too heavy for thieves to make off with. Through the many gaps in the unfinished buildings, across an expanse of barren land, Martin saw a night-site at work, a tower of light and action in the surrounding darkness. Labourers scaled the ladders of the scaffold, heavy hods of stone balanced on their shoulders; bricklayers slowly built up walls, inserting each new piece with steady concentration. The jokes and curses of both echoed along the empty streets. Martin stopped to take it in, smoking reflectively, leaning against a covered mortar-barrel.

A footstep crunched nearby, from inside one of the incomplete apartment buildings further along the row – a man's footstep, heavy and sure, stepping on a bed of gravel. Martin felt a distinct, sobering nip of wrongness. He knocked out his pipe. Quill was further down the street, pointing into the air and gassing on like a true taproom orator. Martin whispered his name, gesturing for silence.

'What's up?' the engineer called back, as loudly as ever, stretching out his arms. 'What's the problem, Mart?'

50

There were more footsteps, and some muttering; Martin went over to Quill's side. 'Someone's here with us, Mr Quill.'

Quill drew on his pipe, making the tobacco in the bowl crackle and glow. 'Footpads?' he asked, speaking excitedly through the side of his mouth, as if eager to fend off such an attack. 'How many?'

'I don't believe so,' Martin replied, glancing over his shoulder. 'Why would such people be out here? There's none about but us. Pretty slim pickings. No, this is different.' He met Quill's eye: this was worse.

The engineer wasn't alarmed. 'What should we do, then?'

Martin nodded towards the night-site, its lamps twinkling between the scaffold poles and slabs of masonry. It suddenly seemed very far away. 'Best bet's to head over there, I reckon. Straight through these buildings here – towards the light.'

Before they could act, however, the trap was sprung. Three men appeared from behind a stack of planks, dressed in working clothes. All three were solidly built and had short, stout sticks in their hands. Martin turned; four more were approaching fast from the opposite direction. They've been stalking us, he thought, from the moment we left the Eagle, waiting for the right moment to strike. He cursed himself for all the pots he'd sunk – for stumbling so unsuspectingly into this crude snare. How could he have been so bloody *stupid*?

'What is this?' he demanded, his eyes darting around, scanning the street for an escape route. 'What d'yous want?'

The little pack started to laugh with the nasty confidence of men who believe their victory to be guaranteed. The tallest of them lifted up his stick and opened his mouth to speak.

His words were never heard. With a wild roar, Mr Quill suddenly charged forward, butting the fellow like a bull and sending them both tumbling into the shadows. The engineer's pipe cracked against the ground, releasing a tiny spray of orange sparks. There was a second roar, and a loud shout of pain. Their assurance rocked, the gang lunged at Quill, trying to drag him off their friend – a difficult task in the murky street. Gritting his teeth, Martin threw himself upon them, landing squarely on someone's back. They went over together, slamming down hard against the newly laid pavement.

From then onwards all was confusion, a virtual blind-fight. One of their attackers was shrieking as though he was bleeding out his last. Martin realised that these men, although determined, had definite limits to their bravery. Searching around in the gutter, his fingers found a single loose cobble-stone. Thinking of Molly Maguire, her green eyes alive with animal rage, he lashed out with it.

This drew forth a yell, followed by the urgent scrabbling of hob-nailed boots; then a blow fell across the back of Martin's neck, sending a dazzling blaze across his sight. He slipped, losing his footing, swinging the stone around again but hitting nothing. They were circling him, keeping their distance, reduced to black shapes only. Off to his left, he heard Mr Quill swear and then exhale with pain. Martin recognised what was happening. He'd been in this situation many times before. The two of them were being overwhelmed.

A powerful kick drove in from nowhere, catching Martin on the jaw. Reeling, he dropped the stone; it struck the pave-ment with a metallic, ringing sound. The gang were on him immediately. Before long, the blows lost their distinctness, blurring together, his foes' grunts mingling with the thumps of their fists and sticks against his flesh. All pain ceased. It felt only as if he was curled up on an open hillside, being buffeted by a powerful wind, Molly's mocking laughter rattling in his ears.

After a time – a minute? two? – something disturbed them. 'Come, lads,' said one, speaking in a twanging cockney accent, 'let's be off. They've 'ad enough for now.'

There was a final kick to Martin's stomach, and the beating stopped.

'Don't you bleedin' forget this, you Yankee bugger!' hissed another. 'We ain't about to stand by all 'elpless and just let this 'appen!'

A strong beam of light was approaching through the gloom, chasing the men away. Martin tried to fix his eyes on this beam; but it dipped and faded, becoming lost in a smother-ing, thickening sensation close to sleep. His clenched limbs relaxed and he flopped over onto his back.

The next he knew he was being helped to sit up, a

bull's-eye lantern in front of him. Gagging, he rolled to one side, his pots of dog's-nose coming up in a long, unbroken jet, splashing hotly across the Pimlico pavement. He gasped for breath, spitting out bile, feeling a great many aches awaken across his bruised, bleeding body. A party of night-watchmen had come to their aid, Cubitt's people from the sound of it, those charged with weeding out the beggars who sought shelter in the empty buildings. He heard them assessing his injuries, and deciding that they were not too grave – nothing broken, at any rate. They already knew that he was from the Colt works, a fact they could only have learned from Mr Quill. Gingerly, Martin turned his head the smallest fraction; his neck felt as if it was being twisted to breaking point, and a flaming claw gripped at the back of his skull.

The engineer was sitting on the steps of an apartment block, streaked with fresh blood, slowly rotating his right arm around in its socket. A grin and a pained wince were struggling for control of his features.

'Christ above, Mart,' he laughed, coughing, 'who the devil were *they*?'

4

Crocodile Court lay near the middle of St Anne's Street, squarely within the Devil's Acre, and it was filled with rowdy conversation. Almost every window in the close lane was open, with lamps and candles set upon their ledges, like the boxes in a shabby theatre where the curtain would never rise. Roughly-dressed women, the majority of them Irish, leaned out in twos and threes, gossiping and quarrelling with each other. As Caroline entered she overheard talk of the evening's arrests, a mysterious murder over on Tothill Street, the rising price of milk – anything that came into the women's heads, in short, and all at the same time. Bottles were being passed from window to window, and even lobbed across to the opposite side. The Court had once been home to the wealthy, back in the age of powdered wigs and sedan chairs, but had long since been given over to the very poorest. Hundreds now lived in residences designed for a single family – residences that were on the brink of collapse. Beams bent and cracked like dry rushes, and plaster dropped from walls in huge chalky sheets. Caroline could never look upon the parliament of Crocodile Court without imagining these ancient piles suddenly overbalancing due to the great weight on their sills, and toppling forward into the lane with an almighty, screaming crash.

She was a visitor to the Devil's Acre, marked out by her clean face, neat straw bonnet and new boots, and had been pursued by a throng of ragged children from the moment she'd crossed Peter Street. Fending them off, picking her way through the darkness, past the stinking puddles, mounds of rotten vegetables and decaying house-fronts, she'd cursed Martin Rea for bringing her Amy to this godforsaken place. It nearly broke her heart to think that this was where Katie, her little niece, was taking her first steps.

As she started along the Court, very glad to be nearing her destination, a great scornful shout went up. Heart thumping, she looked around, thinking for an instant that she must have provoked this somehow; but no, a drunken, filthy husband had staggered in behind her, returning home after a debauch. The women showered him with hoots and bitter catcalls. He waved a dismissive arm in their direction before vanishing through a sagging brick archway.

About half of Crocodile Court's paving stones had been prised up and stolen, creating an irregular chequered pattern and making it impassable for all but the lightest of carts. Caroline hopped from slab to slab, past the rusting water-pump and the rag-and-bone shop, heading resolutely for Amy's building. A game of rummy was underway on the steps, with much swearing and spitting. She took a breath and pushed straight through its middle, slipping quickly through the door.

The stairwell was heavy with snoring, belching, coughing bodies. People were everywhere, overflowing from the rooms onto corridors and landings. Of all ages, they sprawled semi-clothed across the floorboards, lost to liquor; perched upon the stairs, taking their meagre suppers; or huddled quietly in corners, trying to sleep. This was the result of the Victoria Street clearances, which had begun again in earnest, leaving many hundreds without homes. Caroline could not help but kick a few of them as she passed, clutching at the rickety banister. Most did not even have the energy to curse her.

The numbers had thinned a little by the time she reached the third floor. She went to a door at the end of the corridor and knocked three times. Someone came to the other side. Caroline said her name, a bolt slid back and she walked forward into a dell of flowers. Crocuses, lilies, tulips and carnations were gathered into loose bunches, and laid out in baskets and bowls. Their colours were all but lost in the dimness of the room, and there was no perfume beside those of the dyes and inks; but these clean, chemical odours were a definite improvement on those mingling in the musty corridor outside. Caroline shut the door behind her.

Amy was already back in her seat by the fire, a large silk rose in her hands. She was stitching wire-trimmed petals to its cardboard stem by the meagre light of the few coals that smouldered in the grate. The lines on her face deepened as she squinted down at the flower, pushing dark strands of hair behind her ears, searching for the right place to poke in her needle. She looked thin and desperately old for a woman of only four-and-twenty. It seemed to Caroline that her sister, once so strong and clever, was being worn away before her very sight; that life in the Devil's Acre was killing her by degrees.

On the rug between them, rolling around in the weak firelight, lay Katie. The child was trying to rise onto her knees, plump legs wobbling as they took her weight. Hearing the door close, she looked up, mouth open; and seeing her aunt standing there, she cried out with pure delight, lost her balance and tumbled back down onto her side. Caroline felt a sudden rush of love; a tear, a bloody *tear* for Christ's sake, pricked at the corner of her eye. She swooped in on the giggling infant, taking her up into her arms and spinning her around.

'Why hello, my precious darling,' she said. 'And how are *you* tonight?'

Amy gave them both a quick smile but did not stop working. Caroline knew that she had four hundred flowers to deliver to her current employer, a milliner on Bond Street, first thing in the morning. Failure to meet this deadline would certainly mean the loss of the business, and the five shillings it brought in every week. Amy would not let this happen if she could possibly prevent it. Caroline sniffed the top of Katie's head; the girl's skin was sour, her chestnut curls clammy with grease. Once again, Amy had been too busy to bathe her. She glanced over at the cot in the corner that held Michael's tiny form. He was quiet, at least, unlike the three or four other babies who wailed away nearby, somewhere along the corridor. Whether this was a good or a bad sign she dared not consider.

Sitting cross-legged on the floor, Caroline took a small paper parcel from her apron and unfolded it on her knee, revealing half of a slightly wilted ham sandwich. Katie grabbed out for it, gobbling down a mouthful with such hungry haste that Caroline feared she might choke. There had plainly not been much food around that day either. She looked at the grey marble fireplace, a remnant from one of the cramped room's previous, more prosperous lives. The wide central slab bore a relief of a pheasant, spreading its wings as if taking flight from a hunter's hound; an old crack in the stone, black with dirt, ran through the middle of the bird's outstretched neck.

'So I've joined the gun factory,' she announced brightly. 'Mrs Vincent's letter of recommendation did the trick, like you said it would. And it's decent enough work, I s'pose – one and six a day, which ain't half bad. Better than what I was getting before.'

Amy said nothing; her brow creased as she pulled a needle through the rose. Something was troubling her. Caroline took the sandwich back from Katie and tore off a small piece, placing it carefully in the child's outstretched fingers.

'It's a pleasant thing to be out of service, I must say,' she continued, 'and in a new part of town. I'm grateful for you passing on word of this to me, Amy. I mean it. After Mr Vincent done what he done, ending himself in the public road, we all thought we'd be in the workhouse for sure before the month's close. Blind panic, there was, down in the servants' parlour.'

Caroline had witnessed her former master's demise – prompted by a shocking loss on the money markets, or so it was rumoured. Early one cold Wednesday morning at the start of March she'd been on her knees scrubbing the front steps, cursing the butler who'd given her the job, welcoming the warmth of the water on her freezing fingers as she rinsed the brush in the bucket. Mr Vincent had stepped over her, dressed for the City but lacking his coat and hat. *The Times* was in his hand, held limply by the spine, spilling out pages as he wandered to the gate. Reaching the street, he'd stood on the edge of the pavement, peering back and forth, craning his neck as if searching for a cab. A huge coal wagon had passed by, heading up towards Highgate. Mr Vincent had walked out alongside it, crouched down in the muddy thoroughfare and placed his head beneath one of its rear wheels. It had run on over him without so much as a bump, squashing his skull flat; Caroline's first reaction, watching incredulously from her soapy step, had been to let out a yelp of manic laughter.

Amy's needle halted. 'I am glad you have found a position, Caro,' she said quietly.

Caroline fed another piece of sandwich to Katie. 'I saw your Martin, in a tavern near the works. He was drinking with this Yankee engineer. Quill was his name.'

Amy set down her rose. 'He's mentioned Mr Quill to me.'

'A harmless old cove, that one. Likes to talk. Loves his Colonel, this Colt fellow. And he's really taken a shine to Mart. I'm told that he's looking to train him up – turn him into a proper engineer.'

This was surely good news, but Amy made no reaction to it. She looked at her daughter for a moment, and then stared blankly into the fire.

'There were other paddies there as well,' Caroline went on. 'Roscommoners like Mart. Friends of his, from the looks of things. Those I work with said that they're employed in the forging shop, and keep mostly to themselves. One is making a name for himself, though, as a regular hard customer – Pat Slattery, he's called. Word is that he'll serve out any Englishman who dares look his way.'

Amy sighed sharply, her head dipping forward.

'D'you know him?' Caroline asked.

Her sister rubbed at her eyes with a bony, needle-scarred knuckle. 'He was a porter with Mart and Jack in Covent Garden,' she replied, 'but they're old pals. From Ireland. There's a whole group. I – I was hoping that Mart had broken with them, by moving to Colt and all, but I had

me doubts.' Amy hesitated. 'It's just that Pat Slattery is –
is – he's –' Merely saying the name made her slip on her
words and lose her way. She was frightened.

'D'you think they're up to something? Planning mischief
– or thievery?'

Amy shook her head. 'No. *No*. Martin wouldn't. He's a
good man, Caro. He's never been nothing but kind to Michael
and Katie and me.'

Caroline scowled, made immediately impatient by this
unconditional loyalty. 'Oh Amy, for Christ's sake, listen to
yourself! Where is he right now, if he's such a saint? It's the
dead of night, you're alone with your babies in this wretched
place with no coal and no *food* even, and where is your
precious Martin? Out drinking up his wages, that's where,
propping up some bar with the legion of the bloody useless!'

Katie caught the heat in her aunt's voice and gazed at her
questioningly. The girl's almond-shaped eyes – the same eyes
as Caroline and Amy – were open wide, her lower lip starting
to tremble. Caroline made a shushing noise, bounced Katie
up and down rather briskly, and then gave her another piece
of the sandwich.

Amy, too, grew annoyed. 'He is gentle,' she said. 'Not
once has he so much as raised his hand to any of us. And
he is *true* – do you have any notion of how rare that is,
Caro?'

Caroline rolled her eyes; her sister would often resort to
this tactic. 'How could I possibly, Amy, unmarried as I am?'

This sarcasm was ignored. 'Neither does he pay any notice
to the many spiteful things that are said out in the Court.
They call him a traitor to Ireland, to his people, as he is
bound to an Englishwoman with half-English issue. And he
does not pay them any notice at all.' Her pale cheeks were
colouring, and her voice becoming yet more insistent. 'He
is my *husband*, Caro.'

'Only in the eyes of Rome,' Caroline retorted. Her blood
was up now. 'Where was it you was betrothed? A chapel in
an old potter's shed on Orchard Street, weren't it, by some
crack-brained boggler of a priest? You ain't no *Catholic*, Amy.
Your union with Martin Rea is founded on a flaming *lie*.'

Amy didn't respond. She fell quite silent, in fact, reaching over to pick at her artificial rose. Caroline itched with shame. Yet again, she'd gone a step too far; she'd said things she hadn't meant, regretting them even as they passed through her lips. She didn't, in truth, give two farthings for religion of any kind, yet here she was coming on like some doorstep Evangelical raging against Papist heresy. This was often the way between the sisters these days: an almost accidental battle, with the victor plunged into miserable remorse the second it was concluded.

'I'll bet you're right, anyway,' Caroline said at last, as if making a concession, attempting to mask her guilt with breezy cheerfulness. 'Lord, you couldn't steal from the bloomin' Yankees even if you were stupid enough to try. They're far too careful. I ain't so much as seen a complete pistol in all the time I been there.' She cast a look around the tiny, dirty room. 'We stand to turn a decent penny off this Colonel Colt, Amy – your Mart in particular, what with this Mr Quill looking out for him. You'll be leaving the Devil's Acre, I should think, before this year's out. I've found lodgings just along the river, in Millbank, in a new terrace next to a lumber yard. You could do very nicely over there.'

Katie had finished the sandwich but wanted more. Whimpering, she tugged at the front of Caroline's apron. When nothing else was produced, the whimper grew into a low, continuous moan, the infant's smooth little berry of a face crumpling with distress.

Amy stood, wrapping a thin shawl around her shoulders. 'This is our home, Caroline,' she said coldly. 'We ain't going nowhere.' Then she crossed the room and took back her child.

London dirt coated the window beside Caroline's drilling machine like a sheet of cheap brown paper. She had to lean up close to the pane to see anything much through it at all. Her ears had not misled her; down in the courtyard were the thirty or so men employed in the forging shop. Released to take their dinner, they were wandering towards the river, over to the row of costermongers and victual-sellers that had set up on the near side of Ponsonby Street to snag custom from the new Colt factory. All had removed their caps in the April sunshine and were smoking hungrily after their morning's labour. After passing through the tall factory gates, most simply selected a stall, made their purchases and walked back into the yard, eating as they went. A small number lingered, however, taking time to choose or trying to haggle down the price.

There was an angry, affronted shout from the direction of a boiler-cart selling steamed potatoes. Caroline squinted, looking closer. A dark, fierce-looking man, quite short and thin but utterly fearless, was cursing loudly in a strong Irish accent, making an energetic complaint to the stallholder. It was Pat Slattery, the fellow she'd seen with Martin and Mr Quill in the Eagle – whose name alone had caused her sister such alarm. A handful of others, his Roscommon boys, rushed to his side, raising their voices along with his. Martin's stooped, broad-shouldered form was not among them. Caroline supposed that he must be off somewhere doing the bidding of the chief engineer.

Slattery and his friends started rocking the cart back and forth, and a dull clang rang out as one of them struck the boiler with his fist. The rest promptly followed suit, and soon the squat iron tank was under a prolonged, noisy attack. The stallholder did not try to weather this battering for long, driving his dented boiler-cart off towards Vauxhall Bridge in a hail of oaths and stones, whipping his braying mule for all he was worth. The Irishmen patted each other's backs, nodding with the curt satisfaction of a job well done. They paid visits to a couple of the surrounding stalls – which served them quickly, waving away payment – and then came back through the factory gates, joking with each other as they settled against a wall to eat. These were creatures from the Devil's Acre, Caroline thought; that was their natural place. What could possibly have lured them out to this Yankee's factory in Pimlico? It wasn't just the daily wage, that was for certain. Amy was wrong – something was going on here.

Nancy, the girl across from Caroline, cleared her throat

pointedly. This could only mean that Mr Alvord, their over-seer, was approaching. Abruptly, Caroline turned from the window and reapplied herself to her labours. The drilling machine was about the size of a household mangle, but far more intricate and weighty in construction. Everything centred on the pistol part held in its middle by an elaborate clamp. This particular part was called the hammer, but to Caroline it looked more like a small twig or a wishbone. It was certainly hard to imagine this delicate piece of steel fitting into anything as deadly as a gun; hang it on a length of chain, she'd thought when first she saw it, and it would make a pretty pendant. Two different-sized holes had been run through the hammer presently fixed in the machine, which meant that there was one more left to do. The rotating head suspended before her held three drill-bits. At that moment, however, she couldn't for the life of her remember which bit to use.

Compared with other factories that Caroline had seen – a few mills and potteries, glimpsed from the street – the machine floor of the Colt works was almost disturbingly quiet. The labour done there largely involved making adjustments, aligning clamps and so on; the machines were actually engaged for a few seconds only, and would emit no more than a high, rasping whine. There was the slapping of the belts, and the constant background hum of the brass driving cylinder overhead, but for much of the time the floor was swaddled in a schoolroom hush. The sound of men's boots coming up behind her was thus clearly audible, and she stiffened at it; there were at least five pairs of them. Chancing a backwards glance, twisting momentarily atop her stool, she saw that the chubby, bland-faced Mr Alvord was surrounded by numerous others, more than she had time to count. They were all following an imposing bearded fellow, thick-set and tall, who looked like he knew his way around a gaming room – Colonel Colt, her employer.

Frowning in concentration, knowing that she must make a convincing display for the Colonel's sake, Caroline turned the drill-head to the left. It slid around easily, with a heavy, well-greased clunk. She leaned over to pull the lever that would connect her machine to the spinning cylinder ahead.

'Mr Alvord,' said a deep Yankee voice at her shoulder, 'if I'm not mistaken, this girl is just about to sink a second bolt-cam hole through that there hammer.'

This voice, of course, belonged to Colt. Caroline cursed her luck. Alvord was at her side the very next instant, smelling of bad teeth and root ginger, disengaging the belt, rotating the drill-head, apologising profusely for her stupidity. She looked around, thinking to assume her best servant's manner and assure the Colonel that it wouldn't ever happen again.

A small, hard eye was scrutinising her from beneath the brim of a strange Yankee hat. 'That hammer is the most vital part of a Colt pistol, young miss,' the Colonel said, not entirely unkindly. 'It's what marks us out from our main rivals in this city. You be sure to learn how to drill it properly.' He swivelled on his heel so that he faced the overseer. 'And Mr Alvord, p'raps you might like to deliver your lesson again. Although it is true that even the most slow-witted of humans can be trained in the operation of my machines, the rate of success does depend a little on the quality of the goddamn instruction.' With this, the gun-maker strode away in the direction of the jiggers and the lock-frames – the heavier devices that shaped the central parts of the revolver.

Alvord, enraged and humiliated, pointed to the drill-head. 'Start at position *one*, turning *anticlockwise*.' He indicated each bit in turn. 'That's the hammer spring; the bolt cam; the main spring roller. If you don't have it by the end of the day we'll be replacing you in the morning, understand?'

Caroline nodded, repeating the names of the drill-bits. Alvord had already left, though, starting after Colonel Colt. She became aware that one of the Colonel's followers had become detached from the train, and was lingering by her machine. Hands on the drill-head, she aimed a sly sidelong look in his direction. There stood a young man in an English frock-coat and top hat, a junior office type of the sort you saw perched up on the roofs of omnibuses bound for the City, smoking their cigars and surveying the streets below as if they were the rightful owners of all London. She supposed that this particular fellow was part of Colonel Colt's English establishment. He had a cool quality about him, though, a watchfulness, that held an undeniable appeal. He was studying her closely. Pausing in her work, she put a hand on her hip and met his gaze, thinking to embarrass any ignoble intention that might be lurking in his mind.

Caroline recognised him – the straight, short nose and smooth brow, the neat, coppery whiskers, the faint quizzical cast to his lips. It was the gentleman she'd seen in the yard on that first morning, a fortnight previously. He tipped his hat to her and went after Colt.

'The Colonel's starting to fret,' whispered Nancy knowingly. 'That's what it's all about. Word is that he's looking to show the factory off as soon as he can, to the Army and some government toffs most likely. But now, just as he's got the engine running nicely at last, his chief engineer goes and gets hisself knocked senseless.'

Caroline met this rather absently. 'What are you on about, Nance?'

Keen to be the bearer of gossip, Nancy leaned in closer, poking her flat, snub-nosed face between the raised parts of her machine. 'The beatings, Caro – ain't you heard? Mr Quill the Yankee engineer and his paddy assistant. Got served out something proper last night in Pimlico, up on one of Mr Cubitt's sites near Warwick Square.'

The smart young man left Caroline's mind at once. *'What?'*

Nancy was well pleased by this response. Nothing gave this sturdy factory veteran more satisfaction than to adopt the guise of the wise old hand with privileged information to share. 'They'll be all right, best anyone can tell,' she said casually. 'In a week or so, anyway. The Colonel's got 'em laid up in the Yankees' lodging house over on Tachbrook Street. Brought in a doctor and everything. No one knows who done it. There's stories aplenty, o' course.'

This was why Martin hadn't been down in the yard with Slattery. He was lying all bashed up in a Pimlico lodging house. Amy would be going mad with worry. Would he have thought to get word to her? Would he have been able to?

Helplessly, Caroline looked around the long, dingy machine room; at the Colonel's greasy metal contraptions, their operators hunched over them as if they were being slowly devoured; at the complex cat's-cradle of machine-belts, flapping and tensing with the shifting of the levers. It was only late morning. There was no chance of her being able to get away before seven. When she'd been taken on, the foreman had stressed that any unexplained absence from your machine during factory hours would see you slung straight out the gate.

Caroline tried to return her attention to the drill-head, but she couldn't stop thinking of Martin – of what had befallen him and Mr Quill after she'd spoken with them in the Eagle. Why would anyone attack them like that?

She could only come up with one possible answer. It had to be something to do with Pat Slattery.

All fifty of Colt's female operatives were employed in the same region of the works, on the lighter machines, and they took their dinner together. They sat by the water trough in the centre of the yard, chattering and laughing as they ate. Caroline stayed apart from them, having no wish to listen to their excited speculation about the beatings. She'd bought a white onion and a piece of cheese, but frustration and worry had taken away her appetite completely. Pacing the factory's boundary, she peered out through the railings, along the wide river in the direction of Westminster.

The bell rang, summoning them inside. It occurred to Caroline that she could just walk into the forging shop right then, confront Slattery and demand that he reveal everything he knew, for the sake of Martin's wife and children. This was a tempting notion indeed. Crossing the yard to the sliding factory door, preparing to file in behind the other women, she imagined herself simply doing it: turning away from the staircase, weaving between the drop-hammers, approaching the Irishman as he stoked his fire and saying her piece with righteous, unchallengeable anger.

But there was no time; and besides, one of the Yankees would be sure to see her, Mr Alvord would be informed, and she'd be dismissed before you could say 'main spring roller'. Caroline went back up to her machine and drilled hammers all through the grey, everlasting afternoon, fidgeting with agonised boredom. When the final bell eventually sounded she was the first down the stairs and out into the deepening darkness. She left by the pedestrian gate at the rear of the works, intending to learn what she could of Martin's condition and then go to Amy. This gate led onto Bessborough Place, the shadowy, featureless lane that lined the factory block's north-eastern side. From here it was only a short walk to the Americans' lodging house on Tachbrook Street. A large corner residence at the street's southern end, it had the grand, fresh-made look common to all of Mr Cubitt's Pimlico; the Colonel clearly believed in ensuring the comfort of his senior staff. She could see a couple of them through the windows, lounging in a gas-lit sitting room, laughing over something they'd read in a newspaper.

Caroline straightened her bonnet, screwed down her courage and knocked at the front door. It was opened by an elderly male servant who studied her with a knowing leer, no doubt assuming an unsavoury reason for her call. She was about to explain herself when she noticed two people sitting on a bench across the hall, directly opposite the doorway. One of them was Martin. He had a blanket over his shoulders and a wide, blood-spotted bandage wrapped around his brow. His ribs, too, were bound, as was his right wrist; in all, he looked more like a stricken soldier than an apprentice engineer.

Pushing past the servant, Caroline started towards him. The other person on the bench rose to meet her, and she realised that it was the fellow from the machine floor – the smart young man with the coppery whiskers. He was holding his top hat in his hands, as if about to go out; his hair was thick and straight, combed back from his brow in a neat, dark diagonal.

'You are acquainted with Mr Rea, miss?' he inquired.

Caroline nodded. 'He's my sister's husband, sir. She'll be worried half to death.'

Martin hadn't reacted to her appearance in the lodging

house. This wasn't so unusual. Her brother-in-law was prone to strangeness, his gaze icing over as he became sunk in his own private thoughts. That evening, however, he appeared to be barely conscious, swaying slightly where he sat as if drunk.

'My name is Edward Lowry,' the man said. 'I am the Colonel's London secretary.' He spoke in a clear, polished voice, by the standards of the Colt factory at least – this secretary plainly had education, if not wealth or breeding.

'Caroline Knox, sir,' she replied, dropping a small curtsey.

Mr Lowry looked back at Martin. 'The doctor says that Mr Rea here took several rather brutal kicks to the head, and remains seriously disorientated. He is set on returning to his home, though, as soon as possible. At once, in fact.'

'Martin is a determined fellow, sir. Mulish by nature.'

'The Colonel is upstairs, talking with Mr Quill. He has instructed me to honour Mr Rea's wishes – to discover his address and put him in a cab. I was going to take him over to Moreton Street and flag one down.'

Caroline shook her head. 'No cab will go where this cove lives, Mr Lowry. Let me ride with him. I'll get the driver to drop us on Broad Sanctuary. I can get him back from there.'

'Very well, Miss Knox.' He smiled, rather pleasantly Caroline had to admit, meeting her eye for just a second longer than necessary; then he turned to the injured man on the bench and put on his hat.

Martin glanced up at them both, seeming to understand what they'd been discussing. His face looked wrong, lopsided and red, and scratched all over with angry cuts; the bandages had gathered his bushy black hair into a single unruly clump. He winced as if the dim lamp on the wall behind Caroline was painfully bright. 'Let's be off, then,' he managed to croak.

The three of them tottered out into the street, Martin leaning heavily on Mr Lowry. They'd progressed about thirty halting paces along Tachbrook Street when there was movement somewhere behind them – rapid movement. Caroline felt a quiver of fear. Was it Martin's mysterious assailants, come to finish the job, along with any who might be with him? But no; before she even had time to turn, she heard the muttering, the accents, and knew immediately who it was.

The Irishmen came from the direction of the factory. There was an odd, monkish detachment about them. They did not speak to or even look at Caroline and the secretary, closing around Martin like so many pallbearers and all but hoisting him from the pavement. Mumbling something, Amy's name it sounded like, he barely noticed the change.

'All right, men,' announced Mr Lowry from his new position on the edge of this group, recognising the new arrivals as Colt workers and trying to take charge, 'we're moving him up to Moreton Street, just a few yards ahead. There I shall secure a cab, and instruct the driver to transport this poor fellow to his –'

Disregarding him entirely, the Irishmen started off in the opposite direction, back towards the factory. Caroline recognised one of them, a tall, bearded fellow named Jack Coffee, and called out to him. She'd met Jack on a couple of occasions when visiting the Devil's Acre and had found him to be a mild, peaceable soul; a little slow-witted, perhaps, but friendly. Right then, though, he was in no mood to talk to her.

'We'll take him home, Caro,' he replied quickly. 'Don't you be worrying none.'

'I'll come too.'

'Come tomorrow. Our boy here needs t' sleep.'

'What of Amy and the children? I'll –'

'Leave 'em be, will ye?' spat another voice, higher and more nasal than Jack's. She realised it was Pat Slattery's. Half a head shorter than the rest, he was over at Martin's other side. '*Jesus*. Don't you have a life o' your bleedin' own?'

They picked up their pace, carrying their friend off at some speed. Caroline stood watching as they disappeared around a corner, heading in the direction of Westminster, smarting at Slattery's harsh words. He knew who she was, although they'd never spoken before then. She guessed that he'd been given an unflattering report by Martin; he certainly didn't seem to like her. Was he annoyed that she was also at Colt, perhaps, thinking that she'd interfere somehow in whatever they might be up to? She cursed herself for not returning his scorn in kind, and swore that she wouldn't let him get away so easily in future.

'It would seem that we are both surplus to requirements, Miss Knox,' Mr Lowry said with a grin, taking a cigar from his pocket. He lit it, tossing the match in the gutter; then he turned towards her, considering something. 'Would you have me walk you home, since I am already out here in my hat and coat? Whereabouts do you live?'

Caroline remembered the look they had exchanged up on the machine floor, and before that, out in the factory yard; and how both had been terminated. 'Won't Colonel Colt want you, sir?'

'We have an appointment at eight,' he answered, 'which leaves me the better part of an hour. Besides, the Colonel instructed me to see a Colt employee to safety, and that is exactly what I would be doing. Pimlico has revealed itself to be a rather dangerous place of late, as you well know.'

Caroline found that she welcomed the thought of some company. Seeing her brother-in-law so reduced, and then being shooed away from him so curtly, had left her feeling a little odd; jarred, almost. She went over to Mr Lowry and took his arm, telling him that she had a room in Millbank, a short way past the Vauxhall Bridge Road. Together, they walked up to Moreton Street. He asked her how she'd come to be at the Colt factory.

'Believe it or not, sir, it was down to those Irishmen back there,' Caroline replied. 'My sister told me that they'd found work at a new American pistol factory by the river, and that the Yankees were still hiring operatives for their machines. I was in urgent need, you see, having recently lost my position up in Islington.' She paused. 'I was a housemaid.'

'I suspected as much,' the secretary remarked, puffing on his cigar. 'You have the diction of a good servant, Miss Knox, if I may say, and the bearing as well.'

Caroline glanced at him. 'But not the temperament, Mr Lowry – or so they liked to tell me. When the family took a hard knock and half of us were made to go, I was the very first one they picked out of the line. My mistress wrote me a letter, but that was only so I'd leave without a fuss.' She lifted her chin. 'I'd had enough of service anyway, to tell the truth. I wanted a change, and Colonel Colt seemed to fit the bill nicely.'

They arrived at the Vauxhall Bridge Road. Bright and noisy after the stillness of Pimlico, it was blocked by the usual unmoving chain of evening traffic. Fog was growing in the damp air, creeping around buildings, lamp-posts and carriages like soft mould. Caroline and the secretary stepped from the pavement, slipping between the stationary vehicles and the snorting horses reined up before them. As they reached the opposite side, Mr Lowry asked her who she'd worked for in Islington. She gave him a brief account of the end of the Vincent household. He recalled the case clearly, it turned out; it had even informed his own decision to join the Colt Company.

'Four decades of unstinting labour and that is the fate that befalls you. Everything stripped away in an instant. A sudden plunge into despairing destitution, with suicide the only possible release.' He shook his head. 'I wasn't prepared to take such a chance with my life. Like you, Miss Knox, I resolved to move on – to apply myself to something with a sense of real certainty about it.'

Caroline considered the sheen of Mr Lowry's top hat, the crisp whiteness of his collar, the cigar smoking in the corner of his mouth; and she thought, you ain't *quite* like me, though, are you, sir?

The wall of Millbank Prison came into view between two low terraces. Steeped in noxious fog, the monstrous building beyond was like a distant black cliff, forbidding and unreachable.

Mr Lowry looked over at it. 'You live next to the prison, miss?' he asked, the smallest trace of disquiet in his voice.

'A couple of streets past it,' Caroline replied. 'Sometimes, from my window, I can hear those locked up inside,' she added mischievously, 'ranting and raving, and calling for help. They're kept completely apart, you know – alone in their cells for all but one single hour of the day. Drives some of the poor beggars clean out of their minds.'

'Good God.' The secretary took a long drag on his cigar.

She led him on towards the lane that held her lodgings. 'You think our Colonel is a certain bet, then, Mr Lowry?'

He returned gladly to his previous subject. 'As near as is possible, Miss Knox, I'd say. The Colonel's wares are peerless, as is his method of production. There's demand for repeating arms at present – a vast, international demand. We've all been given a singular chance to improve our lot.'

Caroline was sceptical. '*You've* been given a chance, Mr Lowry, that I don't doubt – but I can't see the Colonel doing very much more for the likes of me.'

'You cannot know that, Miss Knox. If you prove yourself a steady worker, you will rise. That's the Colonel's policy. Other departments will open in the coming months – a packing room, for instance – that an intelligent woman such as yourself could easily be placed in charge of.'

She studied his smile as best she could in the gloomy lane. He was perfectly sincere. 'Hark at you,' she murmured, giving his arm a teasing tug, 'Colonel Colt's little organ-monkey, dancing away to his tune.'

Smiling still, Mr Lowry inclined his head. 'A fair description, I suppose.'

They had arrived at the plain mid-terrace house in which Caroline rented her room. Half a dozen other young, unattached women also resided there, mostly shop-girls from the West End; the landlady, Mrs Patten, would be sitting in the back parlour as usual, keeping up her watch on the comings and goings of her tenants.

Caroline released Mr Lowry's arm and went through the gate, rather sad that their conversation was about to end. Taking a walk with a handsome, well-dressed gent who held a clear liking for you would generally be pleasant, of course, but there was more here than that. His hopefulness, his absolute conviction that things would soon get better for them both, was heartening indeed; Caroline wasn't sure that she believed any of it but it was good to hear. Missing the warmth of him at her side, she drew in her shawl and thanked him for escorting her home.

The secretary bowed. 'It was my pleasure, Miss Knox. I can only hope that we will see each other again soon, around the

71

pistol works. And please, do not allow the events of last night to upset you unduly. No lasting damage has been done. Mr Rea will be back in the engine room before you know it.'

Caroline hesitated, thinking of Amy and the children; she would go over to Crocodile Court later on, Pat Slattery be damned. 'Will they try to find out who did it – and why?'

Mr Lowry took a last puff on his cigar and flicked the end into the road. 'I can't imagine that Colonel Colt will just let it pass.'

Caroline nodded, then bade him good night and walked up the path to her door. He was still standing at the gate when she closed it behind her.

5

'What in blazes happened, Mr Quill?' said Sam, leaning down towards the bandaged figure sprawled on the bed. 'What goddamn sons of bitches dared to do this to you?'

The engineer shifted in the amber gaslight. One entire side of his round face was covered by a continental map of angry bruises. His right forearm had been splinted and bound across his chest, the old sailor's tattoos mostly hidden beneath his dressings. 'I counted ten – no, twelve of 'em, Colonel,' he wheezed through his swollen lips. 'Sticks, they had – and great labourin' boots . . .'

Walter Noone turned from Quill's bedside. 'The bottle's done for this dumb bastard as much as any goddamn beating,' he muttered, straightening his military coat. 'He won't be right for a couple of days, more'n likely.'

Sam stood back up, unable to disagree. He stalked across the room to the window. It gave a clear view of the Colt premises, slotted neatly between Bessborough Place and the rusting iron cylinders of the Pimlico gasworks, with Ponsonby Street running across the front. The machines had stopped for the day but lamps still twinkled at the windows, and barrows of coal were being wheeled in through the factory door from a barge moored over at the wharf, ready for the following morning. At last, after countless setbacks, it was starting to look like a decent operation – a viable prospect. But just as there was a chance of some real progress, *this* had to go and happen. Sam didn't have the time for it, quite frankly, not when there was so much pressing business to attend to. A raw ache of vexation pulsed through him; it felt as if his forehead was about to burst open like a ripe boil.

Noone was at his side, arms crossed, a trusted lieutenant ready to draw up a plan of action. 'It was no robbery,' he said. 'Ben Quill ain't the sort to have anything of value on him – leastways, nothing that'd warrant a working-over like this. Any thief worth his salt would see that.'

'So what's your theory, Mr Noone?'

'Ben and his Irishman were targeted. Hunted down.' Noone's voice was insistent. Sam realised that despite his usual stony composure, the fellow was angry; fire-spitting furious, in fact. 'This is a message, Colonel – these cock-suckers knew exactly who they were beating on.'

Sam almost asked who might do such a thing, but found he could easily summon several suspects to mind. 'I'm inclined to agree. We've been denied the one man who is vital to the factory's continued operation. They just about got the engine going this morning without him, but any problems to be seen to or fine-tuning to be done and . . . well, to be blunt, Mr Noone, we'd be in a proper goddamn fix.' Struck by a notion, he turned to address the engineer. 'Were they Bulls, Mr Quill? Were your attackers Englishmen?'

Quill attempted a nod, and tried to lift his unbandaged arm. 'Aye, Colonel, so I believe. They knew I was an American, too, and cursed me for it.'

'Adams,' Sam pronounced. 'Has to be. He's trying to trip us up.'

'We must meet this, Colonel,' said Noone. 'It can't go unanswered. You give the word and I'll gather up some men – pound these motherfuckers flatter'n hammered shit.'

Sam eyed the watchman carefully. This was where the trouble could start. One poorly chosen word and Walter Noone would be out breaking skulls on the streets of London, gratifying that well-known taste for inflicting pain. The Colt Company would be made to leave London in disgrace, and the nay-sayers back in Connecticut would be proved entirely correct. It was a crucial moment, in short, and a firm hand was required.

'Don't you be telling me what I should or should not do, Mr Noone,' he snarled. 'And keep your poundings to yourself. Such measures ain't necessary just yet.'

Noone remained impassive. He wasn't best pleased, but he was still a soldier at heart and could take an order. 'Then we must at least permit our Yankee boys to wear their own pieces when they're outside the works. They must be allowed a fighting chance should they be attacked as well.'

Sam shook his head, growing impatient now. 'I've been making pistols for long enough now to know that if you let our men wear 'em in the streets of London they'll damn well get used. It surely don't need to be pointed out to you that should a Colt Yankee gun down a half-dozen Bulls in their own capital city it'll go very badly for us, regardless of the circumstances. I've been telling these people that the Colt revolver is a *peacemaker*, Mr Noone. I can't be seen to be wrong on that.'

The gun-maker rubbed his brow, trying to relieve the pressure beneath. It was useless; bourbon whiskey was required as a matter of urgency. He lowered his hand into his pocket, wrapping his fingers around the stiff screw of Old Red that lay within.

'Stay alert,' he instructed. 'Patrol the lanes around the factory and this lodging house. If you see anyone skulking about, you chase 'em off with my blessing – but hold your goddamn horses, d'you hear? There'll be a better way to manage this than the spilling of blood.'

The Colt barouche cut across two lines of traffic, sweeping up to the pavement. Sam wiped at the window with his glove, clearing a small rectangular block in the film of condensation that covered it. They were on the edge of Leicester Square, a region of the city which he knew well. During the Great Exhibition two years previously he was to be found there on an almost daily basis; it housed several of London's largest and most popular shooting galleries, and was thus the prime spot to give practical demonstrations of a gun-maker's wares. The building he was looking out at now, however, was an unfamiliar one. They'd come to halt before a set of smart double doors, flanked by glowing gas-lamps and sheltered beneath a striped awning that was fast filling with rainwater. An ornately engraved brass plaque identified this as the entrance to the Hotel de Provence – the designated meeting place.

Sam glanced across at Mr Lowry, who was sorting papers in the barouche's shadowy confines with his customary air of keen efficiency. The gun-maker was pretty satisfied with this young fellow – yet more testimony, he thought, of my skill when it comes to selecting my people. The London secretary was possessed of a cool, understated cleverness, and was already quite committed to the Colt Company. He was prime manager material, in short, the sort who might be given a serious post a few years down the line. Of course, there was still a fair bit of shaping and schooling to be done before then.

'Now you stay sharp in there, Mr Lowry,' Sam told him as he prepared to exit, raising his voice over the steady drum-ming of rain against the carriage roof. 'I don't know quite what to expect from this fellow, but I've yet to encounter a politician who ain't a slippery shark. You be sure to make a damn close record of what's said, for our future reference. And I needn't tell you that if he so much as *hints* at what befell our Mr Quill and his mick last night, you're to deny everything.'

'Naturally, Colonel.'

Hopping out across an overflowing gutter, Sam rushed up to the hotel's doors and pushed his way through. Someone took his coat and hat and directed him towards the restaurant. It was a long, warm saloon, overlooking the illuminated frontages of the various exhibition rooms and billiard halls that fringed Leicester Square. Lively conversa-tion buzzed all around, much of it in French; Sam recalled that the southern part of Soho was home to a great many citizens of France, displaced by the revolutionary upheavals in their own country. An effort had been made to create what he supposed was an authentically Parisian atmosphere, which meant plenty of polished brass and plush crimson upholstery, well-groomed, supercilious waiters with tiny moustaches, and large paintings of idyllic country scenes across the walls. A number of the diners caught sight of Sam; heads turned, and that familiar ripple of recognition ran through the room.

The Honourable Lawrence Street, MP, was waiting at a table at the rear of the room, that weird white-blond hair of his shining against the restaurant's biscuit-coloured wallpaper. The little man was working his way through a newspaper with a cold, systematic air, a pair of silver-rimmed glasses perched upon his nose. As Sam approached he folded it away and stood – awkwardly puppet-like as before – to shake the gun-maker's hand.

'And who is this?' he inquired, eyeing Mr Lowry with some suspicion.

'My private secretary,' Sam replied, 'one of the Colt Company's Englishmen. I hope you don't object.'

Street made no comment. He removed his glasses and tucked them inside his waistcoat.

A yellow rectangle appeared in the corner of Sam's sight; the Colt barouche was cruising past the restaurant's wide windows, its mustard panels glittering in the wet evening.

'That is quite a vehicle, Colonel,' the Honourable Member remarked as he sat back down, gesturing towards the other chairs set around his table. 'It would be a lie to say that I'd seen a finer one this year.'

'I spend more time in that there carriage than I do in my bed, Mr Street,' Sam said, signalling for a waiter. 'An uninterrupted ride across this city is an out-and-out impossibility, what with the omnibuses and the hackney cabs and all the goddamn livestock, so I feel it's best to be comfortable while I wait. Now, would you kindly tell why you wished to see me?'

'Straight to the business at hand, as always.' Street compressed his lips into a tight smile. 'Very well. A couple of matters recommend themselves to your attention. Firstly, I feel it is my duty to inform you that your enemies, alarmed by the great leaps of progress recently made within your factory, have begun to organise themselves.'

Sam sat up. 'Not that bastard Bob Adams?'

Street paused thoughtfully for a second, as if making a mental note. 'No, Lady Cecilia Wardell. You remember her from the reception at the American embassy? She has gathered several supporters around her, Evangelicals I've heard, and aims to cause you whatever difficulty she can.'

The gun-maker snorted dismissively. A waiter had arrived at his side. 'What's it to be, then, Mr Street? Champagne, ain't it, with you Bulls?'

'My thanks, Colonel, but I require nothing.'

Sam ordered bourbon for himself. After the waiter had retreated, he asked to know what the other matter was.

The Honourable Member made a small adjustment to his shirt-cuffs. 'I have heard, Colonel, that you are a great believer in the power of endorsement by a famous name. It has come to my attention that a prominent foreign celebrity is in London – someone whom I believe it would benefit you to befriend.'

Now this was more interesting. 'Who is it?'

'A freedom-fighter in the true American mould,' Street said, delaying the disclosure for a few seconds – attempting, in his low-key way, to build a bit of anticipation. 'Lajos Kossuth, the rightful regent-president of Hungary.'

The gun-maker made no effort to hide his disappointment. Was this meeting to be a complete waste of his time? 'Well, how about that,' he muttered, pushing back his chair and crossing his arms.

Street was unconcerned by this reaction. A flicker of insight passed across his features. 'You know him already.'

Sam sneered up at the ceiling. 'I met Mr Kossuth in the Turkish town of Vidin, Mr Street, shortly after he'd been obliged to flee his homeland and the vengeance of the Austrian Emperor. I was travelling around Europe at the time, acquiring patents and the like, when it came to me that I might find a customer in the Sultan. That gaudy little parrot turned me away – a decision he'll live to regret. Anyways, I had a week or two to spare, there was talk of trouble on the Hungarian border, I had some guns to shift, so I decided to head on over and see what was what. One day I happened to find myself in the same place as the renowned Lajos Kossuth. Naturally I paid him a call.'

Street was wearing that tight smile again. 'You wander the world a good deal, do you, Colonel?'

'Such is the lot of the gun merchant. Conflict don't come to *him*, most of the time, so he must go to it – sniff it out as best he can.' The whiskey arrived in a cut-crystal decanter, accompanied by a single squat glass. Sam reached for it and poured his first drink. 'At any rate, I quickly came to realise that Mr Kossuth and I could do no business together. All he had to offer in exchange for my arms was some fine ideals and a good deal of long-winded speechifying. This is often the trouble with revolutionaries and freedom-fighters, Mr Street, in my experience. They just ain't a decent prospect for custom.'

The Honourable Member nodded. 'Well, poor Mr Kossuth is still rather impecunious, I'm afraid. I've heard that he is obliged to reside at present in a barrack house in Clerkenwell, in fact, as the guest of a chapter of Chartists.' This was said with a measure of both pity and disgust, as if it was akin to setting your bed in a sewer. 'Nevertheless, Colonel, I feel that it could be useful for you to give him a private tour of your factory.'

Sam fixed this queer little man with a long, careful look. Had Street been making promises to the Hungarian exile? Was Kossuth perhaps under the impression that discounted or even free weapons would be offered to him by the Colt Company, so that he could arm his scattered cohorts and re-establish his vanquished republic? This was something that would have to be set straight right away.

'Much as I respect Mr Kossuth and his struggles,' the gun-maker said slowly, 'I must point out that such tours are only worthwhile when there's a chance of a goddamn sale as a result of it.'

Street set his hands together on the tabletop with the air of someone about to embark upon an explanation. 'I take it, Colonel, that you are aware of the ever-increasing belligerence between Russia and Turkey, and the bullying conduct of Russian diplomats in Constantinople?'

Sam indicated that he was. His interest in the grievances that lay behind this deepening dispute was limited – something to do with the supposed entitlement of Orthodox Christians living within the Ottoman Empire to Russian protection. It all sounded entirely contrived to him, a mere excuse for a bit of the sabre-rattling of which these ancient empires were so very fond. He was keeping a close watch on it, though. From where he stood, it was a pretty promising situation.

'Great Britain has taken against Tsar Nicholas,' the Honourable Member continued, 'as he is unquestionably the aggressor, and every Briton shares an instinctive loathing of oppression of all kinds.'

For a moment, Sam considered saying a few words about the British and oppression, but managed to hold his tongue.

'Lajos Kossuth, also, is a notable victim of Russian antagonism. It was the Tsar's alliance with the Emperor of Austria, and the assistance of his massive armies, that enabled the easy rout of Mr Kossuth and the dismantling of his young republic. The regent-president remains a famous and popular man. If he were to visit your pistol works, the press would be certain to attend, and in significant numbers. A great many Englishmen would read of your support for him. It would serve as an effective demonstration of the Anglo-Saxon bond we discussed at Buchanan's.' Street met Sam's eye. 'In addition, you would find that Mr Kossuth has allies of real influence. Being seen to show sympathy for his plight would send out a clear message to these people. It would show them that they can trust you – that you are their kind of fellow.'

Sam knocked back his drink. Something else was going on here, for certain; the Colt Company was being used for some deeper purpose. He looked over at Mr Lowry. The secretary was studying Mr Street with subtle distrust. Street was working a scheme – they both saw it. But whatever the Honourable Member might be plotting, Sam got the sense that the success of his factory was part of the plan. It was worth playing along for now.

'Very well, Mr Street,' Sam said, reaching for the whiskey, 'I'll see what I can arrange.'

6

'He's a pretty slick son of a bitch, ain't he, that Lawrence Street. Lajos Kossuth – Lord Almighty, that would never have occurred to me. Not in a thousand years.'

The Colonel picked up the cut-crystal decanter he'd removed from the restaurant, took another swig straight from the neck and then went back to loading the Navy revolver that hung from his right hand. The pint or so of whiskey that he'd already imbibed was making this rather difficult, however; Edward had already been obliged to chase several dropped bullets across the sand-scattered floorboards.

The secretary was sitting beside his employer, smoking a penny cigar. They were in Marchant's Shooting Gallery, on the opposite side of Leicester Square to the Hotel de Provence. It was a rough-edged establishment, a whitewashed vault with a gun-rack at one end and an assortment of lime-lit targets at the other. A split log had been laid out about twenty yards from the targets to mark the firing line. All of the customers were male, mostly of the sort you'd expect to find clustered around a cock-fight – battered hats, loud chequered trousers and well-patched jackets were present in abundance. There was some money mixed in there too, though, a conspicuous minority of dissolute-looking gentlemen taking an evening away from Society. Rifles were the near-universal choice of weapon. Due to the effects of liquor and a general lack of expertise, the fire across the gallery was intermittent and less than accurate; but several spirited contests were underway nevertheless, with cash changing hands and victors crowing in triumph.

Colonel Colt, with his revolver, his crystal whiskey decanter and his outlandish, fur-lined attire, was attracting the usual amount of attention. He'd been unimpressed by Marchant's at first, declaring it a poor example of its kind and discoursing at some length on the inferiority of the guns on offer. But now, settled on the periphery with his belly full of strong liquor, a wad of tobacco in his cheek and a presentation case of pistols open on his lap, he looked about as comfortable and content as Edward had ever seen him.

They'd left the hotel about half an hour earlier. A waiter had pursued them outside, attempting to reclaim the purloined decanter from the Colonel's grasp; tucking a bank-note in the fellow's waistcoat and waving him away, Colt had run an eye around the coloured lights of the square, soon settling upon Marchant's. The mustard-coloured barouche had drawn up beside them. Opening the door and leaning inside, the Colonel had retrieved a box of Navys from the small stock that was kept on board and headed over to the shooting gallery. Following close behind, Edward had imagined that he wished to fire off a few shots with one of his inventions to dispel the aggravation he'd doubtlessly accumulated during his conversation with the inexplicable Mr Street – who'd remained seated at his table, unfolding his newspaper and returning his glasses to his nose almost before they'd risen from their chairs.

The secretary knew that he had witnessed something important in the Hotel de Provence. This Mr Street seemed to be going out of his way to further the interests of the Colt factory. There could be no doubt that hidden forces were working towards the achievement of their own ends. He'd decided that he would learn more.

'Who would've thought it, though,' Colt drawled, picking up the Navy once more and taking a bullet between thumb and forefinger. 'Kossuth, a committed opponent of tyranny, held up as a hero by the British!'

'Excuse me, Colonel?'

The gun-maker laughed nastily. 'You forget that you're talking with an American here, Mr Lowry! We can still recall fighting our way out from under *your* tyranny, my young friend.' He looked around the gallery with jolly ferocity. 'Why, not ten years ago I myself was occupied with designing weapons – undersea mines of extraordinary power – expressly to keep our American harbours safe from the threat of *your* goddamn ships.'

Edward picked a shred of tobacco from his lip, curbing a smile. This seemed a pretty blatant refutation of the so-called 'Anglo-Saxon bond' mentioned by Street in the Hotel de Provence – and which the Colonel had taken to inserting into his correspondence with British military figures and politicians at every opportunity. The Colt mind was clearly broad enough to encompass the odd contradiction.

Finally managing to slot the last bullet into his pistol, the Colonel worked the loading lever and then set the hammer against one of the cylinder pins. Lifting the revolver up to examine it, chewing slowly on his plug, his meaty face assumed a look of almost reverential appreciation. 'This arm here,' he declared, 'is so much finer than the wretched Adams I held in the office of that idiot Paget as to make any comparison downright odious.'

The shining blue and brass Navy was starting to draw notice, as was surely Colt's intention. Slowly, he turned his head and released a long spurt of tobacco juice onto the range's sandy floor.

'Mr Kossuth is not admired by everyone, Colonel,' Edward volunteered. 'His boldness in attacking emperors and tsars in his public addresses has made him many new enemies in the palaces of Europe. Louis Napoleon wouldn't let him so much as set foot in France – and over here, during his last visit a couple of years ago, the few government men who extended a friendly hand found none other than Queen Victoria herself seeking their removal from office.'

'Queen Victoria *herself*, eh?' the Colonel mused. He took another drink, smacking his lips; and then casually spat out his plug, sending the little brown projectile sailing away into a far corner. 'Perhaps that right there is Lawrence Street's design, Mr Lowry. Colt revolvers may be out of poor old Kossuth's reach, but the spectacle of this fearless republican touring my factory – just taking a friendly interest – might be enough to make your Victoria sit up on her goddamn throne and have a hard think about how long her soldiers can really afford to be without my arms.'

Edward coughed hard on his cigar, somewhat startled by this easy talk of rattling the monarch. Nonetheless, he couldn't help but be impressed by the Colonel's concise strategic summary, and was pleased to have been included in his confidential deliberations. Beneath Colt's coarse, colourful exterior lay a canny businessman – one who would consider a situation in depth, seeking the advantage. But what could Mr Street possibly be looking to gain from all this? Why would he, a member of Her Majesty's Parliament, want it to seem that there was an understanding between Colonel Colt and the Hungarian revolutionary? Who *was* this person?

Before he could frame another query, the Colonel picked up the Navy by the barrel and offered him the stock. Distracted by his ruminations, the secretary accepted it without comment. The weight – and the pistol felt heavy indeed – made him realise what had happened. He looked at his employer enquiringly, but the gun-maker was already up on his feet, hands cupped around his mouth.

'Mr Marchant!' Colt yelled above the chatter and the gunfire. 'Where the hell are you? Mar-*chant*!'

Seconds later, a squat man with a velvet eye-patch was standing before the American, regarding him dubiously. 'What is it?'

'D'you know who I am?'

The man – Mr Marchant – nodded. 'I 'ad a suspicion, sir, and upon 'earing you speak I would say that you're the Yankee what's set up a pistol factory down by the river.'

'Colonel Samuel Colt is my name, and that there in my man's hand is the latest model of my patented six-shot revolver. You ever had a revolver in this place before, Mr Marchant?'

A small crowd had gathered around them. I am to play the squire, Edward thought wryly, rising from the bench.

The Colonel will swagger to the firing line, survey the targets and then hold out his palm with steely nonchalance; I shall approach, obediently place the loaded Navy in it, and retire. Colt was having a fine old time. A rich seam of showmanship ran through him, Edward saw – he plainly relished being up in front of the public with just his wits and his product, making his pitch.

Marchant's doubtful manner had not been altered by confirmation that he had a globally renowned gun-maker on his premises. 'We 'ad one a while back – British made, a five-shooter. Prone to misfiring, it was. I sold it on.'

Colt glowered impressively, his chest swelling beneath his patterned waistcoat. 'The work of an inferior goddamn imitator, Mr Marchant,' he roared, 'and nothing whatsoever to do with me. That there *six*-shooter of mine don't damn well misfire, and it has power like nothing you've ever seen.' He paused, gesturing towards the secretary. 'Mr Lowry here will oblige you with a demonstration.'

Edward barely managed to mask his alarm. There was an expectant murmur from the crowd, and a passage swiftly cleared between him and the firing range. Was this some manner of drunken Yankee joke? The Colonel knew full well that he was the very greenest of gun novices. This had been openly confessed when he'd applied for his position, and had even been accepted as a virtue of his candidacy; he'd argued, rather eloquently he'd thought, that he would be able to see the factory's proceedings as business only, unhampered by the distortions and prejudices of the enthusiast. No one had contradicted him.

Colonel Colt was retrieving his whiskey from the bench, his expression unreadable. In any other circumstances Edward would have considered protesting his lack of expertise, but he could hardly do so now without embarrassing both himself and his employer. A challenge had been laid before him, he realised, and he could not hesitate. The performance must be flawless. He looked down at the long black pistol that jutted from his fist, regarding it anew. *You have in your hand the means to kill a man*, he thought, *this very instant, as easily as pointing*.

Clearing his throat, Edward walked over to the firing line. He placed a boot upon the split log and raised the gun. Although heavy, the weapon was perfectly balanced, the dark walnut stock sitting well against his palm. The mechanism was straightforward enough. He'd watched it enacted on unloaded pieces countless times, but had never once considered picking up a revolver and trying it out. This had plainly been noticed.

The secretary cocked the hammer with his thumb. There was a locking noise in the body of the gun, a sound like the passage of gears rotating towards a decisive, irreversible conclusion. Edward ran his tongue quickly over his top lip. The trigger was tense now, the catch on a coiled spring; he settled it into the first joint of his index finger. He could feel the pulse of his blood against the tempered iron. A cold bead of sweat rolled down his neck. Shutting one eye, taking aim as best he could, he squeezed.

The Navy jolted back against his hand, sending a tremor up his entire arm. The report was deafening, double the volume of every other weapon on the range, with a solid slam to it that was a world away from the weak fizz and pop of Mr Marchant's ageing rifles. Edward did not dare to lower the pistol, in case he dropped it or discharged a bullet into the floor, nor did he attempt to see whether he had hit the large circular target that was mounted before him. Instead, pulling back the hammer, he fired again, and again, until the cylinder was empty and the pressure of his finger produced only impotent clicks. The six shots had gone off impossibly fast, more rapidly than the eye could blink, and without the slightest hint of a misfire; the staggering advantage of the Colt revolver had been ably displayed. Mr Marchant and his customers were completely silent, stunned by the close succession of blasts. As the haze of gunpowder smoke drifted aside, Edward saw that a couple of black dots had even been punched in the outer rings of the target.

'There we have it,' said the Colonel, stepping forward and slapping him on the shoulder. 'He ain't exactly a great marksman, is he, but did you see the speed at which he got those bullets off? Could you feel the raw *power* behind the shots?'

There was a general mutter of agreement. Colt caught Marchant's eye and nodded towards the bench. At one end, the second Navy from the presentation set lay in its case. 'That there six-shooter,' he pronounced, 'entirely virgin and unfired, is now the property of Marchant's Shooting Gallery, with the compliments of its inventor. Which of you fine gentlemen, I wonder, will be the first to shoot six straight bull's-eyes with it?'

The move towards the pistol could only be described as a clamour. Marchant made it first, luckily for him, grabbing the Navy from the case and holding it in the air, shouting for order as he did so. Colt looked on with grave satisfaction, loudly imparting the address of his London sales office and some of his current prices.

Edward stood fixed to the spot, his feather-light guts fluttering around inside him. He brought the Navy down, breathing hard. He'd passed the Colonel's unexpected test. Firing the revolver – reaching out across such a distance and delivering a series of impossibly swift, piercing blows – had been a truly astonishing experience, filling him with an excitement so pure it was almost not to be trusted. The sense of destructive strength as he'd worked through those six shots was dizzying, invigorating; yet also numbing somehow, laced with blackness, utterly devoid of reason. Edward found that he wanted both to set the pistol down for good and reload it immediately for another try.

'Nice work, Mr Lowry,' Colt said with an approving nod. 'Orders'll be the certain result of this little display, from both Marchant and a few of his wealthier regulars. Not worth much in the grand scheme, but it keeps people talking.' He took a last slug from the crystal decanter and then dropped it carelessly on the floor. 'Come, we must be off. We have to unearth that sottish stick-insect Alfie Richards from wherever he's buried himself and start putting together a show for Mr Kossuth. Right this minute.'

Edward looked at the weapon in his hand. A thin line of smoke still twisted from the cylinder. Dazed and a little disappointed, he started towards the crowd at the bench, intending to give it to Mr Marchant.

Colt stopped him. 'I want you to keep that there pistol, Mr Lowry.'

'Pardon me, Colonel?'

'I want you to *keep it*, I said. Hang it on the wall, take it to ranges, show it off to your sweethearts.' The gun-maker slapped his shoulder again. 'Consider it a gift.'

'Lawrence Street is his name. He's in the Commons – a Whig, I should think. D'you know him at all, Saul? Chilly little cove with white-blond whiskers – wears eye-glasses.'

Saul Graff did not answer for almost a minute. He sucked on the cigar Edward had given him, absently pushing a last morsel of devilled kidney around his plate with his fork; then he cast a look around the low brick cavern in which they sat. The Cider Cellars on Maiden Lane, chosen largely for its proximity to the Hungerford Bridge Pier and the steamer to Pimlico, was occupied by the usual early evening crowd, an eclectic assortment of literary, governmental and legal types. It was formidably noisy, a close, smoky basement in which the drinkers and diners were packed together like figs in a drum. Their table was in one of the cellar's furthermost corners, tucked away in a small alcove beneath a candle-blackened archway. Edward leaned back against the wall behind him, feeling the thudding, grinding vibrations of the early evening traffic up on the Strand.

'This is exactly what I imagined might occur in that factory,' Saul said at last, grinding the cigar out in a pool of congealing gravy. 'Manoeuvring. Offers of interested friendship. Back-room deals. And I should have guessed that it would come from the likes of Street. What a blasted *idiot* I am!'

Edward sipped his sherry. 'So you do know of him.'

Saul loosened his necktie, sitting back in his chair. A rather thin, large-eyed creature, dressed as always in a dark costume a little like an undertaker's, he had a dense black moustache and a light manner that he used to hide the deeper analytical workings of his mind. 'I do, Edward, yes. Of course I do. He's a whip on the Liberal side, and something of a tin-pot Machiavelli. Should Lawrence Street come knocking upon your door, there's a fair chance it'll be to do with an intrigue of some kind. They say that his first loyalty is to Lord Palmerston – who in turn places great value in Street's endeavours.' He gave Edward a meaningful look. 'Your Colonel has caught an interesting eye there, and no mistake.'

So there it was: the link with Lajos Kossuth. The famously brazen Lord Palmerston had been the Hungarian's most prominent supporter during his previous visit to England, even going so far as to invite Kossuth to Broadlands, his country seat. This was done in open defiance of the Queen's wishes, leading her to seek his dismissal as Foreign Secretary; only fear of public outcry at the removal of an enduringly popular minister had prevented this. Two governments had fallen since then – events in which Palmerston had not been uninvolved – and he was presently Home Secretary in the coalition cabinet of the Earl of Aberdeen. It was rumoured, however, that he took little interest in his duties there, occupying himself instead with plotting and the careful undermining of his rivals – thus making his current ministry as weak, compromised and ineffectual as every other part of Aberdeen's administration.

'Are you implying that Street is courting Colonel Colt on Lord Palmerston's orders, Saul?'

Graff smiled slyly, knitting his eyebrows into dark diagonals. 'Perhaps. Involvement with an arms manufacturer would be well outside Pam's official jurisdiction as Home Secretary – but then, he's not exactly known for respecting such boundaries. Still sticks his nose into the affairs of Clarendon's Foreign Office without any hesitation whatsoever, from what I hear. The old dog's far more concerned with the goings-on there than in his own department. They say he's making a proper nuisance of himself over this unfortunate business between Russia and Turkey – insisting that our navy intervene and so forth. It's hard to see quite what his angle would be in this affair, though . . .' Saul became lost in strategic musings, poking at the softened wax around the rim of their candle with his forefinger.

Edward finished his drink. He did not have much longer. 'What might your man make of it all?'

Snapped from his meditations, Saul blinked; then he

laughed. 'The Honourable Mr Bannan is a committed *radical*, my friend. He has dedicated his political life to securing the vote for the many thousands of our working men presently denied their rightful voice in the Commons. Our noble Home Secretary is an implacable and very powerful enemy to this particular cause. Mr Bannan therefore welcomes any information I can bring him that may pertain to Lord Palmerston's latest piece of scheming. And this – Lawrence Street seeming to make introductions for the Yankee gun-maker Samuel Colt – will certainly get his attention.' He pushed away his plate. 'You have my thanks, Edward. I wasn't sure, in truth, if you would be prepared to talk with me about matters such as these. It was never my intention that you should become my eyes in the Colt factory, or anything of that nature.'

Edward smiled thinly at this flagrant falsehood. 'I've told you this, Saul, because I'm seeking an explanation *myself*. I'm coming to learn that Colonel Colt explains his actions only up to a point. If I'm to get on in his firm then I feel that I should at least be able to make an informed guess about the rest.'

Saul laughed again. 'My word, how well you're taking to this new world of yours! Such ambition, such initiative! You, old friend, are a natural man of business.' He raised his glass in an amiable salute. 'I am happy to oblige, and look forward to any future exchanges of information – mutually beneficial and entirely innocent, of course – that we two might make.' After drinking down the remainder of his sherry, Saul hesitated, leaned in a little closer and asked, 'What of the women?'

Edward rolled his eyes. The question did not surprise him. In contradiction to his rather cerebral appearance, Graff had always been a keen and active admirer of the fairer sex. Back when both men had been junior clerks at Carver & Weight's, before Saul left for his current career as a parliamentary aide, Edward would regularly be recruited for pursuits over great stretches of London, after a group of dressmakers or governesses or even gay women who'd caught his friend's undiscriminating, ever-vigilant eye.

He looked impatiently at his pocket watch. 'The factory girls, you mean?'

'Several dozen, are there not? Under your very roof?'

'I believe the number is close to that. Most are rather ugly and unkempt, as you'd expect.'

'But not all, eh?' Saul was grinning. 'You blasted rogue, Lowry.'

With a small grimace, Edward relented, telling of how he had walked Miss Knox home a couple of nights previously. He kept his description fairly brief. It did not seem necessary to mention that he'd found himself thinking of her several times since; that he'd taken to imagining her hand slipping around his side, pulling him closer, and her head tilting back to receive his kiss. He was a little embarrassed by this, in all honesty – by the fact that despite all his professional poise he could be so easily affected by a pretty face and an engaging manner.

'And have you sought her out since?'

Edward shook his head. The meeting he was due to attend at the factory that night – with the American staff, after the operatives had been discharged – would be the secretary's first stop in Pimlico in nearly a week. Lajos Kossuth's crowded calendar of engagements had obliged the Colt Company to agree to conduct his tour of the works the very next Tuesday, only four days after the conversation with Street at the Hotel de Provence. Edward's every waking hour since had been spent bound to the Colonel, under the somewhat haphazard stewardship of Alfred Richards, travelling between the offices of various publications, buying drinks and meals for Richards's extensive circle of acquaintances and generally doing anything the press agent or gun-maker could think of to secure some last-minute coverage of the Hungarian's visit in the newspapers. Edward had thus been denied all opportunity to arrange a second encounter with Miss Knox. This was both a frustration and a relief. He wanted to see her again, very much; but he was acutely aware that a dalliance with a drill operator might well hinder his ascent to the Colt Company's upper reaches. On balance, it was best left alone.

Saul was visibly disappointed by this lack of progress. 'Edward, did you learn nothing while we were together at

Carver's? It never pays to linger. You must be *bold*, my friend. This is a factory girl, for God's sake, not some curate's daughter who requires a ring on her finger before she'll even take your hand. You must *act*.'

Edward rose from the table, tempted to point out that Saul's pursuits had almost invariably ended in some form of humiliation for them – and that his friend had met the woman to whom he was currently engaged through the exertions of his mother. Instead, he simply ducked out under the blackened arch, directing a sardonic, sidelong look at Graff as he went.

'I must catch a steamer to the factory,' he said. 'The Hungarian is due at ten tomorrow, and there's a good deal still to arrange. But I thank you sincerely, Saul, for your interest.' He nodded towards their plates. 'I'll let you stand for this one.'

Colonel Colt, clad in a powder-blue Yankee coat, stormed before the bandstand that had been erected over the factory's water trough and threw his arms in the air, urging the dozen musicians perched upon it to play louder. They tried their best to obey the gun-maker's impatient command, blowing hard on flutes and coronets and banging away at drums, but this still wasn't enough to drown out the party of protesters that had gathered outside the Ponsonby Street gate. These people were singing a hymn – the Lord's Prayer set to a rather turgid tune – and held aloft placards on which they had painted biblical passages. The largest read: *The Righteous One takes note of the house of the wicked, and brings the wicked to ruin.* At their head was a pale, majestic lady in a costly emerald-green dress and a black shawl and bonnet. Watching from across the yard, Edward realised that this must be Lady Wardell, the committed enemy of Colt that Lawrence Street had spoken of. Those around her had the upright deportment and sober clothing of city Evangelicals, the kind that one might see taking aristocratic Sabbath breakers to task on Rotten Row or performing missionary work within London's foulest rookeries. Their hymn ended, and one among them, a man of the cloth from the look of

93

him, started to rail against the evils of the weapons trade in a deep, imposing voice. He appealed to the Colt operatives to leave the American's clutches and seek decent Christian labour instead.

'The Apostle Matthew teaches us to *love our enemies*, not destroy them with revolving pistols!' he cried. 'To bless those who curse us, to do good to those who hate us, and to pray for those who persecute us, that we might be the sons of our Father in Heaven! My brothers and sisters, you must turn yourselves away from this infernal factory and the instruments of death it will produce!'

Edward stood with Alfred Richards in front of the factory block's sliding door, beneath a hastily painted banner that proclaimed 'Col. Colt Welcomes Kossuth', and pictured the Old Glory, the Union Jack and the gaudy flag of the short-lived Hungarian Republic intertwined in everlasting friendship. Beside them was the American staff, plainly uncomfortable in coats and neckties, swapping obscene remarks about Lady Wardell and her protesters. Half a dozen newspapermen, all loose stitching, scuffed elbows and four-day beards, were positioned a little further towards the gate, their notebooks at the ready. The main body of the London workforce, numbering around one hundred and fifty, had spread itself across the yard before the warehouse, bunching around the bandstand, chattering loudly. Instructed by Gage Stickney to clean themselves off in the factory washroom before coming outside, they presented a slightly less grubby aspect than usual, but this wasn't saying too much.

It looked, in all, like the setting for some kind of popular ceremony. The visit of Lajos Kossuth was being made to serve as the public unveiling of the factory – the event that would announce Colt's arrival in London to the world. Despite the unruly workers, the Colonel's evident peevishness and the disruptive efforts of those at the gate, Edward was growing excited. This, he thought, is the proper start of it.

Richards wore a frock-coat the colour of old Madeira with a ruffled shirt, and appeared surprisingly well. There was still something tarnished and moth-eaten about him, though, as if he was a rather neglected stuffed peacock instead of the actual living bird. Glancing over at the demonstration he let out a theatrical groan. 'It would seem that we are this week's cause,' he declared, his nasal voice dripping with contempt. 'How confoundedly tiresome.'

As the street sermon continued, intruding upon the jaunty music of Colt's band, the tolerance of the assembled workers was soon used up. They started to heckle, telling the sermoniser to get himself back to church or shut his trap. When this did not deter him they started up a steady barrage of mud, dung and stones. A direct hit to the forehead with a jagged pebble effectively ended the lesson; the preacher stepped back unsteadily among his companions, accepting a handkerchief from Lady Wardell herself with which to staunch the blood that trickled across his face.

Even before this unexpected protest had commenced the morning had not been going smoothly. From the moment it had opened the factory had been alive with talk of a second beating, this time of three English operatives from the shaping machines. It had occurred on Lupus Street, significantly closer to the Colt premises, and limbs had been broken; one of the victims was said to be so badly hurt that he would not be able to return to the works. The general reaction to this news had been fearful, but some among the Americans were angry. Walter Noone, in particular, had been positively incensed, taking the attack as a personal insult. He'd insisted on a private conversation with the Colonel in the factory office, during which he'd no doubt laid out the case for immediate vengeful action. It was fair to assume that this hadn't gone as he'd hoped, however, as he'd emerged from the office even more enraged than he'd gone in. Right then, in the minutes before Kossuth's arrival, the watchman was marching intently along the perimeter of the factory, drawing nervous glances from protesters and Colt workers alike. His weathered, inexpressive features were visibly straining, like a door about to break open before some great force pushing against it from within.

'So, Mr Lowry,' said Richards, chuckling at the smart cessation of the sermon, 'I understand that you were present when this little visit was conceived.'

95

'I was, Mr Richards.'

The press agent grunted cynically. 'He does very well indeed, this Mr Kossuth, for such a wretched failure. Forced to abdicate, driven into penniless exile, sent trailing around the globe like a bloody mendicant – yet still hailed as a living saint by the plebeian million wherever he damn well pokes his head up.' He crossed his arms, leaning back against the sliding door. 'Really rather depressing, is it not?'

Edward was attempting to refute this assessment when he was interrupted by a loud clatter of hooves over on Ponsonby Street, and the sudden flash of yellow panelling. The Colt barouche, sent to collect Kossuth from his Clerkenwell boarding house some hours earlier, cut swiftly past Lady Wardell's party and drove across to the bandstand to hearty cheers; on cue, the musicians struck up a brisk version of 'Hail Columbia'. Colonel Colt strode over to take his place before his men. He turned to Edward and muttered that Mr Kossuth was to be presented with a pair of their finest Hartford Navys if he took to the stand and addressed the factory.

'If he don't,' he added, 'then to hell with him.'

The secretary nodded, thinking momentarily of his own revolver. Still a little intoxicated by his success in the shooting gallery, he'd carried it home that night feeling more alert and intrepid than he ever had in his life. The usual rowdy crowds occupied the pavements of Long Acre, lounging outside taverns, and spilled from the cheaper theatres on Drury Lane. He did not cross the road to avoid them as he normally would have done but walked straight through the centre of their songs and arguments, almost willing one of the drunken roughs to shove him, to challenge him, so that he could produce the Navy from under his coat and face the scoundrel down. It wasn't loaded, of course, but how was anyone to know that?

Edward's very confidence seemed to act as a deterrent, however, and he got back to Holborn without incident. Up in his modest bachelor's rooms in Red Lion Square, he fell to studying the pistol for the larger part of an hour. He cocked and fired mechanically, like a man winding a clock, watching the tiny ships engraved on the cylinder jerk around on their endless voyage; experimented with carrying it hidden in various places about his person; took aim at doorknobs, at the oil lamp on his small table, at the black tugboat in the cheap etching of Turner's *Temeraire* that hung above his fireplace, imagining them being smashed or struck out of shape by his bullets. It was well past two o'clock before he came to his senses, put the gun away in a bureau drawer and fell into his bed.

Lajos Kossuth had an unexpectedly lawyerly look to him, more like a slightly eccentric barrister from Temple Bar than the visionary leader of millions. The years of poverty and exile were starting to show; there were lines upon his broad forehead, streaks of grey in his full, preciously trimmed beard, and his smart, dark clothes, cut in styles over half a decade old, were beginning to fade. He was plainly exhausted, trying to rub some life into his sunken eyes as he opened the carriage door. It had been reported in the press that he'd addressed an enormous meeting of Trades Unions in the East End two days previously, spoken marvellously for well over an hour and received a rapturous response. Privately, Colonel Colt had been supremely unimpressed by this news, being no admirer of workers' organisations of any kind; but as it had only increased the Hungarian's fame, and accordingly the attention paid to his visit to the Colt factory, he'd managed to keep his feelings hidden.

American and Briton alike supplied an enthusiastic ovation as the revolutionary climbed down from the barouche. Someone pushed their way to Edward's side, trying to get a little nearer; he looked around to see Mr Quill the engineer, his arm in a sling, clearly not yet recovered from his beating. Martin Rea, Miss Knox's brother-in-law, stood close behind him, and gave Edward an almost imperceptible nod of acknowledgement. The bandages were gone, revealing a tough face, fashioned by hardship, squinting out from under a grey canvas cap. His age was difficult to estimate – it could have been anything between twenty and forty. Something about him suggested uncommon intelligence, but it was yoked to an aching weariness. Like the engineer, his complexion was still blotted with fading bruises, and there was a sickle-shaped scab across his heavy jaw. Of the two, though, Rea was in considerably better condition; Edward noticed that he was watching out for Quill with careful solicitude, making sure that his injured master did not get into any difficulty.

Kossuth had brought a small party of shabby, intellectual types with him to the factory. Edward detected a certain haste about them, as if they were eager to get the tour over and done with. The Colonel crossed the yard, giving Kossuth's hand a brusque shake, saying a few words and then gesturing towards the bandstand.

His guest shook his head, politely but firmly; he would not speak. 'You are the people, however,' he pronounced in a thick Eastern accent, waving vaguely at the crowd of workers. 'You Americans are the ones – the very ones for making improvements.'

And that was it. They were to hear nothing of the man's famous, Shakespearean eloquence, or his grand oratorical ability. It wasn't enough – especially for a largely English gathering that had just been mistakenly praised for its progressive American character. Colonel Colt turned towards them, directing a bristling, goggle-eyed glare at Richards. His meaning was plain. The press agent pulled himself up to his full height, straightened his ageing frock-coat and adjusted his necktie. Then, with an air of absolute self-assurance, he sauntered over to the platform, tipping his top hat to Kossuth as he passed.

The impromptu speech that followed entirely contradicted the snobbish, dismissive attitude Richards had taken just before their revolutionary visitor's arrival. It was a colourful, sentimental account of Kossuth's struggles, and a truly consummate piece of rabble-rousing. Delivered with a full range of animated gesticulations, it reduced the efforts of the protesters at the gate – who were now singing another hymn – to mere background bleating. The Americans around Edward were soon sniggering into their sleeves at Richards's flourishes, but he held the attention of the London operatives completely, eliciting enthusiastic hurrahs for the brave people of Hungary and fierce boos for their Austrian oppressors. Then he moved on to Imperial Russia, Austria's wicked accomplice, reminding his audience that the Tsar was massing his forces once more, at that very moment, in certain preparation for a strike against poor, defenceless Turkey. The hoots of denunciation grew almost deafening.

Edward shook his head, amazed by Richards's naked fraudulence but unable to remove the grin from his face. Looking around the yard, wondering if he could chance a cigar, he noticed something strange. Martin Rea had left Mr Quill and was standing alone at the furthermost corner of the warehouse, as if waiting for someone at an appointed place. A few seconds later he was joined by the same Irish gang who'd carried him away from Tachbrook Street that night. This little group had a look of tense purpose about it. The men all had a leanness that seemed to border on malnourishment, yet there was not a hint of frailty in any of them; they were like so many gnarled branches, as bleached and weather-beaten as pieces of driftwood. An especially tortured specimen seemed to be in charge, his mouth shaped by constant frowning, his eyes hidden almost entirely beneath a jutting brow. He walked up close to Rea, prodding him in the chest in a none-too-friendly manner. A couple of words were exchanged, the leader casting a furtive glance back at the crowd. Edward turned away sharply; and when he looked back, the men were gone.

'*Mister Lowry!*'

The shout was close to his ear, making him start. Miss Knox was beaming, pleased to have caught him by surprise. The sight of her out there in the spring sunshine, her cheeks flushed, smiling with such bright exhilaration, shortened Edward's breath. He noticed that her eyes were the most unusual shade of blue, as dark and pure as deep water. Since his dinner with Saul Graff, he'd decided that he would have no more to do with her – that he would act like a practical, professional gentleman and maintain the proper distance between them. Now, though, as she stood before him, this resolution evaporated instantly.

'Why, Miss Knox,' he replied, touching the brim of his

hat, trying to make himself heard over a fresh crescendo of cheering. 'I just saw your brother-in-law. I must say that he is making a truly remarkable recovery.'

She set about retying the bow beneath her plain straw bonnet, her smile growing delightfully evil. 'Mart is just well used to being beaten, sir, is all,' she explained. 'He's had a fair bit of practice at it.'

'Some of the Americans are saying that the attackers were from the Adams pistol works.'

Her amusement faded; she'd heard this rumour as well. 'Same as did those lads last night, I suppose.'

The people around them quietened down; Richards had resumed speaking. They both looked over at him. Pointing skywards, he was holding forth about the transformative spirit that was sweeping through the civilised nations of the world, unseating old corruptions and installing a truly popular democracy in their place – a spirit embodied by guest and host alike at the Colt factory that day.

This turned out to be the press agent's closing note. There was an explosion of applause and he dropped from view, his task complete, stepping down from the bandstand. Gage Stickney shouted out that all Colt machine workers were free to take their dinner, and the band struck up once again, lurching their way into a medley of popular tavern ballads. The crowd broke apart, a good portion of it drifting towards the food sellers arrayed outside the gates, who were present in greater numbers that day, attracted by the noise and the spectacle. Lady Wardell and her supporters soon found themselves quite swamped, swallowed up in a jostling, hostile tide; this, at last, obliged them to abandon their protest and take flight.

Edward saw the Colonel leading Kossuth – who had been made visibly uncomfortable by Richards's parade of fanciful encomiums – towards the factory door, the American staff parting before them. 'I must leave you, miss, I'm afraid,' he said apologetically. 'I must join the tour.'

Miss Knox moved a little closer, her lip curving with gentle reproach. 'I ain't seen you around the works.'

'We are really quite busy at the moment.' This sounded

weak indeed. Edward cleared his throat. 'I simply haven't been here.'

'Don't you wish to talk with me again, Mr Lowry?'

'Of course, Miss Knox – of course I do. But the Colonel is a most demanding master. He has me attending on him day and night.'

The light smile that met this was one of ridicule, and almost unbearably pretty. 'Heavens,' she murmured, 'I never suspected that the role of secretary was such an important one. Does he really need you every single night?'

'No,' Edward admitted, 'not every night, it's true. I am usually free by ten o'clock, at any rate.'

'Well, sir, I'm to be found in the Spread Eagle most evenings at present. D'you know it?'

The secretary nodded, now starting to smile himself. 'The masons' tavern on Pulford Street. By the river.'

She inclined her head in a graceful farewell, strikingly incongruous there in the factory yard – a remnant of her servant's training, he realised, wheeled out to rib him a little further – and dropped a curtsey. 'I shall hope to see you there.'

Edward watched her return to some friends from the machine floor, who'd been following their exchange as best they could, hiding giggles behind their hands. A wide grin had stamped itself across his face. Trembling slightly, he was gripped by a sudden, euphoric urge to sprint around the yard; to run up to Richards, clap him on the back and congratulate him on a magnificent speech; to hurry after the Colonel and their celebrated guest and ensure that the tour was a resounding success.

He would go to this tavern. He looked down at the cobbles, putting his hands in his pockets. Yes, damn it all, he *would*.

7

'Did you see that?' Slattery demanded as the Mollys walked down the side of the warehouse. 'Did you? Your sister-in-law, whoring herself to Colt's secretary?'

Martin nodded; he'd seen it, the pair of them simpering away at each other, the nature of their conversation plain even at thirty yards' distance. He had to admire Caroline's nerve, setting her cap at such a smart young gent. Serving in that big house had clearly given her some grand ideas. The secretary he could remember dimly from the Yankee lodging house. Much was being said about this person by the Americans, and none of it pleasant – not by Mr Quill, of course, who never had a bad word for anybody, but by Mr Stickney and numerous others. He was an impostor, they were claiming, a confidence man out to fleece the Colonel for whatever he could get; or a spy planted by one of Colt's English rivals. For his part, Martin could find no sign of such cunning fraudulence. Not that this meant it wasn't there, of course; but to him the secretary seemed to be just another London office type, one of an identical army thousands strong.

'I don't like it,' Slattery stated. 'D'ye hear me, Martin? I don't like it *at all*. Having that bleedin' girl here ain't no good for Molly's ends.'

'She'll be seen to.'

'You've talked with that Saxon wife o' yours, have you?'

Martin ignored the derision in his voice. 'We've had words.'

This was true enough, but rather than firmly telling Amy what was what, as he was now implying, Martin had in fact found himself being asked a series of angry questions, mostly concerning Pat Slattery's presence at the Colt works and what this might mean. He'd managed to throw her off, just about, but Amy was a blasted sharp girl; she knew something was up and would not let it be for long. Caroline was involved somehow, he could tell. The sisters had plainly been nattering. He'd have to think of something to do for them both.

They reached the warehouse's side door. A hot pain tightened along Martin's right forearm as he pushed it open. The tendons in the wrist had been bruised during his beating; more than a week later he still couldn't clench his fist properly. He stood aside, rubbing his palm with his left thumb. Half a dozen of his brothers, Molly Maguire's loyal lads, filed in past him. Lajos Kossuth might have the Colt works distracted, but all of them understood that they had to be quick.

The door led into a large rectangular room. The ceiling was high; although of similar dimensions to the factory block, the warehouse had only two floors instead of three. A row of newly built annealing ovens stood along one wall. Each one had a wide brick working surface stretching from its mouth, into which had been cut a system of pits and channels. Specialist tools, pans, tongs and brushes, were set out across these surfaces, awaiting Kossuth's inspection. On the floor beside each was a bucket of jet-black fish oil, which gave off a pungent, salty odour; this was the stuff, Martin had learned, that gave Colt pistols their distinctive sheen.

'What's this?' asked Slattery tersely, nodding at the ovens. 'Bleedin' bakery or sump'n?'

Martin shook his head. 'This here's the blueing room. They heat the metal and polish it with that oil there – put on the blue, the Yankees call it. Toughens the gun, Pat, so's it don't break or warp or nothin' when it's firing off its bullets.'

Slattery wasn't interested. He strode past the ovens and

off through a door on the room's far side. Martin exchanged a look with Jack Coffee. The three of them, Martin, Jack and Pat, had known each other since before the Hunger. They'd seen Pat in this mood many times before. He was about Molly's business – nothing else concerned him.

Despite this dedication, however, he didn't have the first idea where he was going. Martin alone knew his way around the warehouse; he'd been in there with Mr Quill, who'd been called in several times to advise on engineering matters. He followed Slattery through into an open work-shop area. This was Colonel Colt's proving room, where the testing of the freshly manufactured London revolvers would be carried out. A series of long tables was covered with intricate measuring instruments, arranged in order of size. Ammunition was there also, and in great quantities: neat cartons of pre-made pistol cartridges, flasks of powder, boxes of conical bullets and percussion caps in their thou-sands, heaped in circular tins like so many tiny copper coins. On one side of the room were a pair of heavy steel tubes, about three feet across and mounted at chest height. It was within these tubes that each new pistol would receive its first firing, offering protection for those nearby should one of them burst – 'but that, Mart,' Mr Quill had said during one of their inspections, 'is next to a goddamn *impos-sibility*.' Past these, along the far end of the room, was a simple firing range, a twelve-yard stretch with a thick piece of hardboard at its end.

There was no trace of the revolvers themselves, though. As in the blueing room, the overall impression was of an exhibition of modern Yankee gun-making, rather than an establishment where it actually took place.

Slattery turned towards him. 'So, Martin,' he said, 'where are the bleedin' parts?'

Martin pointed over at a rusted spiral staircase in the proving room's far corner. 'Upstairs. In the polishing shop.'

As they reached it, however, footfalls clanged upon the steps above, slow and regular, descending to meet them. First they saw a pair of shining boots; then a pair of infantryman's trousers, blue with black piping on the side of each leg; then a short military shell-jacket, left open to show the revolver tucked within.

Mr Noone stopped about halfway down, leaning against the rail, showing no surprise at finding them in there. 'The finishing department is out of bounds for all you Londoners,' he said.

The Mollys lowered their heads, shifting apprehensively, not knowing how much Noone had overheard or guessed for himself. Martin came forward, delivering the tale he'd prepared for just such an emergency. Mr Quill had suddenly realised that one of the firing tubes was loose, he said, and had asked him to gather some men from the forge and see to it before the Kossuth tour reached the proving room. The engineer had taken several hard blows to the skull during their beating, and was still having trouble ordering his thoughts. They'd talked about this particular matter after their latest check, and Quill probably wouldn't be able to recall if he'd issued such an instruction or not. Should he be confronted by Noone, Martin's bet was that the engineer would cover for his assistant rather than feed him to the watchman.

It was difficult to tell what Noone made of this story. He continued to study them closely, barely moving, his hand close to the stock of his gun. He said nothing.

'We've dealt wi' it now, though,' Martin concluded. 'Tube's bolted in tight as a drum.' He glanced over at the factory, visible through the warehouse's tall windows. 'The Colonel and his guest'll be over here soon, will they not?'

Noone made a disgruntled noise, relaxing very slightly and walking down another couple of steps. 'The goddamn tube could be the wrong way around,' he growled, 'and that dumb Hungarian bastard would be none the wiser.'

Seeing that they were in the clear, the Mollys let out a conspiratorial chuckle.

'The son of a bitch calls himself a freedom fighter, a *revolutionary*,' Noone continued scornfully, 'yet he crawls to these Bulls like a dog on its belly – these Bulls who keep up the biggest, bloodiest empire in the whole goddamn world.'

Martin saw that anger had been building in the watchman

all morning, throughout the preparations for the visit and the fanfare that had greeted Kossuth's arrival. 'We're all Irish here, Mr Noone,' he muttered. 'You don't need to remind us of the sins of the British. Every man you see before you has lost kin to their misrule.'

Noone stared at him for a moment, looking at the pattern of damage across his face. 'The Colonel has his reasons for asking this Hungarian to visit us,' he said, 'and I'll not question his planning. But by God, it sticks in my craw. You hear the speech? That John Bull cocksucker could talk a cat off a fish-cart, and every last word of it was as phoney as can be.'

The Irishmen grumbled in agreement. Thady Rourke, one of the Mollys Slattery had recruited since their arrival in London, asked the watchman what exactly had happened over on Lupus Street the previous night.

Noone's wrath grew yet further. 'They got three Bulls from the machine floor,' he answered. 'Easy enough to replace, but the message it sends is plain. There's someone out there who thinks they can come at us, at the Colt Company, and suffer no consequences at all.'

There was applause out in the yard; the factory door was sliding back to release Colt, Kossuth and their entourage. Seeing that time was short, the watchman stepped down to the floor of the proving room and addressed the Irishmen in a forceful, confidential tone.

'Now listen good,' he said, his small, yellowed eyes sparking beneath the brim of his cap. 'One of you Irish has been worked over already. Any of the rest of you could be next. We ain't going to stand by and let this go on. I can't allow it. The Colonel don't want to know, but that don't mean that nothing can get done.' He straightened his shell-jacket and began to fasten the brass buttons on its front. 'So I'm calling you micks up for some extra labour. You'll be well suited to it, I believe. Meet me and my boys tonight at eleven o'clock, just along from the lodging house on Tachbrook Street. We'll see if we can't set this nonsense straight.'

*   *   *

The cellar was dark; all Martin could see of Jack was the red eye of his pipe bowl, bobbing and winking over on the other side of the room. It was still open to the elements, rain blowing in through a yawning hole in its front, the night sky beyond only a touch lighter than the black walls that enclosed them. Martin was sitting on a stack of floor tiles, twisting his right hand around with his left, cursing softly whenever he reached a point where the pain made him stop.

There was a coarse, rustling sound: Jack scratching at that carroty beard of his. 'You hang back, Mart,' he whispered in the gloom, 'when it gets started, like. You ain't right yet. No sense risking any further mischief.'

Such solicitude was typical of Jack. That night, Martin found it irritating; he wanted no allowances made for him.

'Don't you be a-worrying,' he said. 'I can carry meself, remember?'

A boot scraped against some brickwork, and a shape moved across the rectangle of sky above them; and Pat Slattery dropped in, bringing with him the smell of cheap sailor's rum. Settling between Jack and Martin, he struck a match to light his pipe, throwing a split-second's illumination over the small cellar and its occupants. Hunched down in their hiding place, neckerchiefs ready to be pulled over their mouths, they looked like nothing more than a gang of footpads. Slattery even had a club laid across his lap.

'Jesus,' murmured Martin, shaking his head, 'how in God's name can we be doing this?'

'Ah, what are you on about, ye bugger?' said Pat. 'This'll be good for us. Making pals with the Yankees – weren't that once your own favoured course o' action? Surely you can see that if we get the favour of the watchman, everything could be a whole lot easier later on.'

'Aye,' replied Martin doubtfully. Molly was quiet in him that night. He didn't like to think about what this might mean. 'I suppose so.'

Slattery drew on his pipe. 'We'll get there, brothers,' he declared; Martin could sense him grinning in the darkness.

'The Gael will get his righteous vengeance upon the Saxon fiend. The Harp and Shamrock will trample down the Lion and the bleedin' Unicorn. Us country boyos will do a truly great thing in the name of our Molly Maguire. They'll be singin' songs about us afore the year's end.'

A shrill whistle sounded somewhere outside – the signal that they were needed. Slattery and Jack knocked out their pipes and the three of them clambered up the slope that led to the street, pulling on their masks. Not a lot could be seen in Cubitt's Pimlico that night, the heavy clouds overhead reducing everything to a few dark shades of grey. They crossed a muddy pathway, entering the beginnings of a smart city square. The other Mollys and a couple of Colt watchmen were making straight for its centre, rushing over the cobblestones and disappearing beneath a stand of newly planted trees. As Martin drew nearer he heard the sounds of a savage, unrestrained fight. A boot squelched in loose earth, and then a body charged into him from the shadows, slamming against his flank. It was a skinny, foul-smelling boy in the garb of a working man – not one of theirs. Martin grabbed hold as best he could but the boy squirmed like an eel, flailing his bony arms around in panic. The scab on Martin's jaw was torn off, and he felt hot blood lick the underside of his chin. Then the injured wrist flared up, catching fire, paralysing his hand completely. He swore; the boy sprang from his failing grasp, darting away into Pimlico, yapping out a cockney oath as he went.

Up ahead, the shutter was slid back on a bull's-eye lantern, projecting a narrow beam of light onto the battle. Four workmen had been caught, jumped on as they moved in to attack two of Noone's people, who'd been wandering the area for the past hour talking loudly in their Yankee accents, serving as bait. The captives were putting on a decent enough show – as Martin watched, one drove a fist into Slattery's stomach – but they were both surrounded and outnumbered. Their cause was a hopeless one.

Noone strode into the light, taking off his military cap and passing it to one of his men. Something flashed in his hand; he'd drawn his revolver and was spinning it around in his palm, expertly reversing it so that the stock was foremost.

He moved on the largest and fiercest of the four cornered workmen, who was swinging a wooden club about while damning them all to hell. Sidestepping a swipe from the club, Noone hit the fellow squarely across the forehead with his pistol, dropping him at once. The watchman planted a foot on either side of his opponent, bringing down the revolver again with precise, brutal speed. Around them, the other brawls had halted; all eyes were on Noone. He struck the unfortunate workman at his feet five more times, with ever greater force, sending a crazy shadow leaping across the tree-trunks behind him. At the penultimate blow, the thud of the stock's impact became a wet crunch, and the fallen man's protests – disbelieving, gasping screams at how much harm was being done to him – abruptly ceased. Noone stopped, examining his handiwork for a moment with a professional air before wiping his gun clean on his victim's shirt. He then turned to the remaining workmen, who were now being held firmly in place by those they had been fighting off a minute earlier.

'I've killed that there cocksucker,' he told them, completely calm, 'and by God I'll do you three as well if you don't tell me pretty damn quick who sent you against Sam Colt.'

'B-Bob Adams!' blurted one immediately, panic-stricken. 'Mercy, sir, do not murder me! I am but nineteen, sir! It were Bob Adams!'

Noone paused, considering this piece of information. 'Know that from this point on, anything you pitch at Colt will come back at you Adams boys double. This dumb bastard here will be just the goddamn start of it.' He looked away. 'Let 'em go.'

The Adams men were released, and given a couple of kicks apiece. They made their escape as quickly as they could. Martin saw one stumble in the mud at the square's edge, lose his cap, and not even bend to pick it up after he'd righted himself. Noone's face showed no emotion: lines deepened by the lamplight, the eye lost in shadow and mouth set in an expression of unreflecting, unflinching sternness, it looked like the profile of an ancient carving.

Slattery approached him, tugged down his mask and

started to offer advice on the disposal of the body in a gruff, comradely manner. 'Grosvenor Canal's the best place in this part o' town,' he said. 'If we weight him properly, he'll find his way out into the river without once breaking the surface – and then he's lost to all men.'

Listening to his brother say these things, staring at the corpse sprawled in the mud, Martin felt a sickening sense of shame. They had abetted in an unjust killing. Molly Maguire had no love for those who did such things. This was why she was staying away – why she would neither move among them nor make so much as a single sound. From where he was standing, he could see something of the dead man's face. The poor fellow had been young, not much older than his nineteen-year-old companion. His neck and brow were pocked with furnace burns.

Noone didn't react to Slattery's advice. Instead, he took the lantern from whoever was holding it and swivelled the thing around so that Slattery and a couple of the other Mollys, Joe and Owen it looked like, were lit up by its beam. Martin tensed. There was another purpose to this mission.

'So you see what happens,' the watchman said, in the same disconcertingly level tone he'd used on the Adams men, 'to them that cross Colonel Colt.'

The Molly Maguires had been played for fools. Noone knew exactly what they were about – and he'd brought them out to this deserted square for a confrontation. Martin counted the dark shapes around the lantern. There were three other Yankees beside Noone, all doubtlessly armed with six-shooters. A half-dozen Mollys would pose no problem for them.

'Did you think I'd let you Papist motherfuckers steal from us? Did you honestly think it would be that goddamn *easy*?'

Slattery was squinting in the bull's-eye's light, squaring up his shoulders, seemingly unworried by this sudden reversal. 'Papist, is it?' he said with menacing lightness. 'You got sump'n to say about the Holy Father there, have ye?'

The lantern moved nearer. When Noone spoke his voice was different, lower yet buckling with violence. 'Let me tell you about that miserable cunt you call a *Holy Father*,' he

110

spat. 'I was born near Donegal. That's right, you dumb micks – I was Irish. We were forced to leave our home after a gang of Catholics, devoted followers of your blasted Pope, strung up my father on the public highway. His *crime*, as you people had the sheer goddamn nerve to describe it, was only to be an organiser of the local Orangemen. I was but five years old. We cursed Ireland, my mother and me, we sailed across the Atlantic Ocean without a backward glance, and we became Americans.' There was a clicking sound: the cocking of a revolver. Martin went cold. 'I am an *American*, damn you, and a Colt man. You Papist sons of whores can go fuck yourselves.'

Slattery was shaking his head, laughing softly. The Mollys knew what this meant. They seized hold of him just as he launched himself towards the watchman, wrestling him back, and managed to march him from the square. The Yankees followed them with the lantern's beam, but did not open fire; a couple sniggered. Shivering with fury, Slattery twisted halfway around and started to shout something. Just in time, Martin clamped a hand over his mouth, and he fought hard to keep it there.

Gage Stickney was waiting for them at the forge doors when they arrived to start their shift six hours later. As they started across the yard he ambled forward, raising up a palm as broad as a spade-head. Behind him, two of the Americans from the square were leaning against the wall of the factory building, smoking cheroots. Both had Navy revolvers hanging from their belts.

'Stop there,' commanded Stickney, 'and turn your grimy mick asses back around. As of right now you're no longer in the employ of Colonel Colt. You ain't allowed in here no more.'

The hulking foreman delivered this news with a smirk, taking a bully's pleasure in using his authority to squash those beneath him, but it came as no surprise to the Mollys. After being denounced by Noone, the Irishmen had slunk back into the Devil's Acre. Settling in their regular bolt-hole, Brian O'Dowd's Holy Lamb off Orchard Street, they'd sunk

111

a few flasks of poteen and made an honest assessment of the situation. Although they hadn't actually stolen anything yet, and Noone had no proof of any wrongdoing, it was plain that his suspicion was enough; that he despised the Catholic Irish and would surely see them ejected from the works. The plan, as it had stood, was finished. At the break of day, however, they'd risen from the table as one, all knowing exactly what they were going to do. It was not the Molly Maguires' way to hand their foes victory. If Noone wanted to expel them from the Colt factory, they would go there and have him do it. They'd filed from the tavern, passing old Brian snoring behind the bar, and joined the early morning tide of costermongers, labourers, beggars and pickpockets that was gushing over the mouldy stones of Westminster into the neighbouring quarters of the city.

Slattery had stayed uncharacteristically quiet since his confrontation with the watchman, keeping out of the conversation in the Holy Lamb, concentrating on his drink. Now, though, at the sight of Stickney standing in his path, he seemed to come back to himself. 'Why has this been done?' he demanded, taking two more steps forward. 'What reason is given?'

They faced each other for a few seconds, Pat Slattery and this great giant of a foreman, like a bandy little monkey before a ragged brown bear. Then Stickney cast a glance back at the gunmen, who duly prised themselves from the wall and tossed their cheroots onto the cobbles.

'There ain't no union here, pal,' he said wearily. 'You ain't going to receive no letter of goddamn explanation from the Colt Company. Just get yourself gone, or we'll fetch the police and have you arrested.'

At this Slattery snorted in disgust, sidestepped the foreman and strode into the centre of the yard. *'Noone!'* he bellowed, wheeling around, glaring at the long rows of windows as if his enemy lurked behind each and every one. 'Noone, ye Orange *bastard*, there'll be a reckoning for this! D'ye hear me? We'll find you, and we'll –'

The two armed Yankees were advancing on him now, hands going to the revolvers on their belts. Martin looked to the other Mollys. There was no noble battle to be fought here. Slattery would have to be reined in once again. Jack made it over to him first, wrapping him in his arms; and the rest of them were there a moment later, smothering his threats, lifting him up and manhandling him towards the gates. Only when they were out on Ponsonby Street, facing the crawling sludge of the river and the dull chimneys that covered its southern bank, did they let him go. Losing his balance, he dropped to the ground, swearing harshly. Martin looked back towards the factory building. The Yankees still had their weapons drawn but had not followed them. They were safe.

'Should've guessed that this would occur,' growled Slattery from down on the pavement. 'It's well known that the Catholic Irishmen who have fled to America since the Hunger are treated little better than their Negro slaves.' He climbed to his feet, shaking a sheet of piss-soaked newspaper from his jacket and gesturing contemptuously towards the pistol works. 'What is this place, anyhow, but a stock-house for our tyrants? That bastard Colonel is here to court the *British Crown*, ain't he, no matter how many failed bleedin' revolutionaries he parades about. Damn him, damn 'em all!'

'Mart,' said Jack, dusting his hands together, 'I do believe somebody's calling out for you.'

It was Mr Quill, drawn from the engine room by the commotion outside. He was waving at the Irishmen with his good arm as he hobbled slowly in their direction.

'This is a chance.' Jack's black eyes were fixed on Martin. 'Go on over.'

Martin looked out at the river. A decent-sized part of him was actually glad that the plan had been ruined and they'd all been thrown from the factory – that the lies and deception could be brought to an end. 'I cannot, Jack. Not alone.'

'We still need those guns, Mart. We need them to balance off some of the evil what's been done to us.' Jack's voice was growing insistent. 'Think of Molly Maguire. Think of what she's endured.'

What could Martin say to this? Their oath had been invoked. He flexed his injured wrist; then he turned away from his brothers and started across the yard, hiding his reluctance as best he could. One of Noone's men shouted at him, but Mr Quill bade the fellow be silent and let his assistant approach. As Martin came closer, he saw that the chief engineer's round, bruised face wore an expression of complete bewilderment.

'What goddamn nonsense is this, Mart?' he asked. 'You've been dismissed for trying to *steal gun parts*?'

Martin shook his head as if a grave misunderstanding had taken place. 'Here's the truth of it, Mr Quill.' He spoke confidentially, as if imparting a sensitive secret. 'We did a piece of work with Mr Noone at his request, late last night – fist-work, sir, if ye catch my meaning. It came out that my friends and I are Roman Catholics, a religion that Mr Noone despises, being as his family is Protestant Irish, and Orange Order to boot. These are old, bloody differences back in Ireland. This is why he wants us run out of the factory.'

Mr Quill had his own doubts about Noone and readily accepted Martin's story. 'Come on, Mart,' he said, 'let's get us back to the engine. We've a devil of a lot still to do. These tales are hogwash, plain and simple. There's nothing I can do for your pals, I'm afraid, but you'll not lose your place over this.'

Stickney tried to stop them. 'That there's a goddamn *thief*, Ben. Will you bring a known thief back under the Colonel's roof?'

'This fellow,' Mr Quill replied, pointing at Martin, 'has the beginnings of a fine Colt engineer, and I need him to ensure the smooth running of the engine. He's as much a thief, Gage, as you are yourself.' Stickney frowned and opened his mouth to reply, but the engineer would not hear him. 'I'll go to the Colonel himself if I must. I'll not see Martin Rea crushed on some moon-struck whim of Mr Noone's.'

Stickney backed down. It seemed that Martin was saved, for the moment at least. As he made to follow his protector inside the factory, mumbling his thanks, he glanced over at the other Mollys. They were wandering away along the riverbank, back towards the Acre. Slattery and Jack were lingering a little behind the others, watching his progress, and touched the brims of their caps to bid him farewell. Martin was alone within the Yankee pistol works. The task before him had become many times more difficult. Noone and Stickney would be on him like a pair of hungry beagles eyeing a cornered rabbit, kept from lunging in only by fear of the master's stick. His brothers, Slattery in particular, would surely be expecting great results. He tried to blink away the hot itch of his tired eyes, but without success. What the devil had he taken on?

Something dark seemed to flit over him; the shadow of a large gull perhaps, flying low before the watery April sun. Martin looked up, shielding his brow. At one of the factory's first-floor windows, peering out between reflections of powdery clouds, was the face of his wife – his dear, sweet Amy, whom he had not seen for almost three days straight. He smiled, not understanding why she was up there but lifting his hand to wave nonetheless; and saw that it was not Amy at all but her sister Caroline, regarding him with unfriendly curiosity. She was seated at her drill, her fair hair tied up beneath a headscarf, lodged securely in the very heart of Colonel Colt's operation. No one is paying any special attention to *her*, he thought. She could get hold of every pistol part up on the machine floor. If she could be made to help –

And then Molly Maguire's voice filled Martin's ears once more, rushing upon him like thick surf surging across an empty beach. It was the voice of both a fresh young girl and the most ancient woman you could imagine; a voice that had known unbearable pain and maddening anger, and would not let those who had wronged her live on in peace. Following his gaze up to Caroline's window, she hissed out a decisive *yes*.

8

Mr Lowry was sat in the middle of the tavern table. Caroline's friends from the machine floor, mostly girls of twenty or thereabouts, were crowded around him, interrogating him with some enthusiasm. She herself stayed at the table's end, on the fringes of his little audience, trying to look like she wasn't paying him much notice.

He had come to them straight from Colonel Colt's side, and was still dressed for splendid dining halls and government houses. He could not have stood out more among the custom of the Spread Eagle had he burst into flames. Caroline liked this. It would have bothered her had he made an attempt to adopt the costume of ordinary folk, as if he felt that he could blend into their company for an evening simply by donning their garments; this tactic, often employed by gentlemen out for adventure in the poorer parts of the city, smacked of trickery to her. He'd approached their table fearlessly enough, ignoring the surly stares of gas-workers and masons, and had taken his place among them without awkwardness. Caroline's friends had all heard about how he'd walked her home, and had seen the two of them talking together during Mr Kossuth's visit to the factory. They'd welcomed the secretary warmly, keen to examine him.

Their first concern was his origins.

'Is this a proper *gentleman* we have here, Maisie? He has the look, don't he, and the fancy togs too.'

'Aye, there's a silver spoon in that there gob and no mistake. What is it, sir? Family fallen on hard times, has it – forced you to do an honest day's work?'

'Ooh, they're the worst, ain't they? Lapsed quality is idle as bedamned, every last one of 'em!'

Mr Lowry's laugh was very slightly strained. 'I must protest that I'm no such thing. I'm but the only son of a penniless schoolmaster, sent out into the world to make his living like every man and woman in this tavern. My own endeavours alone have brought me to the Colt Company.'

This met with general approval. ''Scuse me, sir,' mumbled Maisie, 'for what I said just then. I always been a pepperer, girls, ain't I?'

'Swipey old cow, more like.'

Caroline joined in the mirth that greeted this remark, thinking that the secretary was not so far above her after all. She'd known servants, scullery maids and footmen whose relatives had found employment as schoolmasters. A broader discussion of education began, a couple of veterans of the ragged schools making bitter speeches on the uselessness of lessons to working people and the cruelty common among those charged with imparting them. Mr Lowry sat through this with steady patience. Despite the favour he'd found with the Yankee Colonel, it had to be said that he'd given himself no airs. A pot of ale was fetched for him, and the conversation moved on to the exact nature of his place in the gun works.

'So you're 'is clerk,' said Nancy, the girl who sat opposite Caroline.

Mr Lowry considered this. 'In a manner of speaking, miss, I suppose I am. Although the Colonel does not like letting anyone at all near the factory's account books. He will employ no notaries, on point of principle. There are significant parts of the Colt business that are known to him alone.'

'What does he have you do, then?'

'I run errands. I write a great deal of letters. I offer counsel, at times, on matters of business. I ride with him in his carriage.'

'Ooh, I seen it!' Nancy shrilled, forgetting that everyone

117

had – that it was often parked in the middle of the factory yard for hours at a time. 'A right spanker, that one!'

The secretary smiled. 'And perhaps most importantly of all, I attempt to smooth down the many fine feathers he ruffles with his curt Yankee ways.'

He went on to tell them something of their Colonel's misadventures out in Society; of how, when invited to dine in the grandest houses, he deliberately addressed nobles and gentlefolk by the wrong titles, used the wrong cutlery and glasses, argued fiercely over matters of foreign policy (his oft-expressed view seeming to be that war should be pursued in every circumstance) and dismissed those unfamiliar with revolving pistols and the armament trade as if they were nothing but dismal idiots. The operatives laughed hard at all this, tickled to hear of such open displays of scorn for their betters. They raised their pots and glasses, toasting the Colonel's boldness and honesty of spirit. Caroline found that she was smiling as well, but at the speedy ease with which her smart secretary had won over her companions rather than at his stories.

Before long, their drinks were finished. The group dissolved, a number of them heading for the bar after a chaotic exchange of instructions and coins. As if by accident, a path cleared between Caroline and Mr Lowry. She could feel the other girls swapping glances – could hear the creak of the bench as he rose from it and joined her at the table's end. Knocking back the last of her gin, she kept her eyes on the ale-pots that dotted the tabletop like stout tin chimneys.

'You took your time, sir,' she said. 'Three weeks, has it been? I'd all but lost hope.'

'It is a busy period, Miss Knox, as I told you,' he replied as he settled upon a stool. 'The first London gun is almost made, and –'

'Oh I know, Mr Lowry,' Caroline interrupted, 'believe me I do. Lord above, we talk nothing else up on the machine floor! Honestly, sir, the pride we'll all feel when that day comes will be quite *enormous*.'

He sighed. 'You are mocking me again.'

Caroline turned to him, all innocence. 'There is no mockery in me, Mr Lowry, not an ounce. You are rather out of your element here in the Eagle, and feeling a little vulnerable, I daresay. The truth is that we are very glad to see you here.'

Amusement flickered at the corner of his mouth. 'We, miss?'

She shrugged, pleased by his meaning but deliberately ignoring it. 'It says something, don't it, you coming down here to the riverside and talking with us. Takes a brave soul to pay a call to the Spread Eagle in a blessed frock-coat, that's for sure.'

He hesitated for a second. 'You know that I would endure a good deal more than a labourers' tavern for the chance to sit by your side.'

Caroline let out a loud laugh, banging down her empty glass. 'Dear Lord, sir, are you trying to spin a humble factory girl's head?' She leaned in a little closer to study his face. He meant what he'd said. A warm, woozy fondness flooded into her, and she knew that there was now a distinct possibility that she might have to take this fellow off for a solitary walk before the evening was out; a walk that might well involve a kiss or two.

'Mr Lowry,' she murmured, 'would you be so good as to fetch me another gin?'

He went immediately, smiling broadly, and returned a few moments later with a drink for each of them.

They had perhaps another three minutes together before a finger tapped her shoulder. It was Billy, one of the pot-boys. 'Someone out back for you, Caro. Says she's your sister.'

This was unexpected. Caroline had never known Amy to venture this far west, not at this time of day – and certainly not to visit a tavern. 'Why don't she just come inside, then?' she asked.

'She wouldn't,' Billy answered. 'She's upset – tears an' that.'

Caroline got to her feet without another word, leaving a rather dismayed Mr Lowry with Nancy and the rest and making for the door. It was Martin again, she was sure of it. He'd done something awful. Imagining a host of grievous wrongs, she stormed out into the tavern's yard, ready to tear the name of her thoughtless brother-in-law into tiny bloody pieces. Amy, however, was nowhere to be seen. Caroline peered down the Eagle's narrow alley. Half a dozen men were sharing a ribald joke as they directed hard streams of piss against the bricks; a girl she knew from the machine floor had slipped over while squatting drunkenly nearby, and now shouted out slurred curses as urine and filth saturated her petticoats.

Her temper cooling and perplexity setting in, Caroline looked around more carefully. There was a flash off to the left, from the Equitable Gas-Works, produced by the strange, ceaseless labours underway within; for an instant a sheet of white light was thrown across the row of gigantic cylindrical tanks that loomed behind its walls. She walked around to Pulford Street, heading ten or fifteen yards up it, but there was no sign of a woman with two infants. Had there been a mistake? Had she and her sister missed each other?

Just as she was about to turn around, she heard something; her name, it sounded like, whispered in a begging tone. It had come from the mouth of George Street, a slimy lane that served as little more than a drainage channel for the terrace behind which it ran, and yet was also a popular spot for whores on account of being entirely unlit. As Caroline approached, there was some shuffling and moaning further along; followed by a male oath, a hoarse scream and the sound of someone being struck repeatedly. She stopped, startled, and was on the verge of bolting when her sister came forward suddenly from the shadows and took hold of her wrist.

Caroline barely managed to stop herself from crying out. 'Heavens, Amy!' she gasped. 'You scared me half to death, girl! I thought you was a pouncey, come to cut off me nose!' Her relief quickly switched back to anger. Shaking off Amy's hand, she grasped her sister by the elbow and led her back to Pulford Street, not stopping until they were almost at the Eagle, with the oily river glinting before them. 'What are you doing out here, you bloody fool? You looking to get yourself grabbed – done in?' She held Amy out at arm's length. Her sister was dressed in a cotton bonnet and shawl, and she was quite alone. 'Where's Katie? Little Michael?'

Amy swallowed, her eyes shining beneath the street-lights; she'd been weeping, as Billy the pot-boy had reported. 'With Mart. At – at home.'

'With *Mart*? By my soul, has somebody died?' Caroline almost laughed, but the desolate cast of her sister's features checked her.

'It's nearly as bad, Caro,' Amy replied, leaning weakly against a wall. 'Oh, it's nearly as bad!'

'For God's sake, girl, what is it?'

Amy struggled just to say the word; it finally burst from her lips like a stopper from a holed dam, releasing a great cascade of anguish behind it. '*Debt.*' Her hands closed over her face, her shoulders heaving with fresh sobs.

This wasn't, in truth, that much of a surprise. 'Who's it with?' Caroline asked stonily.

Amy looked up at her, a cloudy tear gathering on the end of her chin and then dripping down to the pavement. 'Some cove back in the Acre. An Irishman named Dickson – a landlord. He's deadly serious, Caro. There's talk of – of Mart and me going to the workhouse, and the children to a – a –' She jerked over as if punched in the stomach, quite speechless with fear.

'How did this happen?' Caroline was unable to keep the exasperation from her voice. 'You've always been so bloody *careful*, Amy, keeping up with those damn flowers – and Mart's always worked, ain't he? Colt's paying him well?'

Her sister shook her head. 'This is old,' she muttered. 'Goes back to Ireland. Something awful and mysterious – they won't say what, exactly. There's interest, Caro, hundreds and hundreds of pounds. And they're all marked for it, Mart and all his pals – Jack Coffee, Thady Rourke, Owen McConnell,' here she paused, drawing in a shuddering breath, 'Pat Slattery . . . all of 'em. They was planning to save up the wages they was getting from the American so they could begin to pay it off. But the Yankee bastard has had them thrown out.'

Caroline sighed; they'd been over this before. 'They was stealing, Amy,' she said bluntly. 'It's said that Mr Noone and his watchman caught them red-handed. It's a bloody wonder Mart didn't go as well.'

This incident, the talk of the factory for the better part of a week, had lifted a great weight from Caroline's mind. Slattery and his followers had been thieving: it had been as simple as that. Martin, although saved somehow from dismissal, was now isolated, and must surely abandon their little scheme. Caroline had hoped that his wage, and his family's well-being, might now become his main concern.

Amy wouldn't have this, of course. Her loyalty to her husband, tested by difficult circumstances, was growing firmer by the day. 'They went, Caro, because Noone nurses a deep hatred of Catholic Irishmen. And I'd wager that filthy demon would be very pleased to learn of the bind we're all in now.'

A timber barge cruised by, its bell clanging and blue night-lights shining, making a late delivery to Cubitt's building yard. Caroline watched it pass. 'You should leave the Acre, then – leave London. Take your husband and the little ones and go back to Aylesbury. No Irish moneylender would think to follow you there.'

'We left no one behind us, Caro, no one at all. Who would I go to? This city is the only home I have now – and you are my only true friend.'

Caroline knew then that she was about to be asked for her help; that Amy was going to make the troubles of Martin and his friends her troubles as well. 'What d'you want from me, Amy? I've told you what you should do. I ain't got no money. My wage at Colt ain't a fraction of what your Martin receives.'

Amy wiped her eyes on her shawl. 'The guns,' she said simply, 'from the factory. They're worth a fair bit.'

Caroline stared at her sister, feeling almost as if she was choking. 'You mean . . . you mean you want *me* to turn thief too?'

'Mart says you're well placed to get all the different parts

– a lot better than he is. And they're watching him now. He can't be seen doing anything strange.'

'Do you have any notion what I'd be risking, Amy, just to save Mart? Why, the Yankees would see me jailed!'

'Not for Mart,' Amy corrected her. 'I'm asking you for Katie and Michael. Please, Caro – for the little ones. If this debt ain't paid they'll be given over to the Parish and they'll never escape. You've seen how it goes. There's something about those places that sticks to you – that can't be got off.' Thinking of this made her well up once more; but she pressed on, determined to state her case. 'Your Colonel's set to make hundreds of guns, ain't that right?'

Caroline looked away. 'Thousands, more like.'

Amy laughed mirthlessly. 'Well then, bless my heart, he won't miss a few of them, will he! It'd be like taking a loaf from the bloomin' baker!'

'But this ain't *bread* we're speaking of here, leather-head!' Caroline snapped. 'These are six-shooting pistols! Who'd they be going to, Amy, d'you reckon? Have you thought about that at all? What might such things be used for?'

Amy drew her shawl around her, pursing her lips. Caroline recognised her mood; any further discussion was futile. 'I can't think of that, Caro,' she said. 'We're facing ruin – the work-house, for God's sake. My family will be broken up, and my babies lost forever. I can't think of anything but that.'

A policeman started down the street as if magically drawn to talk of law-breaking, walking slowly in their direction, his face hidden entirely in the shadow of his black top hat. Caroline could tell that he was studying them, no doubt taking them for a pair of novice whores from whom he could extort some kind of tariff. They had to leave.

'Christ Almighty, Amy,' she exclaimed wearily, 'why's your life always such a blessed trial?' She hooked her arm through her sister's. 'Come, you should get yourself home. I'll go with you.'

'You have to help us,' Amy insisted. 'Please, Caro.'

Caroline didn't answer. Tightening her grip on Amy, she steered them towards the Thames, turning left onto Ponsonby Street. Up ahead were the lights of Vauxhall Bridge, marking

123

a misty line across the wide black Thames. The sisters passed by the Spread Eagle; its low mullioned windows were glowing merrily, and those gathered within were belting out a hearty song. Caroline hurried them on to Westminster, not allowing herself even a single glance inside. Her walk with Mr Lowry would have to wait.

9

The panelled coffee room of the Reform Club covered one entire side of the building. Long rows of tables had been laid out across the tiled floor, and the aroma of a great many different luncheons intermingled in the air; a dazzling variety of creatures of both land and sea appeared to be on the menu that afternoon. There was a civilised murmur of gentlemanly conversation, accompanied by the discreet clinking of fine china and glassware. Political and literary-looking fellows were eating with fastidious good manners, taking coffee from slender silver jugs and reading their newspapers with the infuriating, mincing reserve of well-placed Englishmen. Sam surveyed the room, his chin up, squinting slightly to focus his eyes. He quickly located his ally and strode over to meet him, barrelling between the tables like a ball in the gutter of a bowling alley. Waiters, clad in the club livery of plush-breeches and white silk stockings, were obliged to step smartly from his path.

Commodore Hastings looked up at him, blinking in surprise at Sam's sudden arrival. 'Why, my dear Colonel Colt, I did not expect you to be –'

Sam landed heavily in the chair opposite Hastings. Without speaking, he reached into his jacket, fastening thumb and forefinger around the cold body of the pistol. He whipped the thing out with practised speed, held it up for a moment and then brought it down hard against the tabletop. The wineglasses jumped, one falling over, rolling off the edge and breaking apart on the tiles with a hollow crack.

'*Whiskey!*' Sam bellowed at the nearest waiter. 'Tom Hastings, my friend, let us toast the first London peacemaker – the first London Colt!'

Hastings was staring at the revolver. He had turned a mixture of colours; very pale around the eyes and cheeks, with a deep purple tone building at his neck. 'So it is working, Colonel?' he inquired, almost whispering in the hush that had fallen over the coffee room, mortified by the attention his guest was attracting. 'Your – your factory, I mean?'

Sam turned to the waiter, who was similarly transfixed, a dumb little mannequin in his ridiculous fancy garb. 'I said *whiskey*, man! Are you goddamn deaf?' The fellow shot off like a racehorse from its stall. Sam straightened his collar and addressed Hastings again, his voice proud yet businesslike. 'It is, Commodore – and this here is the very first weapon manufactured by Samuel Colt outside the borders of the American states. The *very first*. A thirty-six calibre Navy pistol made for military use – you'll notice that it has no brass fittings or any other details. No, what we have here is the weapon only, expertly designed and made, ready for use by Her Majesty's forces at their earliest convenience. Neither has it been engraved, apart from the serial numbers and the marks of my inspectors – and this, of course.' He angled the gun slightly, tapping the top of the barrel with his forefinger. There, in neat, mechanical letters no more than an eighth of an inch high, was stamped *Address: Col. Colt, London.*

Hastings leaned forward, plucking a gold-edged monocle from his old-fashioned naval waistcoat, his natural gunman's enthusiasm winning out over his John Bull reserve. There were noises from the other occupants of the room. Sam swivelled his head from side to side, meeting their stares. He saw ire, yes, and disapproval; but also a certain fascination. Even those who thought him a knave were clearly intrigued by his revolver.

'Egad,' exclaimed Hastings softly. 'This is a fine piece indeed.'

'English made in its entirety,' Sam announced, as much to the onlookers as to the man opposite him. 'Every last part fashioned from Sheffield steel by English hands. Physical testimony to the strength of the Anglo-Saxon bond that caused me to establish myself in this great country.'

The waiter returned with a tray bearing a bottle of treacle-coloured bourbon and two short tumblers; he set them down and retired, recovering the broken glass from the floor-tiles as he did so. Sam checked the label and couldn't help but be impressed. Whatever else a man might have to say about these high-born Bulls, they certainly knew how to surround themselves with quality. He poured them both out a measure and drank his down at once.

'I should tell you, Tom, that production is not yet at full strength. But make no mistake – this pistol lying right here is as good a firearm as has ever been made *anywhere*, at any point in mankind's progress. We've proved it ourselves, and rigorously. It's more than ready to be sent off to the Tower to pass the tests of your government.'

Hastings caught the pique in Sam's voice. He sat back, tucking his monocle back into his waistcoat. 'A mere formality, Colonel,' he said reassuringly, 'in your case, at least.'

Sam snorted. 'To be quite frank, Tom, your tests aren't equal to the guns. They might pose a challenge to that rogue Adams, but this here before us now is an expertly constructed weapon.' To stress this point, he lifted the revolver three inches from the table – it had left a greasy impression of itself upon the clean white cloth – and banged it down again. The sound rang through the genteel coffee room like a lead door-knocker.

Hastings had returned to something approaching his usual hue; this second impact of pistol against table, however, brought a fresh radishy rash to the old soul's jowls. 'Will you eat something, Colonel?' he asked quietly, looking to the neatly printed bill of fare lying beside his untouched glass. 'I shall have the beef, I think. It is usually very good.'

Sam shook his head. 'All I require now,' he declared, pouring himself a second drink, 'is a nation to sell my wares to. Pretty soon there will be hundreds upon hundreds of guns piling up in that warehouse by the river. I look in the papers, Tom, and all I read of this promising situation in the

East is an endless dance of diplomats – Russia menaces, Turkey responds, France and Britain flap about like ducks in a goddamn rainstorm. I'm growing impatient with it.'

'My understanding,' said Hastings, 'is that both Lord Aberdeen and Lord Clarendon believe war can be avoided and are briefing the ambassadors to that end.' He summoned a waiter and pointed to his choice on the bill of fare. The man took the card from him with a bow and made for the kitchens.

Sam barely managed to contain his temper. 'Well, Tom, that just ain't good enough. It ain't goddamn *right*. What of this Palmerston fellow? I keep hearing the name from the Englishmen in my employ. They say he is calling for a fleet of gunboats to sail into Turkish waters – to serve as sentinels and remind this frisky Tsar who exactly he's facing here. Now *that's* a course of real courage, if you ask me – and one approved by the British public.'

Hastings cast a faintly flustered look around him, uncomfortable with this sensitive subject matter. 'Lord Palmerston is Home Secretary at present,' he said, a little quickly. 'Such matters are not his area of authority.'

'Perhaps they damn well should be.'

An awkward silence fell between them. Sam overheard someone over by the windows regaling his companions with the tale of the Yankee gun-maker's interview with Lord Paget three months previously. In this rather lively version, the Adams pistol actually went off, blowing a hole the size of a thrupenny bit in the back of Paget's Chippendale desk-chair.

The Commodore's face suddenly brightened; he'd thought of a new topic of conversation. 'I hear Mr Kossuth's visit was a success. Your new friend Mr Street has been talking of it constantly – in this very room and all over London.'

'It won't lead to a sale. The Hungarian fool didn't have enough understanding of what he was being shown even to realise that production had yet to begin, and he ain't got so much as two cents to rub together.' Sam put away his second shot of whiskey. 'Got us in the papers, though. Spot of that ballyhoo's always good for business.'

'Oh, that's not all, Colonel. Not by a good distance.'

Hastings was positively beaming, displaying a row of crooked brownish teeth. 'Your reputation in the Commons – itself a great club, you know, not so very different from the one we sit in now – was raised *enormously* by that one small act. Men who hadn't given a thought to the Colt revolver since the days of the Great Exhibition could speak of little else but the American gunworks, this marvel of engineering that has sprung up by the Thames. You were brought to the attention of England's foremost men. They speak of you as a great innovator and inventor, a business genius, a – a . . .' Here the old sailor's voice trailed off; he waved a hand about vaguely, directing an encouraging smile in Sam's direction.

Sam considered the bourbon bottle for a moment. 'Tom,' he said firmly, helping himself to a third measure, 'call it needless Yankee suspicion if you will, but I'm getting the feeling that I'm being used for some other end here. Exactly whose attention was I trying to get by playing host for Mr Kossuth?'

Hastings laughed, finally picking up his bourbon and taking a sip. 'You have me at a disadvantage there, Colonel. I am no plotter. Cannon, sir; that's my area. Cannon, powder and shot. I am not one of these devious Westminster types.' He set the tumbler down again with a shallow cough. 'Mr Street might be able to help you.'

'I'm sure he could, if he was at all disposed to.' Sam met the Commodore's eye. 'I've been trying to reach the slippery son of a bitch, but I'm fast discovering that if he don't want to see you, he sure as hell ain't being seen. D'you happen to know where he is?'

'Again, Colonel Colt, I cannot help you. Mr Street serves the interests of important men. They keep him busy indeed.'

Sam decided to let this go. What did he really care about the doings of Lawrence Street? He drank his whiskey; three shots down and he was starting to feel it. There was an agreeable fluidity to his thinking, and the stiffness that so often plagued his joints was entirely gone. Outside, sunlight pierced the dense London cloud, laying long strips across the coffee room's tables; these grew rapidly brighter, plunging all else into a pleasant gloom. Sam found himself thinking that he could easily settle in for the afternoon. Then he remembered the letter he'd received earlier that week and the decision it had prompted.

'Listen, Tom,' he said, pushing his glass to the centre of the table. 'I must tell you that I'm returning to America at the earliest opportunity. Friday, most probably.'

Hastings's brow lifted in surprise. 'My dear Colonel Colt! Not for long, I hope?'

'For the rest of the summer, I should think. I'm needed at my Hartford works with some urgency.' Sam sighed; he supposed he owed Hastings a proper explanation, much as it vexed him even to think of what was dragging him back across the Atlantic at this crucial juncture. 'I'm having this dyke built, y'see, to protect my factory from the Connecticut River, which has a famous propensity to flood. An unholy combination of town officials and clergymen has got wind of this project, and seeks to curtail my endeavours, in the rascally way of such people. I must be there to fend them off.'

Hastings's expression was uncomprehending. 'But how on earth can they possibly prevent you from protecting your own premises?'

'Oh, they *won't* prevent me,' Sam informed him. 'There's no chance of that. They've been putting stories about, though, sowing their little seeds. I'm using the very best Dutch methods for this dyke, which I suppose involves a fair bit of excavation. Accordingly, my opponents have cooked up some ridiculous theory that I will *unsettle the river*, and force it to flood further upstream, where there are houses and suchlike. Total nonsense, of course.' Sam laid a hand upon the London Colt, preparing to pick it up. He'd already decided that the gun was going over the Atlantic with him, to be shown off to the staff of the Hartford works – and anyone else who came into its inventor's path. 'Why is it, Tom, that whenever a man tries to do things on the big figure there's always some goddamn chump sat in an office or standing up in a pulpit telling him he can't?'

The old Commodore didn't have an answer to this. 'I am quite sure that you will emerge victorious,' was all he said.

Sam returned the pistol to his jacket. 'Anyways, my friend,

I must leave you. There's a mountain of preparations still to be made, and one particular piece of labour at the Pimlico works that demands my personal supervision.'

'Of course, of course.' Hastings's regret at Sam's departure was tempered by a clear relief that the scrutiny of the Reform Club would soon be lifted from his table. 'But you must promise to return to us soon, Colonel. We cannot allow the momentum that has been built up so skilfully to go to waste.'

Colt stood, dropping a pound note beside the silver pepperpot and extending his hand. 'My people will keep things going, Tom, don't you worry. I'll make sure they know what's damn well expected of 'em.'

The Colt barouche steered away from the Pall Mall traffic towards where Sam stood. He climbed up from the pavement, shouted *'Bessborough Place!'* at the coachman and swung himself inside. His secretary and press agent were seated within, facing each other. As he sat down, taking off his hat and cutting a plug of Old Red, Sam gave them a quick, derisive account of the luxury he had just seen – the fine foods, the magnificent, portrait-lined library, the platoon of overdressed servants – and stated that, in his humble opinion, it indicated a basic hypocrisy at the root of English Liberalism.

'I tell you, the zeal that those worthy fellows in there supposedly feel for reform don't extend to any democratic simplicity of manners or modesty of style, that's for goddamn sure.'

Lowry and Richards grinned at this; Sam felt that the Englishmen had no more respect for the rich Whigs of the Reform Club than he did. We've become a passable team, he thought, me and these two Bulls. They should know my plans; they deserve it. Pushing the plug inside his lip, he informed them that he was leaving the country at the end of the week.

The secretary stared at him in disbelief. 'But how are we to continue, Colonel, without you present to direct our efforts?'

'Consider it a test of your abilities, Mr Lowry,' Sam told

him. 'It's a fine chance to demonstrate to me how much you've learnt in these past months.'

He looked out of the window, feeling an uncomfortable cramping sensation in his midriff that may have been due to the whiskey. They were racing around the boundary of St James's Park. Its lawns were teeming with office clerks and notaries, relieved of their jackets and hats, basking in the summer sun; some were even braving the waters of the boating lake. He slid a hand inside his waistcoat and gave his belly a firm, circular rub.

'Such incredible *faith* you have in us, Samuel,' said Richards, his voice a sly drone. He was sitting on Sam's side of the carriage, and now leaned closer towards him. There was a cut across the bridge of his large, bony nose, and he smelt oddly of candied pears, a sickly, chemical odour. God alone knew what he'd been up to. 'I only hope that we can all be shown to warrant it.'

Sam caught something in the press agent's tone. He narrowed his eyes. 'If that there's a reference to Mr Lowry,' he said bluntly, 'then you can damn well stow it. Three months now he's been following me around, Alfie, watching me conduct my business. The boy has a decent brain on him and he knows what's what. He's good for whatever I want of him, y'hear?'

Richards demurred at once, sitting back and raising his palms.

Lowry himself was grinning. 'I thank you for your confidence, Colonel,' he said, 'and will do all I can to justify it. May I ask what calls you to America so suddenly?'

The carriage swung away from the park, starting down a shadowy avenue of tall buildings. Street bustle rushed around the smart vehicle like a flow of dirty water, threatening almost to carry it on down into the drain of the Westminster rookery. They slid by an omnibus, a loud yellow advertisement for shaving soap blaring across Sam's window. Above the hats of the multifarious crowd he glimpsed the ancient gothic flank of the Abbey, its buttresses like the ribs of some skeletal leviathan; and beyond this the seething Parliament site, swathed in sunlit clouds of dust and steam. The gun-maker

132

rubbed his aching belly some more and recounted the tale of the dyke to his employees.

'It must be owned that my returning home is something of a risk,' he admitted, 'but I'm afraid that nothing less than the survival of my Hartford factory is at stake. Without that dyke it could flood. Can you imagine what a goddamn *flood* would do to a gun works?' He paused, letting this terrible notion hang in the air for a few seconds. 'Besides, I reckon that things ain't really going to pick up round here for a little while. Not by the end of the summer, even. While I'm gone my boys will perfect the machinery and the engine – and when I return we'll be ready to take this government of yours for all she's damn well got.'

They turned hard to the right, pushing Sam against the carriage's side. Through the floor he could feel the vehicle's mechanisms straining and creaking. It grew lighter; he saw they were heading into the Victoria Street clearances, skirting the northern edge of the rookery. Many hundreds of rotten old buildings had been torn down to make way for the new road, the city authorities carving a great track through the district, no doubt envisaging not only a modern thorough-fare but a profusion of neat structures to line it. It was a noble project in Sam's estimation, and a truly improving one, giving the sense that this was a city on the move, ready to purge its filthier regions and enter a better age. Thus far, however, no reconstruction work had taken place. Indeed, much of the earthy, rubble-strewn ground had lain fallow for so long that grasses and even a few small, shabby trees had appeared.

'My expectation,' Sam pronounced as they traversed the relative quiet of this little wasteland, 'is that the two of you will refrain from your sniping and bickering for this short duration and watch over my interests with the correct level of vigilance.'

Richards and Lowry looked at each other. 'Do you mean to say, Colonel,' asked the secretary, 'that you are leaving us in charge?'

'Not exactly. A caretaker has been appointed, but he's going to need your help. That I can guarantee.'

There was more unspoken communication between the two Bulls. Sam saw that behind their spiky exchanges lay a deeper sense of alliance – whether they were fully aware of it or not.

'It's James Colt, my younger brother,' the gun-maker said matter-of-factly, not waiting for the inevitable question, 'a fellow well versed in both the law and the diplomatic arts.' This was a laughably generous description. It rather annoyed Sam to be obliged to give it. 'He's familiar with our situation here – I wrote him a full report only last week – and he'll have the authority to make whatever decisions are to be made.'

This was the real gamble of Sam's trip back to America. Jamie was a man of few accomplishments, his frequent failures thrown into stark relief by Sam's massive and ongoing rise. As usual, he needed money as a matter of urgency, and this time had enlisted their elderly father to help him appeal for a chance in the Colt Company. Such begging letters from his family were a troublesome feature of Sam's life, and long experience had taught him that it was usually easier to give in than resist. His brother wasn't stupid, despite his many other flaws, and Sam had convinced himself that a short trial period in charge of the London works might actually do the rascal good. And after all, he had the right name. The factory belonged to the Colt Company; it felt right somehow to leave a Colt at its helm.

Richards looked doubtful. He was familiar with Jamie's scandalous past – the debts, the womanising, the duelling wounds – and although hardly in a position to judge, he was plainly in two minds about serving under such a person. Lowry was glancing from his employer to his colleague, a trace of uncertainty on that clear, clever face of his. Sam guessed that he'd heard something of John and was getting his Colt brothers confused. The gun-maker could not concern himself with any of this. They would overcome their discomfiture or they would depart the Company. It was as simple as that. Moving forward, a hand still hard against his querulous belly, Sam fixed his secretary with a level stare.

'I have an especially important instruction for you, Mr Lowry. As acting manager, James will be opening all my correspondence – all correspondence, that is, of English or American origin.' He pointed a finger at Lowry. 'Listen well to this, my boy: anything issuing from the rest of Europe you are to forward directly on to me in Connecticut. Is that clear? *Directly to Connecticut.*'

Lowry nodded: he understood. This was a reliable young fellow. Sam sat back, chewing on his plug. A row of Cubitt's identical houses were scrolling past outside, like the repeating scenery in a mechanical panorama. They were almost at the factory. His delicate stomach forgotten, he rose to his feet and lurched awkwardly across the carriage, compelling Lowry and Richards to retract their legs. He brought down the window with both hands and stuck out his head. The corner of Bessborough Place and Ponsonby Street was filled with people. Several carts and a couple of cabs had stopped in the road; out on the river a steamboat was lingering, its paddles working backwards, the passengers gathered at the rail.

Everyone was looking up at the roof of Sam's factory. A party of workmen was clambering over the tiles, light-footed as mountain goats, pots of whitewash dangling from their hands. Across the roof, angled towards the Vauxhall Bridge Road and the city beyond, was now emblazoned the gleaming legend *Col. Colt's Patent Firearms*, each letter twice the height of a man. Sam leaned further out of the window, telling the coachman to bring them to a halt so that he could take it in properly.

Someone whistled sharply; the gun-maker looked around to see almost all of his American staff, standing a little apart from the throng. There was Ben Quill, with his Irishman as always, who had performed the miracle of getting that dud engine to power the machinery; Walter Noone, who had ended Adams's cowardly attacks with quick discretion; Gage Stickney, who along with his overseers had fashioned a workforce from the most unpromising of materials. Sam felt pride, and a deep satisfaction. The British government can dither all it likes, he thought – regardless of what the Bulls do or don't do, with men and premises such as these my London venture cannot help but be a success. Lawrence Street might have his schemes, but Sam Colt would not be bound by these. Why the devil should he be? He was not Street's creature. There were plenty of other routes open to an enterprising gun-maker.

The Americans started to call out his name, prompting others to turn towards the mustard-coloured carriage and slowly join in the chorus. Sam had an idea. Acknowledging the gathering cheers with a brief wave, he ducked back inside, prompting more personal rearrangement by the press agent and secretary. He drew the first London Colt from his jacket and told Lowry to fetch him percussion caps and cartridges from one of the presentation boxes that were stowed on board. The pistol was loaded in well under a minute. Sam then put on his hat, opened the carriage door and climbed out onto the metal step.

They were ready for him this time and let out a great roar; the steamboat wallowing on the Thames added to the acclamation, sounding a long blast from its horn. The shouts grew louder still as Sam lifted the Navy revolver triumphantly aloft and fired off all six shots into the summer sky.

PART TWO

Crocodile Court

1

Edward examined the letter again, angling it in the dusty sunlight that seeped in through the office's single circular window. A dense lattice of black pen-strokes had been scribbled over the original post-mark with the plain intention of eradicating it, but he fancied that he could make out something beneath: a taloned foot, and a feather or two perhaps, such as might belong to an imperial eagle, rendered with the elaborate detail of an official stamp. He compared the two addresses upon it. The first, that of the Colt sales office in Liège, was written in an immaculate hand, angular and somehow alien. This had been crossed out by the same pen which had defaced the post-mark, and a redirection inscribed in next to it with a good deal less precision. Beside the great blot in the upper right-hand corner was a crisp new mark from Liège's central post office.

It was obvious enough what had occurred. The letter had arrived in Liège and been forwarded on by the sales agent there, who'd been unaware of Colonel Colt's sudden departure for Connecticut. This did not explain, however, why such important missives – and this one was certainly important – were being sent to Belgium, which was by any measure a minor outpost of the Colt empire. The Colonel had been in London for several months prior to his return to America. Word of his factory by the Thames had spread far and wide. Anyone of note who sought to do business with him would surely know to send their letters there. And why on earth had the Belgian agent gone to such strange lengths to disguise the letter's place of origin?

There was a knock on the office door, three raps in quick succession. Edward sat up and bade the person enter. It was Mr Alvord, one of the overseers from the machine floor, a sullen, puffy-looking fellow who never made the slightest effort to conceal his dislike for the secretary. He reported in a bored voice that there was a blond-whiskered Englishman standing out on the stairs, asking for their manager. Edward nodded; it had to be Lawrence Street. He knew that the Colonel had been trying to reach Street in the days before he left for Hartford, but without success. Now, a full two weeks after Colt had gone, it seemed that the Honourable Member had finally set aside the time to grace them with a visit.

James Colt, of course, was nowhere to be found. It had quickly become clear that this would be the standard state of affairs. The Colonel's younger brother had visited the factory but once so far, on the day of his arrival in the metropolis. An unfortunate coincidence had brought an irate delegation to the gates on that very same day, demanding the removal of the spectacular advertisement painted upon the factory roof. This party was headed by Lady Cecilia Wardell, who was proving herself a committed and resourceful opponent of Colt. For this particular mission she'd enlisted none other than Thomas Cubitt, the great building-master of Pimlico, who'd stood sternly at her side as she'd asked to speak with the Colonel. James – or Jamie, as he'd introduced himself to them all – had gone out to meet them enthusiastically enough, seeming to think his new managerial responsibilities a bit of a jest or a novel game, smilingly confident that he could talk the Company out of this spot of difficulty and preserve his brother's slogan.

They had beaten him down with a speed that had been embarrassing to behold. Edward had remained in the factory, yet could still clearly hear the black-clad Cubitt – who resembled the more forbidding kind of Methodist minister in both appearance and manner – bellowing that the Colt Company was reducing the tone of his district to that of the lowest commercial lanes of Piccadilly. Jamie had slunk back inside, tugging uncomfortably at his collar and blowing out his cheeks, and told Stickney to get some men up on the roof with buckets of pitch as soon as possible. He'd left shortly afterwards and not returned.

Edward looked at Alvord again. The overseer was staring past him, out of the window, his thoughts elsewhere. 'You'd better show him up then, Mr Alvord. I'll see if I can help.'

As the office door closed, a little more loudly than was necessary, Edward considered the mysterious letter for a final time. His instructions were plain. Everything from Europe or beyond was to be forwarded, unopened, to the Colonel at Hartford. Its origin and its contents were really none of his concern. Decisive, impatient footsteps sounded out in the corridor, approaching where he sat; he brushed the letter into a drawer and set about collecting himself for an audience with Mr Street.

The calculating political operator of the Hotel de Provence was not in evidence that morning. Street's eyes were starting forth in his head, seeming almost to press against the lenses of his eye-glasses, and those fine blond whiskers bordered a complexion bleached by anxious anger. Edward rose from his chair and bowed, welcoming the Honourable Member to the factory. Ignoring him completely, Street paced from one side of the sparsely furnished room to the other, each hard fall of his fine city shoes shaking an issue of dust from the unvarnished floorboards. Then he stopped, studying his left thumbnail with a critical air.

'Where in blazes is he then, this younger brother?'

Edward swallowed. 'Sir, I –'

'Does he have any notion of what is occurring today?' Street interrupted. 'Of what is at stake? The manager of these works is needed *immediately*, do you hear me, to attend a meeting of the utmost importance.' He glared at Edward as if he bore personal responsibility for James Colt's absence. 'Do you even know where he is?'

'I do not, Mr Street. However, if you would care to –'

Street's features struggled to express his incredulity at this answer. 'Do you really not have *any idea*? Are such things

141

not your *duty*, sir? At this essential moment, your chief has truly gone *missing*?'

As Edward was composing a suitably humble reply, the sound of reedy voices joined in Christian song rose up from outside the factory. It was the indomitable Lady Wardell and her followers, gathered at the gates on Ponsonby Street – an almost daily presence since their victory over the roof slogan. The choking miasma given off by the Thames in high summer made such demonstration something of a trial, but while a small number did wilt away, the main body of the group seemed to welcome this call on their stamina and their righteous resolve. In the last couple of days they'd also taken to distributing printed tracts to the Colt workers – which by evening could be seen heaped in grubby drifts along the lanes surrounding the works.

'Dear God,' exclaimed Street irritably, taking off his top hat and dabbing at his forehead with a handkerchief, 'does that blessed woman never rest?'

'They are later today than usual, Mr Street,' Edward said. 'Lady Wardell normally makes sure that she is here for the arrival of the early shift.'

Street returned the hat to his head; the protesters' routine was of no interest to him. He came over to the front of the desk. Fresh perspiration was already breaking out across his brow. His eye-glasses magnified the pupils behind and threw them slightly off-centre, making it difficult to meet his gaze.

'Can you tell me anything of use at all?'

'Mr Colt is a resident at Mivart's Hotel, in Berkeley Square. You might try for him there.'

Street suddenly squeezed up his face into a bitter frown, as if he had tasted something very sour. The effect was oddly infantile; Edward thought that he might be about to stamp his foot. 'It is a trumpery affair, do you hear me? A damned trumpery affair.' The Honourable Member turned away, heading for the door, raging on as he went. 'That the Colonel should have permitted such laxity to overtake his works is quite beyond my ability to understand. This place is at a deuced low ebb – it can not be allowed to continue.'

Edward stood alone in the empty office, the door swinging

open, listening to the distant singing and the sound of Lawrence Street marching back along the corridor and starting noisily down the stairs. Now that, he thought, could not have gone much more badly. He failed to see what else he could have done, however. It wasn't as if he'd urged the Colonel to go back to see to his dyke, or was in any way responsible for the appointment of his idle scapegrace of a brother as the caretaker manager. The secretary closed his eyes for a second. Samuel Colt was an unpredictable, unfathomable master. This was plainly the price of his genius in other areas. Edward knew that impatience or resentment would not help his prospects; the most sensible thing he could do was attend to his other tasks to the best of his ability. He remembered the letter in the drawer, and decided that he would send it right away, from the post office on the Vauxhall Bridge Road.

It was not until he was reaching for his hat that Edward gave proper consideration to what might actually have occasioned Street's ill-tempered visit. He'd taken care to keep up with the newspapers and knew all about the recent escalation in the East. Russia had invaded the Danubian principalities; armies were clashing, men being killed. The British Cabinet remained hopelessly split over the best way to react to the mounting crisis; Aberdeen was hesitant, Palmerston belligerent, and the rest divided more or less equally between them. These two things, the arrival of the strange letter and the visit from Palmerston's man, both seemed to relate to this, but precisely how Edward could not fathom. Pondering it, he headed towards the staircase.

The scream was painful to hear, a clear note twisted horribly sharp as if wrung by malicious hands. Edward was crossing the machine floor landing; his head snapped around instinctively in the direction of this piercing cry. A girl was advancing towards him in the dull ochre light. She'd just walked out from among the small chucking lathes, cutting devices used in the shaping of the pistol barrels. Her movements were odd, the footsteps shuffling and irregular. There was a look of stunned helplessness on her wide, plain face. Edward found that he recognised her. She was a regular in

143

the Spread Eagle; her name was Nancy. Only two nights previously she'd laughed at him from across the bar when he'd looked in briefly – and in vain – after the factory had closed.

Nancy was very far from laughter now. Her hands were clasped between her thighs, and a black stain was spreading fast down the front of her dress. Their eyes met. A question started to form on his lips; but before he could speak she screamed again, even louder this time. Several other female operatives rushed out from their posts, surrounding her, addressing her with firm concern, telling her that she had to show them what had happened. After a few seconds she complied, her left hand jerking out into the open. Edward gulped; the index finger was completely gone, clipped clean off down to the knuckle, and a good portion of the ring finger was missing too. Two little jets of blood, thick and viscous like crimson wax, pumped from the wounds in grotesque symmetry. Those gathered around Nancy gasped out curses and prayers. She herself began to shake uncontrollably, moaning with terror.

Amid the general alarm one of the women took charge, removing her apron and wrapping the mangled hand in it as best she could. She then began looking around, calling for the overseer. It was Caroline Knox.

'Bind it!' Alvord had appeared at the far end of the machine room and was striding down the central aisle. He had the strained air of someone to whom such bloody incidents were simple delays – inconvenient, tedious facts of his existence. 'Bind the wound just below where she's cut! Do it *now*, damn it, as tightly as you can!'

Miss Knox attempted to obey him, peeling back the apron, but as soon as he reached them Alvord pushed her aside and took over. 'Quit your wailing,' he barked at Nancy, tearing off the apron's fastening cord, 'you ain't in any serious danger here. You've lost a digit, that's all – and due to your own carelessness, more'n likely. Now hold still.'

Grimacing, the stout Colt man coiled the cord around Nancy's hand and tightened it without mercy. The injured girl fell directly into a faint, slumping into the arms of the woman standing behind her. Alvord swiftly bound the wound in the remainder of the apron and then gave Nancy's face a hard slap. She came to her senses, retching up a cupful of bile. The overseer asked the operative holding her if she knew her way to the nearest infirmary, where some proper dressings might be applied. She said she did; Nancy was helped to her feet, and the two of them hurried off towards the staircase. They passed Edward on their way out. He overheard Nancy, her voice wobbling with agony, mumbling desperately that she was still good to work her machine and could return later in the day – that the Yankees weren't to give her position to anyone else in the meantime.

The machine room was still and stiflingly hot, hushed by the accident. The driving cylinder spun on above, grinding slightly against its brackets; an incongruous snatch of the protesters' latest hymn drifted in through an open window. Edward glanced at Miss Knox. She was already looking at him, and he could see guilt in her, as plain as day. This brought him a moment's gladness. She does not despise me at least, he thought; there is some other explanation for the determined distance she has placed between us. He'd made many dozens of attempts to meet with her since that first evening in the Spread Eagle, nearly three weeks ago now, when everything seemed to be going so swimmingly well, and all had been thwarted in some way. Slowly, dejectedly, he'd made himself accept that it must be purposeful on her part.

She looked careworn, a little unwashed and ragged even, and very tired. The easy humour that had so animated her during their previous encounters was conspicuously absent. Edward smiled, intending an expression of warmth, of friendly support – but he could feel the accusation upon his face.

Alvord clapped his hands, breaking the bewildered silence, ordering everyone back to their appointed labours and reminding them in the time-honoured fashion of overseers everywhere that their employer was not paying them to take their leisure. Miss Knox immediately headed back to her machine, turning away from Edward with unmistakable relief. He frowned, lowering his head, trying to cover his incomprehension by putting on his hat and then patting his waistcoat as if he had mislaid his pocket-watch.

Alvord was studying the blood and bile that were spattered across the floorboards with weary distaste. 'You lost something, Mr Lowry?' he asked, without looking up.

The secretary excused himself and continued on his way to the post office.

'These fellows,' said Richards, raising his voice to be heard above the music, 'these damned fellows . . . Look at 'em, Lowry. Go on, take a good bloody look.'

'I see them, Richards, believe me.' Edward murmured his words through gritted teeth; the press agent was drunk once again and unable to gauge exactly how loudly he was talking. 'I see them.'

Richards knocked back his latest glass of spirits and then held it aloft to summon the waiter. 'I know London, old chap, I know her thieves and her bloody cads, and this lot right here are the worst specimens I've seen in a good long while. See that coat there – look, there.'

He was pointing across the balcony of the famous Argyll Rooms towards the main body of their company. Discreetly, Edward pinched the bottom of his sleeve and tugged his arm back down. The coat in question was obvious enough. Cut from black velvet in an eminently fashionable style, it was worn by a great glossy hound of a man, broad-snouted and sharp-whiskered, who was leaning in towards James Colt with every appearance of loyal attention. When studied a little more closely, however, it became plain that this character was working on two quite distinct levels. He was speaking with James as a confidential friend; but he was also monitoring the American carefully, waiting for a chance of some kind to present itself.

'That coat is far too bloody *smart* for my liking. The smarter the coat the deeper the trick, my friend,' said Richards, tapping the side of his long nose as if imparting a valuable piece of wisdom. 'The deeper the bloody trick.'

James Colt, however, saw nothing sinister in his predatory cohort. He was lounging beneath a silken canopy at the balcony's rear, doing his best to project an aura of wealth and power – coupled with a strong suggestion of rakish high spirits. Such was his resemblance to his accomplished brother in both face and physique that he was frequently mistaken for him, an error Edward had noticed that he was rather lax in correcting. The secretary had soon learnt that this visual similarity, initially a source of reassurance, was entirely deceptive. Samuel Colt's formidable, demanding nature, his absolute focus upon his guns, his strict intolerance for anything that might waste his time or impede his path to his objective, were replaced in James only by pleasure-seeking indolence; and his gallery of intent, boiling scowls by the vaguely self-satisfied simper that was seldom far from his younger brother's face. James shared the Colonel's taste for costly, colourful clothes (that night, for example, he wore a terracotta-coloured jacket with a waistcoat of sunflower yellow), but his garments also featured odd, dandified touches such as frilled cuffs, voluminous neckties and embroidered lapels. He walked with a slight limp – according to Richards, this was the result of a wound received in a scandalous duel fought over a married woman in the city of St Louis. Edward found this rather difficult to believe. To him, James Colt simply did not seem capable of the sheer nerve that would surely be required for such a dramatic act. Neither could the secretary detect any trace of the political and legal acumen that had been claimed for their new manager. All in all, he seemed to lack a mainsail, a driving shaft – to want for the vital propelling agent that had made the elder Colt what he was.

That evening, James was holding court with a band of followers whom he'd introduced only as 'the Harum-Scarum Club'. Upon their arrival in the casino, it had taken less than a minute for this debauched club to attract a half-dozen of the gay women who haunted its upper regions. Obtaining access into the balcony cost another shilling on top of the door price, and these ladies were accordingly of a superior class to those found fishing for custom around the dance-floor downstairs. Their faces were painted with the utmost delicacy, their rich gowns cut low across smooth, wool-white bosoms, and their smiles immaculately suggestive. They had infiltrated James's group effortlessly, gliding beneath the folds of the canopy, settling among the men like sleek pigeons upon a scattered handful of seed. Batting long eyelashes, the women were putting on an expert show of amusement at the most banal, boorish remarks, and reaching out to touch the backs of male hands with titillating forwardness. James and the fellow in the too-smart coat were discussing one of their number with salacious interest – a slender, feline-featured girl of no more than eighteen who was arranging herself upon an upholstered stool. The younger Colt made an observation, cocking his head to one side; his friend met it with a grin; both shook with unpleasant laughter.

Edward and Richards were positioned at the very periphery of this party. They sat at the far end of a long seat, beside an expansive potted palm at the balcony's edge. The inebriated press agent had been sliding down slowly among the palm's rubbery leaves, which were now threatening to engulf him completely. Below them, through an ornate wrought-iron balustrade, a swirling waltz was underway, all dark coats and vibrant crinolines, the many revolving couples interlocking on the crowded floor like the gears in a massive multicoloured machine. Directly behind their seat hung a huge mirror, its frame embellished with gilded scrolls. Another of similar dimensions had been placed opposite and a couple more off to the side; they'd been arranged to create an impression of size, the reflections artificially expanding the really quite modest proportions of the room and multiplying its compact crystal chandeliers into glittering, serried lines.

The secretary and press agent had been instructed to attend the Argyll Rooms because Colt Company business was supposedly to be conducted there. The only other sign that this might actually be the case was the presence of Lawrence Street, accompanied by an underling of some description. He was sitting across from them, also on the fringes of the gathering; posed rather stiffly in an armchair, he had yet to so much as acknowledge their existence. A man of unchallengeable gravity, the Honourable Member was as out of place in the fashionable casino as a cleric in a Chinese opium den. One of the finer courtesans had been sent over to talk with him and was admiring his fine blond hair; he was replying in frosty monosyllables, looking off in the opposite direction, making her work very hard indeed.

Needless to say, the women all gave Edward and Richards a wide berth, immediately recognising their lack of both ready funds and importance. This was a blessing; Edward really wasn't in the mood to fend off their well-practised advances. His mind was occupied almost entirely with its thousandth restaging of that moment in the machine room when Caroline Knox had turned away from him. Over and over again he saw the resolute rotation of her shoulder, the angle of her head as it dipped down, and the unfathomable haste in her step. He raked through his memory for an explanation, going over every word that had passed between them, yet he could not find so much as a single grain of genuine discord or misunderstanding. Indeed, such reminiscence made him feel only that he might very possibly be in love, however inappropriate or inconvenient that might prove. Her last words to him as she left the Spread Eagle that night had been, 'I must see to this, sir, but I promise you I'll be back before you even know it.' And she had smiled as she said them. What could have happened after this to spoil things so completely?

'My eye, what a blasted *booby*,' Richards sneered from his place in the palm, nodding at James as he stretched out to take a fresh drink from a waiter. 'He fancies himself a Carnival Roman, don't he, cruising the bloody Corso. Rather than a jumped-up simpleton, a – a wastrel, Lowry, who rides upon our Sam's coat-tails like a bloody . . . a bloody . . .'

Before the press agent could recover his train of thought, Mr Street came before them, pushing the departing waiter aside with graceless annoyance. 'Did he honestly think that this would *mollify me*?' he demanded of Edward. 'That this wretched, meretricious place was an appropriate venue for the discussion of our mutual interests?' He moved closer. 'It is offensive, quite frankly. Colonel Colt would never so much as consider such a damnably stupid course.'

Edward got to his feet, offering profuse apologies. He had to agree with Street on this point; it was wholly impossible to imagine the Colonel in the Argyll Rooms, for any purpose whatsoever.

'The Colonel had his priorities in order,' Street continued. 'He knew how to conduct his business. Why he has left this dissolute fool in charge of his London affairs is quite beyond me.' The gay woman who had been making such a determined effort to talk to him came to his side, slipping a neat gloved hand through the crook of his arm. He shook her off. 'I am leaving. I cannot risk being seen in here. I will have nothing more to do with the Colt Company until the Colonel returns, do you understand? *Nothing more.*' Five seconds later he was at the balcony stairs, his lackey in tow, putting on his hat as they went down to the main doors.

There was a loud rustle and an agitation of leaves, followed by the snap of a stalk; Richards was attempting to disinter himself from the palm, with limited success. 'Who the devil was that?' he asked. 'D'you know him, Lowry? You keeping secrets from me, old boy? From Alfie Richards, your fellow Englishman, your one true pal at the Colt Company?'

Edward smiled dryly at this description, one that a more sober Richards would certainly never have made. 'He is an associate of the Colonel's, that's all. I've met him once or twice before.' The secretary decided that he would change the subject, and reveal no more about Lawrence Street. 'Sounds as if he has the measure of our Jamie, wouldn't you say?'

The press agent, as Edward had guessed, was too lost to drink to pursue or even recall his question. 'His godforsaken family are a millstone, a bloody great *millstone* around poor Samuel's neck,' he proclaimed, managing to gain limited purchase on the back of the seat. 'They are the one disadvantage that has attended on his life, and hampered his progress whenever he's been so good as to let 'em. The father is a bankrupt, y'know, always tapping him for money. And have I told you about his bloody *sister*, and what she did?'

There was movement beneath the canopy; James had spotted Street's departure and was rising from his seat, looking their way. 'Quiet, damn it,' Edward hissed, jabbing Richards's ankle with his boot.

The younger Colt drifted over to them in his customarily careless manner. 'Edward, did I just see our guest take his leave without so much as a farewell?'

The secretary, still standing, told him that he had.

James was unconcerned. 'Now there's a rum critter. This entire evening was arranged for his benefit, yet he's run off afore I could say six words to him. Was the scoundrel skylarking us, do you think?'

'I fear that he might have been expecting your conversation to take place somewhere a little quieter, Mr Colt.' Edward nodded towards the gay women. 'Somewhere a little less filled with distraction, perhaps.'

James had fixed him with a questioning smile. 'Why won't you call me Jamie, Edward? How many times do I have to ask you?' He chuckled, shaking his head. 'You might be right, I guess. Too late now though, ain't it? And what's the loss of one jumpy customer, anyways? We're selling *guns*, by God. Another will be along soon enough.'

Edward almost winced to hear this. Did James have no understanding at all of Street's importance – of the connections he had, the opportunities he could provide? Had the Colonel really not impressed this upon him?

James put an arm around Edward's shoulders. 'There's something I need you to do for me at the works tomorrow, my friend, something important.' He turned slightly, seeking out the eye of the young courtesan upon the stool. 'I'm told we had an accident on the machine floor.'

'Indeed we did . . . Jamie,' Edward replied. 'A girl lost a finger in one of the machines. I witnessed it, in fact. A truly nasty piece of luck.' He wondered briefly if James was concerned about poor Nancy's well-being, and maybe wished to see her properly cared for. There were occasional stories of factory managers displaying such benevolence. 'She still suffers terribly, I hear. They say that a fever has set in.'

James's lip was curling slowly as the woman held his gaze. 'It's a mistake to employ females in a gun factory. I can see why Sam chanced it – the cheaper wage-bill and so forth – but the simple fact of it is they just can't understand the machinery, and accidents like this are the certain result.' He looked back at Edward for a moment and then added softly, 'I want you to get rid of 'em for me.'

Edward went quite cold. He found himself staring hard at the pattern of swooping nightingales that was stitched along James's brick-red collar. 'I'm sorry,' he said, 'but I don't think I –'

'The female employees,' James clarified. 'Remove 'em from the works, every last one. Do it tomorrow morning, first thing.' He took his arm from around Edward and held out a hand to the girl, making his selection. She rose from her stool with queenly elegance and started towards him. 'It looks like I'm going to be indisposed until pretty late in the day, I'm afraid, but I'm sure there'll be others around to provide assistance.' James looked down at Richards. 'Like this gamesome true-blood here, for instance. What do you say, Alfie? You'll help Edward out, won't you?'

Richards, jerked from a doze, stuck out his lower lip and nodded gravely, giving James a thumbs-up. He plainly had no idea whatsoever of what had just been under discussion.

'I think it's time for him to head on home before he hashes up his dinner on one of these fine seats. Can you manage that, Edward?'

The secretary said that he could, reflecting bitterly that this foppish fool had finally shown his portion of Colt ruthlessness. One minor mishap and that was it, fifty souls cast from their positions, back out onto the mercy of the city – and Caroline Knox was among them. As James and his courtesan swapped coquettish pleasantries, his fingers quickly finding their way past her elbow to the small of her back, Edward thought hard, knowing that this might be his only chance to save Miss Knox's livelihood. Then, amazingly, it came – a stunning powder-blast of inspiration.

'What of the packing room?'

James was on the seat now, a couple of feet to the left

of Richards; the woman was cleaved to his side, sliding an arm inside his jacket. 'What of it?'

Edward hesitated. The young courtesan was taking him in idly with her large hazel eyes; he saw that she was unpeeling James Colt like a well-ripened orange, and would take her pick of the juiciest segments. 'Mr Stickney mentioned that a dozen more girls are needed over there, to put together our crates and cases, now that production is starting to pick up. Shall I choose them from those already employed on the machine floor? We will have enough recruitment work on our hands finding fifty new operatives.'

James shrugged, utterly indifferent. 'Whatever you think best, Edward – I leave it entirely with you.' He looked away, devoting his attention to the woman who seemed to be edging her way expertly onto his lap.

Edward turned to Richards. The press agent was talking to himself, his head lolling this way and that, apparently reliving some long-past triumph in the courtroom won during his promising, youthful years as a barrister. He was a sorry sight indeed, dishevelled and increasingly emaciated, his face and hands dotted with scabs. Since Colonel Colt's departure he'd given himself over entirely to dissipation; Alfred Richards was not the sort who flourished under a lax regime. Edward went to help him rise but was waved away with a curse. Somehow, Richards stood unaided, plucking a palm frond from beneath his lapel, but after a single faltering footstep he stumbled against the low table directly in front of their seat, knocking glasses everywhere. This won him a growl of unkind laughter from the Harum-Scarum Club, and a few affected titters from their fair friends.

Edward took hold of the press agent's shoulders, heaving him upright. He bade goodnight to James and his assortment of parasitic companions, and then grappled the protesting Richards out into the centre of the balcony. It occurred to him that he didn't know where the press agent lived, but he thought that they could save this particular problem for the cab.

Richards was about to speak, his face contorting with ill-will – his earlier good humour had vanished. 'You are such a bloody *fraud*, Lowry,' he said bitingly. 'I see through you, sir, in a – in a second. In a damned *trice*.'

Edward commenced the laborious process of manoeuvring the press agent towards the balcony stairs. 'Yes, Richards,' he replied, 'I'm quite sure that you do.'

The news of their termination by the Colt Company was greeted by the female operatives with every manifestation of distress. Some simply slunk away, never to be seen again. Others cried and pleaded as they were shepherded from the factory block, telling of debts and the rent and their hungry children, lingering around the gates and lanes outside the works for several hours as if hopeful that a miraculous reversal might occur and they would be called back inside. A few refused to leave, raving against Colonel Colt and his dandy brother, striking out and spitting at anyone who came near. Finally, Noone and his watchmen were summoned; they scooped up the screeching rebels, carried them down to the embankment and dropped them unceremoniously in the clotted, putrid mud of low tide.

Besides Caroline Knox, Edward had chosen the dozen women who would be retained for the packing room from the staff list, picking names completely at random. They were held in a corner of the forging shop until the last of their former co-workers had been removed, and were then escorted from the factory to the warehouse, all barely able to believe their good fortune. Edward stood nonchalantly in the middle of the yard, next to the water trough, thinking that Miss Knox was sure to look his way and realise the central part he had played in preserving her place at Colt. But she hurried straight past him, eyes fixed on the cobblestones before her.

Back up in the office, Edward perched on the edge of his desk with his arms tightly crossed, smoking a cigar with concentrated fury, his frustration champing on him like a carthorse. He'd rescued her from dismissal. Surely she owed him a minute of her attention. He hadn't asked for any of this; he hadn't sought her out. It was she who'd approached him during the Hungarian's visit, and invited him to come to the masons' tavern by the river. How could she turn away from him now – cast him aside like a rotten apple? That he was so angry served to anger him yet further. It seemed absurd that such a trivial thing should be affecting him to this degree. He was twenty-five years old and a man of worldly experience, not some trembling virgin. He'd known women of grace and comeliness; he'd felt the tangled emotions of romantic involvement. For this particular sensation, however, he was completely unprepared. He honestly didn't have any idea what to do next.

Edward glanced at the desktop. Piled upon it was a long report from the steelworks in Sheffield – his supposed area of expertise, he remembered – and a stack of inquiries from all manner of private individuals, forwarded to him by Mr Dennett, the agent in charge of the sales office at Spring Gardens. He could not bring himself to attend to any of it. Crossing over to the circular window, he watched a fierce argument taking place down on Ponsonby Street between the fractious women Noone had dumped in the Thames sludge and Lady Wardell's protesters.

'We ain't *better orf*, damn you,' one mud-blackened specimen shrieked, 'so shut yer bleedin' trap!'

The secretary rested his forehead against the glass, wondering how he had worked himself into such a ridiculous situation.

The morning passed slowly. As the heat in the little attic office grew more intense, Edward sat staring up at the sloping ceiling, imagining the sun melting together the tiles on the other side so that they slid off the edge of the roof in one congealed mass. He was sorely tempted to go over to the warehouse on some pretext or other and have her called out of the packing room, but couldn't think of anything he might then say that wouldn't sound petty, aggressive or aggrieved. When the midday break arrived at last, he spent it standing at the forge door with his hands in his pockets, scanning yard and warehouse for any sign of her. None presented itself; and eventually Mr Quill came over to speak with him, inquiring after his health in a kindly but distinctly pointed manner. Edward realised that his behaviour was

155

starting to draw attention. Americans and Englishmen alike were speculating about what – or who – had worked the Colonel's cool secretary into such an unholy lather, and they were smirking as they did so. He returned to the office at once.

There, back at the circular window, he tried to revive the line of reasoning he'd taken in the days after they'd first met, when he'd walked her back to Millbank. The end of their nascent friendship, he told himself sternly, was for the best – undoubtedly and indisputably. She was a *factory girl*, for God's sake! He was aiming for great things, for the golden pinnacles of business. Was such a woman compatible with such ambition? Could he really see her, a decade from now, being presented at the greatest houses in the city, with a fine silken shawl and a fan, making genteel conversation? He forced his thoughts back to his supper with Saul Graff, and the clear suggestion behind his old friend's words: a liaison with Caroline Knox would only ever be a conquest, a liberty taken with a girl from the servant class, virtue assailed and yielded and that was all. It would be a common, tawdry, short-lived thing. The distance between them, although small enough by Edward's reckoning, was nonetheless real, and would make any lasting connection impossible.

But it was no use. He could not think like this – not about her, the radiant, razor-sharp Miss Knox. In the hot, dusty calm of the office, with the rumbles and squeals of the gun factory vibrating faintly through the floorboards, his mind wandered off in an entirely different direction. He saw them standing together at the rail of a Collins steamer, sailing out of Liverpool harbour, bidding farewell to the old world forever as they headed for the lush vales of Connecticut, far away from England and her paltry prejudices. There, under the mantle of Colonel Colt, they would become wealthy, and respected, and so very happy that merely envisaging it made his heart strain and ache with longing.

At the end of the day, with this tormenting vision still lingering within him, Edward walked resolutely from the factory block and took up the same position beside the water trough – a point which, by his calculation, she would have to walk past as she left the works. The bells rang and the workers crowded out. He spotted the other packing-room girls filing from the warehouse, and caught his breath; but he quickly realised that Caroline Knox was not with them. A couple of these girls stopped to thank him as they went to the gate, smiling and dropping curtseys. They deduced who had made the selection for the packing room, probably on the basis that Miss Knox was among their number. One came forward to talk to him, launching into an earnest speech about how important her post was to her, what with a sick mother, four little children and a husband out of work. Edward tried to be gracious, feigning attention, but his eyes kept wandering past her shoulder towards the warehouse. On and on she went, labouring her points, repeating the litany of her difficulties; but the number of infants changed from four to five, and suddenly he saw that he was being stalled. This woman was deliberately keeping him occupied while Miss Knox made her escape through the Bessborough Place gate at the back of the works. He excused himself and hurried off.

Bessborough Place was crammed with departing factory hands. Craning his neck, Edward caught sight of a single bonnet among the caps, nipping into an alley mouth. He decided that he would give chase. This had gone on quite long enough. If she wanted him to leave her be then he would, of course he would, but he'd be told this by Miss Knox herself. He wanted some explanation for why something that had seemed so fresh and hopeful and filled with excitement had grown so painfully strange. Like most of the workers, she was heading in the direction of Millbank, across the Vauxhall Bridge Road. Edward shouldered his way through the mass of Colt operatives, thinking that he would catch her up, say his piece, and end this one way or another.

He couldn't even get close. Miss Knox was traversing the packed pavements with considerable agility. The secretary, who had of late become used to riding in cabs or the Colonel's barouche, had trouble simply matching her pace. A smothering veil of dust hung over the Vauxhall Bridge Road, stirred up by the tramping hooves and grinding wheels of the city traffic, poisoning the soft evening air. One of the plagues of midsummer London, this dust was yet another instance of the great metropolis perverting Nature, transforming Her into something viciously malign. As he started across the road, Edward pressed his handkerchief over his nose and mouth, squinting so hard that his eyes were almost closed. Miss Knox left his sight, and he feared that he might lose her altogether among the vehicles, animals and swirls of powdered filth. But then he saw her again – coughing against her hand as she walked on into Millbank. He stepped up onto the pavement, following as quickly as he could.

Away from the main thoroughfare the dust thinned a little. Edward glanced down at his jacket and trousers; pale dirt, smelling distinctly of dung, coated both like hoar-frost on a tree-trunk. He tried to knock it off with swift, clapping sweeps of his hand, but with no success. Ahead, behind a row of low houses, rose the dull fort of Millbank Prison, like an austere, geometric remaking of the Tower four miles down the river. Edward guessed that she was heading towards her home – to where he'd escorted her on that first night. He wondered what he might do if she reached the lodging house before he'd managed to speak with her. Would he present himself at the threshold, ready to brave the landlady with a slick tale – or would he take to watching the place, to lurking sadly in doorways like so many of the lovelorn? He couldn't say, but felt strongly that it would be best to catch her before this question became a pressing one.

Miss Knox marched straight past the end of her road, though, away from Millbank and into old Westminster – into the Devil's Acre. Again, it was all Edward could do to trail thirty yards behind her. The streets grew narrow, hemmed in by tight, winding lines of buildings, giving them a shadowy, almost subterranean feel. Everything seemed to slow, the powerful current that propelled mankind throughout the rest of the city slackening off rapidly, as if one was leaving the main course of a mighty river for a stagnant tributary. The denizens of this rotten place leaned and slouched all about, a tattered, aimless crowd, sunk completely in their dismal indolence. Edward tried not to look at them; he knew that meeting an eye, any eye at all, would be unwise in the extreme. Around him, they argued and brawled with drunken, foul-mouthed savagery; or let out febrile coughs and moans, succumbing to the depredations of liquor or some other unknown ailment. He directed his gaze upwards. The last of the day's sunlight, so burningly beautiful, was but a narrow stripe across a sagging rooftop.

There was not much dust here as there was precious little of the lively movement required to provoke it. In its place, though, were flies, many thousands of them, plump as brandy-soaked raisins, that settled upon you if you paused for even a second, crawling for your tear ducts, your nostrils, the corners of your mouth. The smells were enough to stop the breath in your lungs, thick as fish-glue and repulsively over-ripe; Edward imagined that a multitude of deadly diseases were thronging into his body, gaining stronger purchase on his blood with every step he took. In such an environment, Miss Knox stood out like a clean cotton glove dropped on a seething refuse heap, and was therefore a great deal easier to follow. She was forging onwards through the rookery with her head down, deflecting any unwelcome attention with her purposeful haste. Edward became acutely aware of the notice he was attracting himself – of the sheer idiocy of what he was doing. His initial reason for starting up his pursuit was now utterly invalid. He could hardly stop her, amid all this miserable, sickening decay and make his heartfelt declaration. Her sister lived in the Acre, he remembered; that would be why she was venturing out there. She would soon vanish into a tenement of some description, leaving him on the street. He had to turn back, right away.

Just as Edward was about to change course, however, he saw a pair of men in working clothes emerge from the shell of a burned-out building and fall in beside Miss Knox. None too politely, they guided her into a rambling lane, hidden almost entirely from view by the profusion of poles and beams that were literally propping up the ancient houses around its mouth. Disconcerted, Edward came to a halt, unsure of what he should do.

There was a hard tug at the bottom of his jacket. He looked

around to see a score of urchin children; and as one, they reached out to touch him as if he were a long-awaited Messiah, their grubby fingers splayed imploringly, launching into a loud contest of wails and woeful tales, crumpling up their leathery faces as if seized by fits of crying.

'Give us a brown, sir, please do!'

'Oh do, sir – ain't had no vittles since yesterday afternoon, sir!'

Worried that this noisy scene might attract some more malevolent interest, Edward dug out all the coins he had from the pockets of his coat and scattered them across the rutted mud at his feet. The children dropped to the ground with unnerving speed, like so many starving alley cats on a string of sausages, and were soon fighting viciously over their spoils. Edward hopped out from among them and strode away, past the fire-gutted house, deciding that he had to follow Miss Knox and assure himself that she was safe. Slowing a little, he entered the crumbling lane, walking carefully over the baked, undulating earth, welcoming the sense of refuge provided by the dense copse of makeshift supports that ran along it.

Those he sought were standing outside a building some twenty yards down, which seemed to be some manner of tavern. The small, square windows were crusted over with grime, and above the door was a yellowing daub of a four-legged creature the secretary supposed was a lamb. Miss Knox and the two men were talking with a loose cluster of drinkers upon the tavern's crude stone stoop. Edward crept towards them, hiding himself in the nooks and shallow corners that had been formed by the lane's slow collapse.

The secretary identified a couple of these drinkers at once. They were part of the Irish gang who'd carried Martin Rea away that night on Tachbrook Street – and who'd since been expelled from the factory for theft. There was the hulking redhead with the round, simple eyes; there was the ringleader, his raw, gouged-out features arranged in their customary grimace, his knee jigging up and down with pent-up energy. Rea himself was approaching from another direction, muttering a few words of explanation as he walked over. The ringleader said something in response that caused gruff amusement among his men. It angered Miss Knox, though – she boxed his ears with sudden violence, eliciting an uncomprehending bark of pain. Her brother-in-law yanked her back, taking hold of her arms to prevent further blows.

'Your doing, it was, all of it!' Edward heard her cry. 'Damn you to *hell*, Pat Slattery!'

Slattery cursed her in return, a hand over his ear, looking around the lane to see if anyone had witnessed this outburst. Edward pulled back sharply behind a knotty beam; when he dared peep out again a half-minute later, the Irishmen were picking up their pots, preparing to withdraw inside the tavern. Miss Knox went in ahead of them, shaking off Rea and shoving hard against the weathered door.

Edward attempted to absorb what he had seen. She had no liking for these disreputable Irishmen, that much was plain, but there was a connection between them – a connection that in all likelihood involved serious wrongdoing. And what was more, Mr Quill's assistant, whom the good-natured engineer had personally saved from dismissal, was caught up in it too. These were important discoveries indeed, and most unwelcome ones. Where this left his original intentions in following Miss Knox from the gun works Edward couldn't say, but he knew that he would not leave the Devil's Acre without learning what they'd gone into this low tavern to discuss. He'd been into such establishments before, around his rooms on Red Lion Square; they were dingy places, chopped up into a multitude of tiny dens by screens and partitions. The secretary was confident that he'd be able to sneak in, locate a secluded stool and eavesdrop without fear of exposure. He stepped out from behind the beam and started for the tavern's stoop.

The blow knocked off his hat and pushed him into a quick, stunning collision with a pair of iron scaffolding poles. He tried to turn but a body barrelled against his back, throwing something over his head – a length of rope. It came to rest in the depression between the base of his jaw and his Adam's apple and was then drawn in with terrifying force. Edward's entire being focused upon this rope, upon getting

161

his fingertips beneath it and forcing it from his neck, but it was no use. The garrotte was already too tight, and was growing tighter; he felt a hot bloating of blood in his ears, and a dreadful pressure building deep within his skull, dizzying and deadening. His best shout emerged as only a helpless gargle.

Everything grew darker. He was being dragged backwards, through a doorway. There were floorboards overhead, covered with creamy blossoms of mould. Another person was moving in front of him, rifling through his pockets, taking his watch, his money and the pin on his necktie. His throat was wet – was it bleeding? Was he about to be strangled – murdered? The thief was plucking at his boots now, making to remove them. Finding a last urgent reserve of strength, Edward began to thrash about, determined that he would not meet his death in stockinged feet. The garrotte constricted further, sending a white-green bolt across his sight; his bulging eyes seemed to be on the verge of popping from their sockets like a pair of champagne corks.

One of his frenzied kicks hit its target. There was a grunt of pain. 'Bugger this,' said an Irish voice, 'boots ain't worth it anyhow. Let's be off.'

Edward was pushed to his knees, the garrotte whipping away like the string on a spinning top, twisting him to the floor. Gasping and coughing, he fought to take in air, frantically feeling his burning throat, convinced that it must have been slit to be hurting so much; but no, although scraped and bloody, the skin was intact.

The secretary lay still for a minute. One side of his sweat-sheened face was pressed against a drift of loose earth. He lifted his head, a heavy coating of dirt sticking to his cheek; and a sudden, blinding ache was driven into him like a mason's nail through the temple. Trying vainly to blink it away, he took in his surroundings. He lay in a narrow, fly-blown room – and he was not alone. Four small children were watching him intently from a dark corner. They were gaunt and filthy, their hair overgrown, making it impossible to tell their ages or genders. A couple held mackerel heads in their straw-thin fingers, taken from a heaped box of the things that sat against the wall. These unsavoury scraps of waste were plainly a great prize; the children were nibbling at them with hungry relish as they regarded the well-dressed man sprawled out before them.

Edward scrambled to his feet and fled, leaving the tumble-down alley at an unsteady run. It seemed highly likely at that moment that his robbers would decide that boots *were* worth it after all, and perhaps jacket and trousers as well – cases of footpads stripping their victims down to their undergarments were far from unknown. He headed back down the main thoroughfare towards safety, attracting a few mocking catcalls as he loped by, bloody collar flapping loose, shirt-tails trailing down from under his jacket, but most of the Acre's inhabitants were indifferent. The robbed were hardly a rare sight in that lawless district.

As he crossed back into Millbank, Edward slowed to a walk, and then stopped at a recently lit lamp-post, leaning heavily against it and spitting out a thick coil of rust-coloured mucus. He shook his throbbing head, breathlessly cursing his naivety – how the *devil* could he have been so stupid? They'd clearly been tracking him from the moment he'd entered the rookery, waiting until he was at its very heart and thus beyond all possible aid before making their move. For the first time in weeks Miss Knox left his mind completely, supplanted by an excruciating mixture of shame and annoyance at the ease with which he had been over-come. That watch had been a gift from his mother, a token of her pride when he had first been taken on at Carver & Weight's, and now it was gone for good, given over to the enrichment of base villains.

Gingerly, the secretary laid a palm against his clammy, stinging throat. His thoughts turned towards another gift that he'd been given, rather more recently – the Colt Navy revolver. Leaning against that lamp-post, ripped clothes stained with his own blood, he found himself wishing more than anything else in the world that he'd had the pistol with him when he'd ventured into the Devil's Acre. When that cord had gone around his neck he could have pulled it from his belt; loosed his first shot into the ceiling, as a warning; his second perhaps into the garrotter's shin; his third into the air as he chased them away down the lane. By God, how differently things would have gone!

2

Caroline glanced at her knuckle. Beneath the usual persistent smear of gun grease, it was bright red and swelling steadily. She had hit Pat Slattery rather harder than she'd intended and would be bruised as a result. He would have a fine cauliflower ear, though, a real beauty; this thought consoled her somewhat as she took a place at the bar of their rank cave of a tavern, feeling a fetid draught across the back of her neck as the door swung open to admit them.

It was fiercely hot in the Holy Lamb. There was a strong smell of dried-out damp and cess-pools; sticky moisture was gathering in a great dripping patch overhead. Everything in the Lamb was wooden, warped and old beyond estimation. Its low ceiling was crossed with thick beams, making the well-weathered taproom resemble the hold of a river barge. The few pieces of oft-repaired furniture were covered with blemishes and scorch marks, and clearly saw regular use in brawls. Tarnished farming implements, souvenirs of lost lives lived among fields and hay-barns, hung upon the walls. A curling map of Ireland had been mounted behind the bar and garlanded with withered wildflowers, leaving no doubt as to whose place this was. The ale pumps stuck up like a row of worm-eaten vegetables, swollen and discoloured; and behind them lurked the publican, a beady-eyed, hedgehog-like creature, who was regarding her with silent dissatisfaction, as if having a woman on his premises, and an Englishwoman to boot, was a grave affront.

'Don't you gawp at me like that, cock,' Caroline snapped. 'D'you honestly think I'd come into this wretched pit of me own choosing?'

'She's wi' us, Brian,' said one of the Irishmen sleepily, settling against the bar with a suggestive grin. 'Nothin' at all to worry about here.'

Caroline turned towards him, ready to let him know exactly what she thought of his easy manner, when Slattery barged between them, his hand still clamped over his bruised ear.

'Off wi' ye, Brian,' he muttered at the publican. 'Just for a minute, lad.' The hedgehog shuffled off obediently to a back room. They were alone. Slattery glanced at her with angry dislike. 'What d'you have, then?'

She studied him for a moment – the hawkish cast of his features, the black hair greying a little at the whiskers, the pocked skin of his cheek. He mightn't have been a bad-looking fellow once, but he seemed corrupted somehow, moon-struck and dangerous, a nasty threat made flesh. Close up, it was easy to see why Amy had been so upset simply by the sound of his name. Caroline took the revolver cylinder from the pocket of her apron, set it on the bar and rolled it towards him like a barrel. The surface was uneven, covered with dents and nicks, and the cylinder soon went off course; Slattery stopped it with his free hand, looking at her uncomprehendingly. There was a weird flatness to his gaze, but Caroline stared straight back at him, refusing to become intimidated. She would not give this man another bloody inch.

'This is all?'

Martin spoke up from over by the door. Unlike the rest of them, he'd kept his cap on, and seemed scarcely more comfortable with the situation than Caroline. 'You know what it's like in there, Pat – damn hard to get anythin' out. The Yankees watch you every moment.'

Slattery angled his head in Martin's direction. 'Aye, Mart, you are right, I *do* know – full to the rafters wi' gun parts is what it's like. That bastard Colt has a stock room fit to burst its seams. Yet you and Miss bleedin' Prize-fighter here

166

have got us but three of these damn things in a bleedin' *fortnight*. What the devil is that about, eh, Mart? Tell us that, if you can!'

Caroline looked at the row of black bottles behind the bar. All is not well, she thought, between Martin and Pat Slattery.

'We'll work quicker, Pat.'

'By the Holy Mother, Mart, you'd better. That's all I'll say. You'd bleedin' better. You know what stands against us here – what'll happen if we don't get some complete pistols together in the near bleedin' future.' Those flat eyes swivelled back to Caroline. 'You can blame me for this bit o' trouble all ye like, Missy, but we'll all suffer if it ain't sorted out. D'ye follow? *All of us.*'

With that he secured the cylinder in his green canvas jacket and left the tavern, his dozy-looking comrades following after him, exchanging a few words in the strange, thick tongue of their homeland. Only Martin and Jack Coffee remained behind. Jack had sat himself on a stool at the other end of the bar and was scratching vacantly at his red beard.

'They're off to the docks,' her brother-in-law explained, nodding after Slattery and the others. 'There's a chance of some night work at Limehouse.'

Caroline glared at him. She loathed Martin more than any of them. Slattery might be a fiend but he'd never pretended to be anything else: he was a fiend in the Acre, a fiend in the Colt works, and had doubtlessly been a fiend back in Ireland. Martin Rea, however, was a deceiver – a stinking liar. He'd known of this mysterious debt when he first came to London, when he met Amy in Covent Garden that day; when he chose to court her, marry her and sire two children with her. Throughout, he'd been aware that this doom-laded blow would eventually fall, but he'd taken on responsibilities nonetheless, and tied the fate of others, of innocents, to his own. It was the fulfilment of every doubt that Caroline had ever harboured about him – and now she was being made to risk herself as well. When she thought of what might happen if she were caught thieving for these Irishmen she felt sick with fright. Not even Mr Lowry, who continued to watch out for her despite everything and had saved her neck that very morning, would be able to keep Walter Noone off her then.

Martin came in closer, bringing with him the familiar coal-smoke odour of the Colt forging shop. 'I hear that you're up in the packing room now.'

Caroline nodded.

'This is good news. You'll be far better placed to remove a complete gun. These random parts will get us nowhere. We'd need hundreds o' them, and complete sets too – it'd take years. And Pat knows this as well.' He hesitated, growing embarrassed, the lines at the sides of his mouth deepening; he was about to say something he didn't particularly want to. 'What of the secretary, Caro?'

She scowled. 'What of him, Martin? I did as you asked, God help me. Not so much as a word has passed between us since that night you sent Amy to fetch me from the Eagle.'

'Has he made it difficult? Pestering you and the like?'

'He –' Caroline stopped, thinking of his many attempts to place himself in her path, each and every one of which she'd sidestepped with heartbreaking ease. 'Why d'you ask?'

Martin shrugged, looking towards the door. 'He were following you just then, up on St Anne's Street.'

Caroline started, moving away from the bar. 'He was here – in the *Acre*? But he'll be eaten alive! We must go out to look for him, we must –'

'He's gone now,' Martin interrupted, 'back to his rightful region. I got some pals to see to that.'

'What – what did they do to him?'

'Nothin' much. Got him out is all. Just tell me he didn't know where you was headed, or what you was coming here for.'

'No, Martin,' she replied, alarmed by his bluntness. 'How could he? I told you, I ain't spoke to him!'

He wasn't reassured. 'We can't have you romancing the Colonel's secretary, Caro. It'd make you the talk o' the factory. Half the Yankees already hate that poor bugger for the favour he's gained wi' Colt – if they see you and him walking out together it'll bring a load o' notice upon you. The bastards'll be looking out for something just like this thing we have here.'

Caroline grew exasperated. 'How many times can I say it? I have not –'

'He must be put off *completely*, d'ye understand? The fellow can't be let alone to trail after you like a lovesick swan. You must see to him, Caro. If you won't then you can be certain that I will. For the sake of my little ones.'

She didn't respond. Martin made an impatient sound, tugged his cap low over his brow and said that he had to get home to Amy. Caroline doubted this, thinking it far more likely that he was heading off to yet another tavern, perhaps to meet with Ben Quill; but she stayed quiet, too stung by the brutal instruction she'd been given for any more quarrelling. Halfway through the Lamb's door he paused, asking Jack if he'd see her back to Millbank. Jack nodded his assent.

Caroline looked down at the floor, at her scuffed work-boots, feeling Jack's eyes upon her. She was fairly certain that he'd been sweet on her at one stage, but had been too shy ever to act. This suited Caroline; it had saved her from having to put him off. During her years in service she'd heard many stories of the doomed and difficult marriages of the other maids' sisters, cousins and friends, all of which had made her determined only to give herself to a man of brains and ambition – a man who might lift her out of her present circumstances rather than mire her in them forever. Jack Coffee was most certainly not that man.

The publican emerged from his bolt-hole with a tallow candle in his hand, which immediately made the rest of the tavern seem much darker. 'Will ye drink then, Jack?' he rasped.

Caroline glanced up. Jack was looking over to her for guidance. There was a distinct awkwardness in him; he hadn't liked the hard treatment he'd just seen her receive from Martin and Pat Slattery.

She felt drained, dog-tired and thoroughly ashamed of herself. 'I'm finished for today, Jack. Will you just take me home?'

Jack got to his feet at once; he was so tall that he had to

duck to avoid knocking his head against the beams. After pulling on his cap, he retrieved a large sack from the floor, bade farewell to the publican and led her back out into the evening. A small fire was burning in the middle of the lane, encircled by ragged bodies, a loose spiral of insects and embers winding away above it. Caroline looked around for any indication that Mr Lowry had been there. In the fading light, beside some scaffolding poles, she saw a stamped-down hat, once smart but now broken and dirtied beyond repair, its colour lost in the dust. Had she seen a similar hat on the secretary's head? It was too badly damaged to tell.

Jack was adjusting his hold on his sack, preparing to heave it onto his shoulder. Caroline asked him what it held. He broke into a grin, his awkwardness vanishing.

'These here, Caro,' he announced with some pride, 'are me murphies.' He opened the sack's mouth. Inside were dozens of huge potatoes, encrusted with mud; a good number were well past eating, being rotten or covered in sprouting white tendrils.

She smiled back. 'What d'you need so many for, you blockhead? You selling 'em or something?'

'Doin' me turn at Rosie McGehan's, ain't I.' He chuckled. 'No dock work for Jack Coffee, no ma'am! I am a *performin' artiste*, if ye please!'

Caroline had heard of this place, a stable on the rookery's northern border that had been converted by an enterprising Irishwoman into a penny gaff, now famous throughout the city for tuppeny variety bills and lurid, blood-soaked melodramas. 'And what the devil are you going to do at Rosie McGehan's, Jack, with a sackful of bloody potatoes?'

They reached St Anne's Street. Hundreds still milled about, their faces lit by the flickers of second-hand lamplight that fell from the many open doors and windows – and a more sickly-looking horde Caroline had never seen. She'd heard it said that only six or seven years ago the Devil's Acre used to empty itself over the summer, as London's poor made for the countryside to work in fields and orchards, and thus avoid the diseases that stirred amid the filth of the city. This plainly happened no longer. It was the Irish, she supposed, driven over by the Famine. They had neither the knowledge of England nor the ready coin to transport themselves down to the farms of Kent or Surrey – and as a result were stuck crammed together in the festering rookery as the heat continued to rise.

'I will show you,' Jack declared, removing his cap. 'A special performance, Miss Knox!'

With that he lumbered onto a bare patch of ground and began to appeal to those drifting about the street to gather round, launching into a coarse, tongue-tied imitation of a theatre-host's patter. Caroline giggled uncertainly. A handful of rookery people, children mostly, assembled before him in an expectant yet slightly sceptical line. Jack selected an especially large, lumpy potato, the size of two fists placed side by side, cast a meaningful glance around his little audience – and then hurled it straight up into the air with all his strength.

Every eye followed the potato as it rocketed past the rookery's rooftops, a spinning black shape against the flawless purple-pink of the late evening sky. He's going to juggle, Caroline thought, to toss up another after this one, and then another; but no, Jack had left the sack at his feet. Watching the potato as closely as anyone, he was bracing his legs and back as if readying himself to catch it.

The potato struck his forehead with a splitting crack, smashing apart into many pieces. For an instant Caroline thought it was an accident; but then the children around her let out a wild shriek of laughter. Jack wiped his eyes and looked out at them, beaming wide.

'And there it is, me fine friends, Roscommon Jack and his bonce of iron, to which a four-pound murphy is – is snow as a soft-flake – *soft* as a *snow*-flake! Performin' at Rosie McGehan's six weeks a night, twice on Saturdays!'

There was applause, and some of the children darted forward to fetch themselves bits of the splattered potato, which they proceeded to gobble down raw. Passers-by were attracted by the commotion; Roscommon Jack's crowd grew.

'Do it again, Mister, please!'

'Aye, Paddy, I missed it, do it again!'

Jack winked at Caroline, a red welt emblazoned across his brow, his features shining with the potato's cloudy juice. She gaped back at him in astonishment. He plucked out a second potato and prepared to throw.

Mr Churn came through the packing-room door sideways, pushing it open with his shoulder, a bulging roll of oilskin in his arms. He went over to Fran, the oldest of the women at work in there, who'd been granted an informal authority over the rest of them, set down the oilskin and started to unravel it. From the corner of her eye, Caroline could see that inside this roll were yet more Navy revolvers – plain, service-standard pieces, black as pokers, seemingly identical to the twenty or so that were laid out across the table opposite.

'Special task for you, my darlin',' he said. 'Pack these up separate from the rest, in a single box of ten, and leave 'em by the door. Priority job.'

Fran was not the sort to stand for nonsense. She looked at the pistols and put a hand on her hip. 'But they're exactly the same as all the rest.'

The packing room had been running for nearly a week now. Mr Churn was the Yankee who'd been appointed to watch over the women. He was a short, flat-nosed fellow of around forty, whose good-humoured manner formed a poor disguise for the truly spiteful soul beneath. The women had disliked him at once, thinking him a craven spy; and Fran made a point of expressing this unanimous aversion in their exchanges.

Mr Churn sighed. 'Oh Frances, I didn't ask you to think on it, did I? Could you drop the sharkish tone just this once and do as I ask? I'll be back for 'em at noon.'

And with that he left the room. Fran pulled a face at his retreating back and then surveyed the tables, comparing the girls' progress. 'How you doin' there, Caro? Almost done with that one?'

Caroline nodded, tapping home a final tiny nail. It was simple enough work, screwing down hinges and brackets, slotting in partitions and pasting on labels – less arduous, certainly, than operating Colonel Colt's machines. These were only military-grade cases, made for mass sales. No velvet trimming or fine varnish was needed here, just a secure berth for the weapon and its accessories.

The packing room was a small, cramped cell up in the rafters of the warehouse, in which three narrow tables were piled with pre-cut case components, assorted tins of screws or glue, and a jumbled spread of tools and sanding blocks. The mood among the dozen women who toiled there, though, was light-hearted indeed; most of them were still giddy with delight at having been kept on. Caroline played along with all this, joining in the jokes and the chatter, but she was uneasy. This was the one room in the entire works where London employees were permitted to handle the finished guns – the only place the arms stopped on their way to the heavily fortified stockroom at the other end of the warehouse's upper floor – and the Yankees were taking no chances. A single doorway opened straight into the bustle and inevitable Yankee scrutiny of the polishing shop. The windows were so high and narrow that even if you managed to sling something out through one of them you'd have no way of telling where it might land. The opportunities for thievery that Martin had predicted had yet to reveal themselves to her.

Fran rested a finger against her lower lip, considering the guns Mr Churn had brought in as Caroline walked over. 'I don't understand it. They really are *exactly* the bloody same. Why the hurry?' She shrugged, losing interest, turning back to her own half-built case. 'Pack 'em up, dear, would you?'

Caroline took two of the revolvers back to her place at the end of the leftmost table. Even after five days of packing them she couldn't get accustomed to the sight and feel of these gleaming weapons – the leaden heaviness, the deadly possibility of the completed gun. They were made for killing men. You couldn't look upon the perfect shaping of the stock, or the poised hook of the trigger, or the way that long barrel stretched out so purposefully from the cylinder, and be left in any doubt about this. For her first couple of shifts

173

in the packing room Caroline had found herself imagining the usage that might await the virgin revolvers that were passing through her hands. This one might be drawn in Ireland, she'd mused, to drop the ringleaders of a food riot; this one discharged into a savage in distant Africa as he rushed forward with his spear; this one shipped east to the waters around Turkey, to be ready for use against Britain's newest enemy, the Russians. It soon became too wearying, however, to be thinking constantly of slaughter, so Caroline did her best to put it from her mind.

She set one of the pistols down beside the finished case and turned the other over in her hands, making a final check for blemishes. Fran was right – at first glance they seemed no different from the others. By the time they arrived in the packing room the guns had gone through an official proving by the British Government in the Tower of London, as well as the exhaustive tests performed on them by the Yankees themselves. Minute symbols had been stamped on them at each stage in this lengthy journey, attesting to the various procedures that had been carried out. Most prominent among these was the Colt serial number, etched onto each individual part prior to the pistols' first full assembly. This number was the means by which the flow of weapons from the factory was recorded and monitored, and a serious obstacle before the would-be gun thief. The parts Caroline had taken from the machine floor had all been freshly made, unnumbered and thus off the company books; whereas a numbered weapon, even a part from a numbered weapon, would be missed immediately.

Caroline noticed that the number on this pistol was far higher than any other she'd seen. So far they'd all been under 1,000, only three digits long; yet this weapon was marked '103300'. It lay well outside the sequence that had been observed in the London works up to that point. Frowning, unable to account for this, she studied it a little more closely – and made a significant discovery.

The meaning of many of the other symbols on the guns was lost on her, but there was one that she knew. It pictured a crown atop a 'V', and was usually found on the barrel just beneath the lug. It was the mark pressed on in the Tower – the proof mark of the British Government – and it was missing. This pistol hadn't been proved in the Tower. It hadn't been entered into the Government's records. They didn't know that it existed.

Her thoughts racing, Caroline fitted the pistol in the case as if nothing at all was wrong and reached for the other one. It was numbered '103301'; it was also missing the London mark. She placed it next to the first, packed in a handful of fine straw from the bale set at the table's end, and then went back across the room for the rest.

The outbuilding clung to the side of the warehouse like a knot on a log, forming a small interruption in the rear alley that ran between the premises of the Colt Company and the Equitable Gas-Works. There was a padlock on the door, but it was a crude one; using a screwdriver she had taken from the packing room, Caroline loosened part of the mount without much difficulty. She looked back along the alley behind her to check that she hadn't been followed and then slipped inside.

When Mr Churn had made his collection at noon, Caroline had been out in the polishing shop replenishing her supply of nails and screws. She'd watched discreetly as he took the crate of illegitimate guns down the corridor, past the fortified stock room to the warehouse staircase, and pounded his way down into the yard. As she'd emptied a scoop of packing nails into her tray those heavy footfalls had come back into earshot, almost directly below her. Stealing a glance from a nearby window, she'd seen Mr Churn entering this forgotten outbuilding with the crate still in his arms, and had decided right away that this deserved further investigation.

The door opened onto a stone staircase that wound down underneath the Colt warehouse. Caroline followed it into a low, close cellar. She could hear steady dripping and the scratching of rats; and above, through the vaulted ceiling, the blunted pops of revolvers being test-fired in the proving room. A couple of pavement grates on the Ponsonby Street side let in a dribble of sallow evening light, enabling her to make out some forgotten stacks of lumber and a row of mould-blackened barrels.

The pistol crates stood in a far corner – a dozen ten-piece boxes, including the one she had made earlier that day, piled up on a cleared patch of earth. Colt's men had plainly been bringing them down here since production had begun a month or so earlier, skimming them off the surface of the factory's output and hiding them away. Caroline couldn't say for certain why this was being done. The smuggler's motive, perhaps – the evasion of trade duties? Were the Yankees sending them back to America, and resented being taxed by the British Government for shipping arms to their own people?

It hardly mattered. Caroline laid her hands on top of the crates. This hoard could be the answer to her problems. Colt's men were adding to it frequently, that much was obvious; the way that the floor had been cleared suggested that a good many more boxes were to be put down there in the coming months. A few small thefts probably wouldn't be noticed until the crates had arrived at their destination – by which time Martin's debt would be paid off, Amy and the children would be safe, and Caroline would have left the Colt factory for employment elsewhere. It would be a clean escape. Even if the stealing was discovered, this little operation here in the cellars was secret and in all likelihood unlawful. The Yankees might not even risk seeking out those responsible for fear of drawing attention to it, and just move the crates to another place.

Without any further deliberation, Caroline shifted the boxes about until she could get at the bottom one. Using her screwdriver, she prised up a slat from its lid and took out a revolver. Sure enough, it had a six-figure serial number and no proof mark. Arranging the straw to disguise its absence, she replaced the slat and put the pistol in the pocket of her apron.

She left at fast as she could, screwing the padlock mount back on behind her, shivering with fearful exhilaration. Feeling light as a dandelion seed, her head entirely empty of thoughts, she walked back down the shady alley and out into the main yard, trying to keep her pace even and inconspicuous. It was not so late that her still being in the works would be thought odd. Girls often stayed an extra ten minutes to finish off a case; she herself had done so. No one would think anything of it. Darkness was still an hour or two away, but the lights were already lit on the ground floor of the factory block. Work in the engine room would carry on long into the night. Another Yankee engineer, a real master it was said, had arrived in London the week before to help Mr Quill fine-tune the engine. Martin would be in there, of course, toiling alongside them; Caroline longed to see the look on her brother-in-law's face, on Pat Slattery's face, when she produced the prize that neither of them had been able to obtain.

As she was passing by the water trough she noticed a single figure leaning against the wall just by the foundry door, smoking a cigar. It was Mr Lowry. He was looking over at her, his eyes hidden in shadow. They still hadn't spoken; she'd disregarded Martin's instruction, deciding that an outright rejection wasn't necessary. He'd got the message clearly enough. His attempts to talk with her had ceased completely, and he made no effort to approach her now, merely tipping his top hat and drawing on his cigar. He didn't look well, his face pale and lined as if he'd been robbed of his rest. Caroline could see something on his neck, a bruise of some kind, partly concealed by a loose necktie. She had little doubt that Martin's friends had driven him from the Acre with menaces and blows, of which this injury was a probable result, but she couldn't afford any guilt, or regret, or sympathy. Too much was in the balance. Besides, she'd told herself, he was better off not having anything to do with her now. This severance, unpleasant as it might be, would serve to protect Mr Lowry from any accusations that he too had been involved in the Irishmen's scheme.

The pistol in her apron seemed to grow heavier as she passed him, straining against the cotton, forcing its outline into the thin cloth. She dropped him an awkward curtsey, fitting the weapon against the curve of her belly. This was easily done; the Colt revolver was clearly designed to sit closely against the human form. She hurried through the gates and on towards Westminster.

The Holy Lamb was shut up, the door barred from the inside. Caroline hammered against it and looked in through the windows; she thought she could see people inside, hunched around a single candle, but they did not respond to her calls. She stepped back onto the stoop, casting a glance around the derelict lane, and felt a sudden sense of peril. Being with Martin or Jack had shielded her from the worst of this place. Without them, she was as much at risk as anyone.

Caroline started towards St Anne's Street, becoming quite desperate to get the stolen gun out of her apron. She could really feel the weight of it now, pulling on the cord around the back of her neck. Only one option presented itself: Crocodile Court. She could leave it with Amy. Martin would surely seek her out double-quick once he'd come home to a complete revolver. Then she could tell him what she'd found, they could make their plans, and the whole wretched business would be brought that much nearer to its end.

A high-sided cart, of the sort used by tradesmen to move goods, had stopped about halfway down St Anne's Street, a short distance from the mouth of Crocodile Court. Unusually, it had not attracted a crowd; in fact, the inhabitants of the Acre were keeping their distance. As she drew closer, Caroline saw why. A team of workmen, white scarves bound around their faces, were unloading pine coffins from the back of the cart, laying them in the road and removing their lids. Two well-starched, top-hatted gents stalked this grim line, offering direction and reciting passages of scripture. They were the organisers of this undertakers' mission, charitable folk doing God's work among the poor and diseased of the metropolis – for it was an outbreak of disease, Caroline realised with mounting horror, that had brought them there. This was why the Lamb was closed; why the streets themselves were so much emptier than usual. Cholera had arrived in the Acre.

Slowly, the dead began to emerge from the tenements, carried out by friends and relations who were mostly too unwell themselves to make any demonstration of grief. Caroline saw just one of these corpses – wrapped up in a dirty sheet, its grey face beset with flies – before averting her eyes and quickening her pace. The stout piebald mare yoked up to the coffin-cart shook her head in distress at the dreadful smells gathering around her, stamping at the dusty ground.

Crocodile Court was deathly quiet. There was not a single woman at its windows, or cardplayer in its doorways, or ragged child in its gutters. Sickness lay in the bed of the alley like an acrid fog. Caroline ran down to Amy's building and went inside. The stairway was as crowded as ever, and the reek of vomit almost overpowering. Her sleeve pressed against her nose and mouth, she climbed up as swiftly as she could. The hard, flat sound of nails being driven into cholera coffins, rising from St Anne's Street and coming in through the open window, greeted her as she walked into the dark stillness of her sister's room. She saw Katie first, over on the pallet, playing half-heartedly with the remains of a paper carnation. Amy sat in her usual place before the fireplace, but she wasn't at work on her flowers. Instead, she stared numbly at a nest of old blankets laid out on the floor before her, arranged around the tiny form of Michael, her baby son. The child was listless and only half-awake. His skin was an awful colour, a sort of pinkish grey, and he was wheezing terribly, letting out little constricted coughs. There could be no doubt. He had the disease.

'Dear God,' Caroline whispered.

Amy looked at her and began to sob, trying to speak but losing the words in a fit of stammering.

Caroline crossed the room, taking her sister's head against her shoulder and squeezing her tightly. 'Come,' she said, 'we'll find him a doctor. Listen to me. There's still time.'

She released Amy and went to Michael, leaning over him. Even at a foot's distance she could feel the heat glowing from his feverish skin. Gently, she ran an arm beneath his lolling head and another under his legs, bending forward to lift him up.

There was a rattling thump from somewhere beneath her;

179

startled, she glanced down towards it. The stolen Colt Navy had slid from her apron pocket, landing stock-first against the floorboards and clattering onto its side.

3

Reaching the end of the *British Munitions Gazette*, Edward frowned and turned back to the front page, checking the date. He had the right issue. The piece on the Colt factory it was supposed to be carrying, however, detailing the latest advances being made in the engine room and giving some updated production forecasts, was nowhere to be found. Richards had failed to meet his deadline again – for the third time, in fact, since the Colonel had left to see to his dyke. Edward sighed, folding the magazine's thin pages in half and dropping it to the ground.

The secretary was sitting cross-legged on a patch of grass near the eastern end of Rotten Row. It was a warm Saturday afternoon and the fashionable crowd was out in force. Sumptuous equipages cruised to and fro, liveried footmen propped up on every available surface; thoroughbred horses pranced across the Row's fine gravel, shaking their plaited manes, the raucous hoots of their riders scattering birds from the trees.

Edward was not comfortable here. This corner of Hyde Park was given over to the most vapid indolence – it was a lounger's spot, of the sort that would suit James Colt and the Harum-Scarum Club. His cousin Arthur, the soldier whose example he'd trotted out so readily in the meeting with Lord Paget, had suggested they meet there, and Edward hadn't wanted to complicate matters or test Arthur's knowledge of the capital by putting forward an alternative. After a quarter-hour on his patch of grass he'd begun to understand the motivation behind Arthur's choice. There was a sprinkling of military men among the riders and pedestrians in the environs of the Row, resplendent in officers' coatees; and all seemed to be engaged in conversation with admiring young ladies.

Arthur was now ten minutes late, and as usual Edward had a good deal of pressing Colt work to do. Annoyance began to build within him at this wasted time – but he checked it, correcting himself. His cousin had been back from Africa on leave now for almost three weeks and they hadn't yet seen each other. Arthur had written to him a few days before, explaining that he would be in London that afternoon on Army business and proposing that they have a few words afterwards. Edward had sent a note of agreement by the next post.

The *British Munitions Gazette* caught his eye, the close columns of type flanking a technical diagram of a new French rifle. Edward picked it up and started to look through it for a second time. It was possible that he'd missed a page.

Someone pinched the back of the magazine's spine, tugging it from his grasp. Arthur was crouching down before him in his scarlet infantry jacket, a faintly condescending grin on his face.

'By God, Eddie, it's true,' he said with a chuckle, glancing at the *Gazette* before casting it aside. 'You really are a bloody *gun man*.'

Arthur was twenty-one, four years younger than Edward. They looked alike, having the same nose and brow, but Arthur was a larger, stronger version; his legs were a couple of inches longer, his arms thicker, his face half a hand wider and adorned with neat military moustaches. A fundamental dissimilarity of character had always kept a certain distance between them. Edward thought Arthur boisterous and simple-minded, and was unable to understand his passion for field sports, gambling and boxing; whereas Arthur thought Edward bookish and distant, and too wedded to life in London. An affectionate contact was maintained, and letters exchanged on a reasonably regular basis, but they would always be relations rather than proper friends.

182

Edward studied Arthur's uniform. He'd been promoted; more than that, he'd received a commission. 'And you are a subaltern, Art,' he remarked, noticing the hoarseness that lingered in his voice. 'Congratulations.'

'Heavens, Eddie, are you all right?'

There was concern on his cousin's tanned features. He looked well, it had to be said, a little weathered perhaps but full of robust good health – not how you might picture a man who'd been on campaign for the past eighteen months.

'I am fine,' he replied, forcing a hollow smile. 'Rather tired.'

Arthur sat down opposite him. 'What the deuce happened to your neck?'

Edward tried to pull up his collar. 'A tussle in the street. I survived, as you can see.'

'Did they rob you?'

'I don't really wish to discuss it.'

Arthur hesitated. 'Well then,' he said, 'how about this position of yours – working for the Yankee gun-maker? Mother says that you're set to become the first Lowry millionaire.'

Edward shook his head. 'If only that were true. At present we –' He stopped. He wasn't about to share his doubts about James Colt's continued mismanagement with his guileless cousin. 'It is tiresome, Art, to be quite frank. You must tell me of your promotion. Now that *is* a feat, to make the jump from the ranks. You must be pleased.'

Fortunately, Arthur was more than happy with this change in topic. It transpired that he'd initially been given a battle-field commission after one of his company's lieutenants had succumbed to a stomach wound, but had served with such valour and application that his colonel had decided to make the rank permanent.

'Is that why you are in London?' Edward asked. 'For formal approval by a brigadier or somesuch?'

'No, Eddie, no.' His cousin was smiling, a little bashfully. 'That was to confirm my transfer.'

It had only taken four days of leave, Arthur revealed, for

him to grow utterly bored with the pace of civilian life. He'd soon learnt from incendiary newspaper editorials and fervent street-corner demagogues that something major was brewing in the East. Hungry for more adventure, the newly minted officer had decided that he wasn't going to journey back to the end of Africa to sit around uselessly with the 73rd and had requested a transfer to the 44th East Essex. This had been granted just an hour previously; Cousin Arthur, it seemed, was considered a catch for any regiment. Whatever was to happen as a result of this ongoing trouble with Russia, he was now likely to be a part of it.

Edward coiled his fingers around a few long shoots of grass and ripped them up, feeling the dull tearing of roots in the earth beneath him. 'Does your mother know of this?'

'Yes.' Arthur's smile fell. He shifted about, fiddling with one of his jacket's gilded buttons. 'She does not approve.'

Edward's Aunt Ruth, a widow like his own mother, was of a pronounced nervous disposition. She'd almost been broken apart by the wait for news while her only son had been fighting at the Cape; it was easy to imagine what this latest development might be doing to her. 'Well, she has just got you home from one war,' he said. 'I doubt she understands why she must lose you straight away to another. Christ Almighty, Art, I'm not sure *I* understand.'

Arthur slapped a hand against his knee in boyish exasperation. 'Hell's bells, Eddie, it is so *exciting*, don't you see? It is the most noble thing a man can do, and truly glorious to be a part of!'

Edward leaned towards his cousin. 'My dear fellow, this business with Russia is a very different proposition to battling savages armed with spears and a few stolen muskets. We are faced with the prospect of a full-scale war against an ancient and mighty empire – with vast numbers of cannon, and gunboats, and –'

'That's precisely why I must be there! It will be positively *stupendous*. Every fighting man prays that such a war will come in his lifetime. It is a real chance to show your mettle – to distinguish yourself in the service of the Queen. I tell you, Eddie, if the British Army is sent to Turkey's assistance

I'll come back a blasted captain.' Seeing the doubt in his cousin's face, Arthur grew defensive. 'And anyway, old chap, I would've thought that you'd be stoked up for it as well. Your American fellow has a bloody great factory, don't he? How the deuce is he going to shift all those pistols without any battles for them to be used in?'

Edward paused, his brow furrowing, unable to summon a satisfactory reply. What Arthur said was completely true. The Colonel often held forth about the great opportunities to be had in times of conflict, and urged for war whenever he could. We're a part of all this, the secretary thought – complicit, somehow, in the looming hostilities. That men like Arthur were so keen to rush off to fight, that they cheered every ineluctable step towards bloodshed, was in the best interests of the Colt Company. It seemed as if a vast machine had been started up and the British nation was being pulled slowly into it – being pounded, sliced and reshaped – and the gun-makers were among those working this machine's controls. Edward stared down at the torn blades of grass that he still held in his palm, gripped suddenly by a dark, conflicted feeling. He said nothing.

Seeing that he'd prevailed, Arthur became conciliatory. 'I say, you couldn't by any chance see your way to sending me a brace of your Yankee six-shooters, could you? I could tout it for you around the barracks, fire it at the range – become a sort of walking advertisement. I might even be able to get my new colonel to put in a good word at Division, to help you get your contracts and all that.'

'Of course,' Edward answered absently, brushing the grass from his palm, his brow still creased. 'That's a fine idea.'

Arthur got to his feet, well pleased. He straightened his undress cap and looked off towards Hyde Park Corner. 'Let's go across the road to Tattersall's. Word is they've an early running card for the Derby. I'm under orders to catch a train out to Chelmsford this evening – and if I can show up at the officers' mess of the 44th with a few quality tips to pass around it could make me some quick pals.'

The soldier offered Edward a hand, pulling him upright with such force that he almost overbalanced. The Navy revolver shifted inside his jacket; he grabbed at it, just managing to stop the weapon thudding out into the open.

After his garrotting in the Devil's Acre, Edward had found walking down any but the widest and best-lit thoroughfares a disturbing ordeal. Sleep, also, had become elusive, and his hands had begun to tremble so much sometimes that he could barely keep hold of his pen. Eventually, desperate to regain his steadiness, he'd lifted the Navy from its drawer, loaded it with cartridges and caps taken from a small supply he'd found in the office and secured it within his waistcoat, under his left arm. The hard weight of it – the certain knowledge that he could fend off any attack launched at him – had been immediately reassuring. For a couple of days he'd almost longed for such an attack, in the hope that it would purge his tortured recollections of what had happened in the Devil's Acre. None came, however, and he was left peering around him like a hunted man, his fingers starting towards the pistol at the slightest unfamiliar sound.

Arthur was watching him with curious amusement. He'd noticed something strange about his cousin's posture, perhaps even that a heavy object was concealed inside his clothes. Edward took out his cigar case, hoping that this would serve as a distraction.

'Here, Art, try one of these,' he said. 'Finest Havana, from this place over on Oxford Street.'

The young lieutenant accepted readily; and once the cigar was alight he sauntered over to the colonnades of Tattersall's horse repository, forgetting everything but that rumour of an early card for the Derby. Relieved, Edward followed, buttoning up his jacket. For some reason, he felt a powerful need to keep the revolver hidden.

The note was waiting in the factory office when he returned there at around seven o'clock. *He will not leave*, it read, *and his snores and curses have disturbed my efforts to secure a sale on more than one occasion. He must be removed immediately, Mr Lowry, or I will be forced to inform Mr Colt*. It was signed by Charles Dennett, the agent who ran the sales office over in Spring Gardens. Edward was exhausted and wanted only to go home

186

to his bed; but this, he recognised irritably, would have to be attended to first. Screwing the note into a ball and throwing it aside, he headed straight back out through the door.

The afternoon had been spent among the stalls of Tattersall's, listening to Arthur's recollections from the Kaffir War; of marches along rocky ridges aglow with gladioli; of field funerals in wild mountain forts; of the greased bodies of the savage foe gleaming as they darted forward through the brush. The fighting itself – bayonet work mostly, it seemed – was spoken of with bloodthirsty enthusiasm. It was plain that Arthur felt he had a knack for it, and wanted to put this to the test for a second time. Fired up by Tattersall's complimentary sherry, the young officer had predicted that if Great Britain did declare war with Russia, and his cousin came through on his promise of Yankee revolvers, then Lieutenant Arthur Lowry would soon be dropping Russia's best men like they were nothing more than game-birds. Hearing all this had only further unsettled Edward's mind. He'd merely nodded along, saying little himself.

Spring Gardens, a quiet street of small, exclusive-looking premises, was just behind the southern side of Charing Cross. The Colt outlet stood about halfway down, with *Col. S. Colt: Repeating Firearms* stencilled in bold gold and black letters upon its wide plate-glass window. Edward had been here several times before, both alone and with the Colonel. He'd enjoyed the luxury of the place, and the sense that he, as a notable Colt employee, had some kind of special status within. There was no pleasure to be taken in this particular visit, however; the secretary pushed his way inside, thinking that he would get it over with as quickly as possible.

A diagonal block of evening sunlight slanted in through the front window, projecting *Colt* in reverse across the patterned tiles of the floor. The rest of the shop was sunk in an expensive, velvet-trimmed gloom, a black marble counter separating potential customers from the long rank of display cases that lined the back wall. Every variety of

Colt pistol was contained within these cases, from iron-and-brass presentation models of the earliest Connecticut Dragoons to plain, service-issue Navys straight from the Pimlico manufactory. This was where the private sales of the Colonel's firearms were made – where curious Englishmen with a few pounds to spare could purchase themselves a Colt revolver. In truth, though, the sales office shifted a negligible quantity of weapons. Its principal value, as the Colonel had stated numerous times, was promotional. It was the place where a well-connected gentleman with a casual interest in weaponry and its advances could simply saunter in for a look – and perhaps leave with a specimen that he might show around his club, or produce for the amusement of a party of august dinner guests.

The sales agent, Mr Dennett, was a small, fine-featured creature with an oily sheen to his skin. His voice was shrill, with a New York accent anglicised somewhat by a number of years' residence in London. He turned to Edward in an accusatory manner, all but twitching with agitation.

'At last, thank God – get him out, Mr Lowry, this minute! There's an evening crowd that comes in between half-seven and nine, don't y'know, and he must be gone by then – long gone!'

Making the appropriate assurances, Edward walked around the counter to the door that led to the rear room. It was sparsely furnished, in contrast to the front, with pistol cases and ammunition crates piled upon bare floorboards. The Colt Company's English press agent lay behind a desk in its far corner. His long legs stuck out across the floor at right angles, as if he'd been frozen in the act of running and pushed onto his side. He'd removed his jacket and waistcoat at some point to serve as a pillow but both were now bunched up against the wall, caked with dust. He was snoring softly; the clammy, boozy smell of unwashed drunkard hung in the air.

'Richards,' Edward said, taking a couple of steps towards him, 'wake up.'

Nothing happened. Edward repeated the press agent's

name more loudly, this time eliciting a drawn-out groan. Richards pulled up his legs and rolled over. He was cradling an empty bottle of spirit in his arms. A charred cigar-end, cracked and crumbling apart, was stuck to his chin.

'Mabel would have no more,' he croaked, keeping his eyes firmly shut.

Mabel, Edward knew, was the unfortunate Mrs Richards. Every so often she'd grow so tired of her husband's exploits that she'd shut him out of their home up in Marylebone. For some mysterious reason Richards possessed a key to the sales office; and in these times of domestic ruction the shop occasionally served the press agent as a convenient sanctuary.

There were new, unfamiliar voices out in the front. Edward looked over his shoulder. A pair of plump, middle-aged gentlemen were approaching the marble counter, making a jovial enquiry. Dennett went to remove a pistol from a display case, casting a nervous glance in the secretary's direction as he did so.

They had to leave. A chair lay on its back in the middle of the room. Edward stood it up and then bent down to take hold of the press agent.

The noise was loud and very close, wood glancing against wood; the impact jarred along Edward's flank. The stock of his Navy had struck against the desk. Richards's eyes flickered open, the pupils sliding to the side. He looked up at Edward. The pistol was clearly visible inside the secretary's jacket.

'Why, Mr Lowry,' he murmured, 'you appear to be armed.'

Ignoring him, Edward heaved Richards off the floor and into the chair; the bottle dropped from his embrace and span away under the desk. The press agent's hat and boots were standing on the desktop. Edward passed them to him, plucking the cigar from his chin and then retrieving his jacket and waistcoat.

'A most sensible precaution in this city,' Richards continued, 'as I believe you've already discovered, what with that ghastly garrotting of yours. Samuel presented me with a firearm of my own after the Great Exhibition.' He paused to fumble with a boot. 'And I'd be carrying the thing right now if a pressing financial circumstance hadn't compelled me to part with it.'

Edward took a steadying breath. Richards was still rather the worse for drink. It had plainly been an epic debauch that had deposited the fellow in Spring Gardens. They could not wait for him to tie his boots; it could take hours. Grabbing one of his spindly arms, the secretary pulled him up from the chair and led him swiftly through the front of the sales office. Dennett's potential customers – both well-heeled clergymen, Edward noticed – were holding up revolvers as if eager to put them to use. They fixed the passing Colt men with suspicious stares, visibly alarmed by Richards's stained shirt, disordered hair and vagrant's pallor. The sales agent, meanwhile, closed his eyes as if reciting a short prayer for patience.

'Good day to you, Mr Dennett!' Richards called as he was rushed out into the street. 'An *exceedingly* good day to you, sir!'

The sun had disappeared behind the city skyline, sinking Charing Cross in the cool grey of a late summer's evening. There was a faint chill in the air, along with the usual smells of dust and manure. A great cheer sounded over at the base of Nelson's Column, where a troupe of acrobats in multicoloured leotards were somersaulting above the heads of a growing audience. Edward marched Richards through the traffic, across the western edge of Trafalgar Square towards the main pediment of the National Gallery; shut for the day, its steps would offer some refuge from the crowds. Richards sat down heavily and started to lace up one of his boots.

Edward threw the press agent's jacket and waistcoat onto the steps. 'You cannot keep on goading Dennett in that manner, Richards,' he said curtly. 'He will start requesting your dismissal, and I wouldn't put it past our Jamie to oblige him.'

Richards met this with a contemptuous snort and a couple of acerbic remarks about the sales agent's parentage. The walk from Spring Gardens had clearly awakened a whole host of pains within him, though, and he was struggling to sustain his usual flippancy.

'God Almighty, Lowry,' he sighed, giving up on the boot and putting a hand over his face. 'It's all gone a bit too bloody far this time. Mabel Richards has shown herself to be a *viper*, my friend. A Goneril. A Medusa.' He sighed again. 'Why do we let these inexplicable females sink their hooks into us so deeply, eh?'

Edward blinked, his irritation struck out of him at once. His own thoughts had often strayed in this same direction over the past few weeks. In the wake of his ill-fated expedition into the Devil's Acre, he'd resolved to give up Caroline Knox completely – to turn away from her for good. It had been proving astonishingly difficult.

There could be no doubt that she was involved in a scheme of some kind with Martin Rea and the other Irishmen. Rea was plainly a plotter embedded within the works for an unknown criminal purpose, most probably the theft of the Colonel's pistols for distribution in London's most insalubrious regions. Edward knew that it was his professional duty as an employee of the Colt Company to tell Walter Noone what he had discovered. He couldn't do it, though; he couldn't deliver Caroline to the watchman's brutal justice, and the gaol term that would probably follow. He refused to believe that she would freely join the Irishmen in their nefarious schemes. She was being subjected to some kind of pressure by Rea and his cohorts, he was certain of it. He'd looked out for the two of them around the factory, trying to discover exactly what they were up to in the hope that he could somehow extricate her from the plan. Both seemed blameless, however – industrious and punctual.

On a couple of occasions, spotting Caroline out in the yard, Edward had almost rushed over to intercept her – to offer to help her escape the Irishmen in any way he could – but had stopped himself. She didn't want anything more to do with him. That had been made very clear, and had to be respected. Caroline Knox must be driven from his mind. She does not care for me, he thought; very well then, I will care nothing for her in return. This is how it must be.

Such a pledge, Edward soon learnt, was a good deal easier to make than to uphold. He tried to attend to his work with redoubled diligence, but was dogged by a dismal aimlessness that sapped his concentration and his energy. Unanswered questions came back frequently to torment him; he grew quite sick with worry about what Miss Knox and her co-conspirators might be poised to do. As he paced out endless circuits of the factory office, he could only repeat once again that he did not care for her. *He did not.*

'I don't know,' he replied.

Richards studied him for a moment, seeming to conclude that the two of them carried a similar sorrow. 'Come, Mr Lowry,' he said, working an arm into his dirty jacket, 'let's find ourselves a bloody drink. I know a place not far from here.'

Rather to his surprise, Edward found that this proposal held a strong appeal, and five minutes later the Colt men were climbing a narrow wooden staircase just off St Martin's Lane. It led up to a high-ceilinged room set out with small square tables, slim serving girls slipping between them. Plainly a coffee house by day, stronger drinks were now in circulation, and playing cards slapped down upon the tabletops. The patrons were almost exclusively male, drawn from the class that might own an inauspicious printing works, operate a modest photographic studio or pen features for a cheap newspaper. Proper hats and half-decent jackets were on display, but most were a good way past their best. Disappointment speckled the room like rust on an old, neglected blade; these were not men who'd attained what they wanted from life.

Their arrival prompted a stirring of nudges and sidelong glances. Edward realised that Richards was well known in there, and not entirely popular. Oblivious to this, the press agent selected a table by one of the four front windows – a dozen pieces of discoloured stained glass set in a lead frame, left slightly ajar to bleed away some of the tobacco smoke. Balking at spirits after his excesses of the previous night, Richards ordered them a bottle of claret. The smooth, berry-scented wine made Edward feel significantly better, and for perhaps the first time since the attack in the Devil's Acre he was almost at ease. They began to talk of women in general terms, drinking steadily as they did so. Richards was soon holding forth on their unpredictability, their capriciousness, and the fundamental lack of reason or candour that lay beneath their thinking.

'Surely,' Edward interrupted after a few minutes, 'you do not seriously apply this to *all* women?'

'Every one, Mr Lowry,' the press agent answered, emptying the last of the bottle into the secretary's glass and then signalling for another. 'Every blasted one. But Mabel Richards is first among them. She is their queen – the lying bitch before all lying bitches.'

The claret was rapidly restoring Richards's self-possession, topping up both his inebriation and his mordancy. One of Edward's fine Havana cigars smoking in his mouth, he made a slow survey of their fellow customers. Then, quite casually, he revealed that he suspected his much-maligned wife of having taken a lover.

Edward's glass paused on its way to his lips.

'There's this cockney blackguard from the Imperial Gas Company, y'see,' Richards went on, his voice louder now and unmistakably confrontational. 'Five times now in the past fortnight I've returned from my labours to find him in my home. Five bloody times, Lowry! The scoundrel claims he's testing pipes, but that's piffle, ain't it? Purest poppycock.' He hit the table with his palm. 'I ask you, how many blasted times do gas pipes need to be tested?'

'I really couldn't say.'

The secretary took a sip of wine. It now seemed thick and bitter; he set down his glass, his face growing hot. The press agent's words were plainly directed at someone in that room. Richards was trying to stir up trouble. A nearby card game had come to a distinctly tense halt. Four men had been playing; three of them were now watching the fourth closely. Dressed in faded grey with a patchy brown beard, he'd laid his cards face down on the table and was looking at the fan of red rectangles with an expression of fierce attention.

'Blasted cockneys,' Richards continued, blowing out smoke,

'they are so damned *wily*. They see an opening and they go for it, like rats diving into a tub of grain. They'd pimp out their wives for tuppence, wouldn't they – sell their own children to the bloody butcher.'

And then the grey-clad card player was on his feet. More exasperated than angry, he addressed the press agent in a broad cockney accent. 'What the devil is your meanin', Mr Richards? This was over and done with, wasn't it? Why go haggravatin' the sitiwation?'

Richards sat back, smoking his cigar, ignoring the card player completely. 'Show me an honest cockney, Lowry,' he proclaimed, 'and I'll show you a dog that can walk on its hind legs and mimic the ways of man.'

Edward swore that he heard the press agent laugh as he was hauled from his chair. The room erupted with shouts, furniture scraping against the floorboards as people stood up to get a better view. The card player shoved Richards's lanky form against their table, knocking over bottle and glasses.

'I'll show you cockney honesty, cock,' he spat, 'don't you bleedin' worry!'

Leaving his seat, Edward found himself pressed against the stained glass window, all but dangling out above St Martin's Lane. Richards weathered his opponent's first couple of blows as if taking a beating was a terrible bore; then he struggled free and rolled off the table, stumbling to Edward and wrapping him in a long-limbed, clumsy embrace. Their spectators heaved with mirth, someone letting out a sharp wolf-whistle.

'My apologies, old boy,' Richards muttered, turning shakily towards the cockney card player.

Something was different. The weight that had been pulling at Edward's shoulder all day, sending great pulsing aches down his left arm, was suddenly gone. He felt a half-second's relief before he registered what had just happened. His Navy revolver was missing – pickpocketed by the press agent.

The three shots obliterated every other sound in the room and left only a stark silence behind them. A rush of gunpowder smoke spiralled away between the tables, adding to the turbid atmosphere. Those around the pistol-toting Richards were arranged like a petrified tableau; some even had grins still stuck on their faces. Edward could see no obvious signs that any of the press agent's bullets had hit home, and for a moment he dared to hope that Richards had fired harmlessly into the ceiling or walls. But then, close to the floor, he noticed a rich streak of colour – a long crimson splash flicked out across a serving girl's pale cotton slippers. It had come from the card player's left leg. He'd been shot through the calf.

All at once this scene collapsed into noisy chaos. There was a massed scramble for the staircase leading down to the street; trays of glasses were dropped, and a table kicked over; a woman somewhere at the back of the room belted out a mighty, fog-horn scream. Richards's victim fell back into the arms of his companions, his hat sliding off, gasping and grabbing out for support as the colour melted from his skin. They settled him on a chair as gently as they could. The wound was pumping out blood at a startling rate; it drenched his trouser-leg and trickled viscously over the worn boot at its base.

We have to go, Edward thought – this instant. He strode forward, seized the Navy from Richards's uncertain grasp and started to pull him towards the exit. People parted fearfully before them, giving the gun as wide a berth as possible, jostling each other aside to get out of their way. The serving girl with the bloodied slippers had become trapped somehow at the top of the stairs, pushed up against the doorframe by a fleeing customer and now too scared to move. Fourteen years old at most, her thin, freckled face was ashen with fright. She'd clasped her hands before her chest in a desperate prayer; and as the Colt men approached she sobbed out a plea for mercy, hunching her shoulders and lowering her head, trying to make herself as small as possible.

This sight made Edward feel acutely ashamed. 'We won't hurt you, miss,' he managed to say. 'Please believe me. We are professional men – respectable men. This was an accident.'

She nodded, mumbling something, but her gaze did not

leave the pistol in his hand; and as he stepped past her onto the staircase she flinched in terror, squeezing her eyes shut as if expecting execution.

The middle of St Martin's Lane was clogged with bleating sheep. Lost on its way to a market somewhere, this flock was packed in tightly around the drays, cabs and carriages, aggravating horses and confounding the weary efforts of its shepherds to move it up towards Long Acre. This was good; it would prove a certain hindrance to any immediate attempts to pursue them. Still dragging Richards by the arm, the secretary forced a path through the crush of woolly backs, making for a shadowy alley that led away in the direction of Covent Garden.

Edward had been holding the Navy just inside the flap of his jacket. After about fifty yards they rounded a corner; he took the chance to stop, knock out the remaining charges and secure it properly beneath his clothes, shivering slightly at the trace of warmth that still lingered in the steel. The press agent had propped himself against a wall and was panting hard. A gas-lamp flickered to life in an upstairs window, bathing him in yellow light. There was a strange expression on his flushed, angular features – equal parts smirk and grimace.

Facing him, Edward found that he was almost too astonished to be angry. 'What the devil was that, Richards?' he hissed. 'He might well *die*, you know, from such a wound! Why, if they'd caught us in there, we'd –' He couldn't finish the sentence. Everything would surely have been over for them both. 'What were you *thinking*?'

Richards, caught in the grip of a coughing fit, could only shrug.

'That was the cockney gas-man, I assume – the fellow you suspect of seducing your wife. Did you take us in there deliberately, looking for him, once you saw that I had the gun? Was it all planned?'

The press agent tried to laugh but couldn't quite manage it. 'It seemed a rational course,' he protested weakly. 'What more can I say?'

Despite his attempt at offhandedness, Richards was evidently shaken by what had just occurred. Edward's claim

196

to the serving girl had been correct – the shooting had been an accident, the error of an over-excited drunkard.

'You didn't actually mean to hit him, did you?'

Richards rubbed his nose on his sleeve, making a ragged, snuffling sound. He looked haggard and thoroughly out of sorts. 'Dear Lord,' he whispered, 'I do believe I feel rather sick.'

Shouts echoed over from the direction of St Martin's Lane. Edward put a hand on the press agent's bony shoulder, easing him away from the wall and propelling him firmly down the alley.

'Come,' he said, 'let's get us to Holborn. You can stay with me tonight.'

Half an hour later Alfred Richards was fast asleep on the hearth of Edward's parlour, wrapped in the secretary's winter coat. Edward sat in the other room, on the edge of his bed. Holding the Navy, staring at it, he recalled the frantic movements of the wounded man's hands as he toppled backwards; the panicked stampede towards the stairs; the streak of fresh blood on the serving girl's shoes. Most vividly of all, though, he saw the abject fear on this young girl's face – fear he had inspired. Edward believed that he was, at his core, a good man; yet to that girl, when wielding this pistol, he had appeared a thoroughly convincing killer.

This was a raw, mortifying memory. Looking over at the window, he considered going back out into Red Lion Square that very minute and dropping the gun down the nearest drain. Even as he thought of this, however, he knew that he could not do it. He had invested too much of himself in the Colt Company. Throwing away the Colonel's gift would be a betrayal of his own ambition; a rejection, somehow, of the golden future he'd dreamed of so feverishly.

But neither could the weapon possibly go back in the bureau drawer, to be seen every time he reached for some ink or a sheet of writing paper. He took out his oldest shirt, wrapped it tightly around the revolver, and then pushed this awkward bundle as far under his bed as it would go.

4

'A whitebait supper,' said Martin, breaking a long silence. 'That's what's needed.'

He fed his rolled-up cap between his hands, squinting out at the sun-scorched grass and the Sunday crowds that lounged across it. The Rea family sat close to the summit of the hill, about fifty yards from the Royal Observatory, in the deep shade of an oak. The village of Greenwich was arrayed before them, its thriving tea-rooms spilling over into the park. A small fair had been set up in front of the long white colonnades of the sailors' asylum, with a coconut shy and a waxworks tent; music from a fiddle and a drum drifted in and out of earshot, smothered by the torpid, late summer air. Church bells were tolling, in Greenwich itself and all along the valley towards London, announcing the afternoon service; those in the park, however, dedicated solely to recreation, paid them no mind. Behind this scene wound the great river, littered with papery sails. Out here, past the factories and the sewer outlets and the dockyards, the water lost much of its corruption and began to approach its natural colour once again.

'Aye,' he declared, as if the decision was made. 'Come, girl, that'll sort us out. At the Trafalgar, down by the river – a plate of whitebait and a glass of ale.'

Martin looked around for his child. Katie was off investigating the trunk of the oak, supporting herself against the ridged bark. He said her name; she gaped back blankly for a second, and then fell into a sitting position. Amy, curled up on the ground, still had not stirred. Martin patted her haunch, feeling the hard jut of her hip-bone. Grief had denied his wife anything but the very lightest sleep for almost a week now. She was living in a state of exhausted, stupefied despair, unable to work or eat, and barely able to walk more than a couple of dozen steps. This excursion, taking them well away from the Devil's Acre, had been intended to bring her some relief. But their third-class carriage had been brimming with little babies, it had seemed, every one of them screaming with lusty health, and the streets of Greenwich even more so; after a few minutes of this Amy had ground to a halt like a stubborn mule, leaving Martin to carry her, more or less, to this secluded corner of the park, their bawling daughter tucked under his other arm. Here she had collapsed into her current position, not moving or speaking for over an hour. It was good that she'd taken some rest at last, he told himself, but it was time for more – for sustenance, for life and human society. He patted her again.

Wiping the strands of dark, tear-soaked hair from her cheek, Amy shifted onto her back. 'Martin,' she said, her voice hoarse and edged with bitterness, 'do you feel anything at all?'

He sighed. This once more. 'How can you ask me that?'

'I know how you Irish are. You've seen everything, ain't you? Nothing else compares with what you've already lived through. No other loss is as painful. This is – is *measly* to you, ain't it?' She was starting to tremble. 'Nothing very much?'

Martin twisted his cap as tightly as he could, looking down fixedly at his crossed legs. 'I am mourning, in my way. You can be sure of that.'

Amy wasn't listening. She sat up suddenly, rubbing her palms against her eyes, smoothing down her hair and picking up her bonnet from where it had fallen on the grass. 'We must leave this city. I can't stand it no longer. It ain't safe for Katie; Heavens, Martin, it ain't safe for *us*. America – we must go to America.' Her tone grew imploring. 'Talk to your

Mr Quill. Tell him that you wish to go to the Colt factory over there to – to learn more about the engines. To finish your training. He'll listen, won't he?'

Martin found that he could easily imagine a fine new life for them in Hartford. There would be a pretty cottage in a Connecticut lane, with Katie skipping around the flower-garden; formal tutelage in gun manufacture, followed by a long-term contract on a master engineer's wage; a lasting friendship with Ben Quill, continuing until they were both old men. It could not happen, though, not yet, no matter how much he might want it. He had to stay loyal to Molly and his brothers. Caroline was getting them their guns. The moment of action might not be too far off now.

He shook his head. 'It ain't that simple.'

'Because of Slattery, you mean – because of this debt you all kept hidden for so long. You have a *family*, Martin. You have a child. What's to stop us going – making our arrangements in secret and then sailing away from this place forever?'

Martin glanced across at Amy; she was working herself into a rage. The debt she spoke of was an out-and-out lie, a story spun with the Mollys' collaboration to convince her to enlist her sister to their cause. It had been a necessary deception. The truth was too much of a risk. He hadn't liked doing it, and had felt guilt over it since – but he was damned if he wouldn't make her understand exactly what was at stake for him here.

'You're asking me to betray my closest friends,' he answered angrily. 'We are bound together, Slattery and me – all of us. We are *brothers*. I won't leave 'em like that. D'ye hear me, Amy? I bleedin' *won't*.'

This did not chasten her in the least. 'That man hates you, Martin,' she spat back. 'Can you really not tell? He hates you for siring English children, for mixing your precious Irish blood, and will grind us into the mud to show it.'

He looked up sharply; there was something new here. 'What's this? What are you talking about, girl?'

She hesitated, lifting her chin a little. 'I heard him talking. At – at Michael's wake. Saying the most dreadful things. That our boy was a – a half-breed. A Protestant mongrel.'

Here she faltered, shaken by the recollection, brushing away a fresh tear; but she took a breath and made herself continue. 'That it was better that he should have died in his infancy, before he could – could –'

Martin's hand shot out, seizing her arm. 'Pat Slattery said that? He said *mongrel*? He said that to *you*?'

Amy made a vain attempt to wriggle free, frightened by his reaction. 'N-not straight to me face, no, but I heard it clear enough. He was with some of the others – Owen and Joe, I think, and –'

A mighty blaze of light blasted out everything, sweeping away the rest of Amy's words, casting the peaceful park into a roaring forge of blinding whiteness. Martin felt a burning sensation in his throat and chest; he realised that he was out on the hillside, breathing hard, racing upwards in the full glare of the sun; and then he was shoving through a game of some kind, knocking people aside and cursing at the very top of his voice. There was but one thought in his mind. He was going back to Westminster right away, he was going to find Patrick Slattery and he was going to kill him. He was going to wring the life from that wretched bastard with his own two hands. A player from the game he had spoiled grabbed hold of his shoulder, seeking to chide him for his interruption. Martin turned on this fellow almost with gratitude, punching him twice in the face with such un-restrained force that he went straight down and did not rise again.

Then he heard her, singing somewhere in the distance in that cracked bell of a voice. Molly was in the park with him. She'd pushed her way up through the baked turf of Greenwich and was now moving among the trees at the hill's summit, running her bony fingers through the lowest leaves. He tried to look at her; the sunlight was simply too powerful, however, dissolving everything and making his eyes ache. But she knew that he needed her. Was she leading him onwards? Was she beckoning him to her side? Martin continued uphill, and before long found himself at the end of a neat oak-lined avenue with flagstones underfoot. Around him were people with telescopes in their hands, exchanging idle observations, looking off towards London and the distant dome of St Paul's. He paused, panting, momentarily lost; but her song found him again, reaching out to him from the far end of the avenue. And there she was, by God, dancing across the stones like a dark, ragged sprite, skipping through a set of tall iron gates and out into the countryside beyond. Surging on with the last of his strength, Martin went after her.

Molly had led him to a wide, rutted road – the main road back into the city. He was sweating, struggling for breath and sobbing too. Staggering to a halt, he bent over and put his hands on his thighs, watching tears and drops of perspiration splash together against the dusty ground. For the first time in many months, his thoughts were of the Athlone workhouse, of his beloved mother and sisters, all five of whom had met their ends in the same weekend, claimed by a fever that had rushed through the weak, half-starved inmates like a mounted charge. As always, he'd been off plotting a riot or an assassination or the burning of some building or other; and by the time he reached Athlone on the Monday all but Sally, the youngest and last to die, had already been committed to the earth, buried in a mass grave outside the workhouse wall.

The place itself had sickened him past all expression. The moaning hundreds, mostly women, children and the elderly, who were packed into every damp, barren room; the hopelessly thin broth, served but once a day, on which they were supposed to survive; the skeletal dead heaped in the yard, through whom he had to rummage to find what remained of his sister. It was impossible to comprehend the sheer quantity of misery contained within the Athlone workhouse. Every single person under that leaking roof had a tale of terrible injustice to tell – a story to inflame the soul with righteous anger and break the heart with pity. And Sally herself, once able to run a plough truer than any man, was but a faded, broken wisp of what she'd been, with every painful stage of her demise impressed into her teenage face. Martin had carried away her straw-light body on his back, burying her beneath a tree on the borders of what, only a year before, had been the Rea farm. It had been that same evening that he'd caught his very first glimpse of Molly Maguire.

These black memories brought him abruptly to a far more recent time, only a few days past, in the bleak corner of Westminster that served as the Catholic churchyard – where, with Jack, he had carried that tiny coffin to its grave. He felt every sensation anew; the rope against his skin, and the pathetic weight at its end; the smell of wet clay, so strange in the dust and warmth of high summer; the quivering wail that had trailed from Amy's lips, drowning out the priest's final blessing, growing louder and louder as the earth had started to go back in. He could hear the puffing of his so-called brothers, of Pat, Owen, Joe and Thady, as they worked with their shovels – men he'd thought were ready to die for him, who he would surely have died for, yet who'd mocked his loss and insulted his boy within earshot of his grieving wife. Jesus Christ Almighty, he was going to *kill them all*.

Martin swallowed hard, dragged a sleeve across his face and took in his surroundings. The road was quiet, the only traffic being a couple of light Sunday gigs and some solitary riders. Beyond it was an expanse of sun-browned heath; at its far side, shimmering in the heat, was another village, its houses and church arranged like cups around a jug. Off to his left, three horses stood drinking from a small pond, beneath a wilting willow. Molly was nowhere to be seen; nor did her song sound any longer in the dried-out air. He sat down at the side of the road, confusion cooling his blood, the mad fury that had carried him there rapidly ebbing away. What did she want of him? To start for London at once, along this road – to hunt down Pat Slattery and mete out punishment for his unbrotherly words? To dislodge him, perhaps, and lead the Mollys himself? Or something else altogether? Martin asked her for further guidance, for some sign of her will; but she was utterly gone.

A clear image of his wife and daughter, sitting together under that oak, waiting helplessly for him to return, cut through his perplexity. Amy had no money, and was almost certainly too weak and befuddled to get the two of them home on her own. This was a real and immediate duty. A decent man would not allow Molly Maguire's mystifying riddles to keep him from looking after his family. Martin climbed to his feet with a groan and started back towards the park.

Slattery was in his usual spot at the Manticore, right at the ring's edge. He'd pulled his cap low over his eyes and was biting on the stem of his pipe, following the goings-on in the ring with close concentration. As Martin watched he gave a snarl of encouragement, striking the barrier. There was a slip of paper poking from his fist; he had money riding on whatever contest was underway.

Few places offered action as good as that found in the Manticore on a Sunday night. The tavern's modest upstairs room was always stuffed to the gills long before the hour appointed for the first match. This teeming clientele was drawn from every corner of London, and from several different levels as well; there were pockets of black top hats gleaming within the broad silt-bed of workers' caps, and rumours persisted of certain members of the aristocracy paying the occasional visit, sloping across the river on the sly after a long day of sermons and domestic tedium. Attention was divided between the ring itself and the handful of bookmakers positioned at intervals around its edge. Every man in the room was shouting, either to place a wager or to cheer on one they'd made already, holding aloft betting slips, crumpled bank-notes or handfuls of sweaty coins.

Martin elbowed his way to the hexagonal ring and hoisted a boot up onto the top of the barrier. A sturdy, battered-looking terrier was shooting about within, his chewed ears erect, his docked stump of a tail wagging furiously. Before him, a swarm of plump rats was scattering in squeaking terror, pressing themselves into the ring's shallow corners, piling up a dozen deep in their panic. With fierce excitement, the little dog seized a straggler and shook it hard, leaving the body immediately to take a dive at another. This second rodent tried to stand its ground, baring needle-thin fangs, but it did no good; the terrier's jaws snapped shut again, swinging the corpse away to the other side of the arena.

Martin launched himself across the ring towards Slattery, knocking loose the oil lamp that was suspended from the low ceiling with his shoulder. There was a whoop of dismay from the crowd as the lamp dropped from its hook, breaking apart on the sanded floor. Landing at a bad angle in the darkness, Martin stumbled among the rats; he felt their fat, frantic bodies squirming across his calves and starting up his trouser-legs, desperate to escape the dog. Slattery was laughing at him from behind the barrier. Leaping forward, Martin charged into it, pushing it over, the white light roaring up around him once more; and the next he knew they were on the ground together, his foe pinned beneath him in a stream of fleeing rodents, his fist cracking against a nose, then a mouth, then an eye.

'What did you say about me boy, Slattery? *What did you bleedin' say?*'

Around them, arguments began over spoiled bets and quickly grew heated; several vigorous attempts were made to catch or kill as many rats as possible; and somewhere in among it all the little ratter barked in frustration at the ruining of his game. Slattery bucked, struggling hard. Martin adjusted his position, fastening his hands around the bastard's neck. That was it; he had him now. Fingers clawed at his knuckles, trying to work themselves inside his grip, but it was no use. Martin realised that he was grinning. He squeezed tighter.

'*Enough.*'

It was Molly, her voice stern and cold; Martin caught a glimpse of a girlish form gliding through the press of barging men, her hair tasting the air behind her like a long, forked tongue. What the devil is this, he thought – why is she restraining me now? It made no sense at all, but he loosened his hold; and immediately Slattery knocked him back, rocketing up from the shadowy floor and butting Martin's chin with the flat plate of his forehead. This barely had time to register before something struck against the side of his skull, a blow swung in from behind, jolting him into a dizzy, sparking emptiness. When he returned to his senses a moment later he was being tipped down the tavern's narrow staircase. A strapping pot-boy met him at the bottom, taking his place in a well-practised system of ejection; he dragged Martin to his feet, punched him a couple of times and then shoved him out into the street before he'd had time to regain his balance. Carried forward by the momentum of this push, Martin staggered to the centre of the road before falling heavily onto his side.

The Manticore stood next to the fermenting sheds of a small vinegar yard and opposite a sprawling riverside brewery, and the various powerful smells produced by these two establishments – bitterly acidic, cloyingly meaty, revoltingly sour – hung in the surrounding air. Both were dark now, their gates shut; the Sunday night hush was broken only by the tavern sounds leaking from the Manticore and the steady patter of rain. Martin drew up his knees and rocked himself into a crouching position, clutching at his head. There was blood, a tender lump and one hell of an ache, but no serious damage. He'd been lucky. Then Molly's whisper tickled the inside of his ear, slipping between the raindrops, admonishing him softly. He swatted at it as if it were a biting insect.

'Ah, leave me be,' he muttered. 'Ain't you had enough bleedin' fun?'

The tavern door creaked open and Slattery emerged, dabbing at a split nostril with his sleeve. Martin sprang straight to his feet and dived at him again. A body rushed in to stop him, though, clasping thick arms around his chest and holding him back. It was Jack Coffee; Martin saw that the other Mollys were there also, Owen, Thady and Joe, coming out behind Slattery. They must have been in the Manticore as well, away in the crowd.

'Protestant mongrel, weren't it?' Martin cried, fighting against Jack's grasp. 'Ain't that what you bleedin' said, ye miserable louse?'

Slattery came closer, splashing through a puddle. Even in that gloomy lane, unlit save for a single lime-light burning outside the railway yard at its end, Martin could tell that he wore a wicked sneer. 'Look at this, my lads – drunk on his sorrow. Crying in the bleedin' streets.' He shook his head and spat on the ground. 'I'm ashamed o' you, Martin Rea, truly I am. The sons of Eire cannot afford the luxury o' grief.'

Martin took another lunge, almost breaking free from Jack's arms; but something in the way that Slattery squared up to meet this attack quashed his spirit, stripping the fight from him completely. As always, the fellow had transferred all sense of grievance onto himself, admitting no fault in what he'd done. He was ready to beat or get beaten yet would not yield a single inch. Pat Slattery was more likely to remove his boots and cap and leap into the Thames than utter a single word of apology or remorse. Martin stopped struggling. Sensing his surrender, Jack released him and took a step backwards.

Slattery's hackles were up, though; he wanted a battle. Pouncing forward, he grabbed Martin's face between his hands, pressing damp fingertips hard against his cheek and neck. 'You're forgetting the task to which you're pledged,' he declared, clenching his bloody teeth. 'All of us here, *all of us*, are bound by our soul's oath to Molly Maguire. She's looking to us, Martin, to you and me, to get her some bleedin' justice.'

Martin barely managed to keep his voice level. 'I don't know, Pat,' he said.

Slattery was still for a second. Then he leaned in even closer, pressing their foreheads together. His skin was cold; his breath smelled of gin and raw onion. 'Jesus, Mary and Joseph, Mart,' he murmured, 'this is some dangerous ground you're stepping onto here. D'ye not remember Roscommon, and all we did in Molly's name? D'ye not remember Denis Mahon?'

'Aye, o' course I do – how could I not?' Martin pushed Slattery away impatiently. 'I just can't say what she wants of me no more. Not for sure.'

Now Slattery was smiling in scornful disbelief. 'What the devil are you talking about? She wants us to knock over Lord John. Summer's nearly at its end. That filthy Saxon parliament will soon be starting a new session. Our man will be out in the city a good deal. And that's when we'll get him.'

This blunt summary made Martin suddenly perceive their long-cherished plan for what it truly was. The Mollys had convinced themselves that their escape would be easy – that Colt's revolvers would enable them to shoot their way to safety once the deed had been done. It was a lie, he realised, nothing more than a piece of soothing self-deception. They might well kill Russell, and several others besides, but they were certain to be chased down shortly afterwards. A gang of Irishmen armed with revolving pistols would be simple to track, even back into the Devil's Acre. Molly's scheme would surely end in their deaths, either right there in the streets or upon the gallows of Newgate. Martin thought of Greenwich Park – of how he'd returned to the shadow of the oak to find that Katie had wandered off down the hill, fallen flat on her face and was shrieking uncontrollably; yet Amy, slumped once more in a dismal, weeping heap, hadn't noticed. They needed him. To do Molly's will would be to abandon them utterly.

'Oh, see the certainty there, brothers!' Slattery crowed, turning towards the other Mollys. 'See the pure bleedin' *faith* in his eyes! Ain't that the very fellow you want at your side when the trouble starts, eh?'

'The bugger don't want to go through with it,' growled Thady. 'It's plain as day.'

Martin tried to deny this but it was no use; he'd said no more than three angry words before Slattery interrupted.

'Aye, Thady, I believe you're right. He's too afeared for his Saxon wife and the child still living.' He patted at his face as if searching for a bruise. 'Ah, Christ above, I knew this would occur. You were the best among us once, Martin, honest to God. I should've damn well stopped it, and now it's too bleedin' late.'

Curtly, Martin told Slattery that he was not his master, nor had he ever been; that he did as he pleased and no attempt to halt his marriage to Amy Knox would have had any chance of success. And furthermore, he said, he was loyal to Ireland, and to Molly Maguire, and would not hear it claimed otherwise.

Slattery wasn't listening. 'Your union with that Saxon

woman put clear distance between us, and each child you had with her only added to it. And just look at what's happened now. Your boy is dead, finished by one of the plagues of this hellish Saxon city, and all at once you no longer have the heart for Molly's toil.'

Martin knew then what was coming. He stayed quiet, crossing his arms, staring up at the blank, boarded windows of the Manticore.

'You're doing a deal better with the guns, I s'pose,' Slattery continued, 'along wi' that vicious bitch o' yours, the sister-in-law. What is it, three pistols now? Who's got 'em?'

'I have,' said Owen. 'They're safe, Pat.'

Slattery nodded, strolling back over to the other Mollys. 'Here's how it will be, Mart. You get us the rest o' the dozen, wi' bullets and powder and whatever else these Yankee contraptions need. And then we'll let you go.'

There was a short, significant silence. Martin could feel their grins through the darkness; behind him, Jack cleared his throat, shifting about uneasily.

'What d'ye mean?'

'Get us the guns,' Slattery repeated slowly, 'and we're through wi' you. We don't need you for the job itself. We don't bleedin' *want* you, chum, if truth be told. Molly Maguire don't want you. Not for this.'

A week earlier, Martin would have protested this ruling with all his might, and demanded the chance to demonstrate his commitment in various hot-headed ways. Now, though, he thought only of flight, of doing as Amy had begged him to back in the park: of going to Mr Quill and asking him to arrange a transfer to the Colt works in Hartford. Slattery was right, it seemed. He'd lost his heart for their task.

'You've a month, Mart, before the Saxon parliament opens again and Lord John returns to London. After that, if we've got what we need, you can take your little Saxon brood off wherever you damn well please.'

With that he led the Mollys back into the Manticore. The tavern door opened, throwing a shaft of warm light across the street, allowing Martin to see the contemptuous glances being cast at him by those filing through it – those he had so recently counted as his brothers. And there she was, Molly Maguire, slipping from the deep shadows around the vinegar yard to go in with them, drifting ghost-like along the tavern wall, quickening her step to reach Pat Slattery's side. She was cackling to herself as she went, a cruel, rattling sound, unlike anything he had heard from her before; his casting-out seemed to amuse her.

The door closed again, restoring the street's darkness. Martin stumbled over to the brewery gates, leaning against them, sliding down until he was sitting on the ground. Gingerly, he touched the lump on the back of his head. It had grown to the size of a half-walnut, and was even sorer than before. His headache was getting worse as well, curling slowly around the top of his spine, squeezing the wakeful-ness out of him; he felt as if he could sleep where he sat, out in the rain. At that moment he was thinking not of Slattery, nor of Molly's scheme, nor even of his wife and daughter and departed son, but of the work that awaited him in the coming morning. He was expected in Colonel Colt's engine room at seven o'clock sharp. The new Yankee engineer, Mr Ballou, was a stickler for punctuality, and both he and Mr Quill would expect the usual long day of intel-ligent labour. How could he, so battered, dazed and exhausted, possibly hope to supply it?

Jack had remained outside, and was standing in the centre of the lane, regarding him uncertainly. 'Are ye going back in, Mart?' he asked. 'To watch the ratters?'

'I don't think they'd have me, pal.'

'I ain't neither.' Jack looked off towards the light outside the railway yard. 'Got to get me to Rosie McGehan's for ten, so I have.'

'What, she has you smashing murphies on the Sabbath?'

'Aye, she's a tough mistress, that one.' Jack paused, kicking at a loose cobble. There was something he wanted to say. 'You are doing a good thing, Mart, whatever Pat might think. You must see to your family. Too much has been lost already.'

'Aye, Jack,' Martin replied warily, 'it surely has.'

Jack was satisfied; he'd spoken his mind. 'Shall we walk back to the bridge, then?'

Martin nodded. Jack extended a hand, heaving him to his feet, and together they started along the street.

Word reached the engine room shortly after noon – Walter Noone had rooted out some more villains who'd hidden themselves among the workforce. Following some questioning in an empty chamber of the warehouse, their source reported, the watchman was about to expel them from the works. Martin's first thought upon hearing this was of Caroline. A cold cramp twitching in his stomach, he set down the spare piston ring he'd been cleaning and climbed up onto the workbench beneath the room's single narrow window, set high into the yard-facing wall.

The moment for the expulsion had been chosen carefully. The yard was full of operatives taking their dinner break with the usual clamour; all fell silent, however, as the front door to the warehouse opened and two men were pushed through it into the sunlight. Both were bleeding from the nose and mouth, their eyes closing fast under the weight of bright, bulging bruises. One of them was sobbing, cradling a shattered hand in the crook of his arm. Noone and a couple of his henchmen came behind, clad in their dark army-style uniforms, shoving the pair towards the main gate. Martin breathed a short, hard sigh of relief. There was no sign of his sister-in-law. She had not been caught, thank God. There was hope; they could still get the guns.

The straight-backed watchman looked over at the engine-room window, seeming to spot him there – and promptly reached out to seize the collars of his prisoners, bringing the little procession to a halt. 'How 'bout it then, Mr Quill?' he shouted, his stony features somehow expressing livid amusement. 'How 'bout it, sir?'

Martin realised that the chief engineer had got up onto the table beside him and was peering out through an adjacent pane. He'd been so lost in his fears for Caroline that he hadn't even noticed.

'Spies, these two, from the workshop of none other than Robert Adams,' Noone went on, speaking with mocking clarity. 'Here to jot down the details of the Colonel's machines and then wreak as much mischief upon them as they could. So please, Mr Quill – have I your permission to continue? Does their removal from the Colt Company meet with your approval?'

This was a crude reprisal for Quill's intervention in Martin's own case, which had obviously left a nick in Noone's pride. The stocky engineer was scowling, muttering oaths against the cracked, sooty glass of the window. His point made, the watchman slapped each of his captives about the head, prompting them to continue their shambling progress towards Ponsonby Street.

Martin jumped back down to the engine-room floor, sat on his stool and tried to return his attention to the piston ring. Despite his staggering fatigue, he'd lain awake throughout the previous night, turning the situation over in his mind. He'd considered fleeing with his family – going to Mr Quill and requesting an immediate transfer to Hartford, as Amy had begged him to – but soon saw that it would be futile. To leave London now was to make the Molly Maguires his sworn enemies. He honestly did not want this; and besides, he knew only too well what the consequences would be. The Hunger had scattered the Mollys far and wide. They were certainly in America, and in numbers. Were he to make it across the Atlantic, there'd surely be a gang of knife-wielding Tipperary boyos waiting for him on the docks at New York.

The simplest way out of it all, he'd concluded, was to go along with what Slattery had proposed; and at dawn he'd left Crocodile Court determined to double the tally of stolen Colts before the day was over. He'd cornered Caroline at the Bessborough Place gate, demanding to know the source of her mysterious revolvers so that he could lend his hand to their removal. She'd refused to tell him, saying that something was afoot – that Noone had got wind of wrongdoing and had every department of the works under a close watch. There was still little love lost between them; Martin knew that she even blamed him in part for Michael's death, in

212

fact, as it was due to him that the boy's short, fragile life had been spent amid the disease-ridden squalor of the Devil's Acre. He was sure that he'd detected a trace of pity in her, though, somewhere behind the knot of her frown, and this had irritated him enormously. She'd plainly thought that he, veteran of a hundred dangerous adventures, wasn't fit for a simple piece of burglary. He'd tried again, growing angry, repeating the lie about the debt, yet she would not budge – and now he saw that she'd been entirely in the right. Noone and his men would surely be at their most alert after an incident such as this, making any irregular movement about the works nigh-on impossible. Caroline was showing herself to be quite the thief; she had a clear instinct for it. Martin was honestly not surprised.

Mr Quill clambered down after him, shaking his head. 'What the devil is it with that fellow, eh, Mart? Why does he have to be such a confounded jackass?'

'I take it,' said Mr Ballou from over by the engine, raising his voice over its constant clank and hiss, 'that this Robert Adams is a rival gun-maker.'

Loren Ballou, 'Lou' to every Yankee in the works, was a neat, pale man, bearded and bespectacled, almost professorial in his manner despite his engineer's corduroys and leather apron. His accent was slightly different from the other Americans, softer somehow; Mr Quill had told Martin that he hailed from Kentucky rather than New York or Connecticut, and had cut his teeth laying the Kentuckian railroad. Now, though, he bore the lofty rank of general overseer, and was said to possess a complete knowledge of the Colt industrial process rivalled only by the Colonel himself. The Yankees certainly deferred to him on all matters. Even Mr Quill, better qualified perhaps on the specific workings of the London steam engine, listened very closely to Lou Ballou and allowed him to work alongside them in the engine room without a whisper of complaint. Their diligence had also increased markedly; drinks in the Spread Eagle had almost become a thing of the past.

Mr Quill leaned against the table, crossing his serpent-covered forearms. 'Robert Adams, Lou, is an Englishman based on the other side of the city, who sees the Colonel as the very nemesis of his trade. He makes this double-action five-shooter, y'see – a distinctly inferior device, if truth be told, but he hopes that the John Bull government will take it on for patriotic reasons. Things got rather hot between Colt and Adams back in the spring. There were a few rows in the streets hereabouts – nasty business. We did our part, didn't we, Mart?'

Martin said nothing. His head felt empty; his eyes were burning. He concentrated on the steel ring in his hands, rotating it slowly, looking for imperfections.

Mr Quill chuckled on regardless. 'Anyways, the Colonel didn't put up with it for, as I'm sure you can imagine. Noone put the whip-hand to 'em and they soon backed off.' He sighed, picking up a spanner from the table. 'But here they are having another try, and with a rather more sly tactic than beatings and suchlike. I'll wager they've heard about your arrival, Lou, and the great things that we three are bringing about in here. They know that Colt production is ready to soar up to the heavens, leaving them behind in a world of trouble!'

Ballou took this in impassively. He was never particularly impressed by Mr Quill's efforts to include Martin in their engineering accomplishments. 'I suppose that fighting off a determined rival will keep Mr Noone happy, at least,' he mused. 'It wouldn't do for the poor fellow to get *bored*.' The general overseer had known of Noone before he came to Pimlico. From what Martin could gather, the watchman's hiring had caused serious division among Colt's senior staff members back in Hartford. Why he could not discover; it was clear, though, that Ballou had been one of those who'd opposed the appointment. 'D'you think he's sent word to Jamie of this revived threat?'

'Aha, no,' Mr Quill replied, 'I think the Colonel's brother has some pressing personal matters to worry about of late. Besides, simply reaching him has become pretty difficult.'

The two Americans shared a laugh. Stories were going around of how James Colt had disgraced himself with the wife of a military figure he was supposed to be charming on behalf of the company. What exactly he had done was unknown, but it was bad enough to force a rapid retreat to a distant corner of the English countryside. There was a bitter edge to Quill and Ballou's amusement; like many among the American staff, they were starting to feel that the London factory was a rudderless ship, drifting aimlessly, failing to avail itself of some real opportunities. War with Russia had not arrived, but the word was being printed in every newspaper and journal in letters three inches high on an almost daily basis. This feverish climate, they said, was one in which a gun-maker could thrive. Yet there they sat, stagnating by the Thames, taking only small private orders; their enemies were resurgent, and showing new levels of deviousness; and their supposed captain was nowhere to be seen.

A flat clang made Martin jump and rock back on his stool. The piston ring had slipped from his grasp onto the brick floor. Some time had passed; he realised that he'd fallen asleep, and had been seeing Michael in his dreams, those little legs kicking up in the air – feeling the infant's pink fingers close so gently around his thumb. Mr Quill and Mr Ballou now stood together before the engine. The general overseer was examining the condenser; the chief engineer, alerted by the sound, was looking over at him. Martin bent down to retrieve the dropped ring, but it seemed to blur before him, blending in with the bricks. His eyes were brimming with tears. Hurriedly, he wiped them away; but more welled up immediately, one escaping the stroke of his sleeve and rolling across his face.

A hand was laid upon his shoulder. Mr Quill had come to his side. 'We're stepping out for a minute or two, Lou, me and Mart. Nothing to worry about.'

Ballou glanced around impatiently. 'But I may need your help, Ben, with the –'

'Damn it, Lou,' Quill snapped, 'I'll be gone a moment only. You can manage until then, I'm sure.'

Soon afterwards Martin was sitting against the factory wall in the still, dead heat of the afternoon, leaning against his knees and weeping hard, a hot, salty mixture of tears and snot running around his mouth and dripping off his chin. Mr Quill was beside him on the cobbles, one of his tattooed arms wrapped around Martin's shoulders, puffing stoically on his pipe.

'The first month is blackest torture, Mart,' he said. 'I'll not lie to you. It's like madness. After my Jenny was taken – scarlet fever, it was, at the age of three – I lost the winter of forty-two completely. Can't say where I was or what the hell I did. But when I did finally return home, my wife was gone, bless her, and my house sold on to a taxidermist named Bowley.' A curl of white smoke wound from the corner of his mouth. 'That's what first put me on the steamers, matter o' fact.'

Taking in a breath, Martin pulled up his shirt front and mopped his streaming face with it. 'I can't *sleep*, Mr Quill. I ain't had a bleedin' wink for days.'

The engineer nodded, as if this was to be expected. 'When was your last square meal?'

Martin couldn't say. He remembered something about whitebait, but they hadn't done that in the end, had they? He shook his head. 'My baby boy died because of me. Because of this bleedin' city, the filthy air, all the – the muck and the bleedin' dirt. I let him be born here, and by God I let him perish here.' He was growing restless once again. 'I've got to get us *out*.'

Mr Quill tightened his embrace. 'You are *not to blame*, you hear me? Christ, Mart, if only you knew – I thought the very same things myself, my friend, the *very same things*, but it just ain't so. Some souls are too pure for this Earth. Almighty God has to gather 'em in early.'

Martin's brow darkened; he shrugged the engineer off. 'Why does He choose to put them here in the first instance then, Mr Quill? Michael was but seven months old. What the devil does God get from putting us through this? My wife, my poor bleedin' wife can barely *stand*, she –' He stopped. This was unfair of him; he adopted a calmer tone. 'I'm sorry, I – I don't know why I . . .'

Mr Quill, who had coloured slightly, waved his apology

away. 'You're angry, Mart – I understand, believe me I do.' He knocked his pipe out against the wall and tucked it in his apron's front pocket. 'But look, you must think on this. One day not so far from now we'll leave this place, you and I, and your wife and little daughter as well, and we'll go over to America. All we need to do is really make our mark in this blasted factory and I'm certain the Colonel will agree to it. Another year, say – two at the most.'

Martin wiped his stinging eyes. This glorious escape to Connecticut could never come to pass. Even if the Mollys' plan went off perfectly, his involvement in it was sure to be detected. The safest place for the Rea family would be Ireland – Roscommon, most probably, with all its old miseries.

Quill could see that Martin hadn't gained any comfort from his words. 'You're wondering how the hell we're going to get anything done in this here pistol works when our manager is hiding away somewhere, and we make guns just so they can be stacked up in the goddamn stock room. Well, Mart, take heart – all of that is about to change. Word arrived this morning. We've been instructed to keep it to ourselves, but I can't see the harm in you knowing.' He hesitated, casting a quick glance about him. 'It's happening at long last. Colonel Colt is coming back to London.'

5

'*Colt!*' Sam roared as he burst through the doors of Mivart's Hotel. 'Colt is the name! Where the hell is he?'

The startled clerk did his best to halt the gun-maker's furious charge, but it was like setting pasteboard before a typhoon. 'It is against hotel policy to reveal such details,' he protested, 'and quite out of –'

'Mr James Colt.' Sam gripped the edge of the counter as if he was about to tear it free and use it to hammer the clerk into the floor. 'Directions to his room, right this instant – or by thunder I will see you removed from your post and tossed out into the street like so much goddamn garbage.'

James was installed on the top floor, of course, five storeys up; Sam was leaning heavily against the sumptuous mahogany banister by the time he reached it. Staggering on through the carpeted hush of the corridor, he beat his fist against his brother's door. Sam had sent no word of the precise time of his arrival in London to anyone, preferring as always to catch his people unawares; accordingly, James was most surprised to see him standing there, red-cheeked and panting with necktie loosened, his eyes starting out like black spikes from his head. The gun-maker pushed his brother aside and walked into the middle of a large, well-furnished sitting room, all rich drapery, polished sideboards and upholstered chairs, with a fine view of the copper and gold treetops of Berkeley Square. It was early evening, about five o'clock; coals glowed softly in a wide stone fireplace and a moulded gas fitting hissed away between the two large windows. The overall effect was one of elegant, costly comfort.

'What's this here, then,' he growled, his first words to his younger brother in nearly four years, 'the most expensive set of rooms in the hotel? In the entire goddamn *city*?'

He'd given James a few seconds to think since opening the door; the rascal had realised that there was to be a clash between them. Somewhere inside him he must surely have been expecting it. 'It is important, Sam,' he said now, as coolly as ever, 'to make a display of wealth. You know as well as I that no one at all will buy from a shabby or desperate-looking salesman.'

Sam spun around so hard that the thick rug on the floor bunched up beneath the heel of his boot. 'Oh, ain't you wise, all of a sudden! Ain't you the noble authority, the voice of goddamn experience! Desperate-looking indeed! How d'you think we look right now, Jamie? How d'you think *I* look after three months of your wondrous stewardship?' He shouted out a couple of oaths before putting a hand to his brow, trying to calm himself to the point where he was capable of normal speech. 'You tell me about Major Dyce's wife. I want to hear it from you, from your own lips.'

James stiffened defensively, the fatuous grin dropping from his face. He had a plump, well-rested look to him; his clothes were new and distinctly English in style. This fellow has been playing at being a London dandy these past weeks, Sam thought, and on the Colt Company's dime. 'Then let me say that I was not at fault – not at fault at all. Major Dyce is a jealous lunatic, Sam. I've crossed his sort before, back in St Louis – they can't bear the sight of anyone they don't know so much as *talking* to their wives. And I was talking only. I swear it on Mother's grave.'

Sam was not convinced. '*Improper attention* is what I heard, you unmannerly dogger, which I take to mean that you were making your oily advances on this woman before a roomful of people – whose number just happened to include not only her goddamn husband but also several of his close friends from the Woolwich Arsenal! The *Woolwich Arsenal*, Jamie! What in Christ's name is wrong with you?'

His brother was smiling bitterly, shaking his head. 'Well, you may have heard that, Sam, but it was not the case. I merely took Amelia through to the garden for –'

'*Amelia*, is it? Lord God Almighty!' Sam considered crossing the room and giving James the resounding slap he so deserved, as he would have done in their youth; but instead he just cursed some more and looked about for a drink. Several decanters were arranged upon a corner table. He went over and poured himself three fingers of bourbon. 'What of the works?'

James followed him, affecting concern. 'You look worn right out, Sam. How long have you been back in London?'

The gun-maker drank down his liquor in one swallow. This was a fairly transparent bit of evasion. He didn't feel that it deserved a reply.

'You must tell me how things are in Hartford,' James tried next. 'Did you see Father? Or Miss Jarvis?'

Sam had forgotten that James knew about his engagement. It vexed him to be reminded of this. 'I saw 'em both.'

James reached for the whiskey decanter, knocked a little by this terse reply; his older brother's tone had left no doubt that nothing more was forthcoming. He was visibly wracking his flabby brain for another topic. 'And what of the dyke?' he asked at last.

'It's going ahead, full steam. Those self-appointed bores could not stand against me. The South Meadow will be drained and the Hartford factory will be extended. It's already well underway, in fact.'

'I knew it.' James was grinning again. 'I knew you would prevail, Sam. You always do.'

That was it. The boundary had been crossed. Sam slammed down his glass. 'Do I now, Jamie? Do I *really*?' he yelled. 'What of my slogan, then, painted so boldly across the roof of the London works so that every ship passing down the mighty Thames would see it? What of my *slogan*, you worthless son of a bitch? Have I *prevailed* there, would you say?'

James blanched. He replaced the whiskey on the table without pouring himself any. 'That was . . . unfortunate,

I'll admit. But you didn't hear the case that was made against us. Lady Wardell and her –'

'You gave in to that harpy? That John Bull bitch so puffed up with her own righteous authority over the rest of us – professional men just trying to turn a bit of business?'

'There were others with her, Sam,' James came back weakly, 'a Mr Cubitt, for one, who accused us of bringing down his neighbourhood, and –'

'Cubitt's a blasted *builder*, that's all, a fellow with a ser-iously overblown sense of his own importance. He ain't nothing to us. That there slogan was a prime piece of ballyhoo – one that I'll struggle to replicate.' Sam walked to a window. 'And you've barely been in the city since, I hear – after you'd mortally offended half the goddamn British army, that is.'

His brother frowned, as if affronted by this suggestion of negligence on his part. 'Who told you that?'

'I've already been out to Pimlico. I've talked to the foreman, the overseers, the engineers. They gave me a full account of your tenure as manager, if it can rightly be so described. Did you honestly not realise?'

James swallowed. 'Everyone of quality leaves the city during the summer. There was quite literally no one useful left for me to talk with.'

'Horseshit,' Sam declared. 'What about Lawrence Street?'

The name elicited only a blank look. 'I'm afraid you'll have to –'

Sam plucked a vase of dried flowers from a shelf and hurled it into the fireplace. It broke apart in a puff of dust and old pollen, scattering brittle purple blooms across the hearth. James's instructions regarding Street had been plain to the point of bluntness. It had been stressed in several letters that the fellow was possibly the most important man in all London for the Colt Company. For a weapons manu-facturer, Sam had written, politicians were the real prize, of more worth than any number of soldiers or ordnance offi-cials. Yet James had failed him here as well. Sam glared into the fire, the energy draining out of him.

'This is my own doing, I suppose,' he admitted. 'I should've known that you'd be useless for a delicate piece of work like this – Christ, way *worse* than useless.'

There was a creak off to his left. Sam looked around to see that the door to one of the apartment's adjoining rooms was open just a crack; an eye withdrew from it swiftly, and a pair of dainty feet danced away across the floorboards.

The gun-maker stared at James in disbelief. 'Tell me you ain't bringing back whores to a place like this.'

'She ain't no whore, Sam. That's –'

'By Heavens, Jamie, you really are dumb as a pile of goddamn rocks.' Sam paced over to his brother, stopping only when their faces were a few inches apart. The idiot had to be dispensed with before he could do any more damage. 'You listen to me, and you listen well. Keep away from Bessborough Place from now on. Don't even think of showing yourself there, nor over at the sales office neither. D'you hear me?'

James's expression, clearly intended as a wry, defiant smile, came out half-cocked; he seemed almost on the verge of tears. 'Are – are you ordering me back to America, Sam? Is this how it is to end?'

Sam started for the hotel corridor. 'I don't give a good goddamn where you go, Jamie,' he replied, without looking back. 'Just keep the hell away from my factory.'

The left paddle-wheel began to reverse, sending black smoke belching from the steamer's single chimney as the vessel turned against the current of the river. There was a sudden retreat of passengers from the rail as a gush of noxious foam splattered up the side of the hull; Sam watched a leathery turd the size of a brick arc through the evening air and slap wetly against the deck planks. The dank stone arches of London Bridge passed overhead, and the long double row of stationary traffic that stood forever stranded upon it came into view, hooting and whistling in useless complaint. Off across the Thames, a short distance downriver, stood the battlements of the Tower, with that pale, pepperpot fortress rising in its centre. Sam gave this ancient stronghold a moment's contemplation, gazing out across the greenish waters and the boats that swarmed about them. That was where his state-of-the-art firearms were being sent to be subjected to the indignity of government tests – to be picked over by hare-brained British smiths and branded with crowns and suchlike, as if they belonged to Queen Victoria rather than Samuel Colt, their inventor and manufacturer. He couldn't help but resent it.

On the other side of the vessel, along the river's southern bank, stretched a row of plain brown buildings, warehouses and tanning shops from the look of them. The top hats pressed in around Sam began to stir; newspapers were being folded tightly and stowed under arms. These were the men of modern London, departing their workplaces at the day's end to ride locomotives back out to suburbs and villages, and they were preparing to fight their way onto the shore – to barge aside their fellows so that they could catch that train, win their preferred seat in the carriage, secure themselves a few more minutes of precious rest. The crowd jostling upon the wharf seemed a mirror image of the one on the deck of the steamer; Sam almost expected to see his own smart blue coat reflected among the wall of black. He carved a path through them without difficulty, leaving the quayside and starting along Tooley Street, a busy avenue of shops of the more modest, practical variety.

The place he sought was in an alley about fifty yards down. Its frontage was humble enough; it could have been the premises of a carter, or perhaps an undistinguished instrument maker. Only the revolving pistol rendered upon the sign – a double-action model, lacking a hammer, drawn with expert precision – gave any indication of what went on within. He went through the door without announcing himself. The interior was no more impressive. It reminded Sam of his own very first pistol manufacturing venture, in fact, which he'd set up in a Hartford attic more than ten years earlier. The tables were fitted out with crude clamps and pedal-drills – *pedal-drills*, for Christ's sake! Small wonder that the son of a bitch's guns didn't shoot straight!

Sam's timing was good; the bulk of the workforce had already retired for the day. Only one other person was in there, a skinny boy who had been sweeping the floor and was now gaping at him in obvious recognition. Without daring to utter a word, he gave his forelock a tug, dropped his broom and rushed up an open wooden staircase set against the far wall. Left alone for a moment, Sam took the chance to make a closer study of the main shop. Over in a far corner stood several huge crates, of the sort used to transport pieces of steam-driven machinery. He was walking over to them, thinking to look for a maker's stamp, when he noticed that an internal wall had recently been demolished and the area beyond cleared. The meaning of all this was plain. Mr Robert Adams of London Bridge was planning an expansion.

'Colonel Colt,' declared a slow voice, marked with a rustic-sounding burr. 'An unexpected pleasure.'

Sam turned; a stout, long-nosed man in sober clothes was descending the stairs: his English competitor, in the flesh. The fellow looked like an apple farmer in a borrowed coat – a simple soul ill suited to the vigorous cut and thrust of the armaments business – but Sam knew from experience that this impression was deceptive.

'Mr Adams,' he replied with a civil nod. 'How long has it been? Two years, ain't it – that test at Woolwich?'

Adams stopped three feet from the bottom of the staircase. 'I'd invite you up to my office,' he said, ignoring Sam's question, 'but I'm afraid that I have none at present. The company of Deane, Adams & Deane is undergoing a few changes.'

'I can see that, Mr Adams.' Sam nodded towards the crates. 'What are these, chucking lathes? Drop-hammers, perhaps? Are we mechanising at last?'

A scoundrelly smile twitched at his rival's face. 'We must remain competitive, Colonel, must we not?'

'Indeed you must, Mr Adams,' Sam answered, marvelling at the fellow's shamelessness, 'indeed you must. Now, as you might know, I have only recently returned to your delightful city after a stay in America. Imagine my dismay when my watchman told me that over the summer he was obliged to weed out a couple of your employees from my factory floor – *spies*, Mr Adams, who'd burrowed their way into my works like ticks, with the intention of copying my machine designs and committing acts of sabotage.'

Adams was shaking his head in flat denial.

'I've come down here as an act of courtesy,' Sam continued, strolling off between the tables, 'one gun man to another, to give you the chance to explain yourself. There was some trouble between our people back in the spring, I believe – but that had reached a natural resolution. Why the devil are you setting your sights on me again?'

'Colonel Colt,' Adams came back, cool as a cucumber, 'I don't know how things are done in America, but an Englishman would blush to come to another's place of business and make such wild allegations. What proof do you have that these villains were in my employ? You're prepared to take them at their word, are you?'

'My watchman found 'em convincing enough.'

Adams shook his head again. 'Nay, sir – this is a common enough circumstance in London, believe me. They were but thieves, throwing my name out either to keep your torturers at bay or to stir up a bit of trouble as revenge for their capture. That's all it was.'

Sam grinned up at him. A rehearsed answer, plainly – the devious bastard had been ready for this. 'You're quite right, Mr Adams. I have no proof at all that you sent 'em. But you should know that I am now in a position to bankrupt you utterly – to have you run out of this cosy little shop into the goddamn street. You no doubt think of the competition between us as a sort of David-meets-Goliath situation from which you'll eventually emerge the plucky victor. That, sadly, just ain't the case. My machines are going full pelt, with a thirty-horse engine behind 'em. Fifty Colt pistols a day will very soon be a reality.'

To Sam's satisfaction, Adams squirmed ever so slightly as he listened to this. Like all accomplished liars, he knew the truth when he heard it.

'Here's what I propose. Keep things between us on the level from now on – no more beatings, or spies – and I'll give serious thought to buying you out while your firm is still worth something.'

'On the level, you say?' Adams remained composed, but a blotch of angry red had broken across his cheek. 'Since you came to London, Colonel Colt, several of my men have vanished – vanished into thin bloody air. Can you explain that, sir, given that you are so very much *on the level*?'

Sam narrowed his eyes; he didn't know what the fellow was on about. 'Perhaps they saw better opportunities elsewhere, in a company with a more stable future.'

'You can take your condescending offers,' Adams pronounced firmly, 'and feed them to the cat. I will meet you, sir, on the field of commerce. Don't you be doing me any special favours. You might have your hundreds of men and great rows of machinery, but I have my friends; I have the national interest; and I have a superior weapon.'

'Do you now?' Sam couldn't help laughing at the Englishman's nonsensical pride. 'A *superior weapon*, Mr Adams? Is that so?'

'It is. There can be no agreement between us, Colonel Colt.'

'Ah well,' Sam sighed, 'you're correct there, at least. In my heart, I knew it all along.' He made for the shop door, fishing out his screw of Old Red and opening up his clasp-knife. 'Interesting times ahead, Mr Adams. Interesting times indeed.'

First had been the oysters, great platters of New York natives shipped over live in barrels of brine and served raw, stewed and fried. Then came the terrapin soup, so devilish spicy it made your nose run; then American pork and beans, baked in the Yankee style; then, to applause, a pair of enormous American turkeys, their skin roasted to a rich golden hue; then a healthy round of rare American beef, so much more tender and flavoursome than the grey, stringy British stuff on which John Bull placed such unwarranted value. And finally, when all were at the point of gastronomic exhaustion, there had been half a dozen glazed, canvas-backed ducks, which Sam had permitted to be carried on with the sweets in the usual English fashion.

The diners lounged in poses of satiety, rubbing their bulging bellies and picking at the few morsels that remained on their plates. The air above them swam with the smoke from costly cigars, ordered by Sam to be brought in their boxes from the divan downstairs. The table before them was strewn with the wreckage of their feast; the turkeys' forlorn-looking carcasses, torn asunder by hands unschooled in polite manners; various bones, half-eaten potatoes and slicks of soup and gravy; the many ale pots carried up to cater to palettes unsympathetic to wine. Early on, Sam had instructed the waiters to hang back, so that they were not constantly underfoot, clearing things away.

'We are but simple fellows, y'see,' he'd explained, 'mechanics and suchlike, and we'd rather the dishes were left until we're quite finished with 'em.'

This had been understood immediately, the staff becoming all but invisible. It was a fine, accommodating place, this Royal Divan; they'd set up Sam's Yankee banquet with professional thoroughness, attending to every one of his very particular requests. Only a short stroll up Piccadilly from his own rooms, the Royal sat in the middle of an imposing row opposite the iron railings of Green Park. It was damn expensive, of course, and far better than his men were accustomed to. Their attempts at gentlemanly dress – odd combinations of cheap dandy garb and moth-eaten Sunday best – demonstrated this clearly enough, and were a comical sight indeed for any discerning eye. But that night was a special celebration, both of Sam's return to England and of the significant advances made by Messrs Quill and Ballou in his absence. He wanted to treat them, to unite them in comradeship – and to reaffirm their loyalties to the Colt Company after a summer under James. The gun-maker looked around the table. All were there, from engineers to fitters, and all were taking advantage of his generosity in the intended manner. Mr Noone and his lieutenants, in particular, were tipping back whiskey like they were engaged in some kind of contest. It's going pretty goddamn well, thought their employer; then his gaze reached the figure of his London secretary, who sat a few places to his left, and his satisfaction diminished somewhat.

The word to describe Mr Lowry that evening was *contained*. This could hardly be attributed to some innate British reserve, brought out by the very American character of the gathering – good old Alfie Richards, his countryman, was in the thick of things, waging a heated debate about horse-racing with a couple of the polishers, gesticulating wildly with a well-gnawed duck drumstick. No, a definite change had come over his secretary during the summer months. The boy had handled the European letters with prompt discretion, it was true, but he seemed guarded, lacking in spirit. Sam was inclined to attribute this to his experiences under Jamie – to having watched his block-headed, profligate brother squander so much of what they'd accomplished in the spring. Since his return, Sam and Mr Lowry hadn't spent more than a couple of hours together. The gun-maker decided that they would have a private word before he left the dinner, to restore some of the confidence that had existed between them and perhaps get an idea of what was amiss. This was a man he'd once thought of as a potential manager, after all; it would be a crying shame if the London secretary was permanently dulled and had to be cut loose.

Collecting himself, Sam put in a new wad of Old Red, refreshed his bourbon from the bottle beside his plate and got to his feet. A hush fell, and every head turned his way. 'I thank you, my friends,' he began, 'for joining me here this night to partake in what I believe you'll agree was some superfine Yankee cuisine . . .'

Their cheers were so loud that he was obliged to stop. The twenty-five men rattled spoons inside tankards, whistled and whooped; Alfie Richards shouted *'Bravo!'* like he was giving an ovation at the close of a grand opera. After a minute or so of this, Sam gestured for quiet.

'I wish to express my earnest thanks to the two gentlemen seated over there on my right, Mr Loren Ballou and Mr Benjamin Quill. I owe them both a great debt, and it is in their honour that I have thrown this little gam. Without their noble and learned efforts, our fearsome son of a bitch of a factory would not have half the goddamn poke that she does at this present time.'

They erupted again, pelting the engineers with cigar ends, corks and anything else that came to hand. Quill's beam split his red face in two; he waved those tattooed arms of his around to deflect the rain of missiles, swearing good-humouredly at his attackers. Ballou was less impressed, recoiling slightly from the barrage, wincing as the bright orange beak from one of the ducks bounced off his dome-like forehead.

'I have often had cause, my friends, to remember something that my mother once told me when I was but a tiny infant. It is better to be at the head of a louse, she said, than at the tail of a lion. I have always held this close to my heart. I have taken charge of *every stage* of my life, and would advise any other man here to do the same. I have struggled – by God, have I struggled – to keep myself free from any arrangement that would have me beholden to governments, or kings, or boards of goddamn directors.' Sam paused, taking a good chew of his tobacco, savouring the earnest respect that emanated from the table. 'As I stood in those brick barns by the river yesterday morning, looking over what these two fine men here have done – Christ Almighty, what every one of you has done – to make my bold plan real, I found myself reconsidering Ma Colt's old saying. It is better to be at the head of a louse, for certain – but you fellows have placed me at the head of a goddamn lion. And I drink to you all.'

The gun-maker lifted up his glass in a salute, swallowing the contents in one gulp. His men did the same, and their empty cups and glasses banged down upon the table in a ragged but enthusiastic percussion.

'Now, my lads, I know that the summer has not been easy, for one very obvious reason. But I'm back now. Soon we will start to really do things, all of us – to show John Bull what Yankee boys are capable of when we set our minds to an object.'

The men exchanged grins and refilled their glasses in expectation of the next toast. Sam straightened his coat and spat some juice on the floor beside him. It was time for the real news.

'Things are afoot on the fringes of Europe,' he declared. 'I won't bore away your merriment with the details, but Turkey has demanded that Russia retreat double-quick from the Principalities – from the lands she has occupied. I have it on good authority that the Russians will not go along with this demand. Their Tsar, on his throne now for thirty years, considers himself appointed by God Himself and thus beyond all error. Such is the folly of the old world, my friends. Be damn glad that you are free of it.' He picked up the bourbon bottle, drawing out the cork, pouring as he spoke. 'As I'm sure you already know, our British hosts have committed themselves to aiding Turkey. Gunboats have sailed for Constantinople, and there are voices in their cabinet calling loudly for action. It is underway. The hammer is falling, and nothing can stop it. War is coming – war at last.'

They cheered again, even more loudly than before, throwing back their heads and baying like mountain apes.

'War, of course, is a very terrible thing,' Sam went on with mock gravity, drawing a wicked laugh from the company, 'and it brings misfortune to millions. But to a few, to men like us, it brings incredible opportunity. We are well placed here in London. These old Bull generals will be looking out for weapons that will give their troops a real advantage – of course they will. And what could be better than the very latest model of Colonel Colt's six-shooting Navy revolver, the best goddamn peacemaker on God's green earth, expertly manufactured on their own goddamn doorstep?'

Mr Quill rose unsteadily from his chair, raising a black beer bottle so high that it sounded a tolling note against the brass chandelier above his head. The others began to follow his example, and within ten seconds all were standing with their drinks held aloft.

'To war in Europe, gentlemen,' Sam bellowed, 'and the Colt arms that will surely be bought to fight it!'

6

Edward was the first to return to his seat. He set down his port glass. Richards had filled it to the brim but he'd been unable to take so much as a sip. He felt nauseous, a sour redolence of the procession of rich, meaty dishes he had eaten, of the various wines and spirits he had drunk, coating the back of his throat like silt in a drain. Pushing his chair away from the table, he rested his elbows on his knees and put his throbbing head in his hands, trying to order his thoughts.

Cousin Arthur would be sent to fight against the Russians. This seemed almost certain now. Edward could not drink a toast to this, and was finding all the brash jollity around him difficult to bear. There could be no escaping the fact that as a Colt man he was involved in the coming war – but in an entirely cynical, opportunistic way. The secretary felt something close to guilt, and cursed his wretchedly illogical, contradictory nature. What the devil did you think this enterprise was building towards, he asked himself – the factory, the machines, the meetings with government officials? What conceivable purpose did you think those thousands of firearms would serve, if not this?

The month before, rather reluctantly, Edward had sent Arthur the pair of Navys he'd requested. He'd reasoned that they would help to keep his eager young cousin safe, and could prove vital in fending off the enemy. Arthur's letter of thanks, however, had openly extolled the revolvers' offensive potential, stating that they would surely enable him to perform yet greater feats of daring on the battlefield and thus guarantee him a lion's share of glory. The lieutenant was absolutely determined to be at the forefront of any action, in the fiercest fighting. That he had appeared to give such recklessness his tacit support brought Edward deep disquiet.

Colonel Colt had started off again. He was predicting that the cavalry would be the first to take his pistols, followed by the guards' regiments maybe, and then the rest; adding that he was also secretly confident of interest from the London police, who he thought could be convinced to buy a few ten thousands. 'Who knows, my lads, p'raps such a purchase would bring some actual *order* to this goddamn city, eh?' There was another burst of laughter and the clink of glasses.

Richards flopped into the chair beside Edward's, throwing a long arm over its back. 'Are you quite all right, Lowry?' he inquired. 'Only I must say that you look to me like a chap who's about to reconsider his supper, if you catch my meaning. It's a look I happen to know rather well.'

The press agent was enjoying their American feast immensely. There was a decanter of good port at his elbow and a fat, fresh cigar between his teeth – neither of which had cost him a farthing – and he was in a lively company to whom he owed no money whatsoever. He looked well, relatively speaking at least; he'd managed to shave and find a clean coat, and his face bore only a single modest lesion, just below the left eye. His wife had permitted him back into the marital home after a month of exile, which he'd passed mostly in a cheap boarding house in Euston. This reunion with his Mabel, as well as an equally significant reunion with Samuel Colt a few weeks after that, had served to restore him to an approximation of his normal self.

They had spoken of the incident in the coffee house only once. Richards had sloped into the factory office and casually informed Edward that the man he'd shot was reported to be on the road to recovery. The fellow wouldn't be contacting the police over the matter either, the press agent had revealed, as he had some pretty compelling reasons of his own for wanting to keep it quiet. And that was all he had to say. He treated Edward rather less acidly than previously, but in every other respect seemed to have put the shooting completely from his mind.

Edward could not do this. He'd witnessed the result of a moment's drunken stupidity with a revolver, and had seen the profound fear that the weapon could inspire. He often found himself imagining how much worse it could have been – how many innocent lives might have been claimed by Richards's haphazard blasting. Yet an inevitable consequence of their work, of the factory at Pimlico, would be to make many more of these guns available to the people of London. And mass-produced Colt revolvers, as he knew only too well, were among the cheapest firearms ever made.

Richards studied Edward for a second or two. 'Nothing has actually *happened*, y'know,' he said, leaning towards him in confidence. 'We're all cheering this bloody war, but it's quite probable that it won't even be fought. I needn't tell you what diplomacy is like. The Turks may still be talked down; the Russians may lose the stomach for it. In a way, it is the perfect situation. The Army will buy to ensure that they are ready to fight, yet the odds are good that they won't have to – so we acquire our contracts, make our money and no blood is spilled.' He nodded at Colt, who had concluded his speech, retaken his seat and was applying himself single-mindedly to his bourbon. 'Old Samuel there wants to make the most of it that he can, naturally, and talk up Great Britain's imminent war to anyone who'll listen. But talk is all it is.'

'I suppose so,' Edward muttered doubtfully, rather annoyed that his discomfort with the Colonel's speech was so obvious.

The press agent slapped him on the shoulder. 'That's the spirit, old boy! You must think of your work for these Americans as an *indirect path* to your patriotic duty. The Colonel's guns are the very bloody best, and will certainly speed along a British victory.' He sucked on his cigar for a moment, remembering what he had just asserted. '*If* we fight, that is, which I think is rather unlikely.'

Before Richards could add anything more, someone across the table with whom he'd been arguing earlier about an obscure point of horse-racing issued a new challenge to him on the subject of fetlocks, and he leapt back happily into the fray.

A summons from the other side of the dining room made Edward's head snap up with instinctive obedience. Colonel Colt stood in the doorway; seeing that he had his secretary's attention, he nodded towards the corridor, indicating a wish for a private conference. On his feet at once, Edward skirted the dining table, drawing some unfriendly glances from the American staff. One of Noone's men, feigning inadvertence, slid his chair back into the secretary's path. Edward side-stepped it coolly and strode from the room.

The Colonel was at the top of the staircase, blocking it with his bulk, shifting the tobacco plug in his cheek around with his tongue. He looked a little heavier, as if he'd eaten rather well during his sojourn in Connecticut and the long weeks at sea, but those small, hard eyes still shone with purposeful energy. Having settled the business of the Hartford dyke to his satisfaction, it was plain that Colt was now focused entirely upon setting right Jamie's neglectful reign and putting his London works back on course.

Edward went before him and awaited his instructions. There had been an unmistakable distance between them since Colt's return. He was worried that in his conflicted state he might have worn his qualms a little too openly. The Colonel was capable of singular perspicacity, and might well have realised that his secretary's commitment to the goals of the Colt Company had taken several hard knocks during his absence. Edward had resolved to address this, to show that he remained an effective employee – a professional man before all else. Losing favour with Colonel Colt would help nothing.

'I've got us back in with Lawrence Street,' the Colonel announced flatly. 'Didn't take much, in truth. He could see that James's thick-headedness was his own – and not any wider reflection on the rest of us. He's trying to win me some time with his master, this Lord Palmerston.'

Edward nodded, attempting to unravel the various possible meanings here. Colt's brusque manner seemed to contain an implicit criticism of his failure to keep Street content while he was in America. At the same time, though, he found that he was flattered to be told of this latest development – to have such privileged information shared with him. He felt a stirring of that old excitement, that sense of limitless possibility; and the doubts that had been troubling him during the meal faded from his mind.

'I will ensure that we are ready,' he said.

Colt contemplated him for a second, as if reaching some unknowable conclusion, and then turned towards the stairs.

'You are leaving us, Colonel?' Edward asked in surprise.

'Never have more than a couple of drinks with your people, Mr Lowry,' the gun-maker replied as he started to descend. 'That there's a basic rule of business. A fellow might wind up making promises and declarations that he'd later regret.'

Back in the spring Edward had seen Colt the worse for drink on several occasions. Was he being paid an oblique compliment here – was the Colonel suggesting that he was more than merely another subordinate? Or had he simply forgotten?

'Besides,' the gun-maker added, 'I have someone to see – a soldier my idiot brother managed to offend.'

Edward moved to the edge of the staircase. 'Shall I accompany you?'

'No, Mr Lowry,' Colt said curtly, not looking back, 'that won't be necessary. You get in there and enjoy the damn dinner. I'll see you in the morning.'

And with that he thundered down to the room below. Edward remained on the landing for a few seconds, staring in confusion at the red and green pattern on the rug beneath his boots. He'd just been tested, he was sure of it – drawn in and pushed away at the same time, a tactic intended to knock him off balance. Although undeniably pleased that he'd retained his place at Colonel Colt's side, he was also ashamed at the speed with which his misgivings about the war and everything else had left his thoughts – at how pathetically eager he still was to do the Colonel's bidding. Shaking

235

his head, he went back to the dining room, wishing he hadn't drunk quite so much port.

A debate was underway around the table.

'Who would've thought it, eh, Ben?' Walter Noone was calling out to Mr Quill. 'A fourth-generation Yankee boy like you angling for the custom of the goddamn *redcoats*! Your own father, I believe, fought these John Bull cocksuckers on the streets of Baltimore, and saw the flames rage after they'd put Washington to the torch. What would he say to the work you're doing now? He'd be so goddamn proud of you, wouldn't he?'

Mr Quill's voluble good humour, a constant feature of the gathering, quickly subsided. Edward had heard that there was a problem of some kind between these two men, but knew no more than this. He went back round to his seat as swiftly and unobtrusively as he could.

'That was many years back, Walt,' the engineer replied, wiping ale-froth from his top lip. 'All this here is just business. The Colonel's business.'

'If I may, gentlemen,' Richards interjected, 'speaking as one of Mr Noone's *John Bull cocksuckers*, there is a phrase that our Colonel uses a good deal to express the fellow feeling that should now rightly exist between our two lands. He describes an *Anglo-Saxon bond* – a bond that places the friendship of Great Britain and America in the utmost rank of international alliances. And there is a truth in it, is there not? I think, at any rate, that our two countries have certainly fought their last war.'

'Don't speak too soon now, Mr Richards,' drawled Noone, to the amusement of his men.

'Tell me, Mr Noone,' spoke up the other engineer, the bespectacled man called Lou Ballou, 'how valuable do repeating arms actually prove on the field of battle? Forgive my directness, friend, but I believe you are the only person here who knows from first-hand experience.'

Edward couldn't tell if Ballou was asking this question to move the conversation on and thus rescue Quill from Noone, or because he wanted to know the answer. Either way, it immediately won them both the undivided attention of the room.

'S'alright, Lou,' replied Noone a little warily, sipping his drink. He shifted in his chair, preparing to reply. Without his military-style cap he looked considerably older, with tufts of spiky white hair sticking up around a bald pate; but that weathered rock of a face was as formidable as ever. 'They were beyond all worth. Plain as that. My six-shooters saved this sinner's hide on more occasions than I can remember. I owe my life to Sam Colt, and I've told him as much.'

Noone's sneering attack on Mr Quill had split the company; a number of them had family who'd fought in the war of 1812, and the War of Independence before that, and resented his suggestion that they were being disloyal to their ancestors. But this simple statement of loyalty, of indebtedness to their chief, earned the watchman a murmur of unequivocal approval.

'There was this one time down in Mexico,' Noone continued, warming to his subject, 'during the taking of Monterrey. My company was sent to the western quarter of the town, away from the main advance. We were in the second wave, and it seemed that the fun was pretty much at an end. The Mexicans were a worthless foe, cowardly and badly trained – but they knew how to stage a goddamn trap. Me and two of my corporals were sent to scout out this little square, just three rows of their mud houses thrown up around a whitewashed church, a real spot of nothing. Anyways, some genius in the 10th Infantry decided to start a fire somewhere, and fires in Mexico spread damn fast. Before we knew it there was smoke all about, and these great jumping flames too, the whole place hot as Satan's hoof. Right away we're severed from the rest of the company. This barn door opens across the square from us – Mexicans, ten of the motherfuckers, muskets ready in their shoulders like a goddamn firing squad. That's it, thinks my two corporals, we're finished. One of 'em started to damn well *pray*, right then and there. Shaming, it was.'

Noone paused, a cigar smouldering unsmoked between his fingers. No one made a sound, the entire room willing him to continue. Then, slowly, the curved line at the left side of the watchman's mouth deepened, twisting his top lip; for Walter Noone, Edward realised, this was a smile.

'I had my Colt Dragoons at my belt, a fine pair of 'em, loaded and set to go. Five of the Mexicans were back with God afore the dumb bastards even realised what the Drags were. The rest didn't even bother to fire, just turned and ran like cats from a goddamn skinning shop. Them grey Mex uniforms made for some easy shooting, though – I brought down three more of the cocksuckers as they tried to get away.'

Abruptly, the watchman looked up, his eyes going straight to someone at the back of the party. Edward followed the direction of this stare; it was fixed on Martin Rea, Caroline Knox's devious brother-in-law, who was sitting away in a corner of the room, behind the ample form of the chief engineer. The Irish plotter had been keeping a low profile – so much so, in fact, that the secretary hadn't even noticed him before that moment.

'This was the thing, y'see,' Noone said loudly, grinding out his cigar. 'In a practised hand the Drag could take down men so quick it was like they were all falling at once. Up in California after the war, when I was with the 1st Cavalry, I got myself known for being able to shoot Pomo braves clear out of their saddles – three, four of 'em from one cylinder. And this is me on horseback too.'

The room remained admiring, by and large, the Colt men raising eyebrows at this feat of gunplay; someone said that Indians were savage bastards and often gave you no choice but to reach for your gun.

'This is the power that the revolving pistol gives a man,' Noone continued, his eyes still on Rea. 'Christ, with a Colt Drag in each hand you could ride into a ring of their teepees and put a bullet in *everything*, more or less – the old crones hunched around their fires, the crazy squaws that charged out at you with those tiny goddamn axes, even the little ones as they scattered into the brush.'

There was a short silence. A couple of Noone's men guffawed. The rest of the party stirred uncomfortably as if struck by a simultaneous bout of indigestion.

'Good Lord,' murmured Mr Quill.

'Oh yes, we did their children in my unit. Some men wouldn't but I had no trouble with it at all. They're all just goddamn vermin to me, I said, at the end of the day. Leave the dirt-worshipping heathens to grow and in ten years' time they'll just be coming at you like the rest, creeping into Christian houses to scalp us in our beds. Best just to get 'em at the start, I said, and plenty agreed with me.'

Heads were shaking now, and brows furrowing with disapproval, even as Noone and his men knocked their whiskey glasses together in hearty camaraderie. Edward couldn't be sure of what was going on here. Were these foul boasts true? Was this butchering past the reason that the watchman had such a dark reputation – why his appointment had caused the Colonel so much difficulty? Or were they a fabrication, part of a distasteful, pitch-black Yankee joke – their liking for 'tall tales', of which he had been warned by Saul Graff when he started at Colt back in the spring? And also, regardless of their veracity, why was Noone directing them so pointedly at Martin Rea?

'I did have my limits, though. I knew this one moon-struck cocksucker, a sergeant he was, who took pleasure from gunning babes from their mothers' arms. This I would not do. I told him: I will not shoot anything that cannot walk unaided.' Noone stopped to take a drink. 'No, in my unit we just brought down all the others and left 'em for the goddamn wolves.'

A chair was propelled violently backwards, tumbling to the floor. The Irishman was up and storming from the room, his face contorted with fury. Noone's men laughed at him, rocking in their seats. Mr Quill got to his feet, directing a disgusted look their way as he followed his assistant onto the stairs.

Suddenly, Edward saw that the purpose of Noone's stories had been blunt intimidation. He'd uncovered Rea's shady scheme somehow and was trying to panic the engineer's assistant, to scare him into revealing himself. A cruel game was underway.

One inescapable thought now filled Edward's mind: Caroline Knox, as a party to the Irishmen's plan, was surely in the gravest danger. The fragile pretence of indifference that he'd worked so hard to maintain since the summer collapsed at once. He had to warn her.

7

By the end of the day the women of the packing room were always very eager to be out of the Colt works, making it easy indeed for Caroline to slip away from them unnoticed. As they all left the warehouse she stopped in the semicircle of gaslight around the doorway, pretending to refasten her bonnet, letting them continue without her; and then, when they were off, heading determinedly across the yard, towards the lamps of Bessborough Place, she slid into the lake of shadow that pooled around the left side of the building.

Every single part of this thievery was utterly terrifying. The empty winter darkness; the echoing stone that could betray you with just one misplaced step; the ceaseless squeak, scrape and rummage of rats down in the cellars; the sickening fear of discovery and capture, of being at the mercy of of Walter Noone and his gang. But Caroline found that she actually looked forward to it, as you might to a ride on a sledge down a steep, icy hill – that she was frustrated when it could not be done and regarded her tally of stolen guns (three off with the Irish now, and one more ready to be handed over) with furtive pride. With the fear came a tingling flood of energy. Chancing everything like this, turning away for just a few minutes from the dull path that had otherwise been allotted to her, made Caroline feel properly aware of herself, properly *awake*, for perhaps the first time in her entire life.

Nothing had been taken for almost two months. What with the Adams spies, and then the return of the Colonel, the watch upon them all had simply been too close. That evening, however, an opportunity had presented itself. There had been a lavish celebration the night before, thrown by Colonel Colt for his American employees in an upmarket dining room – a right buster of a meal, it was being said, with enough liquor on hand to float a coal barge. The result of this was that none of the Yankees were at their best. Up in the packing room a grey-faced Mr Churn had barely been able to keep himself from his vomit-pail for long enough to count their crates. A good number had retired to their lodging house as soon as they could, and most of those still within the works' walls were now gathered in the factory where Colt was holding court. The route to the cellar – and then back out into the city – lay wide open.

Caroline had known at once that she had to act. Martin was better, but he was still too addled by his grief for Michael to be of any reliable help. The debt sitting over her poor sister and her family had to be paid off as quickly as possible. She was the only one who could do what was needed. Pausing for a half a minute to let her eyes adjust to the darkness, she watched her misted breath drift back towards the yard; then she crept along to the cellar door, removed the lock and went beneath the warehouse.

The gloom was soupy and suffocating. Finding a wall, ignoring the musty smells that pressed in on her, Caroline started to feel her way along the slime-coated bricks, trying to recall the cellar's layout. Before very long there was a rustle of oilskin beneath her boot. Cautiously, she extended her fingers into the murk before her until they met corners of rough wood and the cold, round heads of packing nails. She'd located the pistol crates, and rather sooner than she'd been expecting. The store of pistols had almost doubled in size, she realised, spreading out of the area it had originally occupied. Mr Churn had continued to bring in his 'priority jobs' every week or so, but he'd ordered that they be assigned to a different girl each time, making it difficult for her to keep track of them. Down there in the cellar, though, it was plain that this was an ambitious project indeed, far more so than she'd first thought. These guns now numbered well into the hundreds.

Selecting a crate close to the back of the pile, she took out a Navy revolver, resealed the box and headed back up to the yard, the gun tucked beneath her shawl. The works were quiet. She left by the Ponsonby Street gate, intending to hurry back along the river to Millbank.

Sight of Vauxhall Bridge brought her to a halt. A vast, unruly procession was advancing across it, engulfing the evening traffic, singing songs and chanting with enormous vigour. Many of the marchers held torches or long poles with lanterns dangling at their ends. There were flashes of bright colour, accompanied by bangs and the odd scream, as small fireworks were lit and tossed into the air; Caroline saw a ball of fizzing green light drop over the bridge's side, rushing to meet its reflection in the water below. The leaders of this enormous parade were just emerging onto the Thames's northern bank, pushing their way through the toll gate. They were carrying a strange, outsized mannequin between them, bearing it aloft as if it were a criminal being taken to meet some bloody mob justice. She remembered the day's chatter up in the packing room, and the various plans that had been under discussion. It was the fifth of November, Guy Fawkes Night. Revellers would be crowding through London's streets and parks, heaping a hundred different likenesses of that infamous Catholic plotter onto roaring pyres, consigning him once again to hellfire.

The Guy leaving the bridge was a fine example of his kind, with a pointed black beard, a broad-brimmed hat and a large bundle of matches pinned to his cloak. As Caroline watched, he lurched a little to the right; the procession was turning onto the riverside road, the very route she'd been about to take herself. Their destination was likely to be the square before Parliament, next to the New Palace Yard. They would be passing within a few streets of the Devil's Acre, one of the greatest gatherings of Catholic Irish in the city. As the people streamed onwards, another mannequin rocked into view, very different in appearance from the first. This figure was grotesquely fat, dressed in lurid robes with an upside-down cross painted on its belly; the face was little more than a greedy leer, above which wobbled a huge bumblebee's arse of a hat. It was the Pope.

'Burn him in a tub of tar,' sung those around him, 'burn him like a blazing star, burn his body from his head, then we'll say old Pope is dead! Hip hip hoorah! Hip hip hoorah, hoorah!'

This was a deliberate bit of baiting that the Irish were sure to snap at, and in numbers. Brawling between Catholics and Protestants had become a feature of this night in London's poorer quarters, and one relished by both sides as far as Caroline could tell. The police would be on hand, but they had allegiances of their own. It seemed to be a fight that everyone wanted – and one that could surely know no possible resolution. Caroline cursed the whole foolish business and cut back along Bessborough Place, thinking to cross the Vauxhall Bridge Road fifty yards further up. She reached the wide thoroughfare to find it empty of traffic and echoing with terrified shrieks. A pair of Irish girls had been discovered heading for the Acre, and were being pelted with stones and rotten vegetables by a snickering group who had split off from the main procession. Lowering her eyes, Caroline checked the pistol and continued on her way.

She soon pulled ahead of the Guy Fawkes parade. The lanes around the prison were clear, save for the beer-sellers rushing down with their barrels and hand-carts to secure the best spots along the procession's route. There was a strong odour of bonfires coming from the direction of the Victoria Street clearances. Many of the penitentiary's inmates were joining in the chants of those marching past its gates, and Caroline could hear a robust, disembodied chorus drifting out over the walls and away through the smoke-hazed air.

'*Remember, remember the fifth of November,*' the prisoners were singing, '*gunpowder, treason and plot . . .*'

Reaching her boarding house, she bade her landlady good evening, went up to her room for a length of cheesecloth and then crept out of the scullery door. Across the alley at the rear of the house lay Selby's Lumber Yard. It had a high wooden fence with a loose slat at one end; a little pressure and it creaked aside, creating a triangular crack that Caroline could just squeeze herself through. The yard beyond was shut up for the night, and lit only by a single oil-lamp over in a window by the front gate. There was a watchman, but he was a drinker and would be fast asleep in the office by now. She sneaked down a shadowy corridor between two tall timber stacks, coming to a pile of lichen-spotted logs heaped up against an old brick wall. Caroline knelt down, leaning around the logs and feeling for a particular brick, close to the wall's base. Like the slatted fence, this wall had been cheaply built and poorly maintained. Finding the brick she was looking for, she pulled it loose. There was a size-able cavity behind.

This was where Caroline stowed her pistols before she delivered them to the Irishmen in the Devil's Acre. She'd concluded that it was far too great a risk to have them in her room or anywhere in the boarding house. It would be the first place a policeman – or Colt watchman – would look. A couple of hours spent hunting around outside in the dead of night had brought her to this Selby's wall. Should she ever be exposed to suspicion, this one simple measure might well prove to be her salvation; she could not help but be a little pleased by her own cunning. There was already one other gun in this secret nook. Caroline had decided to start handing them over two at a time, partly to limit her contact with Slattery as much as possible, but also to make him look a fool in front of his lads. He'd derided her, doubted what she could do. She saw herself walking before him, telling him exactly what she thought of him and his precious bloody Ireland, and then throwing down not one more Colt revolver but a bloody *pair*.

She'd been planning to go on to the Acre that evening, but the Guy Fawkes parade had changed her mind. It could wait until tomorrow. Caution was everything, after all; she was coming to believe that a sufficiently cautious thief would never be caught. Taking the latest stolen revolver from her shawl, she wrapped it up carefully in the material she'd fetched from her room and then reached into the hiding place to arrange its brother so that both guns would fit. Where there should have been a length of finely shaped steel swaddled in cheesecloth, however, there was only coarse mortar dust – an empty space.

For several seconds Caroline couldn't move. Blinking, she searched again, forcing her fingers into the furthermost cracks of the wall cavity. But the pistol was gone. There could be no doubt of it. Her shoulders sagged and she slumped onto the log pile, feeling as if a butt of ice-water had been tipped over her, robbing her of breath and weighting down her clothes. Suddenly wild with panic, she looked behind her, fully expecting to see a policeman's light approaching between the banks of wood.

No one was there – only the dark stillness of the deserted lumber yard, backed by the distant carnival sounds of the Guy Fawkes procession. Letting out a shivering gasp, Caroline attempted to recover some of the crafty intelligence for which she'd been congratulating herself only ten seconds earlier. She got to her feet, fighting back a wave of nausea, and tried to think things through. It seemed very unlikely that a lumber yard employee had stumbled across the pistol. The hiding place was too good. No, she'd been seen. Had a passer-by spotted her pushing back that fence-slat, or someone looking out of a window perhaps, and then come over to investigate after she'd left? Caroline couldn't believe this. She'd made absolutely sure that there hadn't been a soul around, every time she'd crept in there.

There was but one answer. She'd been tracked by a true expert, all the way from the pistol works. Only one person could possibly have done this – the Colonel's watchman, Walter Noone.

Barely three minutes later, Caroline was on St Anne's Street, running for the Holy Lamb. The stolen Navy was no longer under her shawl; she'd made a quick diversion on the boundaries of the Acre to drop it into a cesspit, where it had vanished with a soft, sucking *plop*. Her thoughts were of getting word to Martin; of collecting Amy and Katie and fleeing the city. The debt would have to remain unpaid. They had to run away, that instant, as far as they could. Amid this frantic worry came the first sharp pricks of resentment. She'd done all this reckless thievery for *them* – they'd better make sure she escaped Colonel Colt's vengeance.

The streets of the Acre were braced for a storm. All the women apart from a few desperate whores had sought refuge indoors, and the only street sellers doing any business were those peddling strong drink. Gangs of men and boys were gathering on corners, smoking pipes and cheroots, listening closely to the sounds of the procession advancing along Millbank Street, now just a few roads over. The enemy was drawing near; a good number of them hefted sticks or metal bars in their hands, ready for battle. A black-robed priest was wandering among them, appealing in an educated English voice for calm, for Christian forbearance in the face of heretical provocation. Caroline heard an Irishman advise him to get well out of sight before the Proddies arrived.

As she came to the junction with Old Pye Street, a large labourer tried to step in her path, demanding that she prove her allegiance to Rome or face the consequences. She weaved around him without answering. A hand hooked in her elbow, yanking her back; and for a moment she thought that she might face a similar ordeal to that of the two Irish girls on the Vauxhall Bridge Road, only inflicted by Catholics rather than Protestants.

'Stop that, ye bleedin' eejit!' said someone else. 'I seen her before – she's wi' Pat Slattery!'

The hand withdrew immediately; there was even a muttered apology. Caroline hurried onwards.

Like many of the Acre's shops and inns, the Holy Lamb was locked up against the night, its windows boarded over. Light shone between the planks, though; Caroline rushed to the stone stoop, feeling as if she were pursued by slavering hounds, ready to pound on the door with her fist and demand admittance. She was checked, however, by a truly brutal burst of shouting from inside.

It was Slattery. 'Damn them all to hell!' he yelled. 'God

help me, I will go out there and I will shoot them down! I swear it on Molly's honour, on the honour of all bleedin' Ireland!'

There was the sound of chairs being knocked over as men grappled with one another. Caroline glanced behind her; the tumbledown alleyway was empty but for a few shambling drunks, their shoulders hunched in the cold.

'You'll do no such thing!' This was Martin. 'We've got to stay put!'

'If they make to attack Catholic Irish, I bleedin' will, I tell you!'

'Think for a moment, Pat. If you fire off a Colt revolver in the Acre tonight, the Yankees'll be sure to hear of it afore the morrow. They'll seal up their factory tighter than the bleedin' quod. Caro won't be able to lift any more guns. And then where will Molly's scheme be, eh?'

Caroline's brow furrowed. What was this – who was Molly, and what did the stolen guns have to do with her? In fact, why did the Irishmen still have the Colts at all? Why had they not already passed them on to their creditor? She moved closer to the window.

'What in blazes would you know about *Molly's scheme*, Martin Rea?' Slattery replied with biting scorn. 'It ain't your concern no longer. You just need to make sure we get our bleedin' guns.'

This brought forth a growl of agreement from the rest of those gathered in the Lamb. Martin had been beaten down. Caroline was taken aback by the contempt in their voices. Some kind of quarrel had plainly taken place – a serious one.

'We've waited too long now,' Slattery continued. 'It was going so damn well, and now nothing. What's the reason for this delay? Why has that Saxon bitch grown so bleedin' slow?'

'Trouble at the works,' Martin replied. 'Spies and so forth. She'll come through. You can't expect her to –'

'I saw him t'other day, ye know,' Slattery interrupted, his anger reaching a new ferocity. 'I bleedin' well *saw him*, Lord John Russell, the shrivelled little *cunt*, hobbling into that stinking Parliament like a little hunchback. I saw the man that passed a death sentence on Catholic Ireland and thought nothing of it at all. He has to die, my brothers. He has to die, and soon. We'll get our guns, our holy dozen, and we'll end him on the steps of that Parliament o' theirs. For our lost ones, for Molly Maguire, we'll bleedin' well *end him*.'

Caroline sat down on the stoop, her head falling into her hands, staring disbelievingly at the ground. What a miserable fool she was. She'd swallowed that lying story about the debt almost without question. Those Irishmen in there were planning a bloody *murder*, and someone important from the sound of it. This was an entirely different order of wrongdoing. If she was captured and connected with them, identified as someone who'd aided them, she could go to the gallows. She didn't give any consideration to their motives. The crazed talk of Catholic Ireland, their 'lost ones', and this woman Molly Maguire meant nothing to her. All that mattered now was finding her sister and niece and making good their escape before Walter Noone arrived with the police.

Without Martin, however, it was impossible. Shortly after Michael's death he'd taken his wife and daughter out of Crocodile Court in order to escape an official quarantine imposed on account of the cholera. Caroline had welcomed this at first, but soon came to realise that he did not plan to settle them anywhere else. They went from room to room, all over London, staying nowhere for more than a couple of weeks. The sisters would only see each other when Amy called at Caroline's boarding house. She'd thought this strange, perhaps another manifestation of Martin's grief – although now she understood that it was rather the behaviour of a man preparing to make a quick, clean break. Right then, at any rate, she had not the faintest idea where Amy and Katie might be.

A deadening numbness began to spread through her. In a single dreadful hour she'd lost everything. Those she'd been in league with had revealed themselves to be villains of the most deceitful kind, plotting murder with guns she'd got for them – and one of their number stood between her and all that remained of her family. She was surely being hunted by Colonel Colt's men, and could never again return to her home or her place of employment without falling into their hands. Her few possessions, including her clothes and spare pair of boots, were gone for good. She had no money, and no friends who she could trust not to fetch the police on her when they learnt what she'd been doing.

An unexpected sob surged up Caroline's throat, bursting loudly through her lips like a sneeze. There was movement inside the Lamb, and a moment later a bolt drew back. She took to her heels at once, running as fast as she could, making it to the end of the alley before the door opened. A man shouted her name, Jack Coffee it sounded like, begging her to stop. She didn't care; lifting the front of her skirts, she headed off into the Acre.

There was one last person she could try.

Keeping to the shadows of Bessborough Place, Caroline made a hasty survey of the Colt works. It felt odd to look upon the deserted yard, a place so familiar to her, that she would surely never set foot in again. The factory still seemed to be running, despite the lack of operatives. Lights were burning in the engine room and some of the upper windows. This was a good sign; the person she sought might well be inside, attending to the Colonel. Questions continued to itch away at her, however, like so many angry flea bites. What if he wasn't in there? What if she waited and waited for nothing? Or if he left with Colt, on his way to some fancy gathering – would she then give chase, and pursue them into Belgravia or Mayfair, trailing behind that glaring yellow carriage in the stupid hope of somehow catching the secretary's eye?

Caroline had no answers. Her situation had the simplicity of absolute desperation. The choice was this or a leap from the nearest bridge. She made for Ponsonby Street, intending to hide herself among the mismatched huts and outbuildings that were scattered along the wharf, from where she'd be able to keep a close watch on the factory door.

Mr Lowry was standing opposite the Spread Eagle, just

thirty yards down the riverbank. She stopped dead, dazed for a moment by her good fortune. It looked as if he'd been there for some time, maintaining a vigil outside the tavern, and was so absorbed in his own thoughts that he didn't notice her approach. She took his coat cuff between thumb and forefinger and gave it a tug.

He turned with alarming abruptness, lifting a hand as if to shove her away. Sight of her stopped him at once. 'Miss Knox, thank God!' he exclaimed. 'You are in trouble, I fear – terrible trouble!'

Glancing around them, Mr Lowry steered Caroline away from the merry windows of the Spread Eagle, down the side of a wooden rope-shed. 'I am certain that Walter Noone is after your brother-in-law,' he said urgently. 'He will surely be coming for you as well before very long.'

There was a new disquiet in the secretary; his light-hearted charm was quite gone, as if fine varnish had been stripped away to expose the raw wood beneath. She'd been preparing a full confession, and was ready to tell him about the guns in the cellar, the Irishmen's murderous plot – how she'd been lied to, manipulated, and made to give him up. This had to happen, she'd thought, if she was to have a chance of regaining his trust.

Mr Lowry wouldn't hear it, though, cutting in before she'd said half a dozen words. 'There's simply no time for this. We have to get you away from here as quickly as possible, or you will be caught.'

Caroline leaned back heavily against the side of the shed, realising all of a sudden how very tired she was. 'Do you have any notion of what I've done, Mr Lowry?'

His eyes narrowed slightly. 'I saw you in the Westminster rookery with those Irishmen. I'd say you were stealing.'

She stared at him. He'd known since the summer – for months. 'Why – why didn't you tell anyone, then? Any of the Yankees?'

'It was plain to me that you were involved against your will.' Mr Lowry looked away from her, a little embarrassed. 'I – I suppose I wanted to find a way to untangle you from Rea and his accomplices – to rescue you before Noone

251

found out. But I was too slow, too hesitant. And now it's too late.' He sighed ruefully. 'I've been trying to get away from the Colonel all day to deliver a warning to you. I considered going to your lodgings at Millbank, but it seemed too likely that Noone would have someone posted there. Waiting outside this inn was all I could think to do, in the slight hope that you still visited it. And here you are, thank the Lord.'

A blush rose in Caroline's cheeks as she listened to this; she felt herself smiling even as new tears stung her eyes. This man alone had placed her before everything else, before his own concerns even, despite the cruel treatment he had received from her – and for which he still had yet to receive a proper explanation. Amid all the trickery and treachery, it seemed that she had stumbled undeservedly across a true friend.

'Oh, they lied to me, Mr Lowry,' she said, starting to weep, 'how they *lied* to me. They used my sister against me, and her children . . .'

'Miss Knox, I promise that I will hear all of this later, gladly, but we must leave. If you are willing, I propose that you come back to my rooms in Holborn.' He hesitated. 'I would never normally suggest such a thing, of course, but I don't believe that Noone would think to look for you there. My building is a busy one, and large – no one will pay you any mind. And first thing in the morning I will withdraw a sum of money from my bank, enough to take you from this city and set you up elsewhere.'

She shook her head. 'You're being very good to me, Mr Lowry, but I can't possibly think of leaving London without my sister and her daughter. They are caught up in this too. I don't know where they might be. I must find them and take them with me.'

The secretary consulted his watch in the light from the Spread Eagle's windows. 'Very well, Miss Knox, but we must leave now. The last eastbound boat will be docking shortly. We will locate them tomorrow, I promise you, but we must go.'

He held out a hand and together they went back out onto Ponsonby Street, hurrying along the riverside road to Pimlico

Pier. Caroline heard the clanging of a bell out on the water, and the thrashing of paddle-wheels; a small passenger steamer was pulling in, sounding its bell, two blue signal lights blazing and smoking upon its prow. The gates opened and a handful of passengers walked across the raised wooden platform to the boat's gangplank. Mr Lowry bought their tickets at the booth; she kept herself out of sight as best she could.

They stood in the centre of the vessel, next to the chugging chimney block. Gratefully, Caroline closed her eyes. The steamer rocked beneath her feet as it nosed back out into the main current of the river, and a bank of freezing winter wind swept across the deck. Soon afterwards the sounds of the boat and the curt exchanges of its sailors gained a dull, metallic echo; they were passing beneath the iron arches of Vauxhall Bridge, leaving the Colt works behind them as they headed steadily downriver. For now, at least, she was safe. She tightened her grip on Mr Lowry's hand, feeling the warmth of his palm through his calfskin glove. He turned slightly, protecting her from the wind; she laid her face softly against his upper arm, her tears soaking into the sleeve of his coat.

8

Martin and Jack returned to the Lamb. Slattery and the others were on the stoop, smoking their pipes. Their numbers had grown, Slattery having gathered in a couple of new recruits from the huge reserve of aggrieved Irishmen living in the Acre. Martin hadn't learnt their names and didn't care to. He knew very well that they'd been taken on to replace him.

'Well?' Slattery demanded as they approached. 'Who was it?'

'Me sister-in-law, I think,' Martin replied. 'Hard to see, though. She was gone by the time we reached the alley's end. We hunted about a bit, but there's just too many out tonight.'

'It were Caro,' asserted Jack, 'for certain. Saw her with me own eyes, so I did.'

'Oh, you *saw* her, did you, Jack Coffee,' Slattery sneered, 'you who makes his pennies smashing bleedin' murphies against his bonce all evening long! Was it the Virgin Mary Herself came down from Heaven and pointed the girl out to you, Jack? Or just a couple o' the bleedin' angels?'

Jack's performances at Rosie McGehan's theatre had become a sore point between the Mollys. Several of them, Slattery included, had recently got six months' navvy work on the Parliament site, as part of a push to finish off the great entrance tower at the southern end. Slattery was well pleased by this, believing that it would allow them to get familiar with both the layout of the building and the details of Lord John's routine – and thus deduce the best time and place to strike at him. Toiling away in the cold rain to run up the palace of their tyrants was a price worth paying, in Slattery's view, for such knowledge. He wanted to get as many of them on the site as possible; but Jack, wedded to the boards it seemed, had so far resisted, earning him frequent jibes and gestures of contempt.

'She'll have heard about the plan for Russell,' Martin said through the laughter. 'This could prove a problem, Pat.'

'I don't for the life o' me see why.'

'She'll stop helping us. She was doing it for Amy. She won't want any part of the scheme for Lord John.'

Slattery wasn't worried. 'Ah, the Saxon bitch is ours, Martin, and for as long as we bleedin' want her. What she's done already would damn her in the eyes o' the law, and she knows it. And if she does try to buck the bridle, well, we'll just have to think up a way to hush her back down.'

There was more laughter from the gang standing around him. Martin understood his meaning clearly enough. If Caroline had stolen from Colt to save Amy from an imaginary threat, she could surely be made to keep at it to save her from a real one – one that Pat Slattery would have no qualms about supplying.

'If yous so much as think about hurting me family,' he stated simply, 'I'll knock yous stone bleedin' dead.'

This only increased their mirth. 'Would you now?' Slattery hooted. 'Would you indeed? Well, it's good to know that there are still some things that put some blood in your pizzle, Martin! Shame that Molly's justice ain't bleedin' one of them, eh?'

Martin moved towards him. 'I mean it.'

Slattery took a drag on his pipe, squinting nastily in the dark lane. 'How can you turn away from your people, Martin Rea? How the devil is it done?' He blew out his smoke. 'I lost less than you in the Hunger, for certain I did, but I would sooner cut off me bleedin' hand than lie down in the manner that you have.'

This exchange would have ended with them fighting in the

mud had a great cheer, hundreds upon hundreds of voices, not rolled across the rookery from the direction of Parliament, rattling windows with its tremendous volume. It was the type of rousing shout usually stirred up by some singular public spectacle – the appearance of a monarch or a murderer's final drop from the Newgate scaffold.

'Proddies have reached the Abbey,' Thady said. 'They'll have got that bleedin' fire going, Pat.'

Slattery backed away from Martin, knocking out his pipe-bowl and starting from the alley. 'Best get over there double-quick, then. Wouldn't want to miss the caper, brothers, now would we?'

At first, Martin stayed put. Jack asked if he was coming and he shook his head. He was no longer one of them; that had been made clear enough. Let them wage their impossible battles without his help. He would return to the room in Soho where he'd lodged his wife and child and consider what to do next. But then, in the light of a gas jet out on St Anne's Street, he noticed that Slattery was carrying himself strangely. Something heavy was concealed beneath his black fustian coat, weighing his wiry frame down on one side. It had to be a revolver. Owen had brought one to the Lamb that evening so that they could all practise loading it – Slattery must have taken the thing from the tavern while Martin and Jack had been chasing after Caroline. Martin swore; there was no telling what the hot-headed fool might end up doing with it. This could make things far worse than they were already. He had to get that pistol back.

The Acre was in uproar, its residents now under steady attack as restless mobs that had splintered from the parade moving along the riverbank came over to confront their Catholic foe. Martin shoved his way through brawls and beatings, ducking volleys of stones, mud-pies and random rubbish. Furious insults were being hurled back and forth; women screamed and spat from windows, and struck out at any who came close. He just managed to keep sight of Slattery and the rest. They were avoiding the worst of the fighting, striding across Orchard Street and past the tall, solid walls that separated the fringes of the rookery from the precincts of Westminster Abbey.

Martin pursued the Mollys out onto the open expanse of Broad Sanctuary, past the Abbey's pale, soot-streaked towers and blackened stained glass. The enmity of the Acre was left behind as entirely as its cramped, winding lanes – as if it had been another world or a particularly shallow region of hell. Everyone here was concerned only with advancing down Broad Sanctuary to the square at its end. Martin could hear the rumbling chatter of a very large crowd, and the smell of smoke was growing stronger. He came to the church of St Margaret's, as chalky and ancient-looking as the Abbey but only a fraction of its size, standing next to its vast neighbour like a calf beside its mother. Just past it, around the corner of its façade, was a sight that made him promptly forget the Colt hidden beneath Pat Slattery's coat.

In the centre of the square, upon a rectangle of muddy grass, was the bonfire, a two-storey pyramid constructed from numberless branches, planks and beams. Atop it was a crown of flame, already leaping six yards high. People were packed in close to this inferno, as if seeking to toast themselves before it. A few among them were darting in closer still, to toss on more fuel or to poke bravely at its glowing heart; and then they were rushing back away again, alarmed by sudden pops of combustion or the crash of a collapsing branch. Around this blaze had sprung up a bustling winter fair, generously furnished with stalls, street performers and musicians, and the odours of roasting and frying mingled with the wood-smoke. The mighty bonfire, a multitude of torches, lanterns and spitting, flare-like fireworks, and several lines of smart iron street lamps all combined to make the square seem like the most brightly lit spot in the whole of London. Were it not for the chill of November and the scattering of dim stars overhead, Martin thought, you could almost pretend that you stood in some cavernous assembly hall rather than the open air.

The crowd was typically metropolitan in its make-up. Martin saw red infantry jackets, trailing whores like gulls behind a fishing boat; a crew of bemused Lascar sailors who'd found their way over from the docks of Limehouse; a clean-collared, well-supervised crocodile from a respectable boarding school being harassed by grubby street children; numerous rowdy, well-oiled parties from every kind of office, shop and factory; and the standard smattering of rascals and adventurers, trying out their tricks on the scores milling around them. Advertising placards nailed to poles stuck up above the hats, bonnets and caps like so many sails on a lake, announcing the usual amazing exhibitions, affordable guest houses and quality goods. One caught Martin's attention; it was light blue, about five feet by three, with a tolerably accurate drawing of a single-action revolver at its top. Beneath this, in large, plain letters, was painted *Colonel Colt's Repeating Pistols of British Manufacture – Beware Counterfeits and Patent Infringements!* There was a paragraph in smaller print trumpeting the virtues of Colt's revolver and providing the address both of the works by the river and the sales office in Cockspur Street. And under that was a sketch of some horsemen, American cavalry Martin guessed, routing a band of Indian braves, the ground around them carpeted with the dead.

Remembering his purpose, Martin wheeled about, hunting for Slattery. He was easily found; the Mollys were locked in discussion with another, far larger gang, Irish navvies it looked like, over by the white wall of St Margaret's. Their faces were grim; they were not there to celebrate. All of them started along the side of the church, in the direction of the river. Something was going to happen. Martin followed as quickly as he could, barging through a game of dice. Before him now was the sturdy fence of the Parliament site, lined with blue-coated policemen. He could see the roofs of the small hamlet of temporary wooden structures that clustered around the base of the building; and beyond them, receding into shadow, the unfinished palace itself. Much of the crazy, eye-crossing decoration was lost to the gloom, leaving only the impression of a tight grid of stone spanning its immense surface – and those narrow windows, more than he could possibly count, each one reflecting an orange shard of firelight. At the northern end was the hollow stump of what would one day be the clock tower, already over a hundred feet tall, with a lifting engine squatting atop it like an iron spider crawling from a drainpipe.

Martin was drawing close to the Mollys and their friends when a clamour of enthusiasm spread across the entire square. The figure of the Guy, the thwarted Catholic revolutionary still so hated by these Protestants, appeared from the direction of Millbank, and was borne past the new Parliament to a deafening chorus of jeers. A chant started over at the mouth of the Old Palace Yard and was soon taken up by all: *Guy, Guy, Guy, poke him in the eye, put him on the bonfire and there let him die!*

'Steady, now, brothers,' Slattery was saying, 'steady . . .'

The Guy had a long boat-hook inserted under each of his arms and was lifted high into the air, at which the chanting grew louder and faster; slowly, he floated over the crowd to his pyre and was balanced at its summit. The flames claimed him at once, wrapping around him ravenously. Two minutes later Guy Fawkes was all but gone.

'The Holy Father!' someone yelled – was it Slattery? 'They're going to *burn the Holy Father!*'

There was a great push forward, causing many to fall; Martin staggered, losing his balance. As he struggled to recover, he glimpsed a hideous, grinning model of the Pope, coming into the square from the same direction as the Guy. Pulling himself upright, he stared over disbelievingly at this horrible and deliberate slur upon his religion – the dearly held religion of his parents and sisters. Irish hands were already pulling at its gown, making it slump to one side and the striped hat topple from its head. Martin felt the cheerful mood of the people around him darken swiftly at this disruption of their festivities. A ring of determined defenders closed around the fake Pope, heaving back the press of Irishmen, set on preserving him for the bonfire. Blows were traded; women shrieked; large numbers both fled the brawl and hurried towards it.

Standing in the midst of it all, Martin experienced something unforeseen: a bright flash of exhilaration. He wanted to be there. Pitching in eagerly, he made for the Pope, thinking that he would see this insult to his people ground into the dirt, along with any who tried to stop him. For the first time in many days he heard the voice of Molly Maguire, hoarse with passion, urging him on; he could feel her hovering above the swell of bodies like a tattered kite, guiding him with her gaze. To his left, Thady Rourke went down, a man clinging to his back. Martin was at his side in seconds, kicking off his attacker. Then he was back at the Pope, a stout stick in his hands, swiping at the kneecaps of one of its bearers. This did the job – down came that revolting form, falling into a jumble of stuffed sacks and outsized autumn vegetables. Molly was chuckling happily, a sound like a handful of rusty tacks jangling together in a jar; Martin looked around, grinning, wanting to share his victory. Through the struggling, swearing crowd he caught sight of Pat Slattery, sprawled awkwardly in the mud. His face was smeared with blood, his black coat all but torn from his back. Molly's mirth stopped dead. Sensing disaster, Martin ran straight over and started helping him to his feet.

Jack was there too, a moment later. 'Knew you'd come wi' us, Mart,' he muttered. 'Knew it.'

They got Slattery to the high pavement next to St Margaret's. His nose had been broken again, and badly. Jack peeled back his bloody shirt; someone had stamped on his shoulder so hard that the curve of a boot-heel had been cut into his flesh.

'The gun,' he panted. 'They swiped it.'

Martin looked at Jack. 'Who, Pat? Did ye see?'

Slattery shook his head, angry and ashamed; he didn't want to say. 'Whipped it from under me coat, he did, easy as ye damn well please. The cunt *thanked* me for it afore he lammed into me – can you believe that?' He tried to touch his burst, crooked nose but the pain was too much; he tore the hand away in disgust. 'Damn it all, he was a bleedin' Yankee!'

It had been Noone. There could be no doubt of it. The method was his: the careful selection of the moment, the sudden, violent action, the deliberate sowing of fear and confusion among his stunned victims. Martin had been certain that those tales of massacre and child-killing that Noone had spun at the Yankee dinner had been both an attempt to rattle him and a clear signal that the watchman was preparing to strike. He'd tried to warn Slattery about this in the Lamb, but he hadn't wanted to hear it.

'That Orange bastard is nothing to us, Martin,' he'd snapped. '*Nothing*. He ain't got the brains, he ain't got the heart, and he ain't got the bleedin' strength neither. The Molly Maguires ain't concerned, ye hear?'

And yet now Slattery was a battered mess, one of their three Navys was lost and the Mollys were properly spooked. It was obvious that Noone had been watching them closely, probably since the ejection of Slattery and the rest from the works, following them throughout the city with a practised eye. As he'd stormed back along Piccadilly towards the circus, with Mr Quill chasing behind him calling out some more of his well-meaning words, Martin had wondered how the devil Noone had heard about baby Michael – for he surely had, with his pointed talk of infants being left for wolves and so forth. Here was the answer. The spying watchman had made it his business to learn everything about them.

Martin knew that he could never return to the Colt works now. This was a bitter realisation. Noone would be on him the instant he passed through the gates, dragging him around the yard by his hair most likely, seeking to humiliate Mr Quill with the capture of a thief whose ejection he had prevented the first time around – whose good character he had vouched for. Not, of course, that his disappearance would protect Quill at all. The watchman would enjoy making the details of Martin's duplicity public, and would certainly stress the vital role played by the foolish, trusting chief engineer. It might even end up costing Quill his position with Colt. He would soon have very good reason to curse the name of Martin Rea.

After setting Slattery down on a pallet in the upstairs room, the Irishmen held an urgent meeting in the bar of the Holy Lamb. They agreed that the two remaining revolvers should be separated, to lessen their chance of discovery by

Colt's men. Owen produced them; young Joe took one, saying that he would hide it in his uncle's butcher's shop on Golden Lane, over in the East End. He walked from the tavern and vanished without trace. Neither man nor gun was ever seen again.

They gathered in the Lamb a couple of days later. Slattery was up from his sick-bed, heavily bandaged, grey-skinned and drinking hard. He had a simple explanation for this latest setback.

'The bugger's fled,' he said. 'Pawned the weapon and used the coin to get hisself as far from London as he can. Lost his damn nerve, ain't he, the bleedin' coward.'

The others weren't so sure and started to murmur uneasily, suspecting that this was more of Walter Noone's handiwork.

'Now yous *listen to me*,' Slattery shouted, striking the bar. 'Yous are Molly's lads, and you'll do her biddin'. Lord John Russell will still die at our hands, and in the same manner as before. It can still be done.'

'How, then?' demanded Martin, his patience gone. 'I've no place in the factory. I can't find me sister-in-law anywhere – she sure as hell ain't at Colt no more. How we going to get your bleedin' guns, Slattery?'

'Oh, we'll get them, don't you worry. And what's more, we'll give this jumped-up Yankee a bit o' bleedin' punishment for sending his men out after us. D'ye hear me? We'll have our revenge on Colonel Colt for what he done. That's right, brothers – Molly's got us a *new plan*.'

Martin glared balefully at the bar's scratched surface. He'd come to the Lamb that night hoping to hear the scheme abandoned, and escape routes discussed; he saw now that he really should have known better. Slattery's pride had taken as sound a beating as his body, and he was bent on a reckless gesture. It was a sure bet that this new plan would involve even more mortal danger than the first.

'Enough,' he announced angrily, rising from his stool. 'I'm leaving. It's over, Slattery. There's nothing more that can be done here. This bastard Noone is after us, and I've a wife and child to consider.'

Arriving back in Soho after the unholy chaos of Bonfire Night, Martin had found Amy asleep on the floor with Katie whimpering on her breast, an empty gin-bottle at her side. He'd woken her up and told her that it was over – that the thefts had been discovered. Caroline had already done the sensible thing, he'd said, and made herself scarce; and they would be following her as soon as he'd squared things with his friends. She'd nodded blearily, worried for her sister but trusting Martin, and clearly relieved to hear that they would be departing London at last, whatever the circumstances. He'd put them both to bed, feeling a familiar queasiness at his own half-truths and omissions. At least, he'd thought, we'll soon be free of all this.

Thady stepped forward, blocking his path to the tavern door. Martin looked around; the Mollys were drawing in, ready to stop him going. Even Jack, dear old Jack who he'd hoped might want to come with him, seemed set to wrestle him to the ground.

Grunting with discomfort, Slattery heaved his aching carcass over from the bar. 'Then *consider them*, Martin,' he hissed. 'We'd certainly catch you if you tried to run out on us now. We *know* you, remember. We know the routes you'd take, the hiding places you'd pick. A woman and an infant really slow a fellow down as well. You wouldn't stand a chance – and by the Holy Mother, there'd be bleedin' consequences for that sort of betrayal.' He jabbed an angry finger in Martin's face, shaking loose the blood-encrusted dressing stuck over his nose. 'We'll let you go when we have our pistols and are set to knock down Lord John, and not a second before. You might not be in that Colt's factory no longer, but there's plenty else you can do for us.' Slattery sucked in some air with a rasping snort and then spat a thumb-sized gobbet of blood and mucus onto the sawdust floor. 'Your debt to Molly Maguire ain't paid yet, pal, not by a good bleedin' distance.'

9

'Well, Mr Noone,' Sam said, rising from his chair, 'what d'you have to tell me? Good news, I take it? Quickly, man, I've got to be off.'

He looked over at the watchman. The mad mutt appeared distinctly pleased with himself; the thin little cracks of his eyes were glinting in the winter light, hard as twice-baked biscuit. Heavens, thought Sam, what mayhem and agony must he have inflicted?

'I've found the thieves, Colonel. Motherfucking Gaels – that man of Ben Quill's, the one I tried to throw out back in the spring, and a female relation of his from the packing room. There's a gang, too, over in the Westminster rookery. Each and every one of 'em dumb as carthorses.'

Sam scooped up his hat. 'I don't know about that, Mr Noone. They got a bunch of my guns out of this factory, and from right under your goddamn nose. How many was it – five? Did you get 'em all back?'

Noone shifted his weight from foot to foot, a good deal of his satisfaction departing. 'Three of 'em, yes. One was disposed of by the girl from the packing room – she panicked once she realised we was on to her and got rid of it somewhere. They still have one.' He looked over stiffly at the office's circular window. 'We'll recover it soon enough.'

'See that you do. I needn't remind you, Mr Noone, just how important it is that this particular pistol don't fall into the clutches of any kind of British official. All we need is for these Irish fools to try a spot of robbery with the thing, and get caught – and we might as well pack this whole place right up and go back to Hartford.'

'Won't happen.' The watchman's head swivelled back around. There was absolute certainty in his voice; he crossed his callused hands in front of him. 'I'll stop these fuckers, Colonel. I'll stop 'em dead.'

Sam flattened his hair and fitted on the hat. 'Don't you go getting carried away here, Mr Noone,' he warned. 'These ain't your Pomo Indians, y'hear? The Colt Company don't need the kind of attention that a massacre of Irishmen would bring. It really don't.'

Noone didn't like this. 'I've done pretty well by you so far, ain't I, Colonel?' he growled. 'Three guns back, and not so much as a whisker of the law? It'll end the same way.'

The gun-maker sighed; their meanings were not quite the same. He considered explaining the difference to his blood-thirsty underling but decided it would only be a waste of his time. 'You got any leads on this missing gun?'

'The Irishmen are gathered in their slum-tavern. They're under watch – we'll keep picking 'em off until we get the pistol. The packing-room girl's slipped us for now, but we'll track her down.'

'What d'you know of her? Anything?'

Noone paused, raising his chin a couple of inches. 'She was friendly with your secretary, Colonel. *Proper* friendly, if you follow me. I saw 'em together a while back, when that Hungarian fellow visited the works. Seemed to go cold, but I reckon that could've just been part of the scheme.'

Sam started across the office, shaking his head. 'Coincidence,' he declared, 'and that's all. By God, Mr Lowry ain't in on this! You're off course there, Mr Noone – way off course. Just get me that goddamn pistol back.'

Noone eyed him inscrutably as he opened the office door. 'Right you are, Colonel.'

Normally when Sam rejected a notion it left his head completely, jettisoned like slops from a transatlantic steamer. Not this one, though. The watchman's comment about the secretary nagged at him all the way along the corridor, down the staircase and out into the yard, riling him with its sheer absurdity. Noone had a determinedly suspicious way of thinking that could lead him in some truly nonsensical directions. Mr Lowry was a businessman, a professional to the bone – that was why he'd been taken on. His ultimate goal was to assume the management of Colt's European operations. Sam was sure of it. Such a fellow would never risk all that for a few stolen guns, for a few pounds in ill-gotten profit. At a stretch, Sam could imagine him defecting to a rival, to Adams perhaps – which would make him a louse and a cocksucker and a miserable ingrate bastard – but base theft, and on such a piddling scale? It was so goddamn *unambitious*.

His secretary was waiting by the side of the Colt carriage, chewing on an unlit cigar which he promptly stowed away in a pocket. Sam slowed his march across the freshly swept cobbles, studying him for a moment. Mr Lowry was no thief, of that he was certain, but he couldn't deny the slight distraction that continued to mar the boy's otherwise impeccable business manner. Sam had yet to uncover a satisfactory explanation for this.

'You've got it all, do you, Mr Lowry?' he called out as he approached. 'All the figures?'

'I have, Colonel,' he answered smartly, lifted up the folder under his arm, 'every piece of coal burned, every bar of steel forged, every Colt pistol made in London so far, entered and accounted for.'

'Good work,' said Sam – who knew very well that this was far from the case. 'We're ready for Mr Street's man then, eh? Ready for the inner chambers of British government?'

As ever, the secretary made all the right sounds, professing his enthusiasm for this and his expectation of that. Sam looked at his quick, bright face, his firm jaw, his sideburns untouched by grey; and he remembered the wan, jowly reflection that had met him in his dressing-room mirror that morning, inexplicably flabbier and more lined than he felt it had any right to be. Mr Lowry turned from him to climb into the carriage, and he caught something – a misty half-smile, as if the boy had suddenly become lost in a tender recollection. It lingered around his lips as they took their seats.

Sitting back, Sam made his assessment. 'By Heavens, Mr Lowry,' he pronounced, 'I do believe you're cunt-struck. And it's a bad case indeed.'

Mr Lowry demurred, colouring a little. 'I assure you, Colonel, that I am in no way, as you put it –'

'Let me guess,' the gun-maker cut in. 'She's the daughter of some distinguished professional gentleman, well schooled, with modest accomplishments of her own – painting, perhaps, or the teaching of music or arithmetic. These are the best sort of girls for men like us, Mr Lowry. They have brains, yet they are used to the needs of a strong male character.' Sam decided to make a personal revelation, thinking that this might induce the secretary to reveal something of his own. 'I myself am engaged to such a woman, in fact.'

The boy stared. 'You are *engaged*, Colonel?'

Sam nodded, having expected this reaction. The few people he'd told tended to assume that his roving life would make such a commitment impossible – not understanding the rather sedate pace of Connecticut society. 'To Miss Elizabeth Jarvis of Middletown, and for upwards of eight years now. Her father is an Episcopalian rector, and he has developed in her a serious mind indeed. Time spent with Miss Jarvis has a positively wholesome effect on a fellow.'

Mr Lowry was smiling. 'I'm sorry to disappoint, Colonel, but Almighty God has yet to favour me with such a salutary companion.'

Sam's tone hardened. 'Well, that simpering face ain't made for no *whore*,' he said. 'Tell me you ain't meddling with the lower orders, Mr Lowry. Tell me you ain't finding your fun up in my goddamn packing room or someplace.'

The smile dropped away. 'I assure you that I am not.'

These words were delivered with the flat ring of finality; an iron gate had been shut in the path of Sam's enquiry and bolted from the other side. That's real resolution there, the gun-maker told himself. He ain't saying any more on the subject. Sam looked out through the window. They were passing through the main gates onto Thames Bank, ready

267

to drive up the river to Parliament, and then on to St James's Park. He glimpsed a well-dressed party clustered around a brazier – and all deliberation of Mr Lowry's reticence ceased at once. His fingers went straight for the grooved brass bar at the top of the window pane; he wrenched it down and leaned out, treading on the secretary's toes as he did so.

'Why, Lady Wardell!' he called out, as if spotting an old friend. 'By God, ma'am, it's been a good long while since you graced my humble establishment with your attentions! Was it the pong of the river or the call of some nobleman's country house that caused you to abandon us? Would Christ have left off his righteous duty so easy, I wonder?'

A score of middle-aged faces turned up towards the gun-maker like a sour parody of a sunflower patch, every one of them puckered with dislike. Sam's coachman, hearing his employer's voice and then seeing his head and shoulders jutting from the side of the vehicle, drew it to a rapid halt, murmuring a few soothing words to the horses.

Lady Wardell herself towered above her comrades, looking really quite magnificent in her outrage, Sam had to admit. 'We will be coming out here, Colonel, for as long as your infernal factory is producing its death-dealing instruments.' This met with a muttered chorus of amens. 'We have seen the revolting advertisements you have been circulating around the city. We have seen how they actively celebrate the part your guns have played in the butchery of your country's heathen tribes – of poor, simple people who should rightly have been offered the true salvation of the Christian faith, but met with senseless murder! And we mean to put a stop to them – to *you*, Colonel Colt – once and for all!'

There were more amens, louder this time, and a fat, pasty creature behind the noblewoman started up with a bible quotation, delivered in an irritating, reedy voice – something about how evil men will soon wither away like the grass.

'Yes, well,' Sam interrupted, trying his best to stay civil, 'those boards are only intended to attract private customers, of which we've never had more than a handful in this country, to be perfectly honest with you. Our real focus at present, ladies and gentlemen, is the upper regions of the government. Why, I'm just on my way to see a cabinet minister right now, in fact!'

This quietened them down a bit. 'And which minister is that, pray?' asked Lady Wardell, her eyes cold and sharp as icicles.

Sam looked straight back at her. 'Now *that* I'm not inclined to reveal, ma'am. Let's just say that he falls well outside your particular sphere of influence.' He cast a glance up at the rain-clouds that were cruising over from the east of the city. 'You all be sure to have a pleasant afternoon out here.'

The gun-maker ordered his coachman to carry on, ducked back inside the carriage and closed the window with an emphatic *thud*.

'Jesus Christ on a donkey,' Sam thought as Lord Palmerston walked across the hall of his mansion-house to greet him. 'What kind of a man is this?'

Decked out in finest Harris tweed, the Home Secretary was a shade away from seventy but conducted himself in a very lively fashion, moving with a weird, mannered grace as if about to take his place in a grand dance. He wasn't physically impressive, possessing a short stump of a torso, long, simian limbs and a rather outsized skull. His hair was neatly cut and brushed in a style too modish for one of his years, artfully arranged to hide some thinness at the temples, and copious whiskers gushed over his collar. The colouring of both was strange; brown, broadly speaking, but weak and yellowed in places. Sam suspected that dyes had been employed. His folio of portrait engravings of British political figures had led him to expect a supremely dignified statesman, radiating a diamond-hard intellect. The reality was a good deal more bizarre, but pretty daunting nonetheless; his servants stood about that marble hall at rigid, terrified attention, like men facing a firing squad.

Lord Palmerston was fond of raising his voice without warning, and at unexpected times; having roared Sam's name, he then adopted a normal tone only to bellow out a commonplace observation about the weather a few seconds later. The gun-maker's equally commonplace reply caused a sudden, wild smile to grip the minister's face, exposing a set of false teeth as ivory-white and even as the keys on a piano, and wrinkling up his eyes so tightly that they threatened to vanish altogether. And then, just as completely, the smile was gone, the nobleman's thoughts seeming to have switched abruptly to something else. They strolled across the crimson carpet, the conversation continuing in a general vein. Palmerston asked whether the Colonel was taking full advantage of the pleasures of the season, the balls and theatres and so on – London really was at its most brilliant, he opined, during the six weeks before Parliament broke for Christmas.

'I pursue my customers,' Sam replied, 'but beyond that –'

This prompted a gale of jovial laughter, terminated as swiftly as the smile, followed by an enquiry about Sam's metropolitan residence. 'Piccadilly, eh?' Palmerston noted with approval once he'd received his answer. 'It is the proper region for men of the world such as ourselves. A vivacious place – a place of possibility, of variety. I shall be up there as well before very long, out of this wretchedly dull part of town.'

And then Sam saw it. This here was a faded dandy-gentleman who, despite all his wealth and power, still fancied that he had the strut of fashion left in his warped old bones. He looked around the hall, and the corridors and stairways that led off from it, decorated in the usual overblown aristocratic style; the gilded grandeur was so rich and intense that it jaded the eye. How could a man who dismissed all this as if it were a Bowery garret possibly govern a nation of equal men? These John Bull politicians truly were a rum lot. In America they were lawyers and soldiers, professional fellows who took to the hustings to do something for their country. Over here, though, so many of the most powerful had simply been born to it. They knew nothing else. For them, the governance of millions was but an arena for petty personal contests. There was little method or principle at play, just lordly men expressing their characters, and executing their endless plots and plans against each other. It was a damnably unpredictable system, and a difficult one indeed for even the most resourceful businessman to navigate.

Lord Palmerston led his guest through to a large smoking room at the back of the house, the walls covered with wide, vaporous landscapes. Lawrence Street was there, along with a couple of others, all of whom rose to their feet at the minister's entrance. Street met Sam's eye, and the coolness of his demeanour gave the gun-maker heart. Business would certainly be done that afternoon. Mr Lowry waited by the door, a dapper mouse in a lion's den.

Palmerston walked to the fireplace and swivelled around on his heel, striking an oratorical pose. 'Colonel Colt,' he began, 'I am certain that I need not tell you of the situation in the East. You read your *Times* and your *Morning Post*, as does every man here. Our Prime Minister, poor Aberdeen, still holds out for peace, and with every passing day it becomes plainer that his feeble-minded indecision will finish him. Now, I have long pressed for action, proposing most recently that the Navy sail into the Black Sea and occupy it, thus preventing any further Russian manoeuvre. We must show this blood-steeped Tsar that we are serious, Colonel – that we will halt his aggression towards his neighbours at the point of a sword!'

His voice had been getting steadily louder, building to a rousing, flourishing finish and a defiant snap of the fingers; the assembled aides, Street included, seemed ready to applaud.

'There will be war,' the minister added carelessly, 'it is quite certain. Nothing less than British honour is at stake. Turkey, our weak and brutalised ally, must receive our protection. I'm trying to push this question of the Black Sea to a division in the House. We'll see what happens there, eh?'

Sam revised his initial, rather dubious opinion of the flamboyant old fellow before him. There was plainly a rod of best steel running up Lord Palmerston's spine; this was a man who faced the goddamn situation, who called it what it was and did not shy away from the prospect of a necessary conflict. He met the minister's speech with an impassioned rendition of his own about the fabled Anglo-Saxon bond that had first inspired him to set up a manufactory in London – glancing

271

over at Street again as he did so. Palmerston seemed well pleased by this, and continued to pay close attention as Sam described the Pimlico works' unrivalled production speeds, mounting stockpile and extremely competitive prices.

'So, my dear Colonel Colt,' the nobleman asked with another of his savage smiles, 'if a man was so disposed, might an order – a really very *large* order, I think – be placed with you right now, this minute?'

'A fair price will get you however many you ask for,' Sam answered. 'Under five thousand and you can have 'em today.'

He waved Lowry forward to present the pair of pistols they'd brought along with them, which he did with a low bow. Palmerston was delighted by this gift, opening up the case at once; and there it was, Sam's beautiful Navy, engraved and blued and glinting fiercely in the firelight. The minister started to wave it around, advancing playfully on Street, jabbing at him as if it were a rapier. Sam managed a pained smile, and gave a quick explanation of the firing mechanism. He stared at the landscapes for a minute, at the soaring mountains and shady plains, hearing the soft *click-click* of the hammer drawing back – and then the sharp *clack* as it sprang back into the body of the gun. This was repeated several times, and the weapon declared a positive *wonder* of engineering in tones so loud that they almost jingled the coins in Sam's waistcoat pocket.

Something seemed to occur to his lordly host; turning around, he let the shining pistol go limp in his hand, the barrel angled towards the floor. 'You gave a tour of your marvellous factory to my dear friend Lajos Kossuth, did you not, back in April? I noticed it in the newspapers and meant to see you then, but events got the better of me. You are a supporter of his, I take it?'

'I am,' Sam said with a grave nod. He noticed that a tiny ironic line had appeared at the side of Lawrence Street's mouth. 'A true American always backs the cause of liberty.'

The minister inclined his head in polite acknowledgement, raising his eyebrows. 'Of course he does. Not that such admirable sentiments will help Mr Kossuth, I am afraid. The poor devil is doomed to fail. He has too many foes, and of the most inconveniently influential variety. Why, when I attempted to have him to stay at my country seat a few years ago – as a rather modest demonstration of support – the cabinet, including several close colleagues of mine, passed a vote expressly forbidding it! Imagine that, Colonel!' He sighed, laying the Navy on the oval table that stood in the centre of the room. 'Have there been any other noteworthy guests since?'

'There have not. I've been back in Connecticut, y'see, and my brother –'

Lord Palmerston exchanged a look with Street. 'We really should remedy that with all haste, I think. Your renown must spread yet further, my dear Colonel – you deserve it, and I will do everything I can to ensure it. Come, let us drink to your amazing invention! What would you care for?'

'Bourbon,' muttered Sam gratefully.

'Bourbon, then, for Colonel Colt!' cried Lord Palmerston, sending a servant scampering immediately from the room. 'Bourbon for us all!

The drinks came in moments, far more quickly than Sam would have thought possible. He swallowed his down at once and was promptly poured another. They settled themselves in a ring of high-backed chairs, upholstered in oxblood leather – apart from Mr Lowry and a couple of the minister's more junior aides, who remained by the door and windows respectively. Cigars were lit and snuff taken. Sam cut a plug of Old Red, thinking to make use of the wide fireplace; but to his surprise, a fine silver spittoon was brought in and placed at his feet.

'Presented to me by an American friend,' Palmerston said. 'Suitable for all manner of expectoration, I find.'

As evening approached they talked their way through the meatiest issues of the day, the minister leading the conversation in his expansive, erratically voluble manner. Sam did his bit but grew increasingly unsatisfied; after such a promising start, their discourse stayed well away from the definite pledges of government custom that he'd been pretty confident of receiving. He reminded himself that the Home Secretary's area of authority was domestic issues. Lord

Palmerston was in no position to patronise the Colt Company, whatever his views on the necessity and inevitability of war and the superior quality of the Colt revolver. Finishing off his fifth whiskey, Sam tried to raise the subject of the police, and how fearfully under-equipped they were for what was a damnably dangerous job – only to be knocked back down at once. Englishmen, he was informed rather pompously, instinctively deplore the idea of an armed police; the sure and certain result of such folly would be an enormous rise in shootings by policemen, and a new breed of criminal who carried a gun of his own as a matter of course.

Chewing hard, the gun-maker fixed his gaze on the Navy that lay on the table before him, trying to halt the turning of his temper by running his eye over its perfectly fashioned lines. An invitation to dine was extended. Sam wasn't inclined to accept at first, but the expression on Street's face made him reconsider – the purpose of this meeting, it seemed to say, has not yet been attained. Leaning around in his chair, the gun-maker instructed Mr Lowry to return to the factory and see to the close of the day's business.

It was fine enough fare, some woody-tasting game-birds followed by baked turbot and a rich macaroni pudding; Sam got the servant to leave him the bourbon bottle, deciding that he would make the best of the situation. There was no sign of a wife, or indeed women of any kind. The minister simply stated that Lady Palmerston was out of town visiting a friend, and called for another bottle of Bordeaux. As they ate, their host regaled them with the story of his latest ingenious play in the Commons, in which he outsmarted his rivals (who, it seemed, were legion) and saw his own murky political ends achieved. Here was a man, Sam mused, who revelled in cunning and subterfuge at the highest levels – Lawrence Street's true master. This dinner would not be innocent. Something was up.

At some advanced point the discussion moved on to America, specifically the Kansas-Nebraska Act that was just about to be introduced to Congress. Sam had heard much about this over the summer. Slave-owners and antislavery abolitionists were both pouring into the same western regions, and President Franklin Pierce, in an ill-conceived attempt to calm the situation, was going formally to create the territories of Kansas and Nebraska, and then allow the residents to vote on whether or not they would have slaves there. This potentially meant the expansion of America's slave ownership; everyone Sam had spoken to in New York and Connecticut was staunchly opposed to the Act, considering it a presidential sop to the slavers made by an openly pro-Southern Democrat, a doughface of the weakest kind.

Palmerston was very interested in this affair; he'd obviously been following it closely, and had in fact given it a good deal more thought than Sam had himself. 'Your President is storing up trouble there, Colonel, you mark my words. The people in these new states will not separate themselves neatly, in accordance with some unseen celestial plan. There will be violence, bloodshed, conflict even – in the western territories, yes, but also in America at large. I fear that the evil of slavery is set to bring your young nation to a very dismal head.'

Street spoke up from the end of the dining table. 'Surely, Colonel, as a proud Connecticut Yankee, you are as fierce an opponent of slavery as any man in this room?'

Sam sat back, frowning, swilling the bourbon around in his glass. The pious tone of these Englishmen was annoying him; he felt that they were passing judgement on something they could never hope to understand. 'I've seen the South,' he answered slowly. 'I sailed along the Ohio River in the thirties, and I've spent some time in New Orleans. And I have to admit that slavery is a deeply wrong-headed system.'

'Hear, hear!' hollered Palmerston, banging the tabletop.

'Bravo,' said Street, rather more quietly.

'To my mind,' the gun-maker went on, 'it is above all very wasteful and inefficient. The blacks are ignorant and idle beyond belief, and they do nothing well. And the whites, so used to being slave-masters, have forgotten how to perform even the smallest service for themselves. The result is a society where every meal is lukewarm, every bed

275

unmade, every shirt but half-washed and burned by the goddamn iron.'

There was an uncertain pause.

'You favour emancipation, though,' Street said. 'Surely.'

'More than that,' Sam came back, 'I believe that every Negro in the American states should be returned to the African lands from which he was originally taken, without delay. The southern states would improve beyond measure if they had decent workers toiling for a decent daily wage. And I can tell you, gentlemen, that could such a thing be arranged, there wouldn't be a single plantation owner who'd oppose it.' He knocked back his whiskey, barely feeling it pass down his throat. 'But it's impossible, sadly; there's already far too many of 'em. And I'm told they breed like goddamn rats.'

The Englishmen were looking at each other over their half-filled wine glasses. Someone, one of the aides, coughed.

'At any rate,' pronounced Lord Palmerston after a couple of seconds, 'whichever way it all proceeds will be favourable for you, eh, Colonel? Ah, the great comfort that must reside in manufacturing weapons for one's livelihood! No danger at all of the market for your worthy productions drying up, now is there?'

He gave Sam that smile again, the inside of his taut upper lip blackened by red wine. Sam looked back at him, feeling adversarial and pretty goddamn drunk. He couldn't make this old bastard out. Was he mocking Sam, or the divided people of America, or both? Or neither?

The gun-maker picked up the bourbon bottle. 'As I often have cause to remark, Mister Palmerston,' he snarled, drawing out the stopper, 'the Colt revolver is a *peacemaker*. Brought to a dispute of any size, in any part of the world, by any man, it will make the goddamn peace. You can take that as the seller's guarantee.'

This bold claim brought Sam's gift of pistols back to the minister's mind, and he proposed that they go out into his garden right then to shoot off a few bullets. Sam consented without really thinking, and lurched through the mansion's luxury out into the darkness. The evening, he realised, had slipped past him entirely; it was night, full and proper, black

276

as the bottom of a pond. He was aware that it must be cold as the breath was coming out of their little party like rushes of steam, but he hardly felt it. The garden was seriously big, far more space than should rightfully be reserved for one man in the heart of the largest city on earth. Two lanterns had been set against the base of a wall, and for a second Sam thought that they were to serve as the targets; then he saw the half-dozen old boots arranged in a line between them. Someone had loaded one of the pistols, and by general consensus it was offered to Sam.

'Show us how it is done, Colonel!' they cried.

Sam refused, pushing his trembling hands deep into the pockets of his coat, which some obliging flunky had brought over and helped him into. He found himself longing for the rocking of a railway carriage, for the swell of the sea against a steam-ship's hull; for the sweet freedom of travel.

The company proved insistent. 'Come, sir,' urged Palmerston. 'Why, a revolver-shooting lesson from Colonel Samuel Colt is akin to instruction in music from Charles Hallé – or in sculpture from the immortal Buonarroti! Do not deny us, I beg you!'

The gun-maker shook his head, turning to spit his plug away into some bushes. 'I don't shoot at targets,' he said firmly. 'Not ever.'

After a short, quizzical silence, the minister gestured for the pistol to be given to him instead, briefly weighing it in his hand before taking aim with offhand confidence. His first shot sounded rather muted to Sam, a dry pop more than a bang; then a split-second later it echoed back from somewhere with its volume doubled, setting several distant dogs off into frenzied peals of barking. The old fellow fiddled with the hammer and fired again. One of the boots spun and flapped like a leathery bird, prompting a round of huzzahs – the loudest of which came from the shooter himself. Curtains started to open in houses all around the garden, and faces both irate and fearful peeped out. Palmerston glanced up at them with clear satisfaction before loosing the remaining four shots in a deliberate, emphatic rhythm. Only one hit home, shearing off a toecap before striking the brickwork behind.

Sam was caught in the cloud of powder-smoke, and a mighty sneeze ripped through him, nearly doubling him over. As he recovered, wiping his eyes with a handkerchief, he heard a visitor being announced – Lord John Russell, no less, another senior member of Lord Aberdeen's cabinet. Sam had courted this fellow in the past, back when he'd been prime minister, yet his advances had met with complete indifference. Russell's current position – Leader of the House – was a useless one as far as Sam was concerned, and he resolved to leave. He'd had his fill of these John Bull politicians for one night, quite frankly, and desired only the peace and solitude of his rooms.

Palmerston passed the smoking revolver to a lackey, proclaiming the experience great fun. Rubbing his hands together, he turned to meet his latest caller. Russell had been brought straight through from the hall and was still in top hat and greatcoat. His face was fine-boned, aristocratic, almost feminine; Palmerston looked like a positive brute beside him, which was no mean feat. He, too, was old and strikingly small, but wizened rather than bandy, and brooding where his colleague was brash. It emerged that he'd come straight from Parliament, and was there to discuss what was described only as 'reform'. Looking to the revolver, he said that he'd heard the gunfire out on Carlton Gardens, and had simply assumed that Palmerston had taken to using firearms on his beleaguered servants – 'as it is surely the next natural step'.

The Home Secretary introduced Sam with great fanfare, going on to provide an enthused, rose-hued description of an afternoon-long discussion of production methods and pricing that had culminated in a little practical demonstration.

'All fascinating, *fascinating* stuff, Russell,' he boomed. 'The shape of the future, I tell you.'

Russell nodded, feigning a casual interest, plainly suspicious. These two were seasoned political operators and had clearly been sparring against one another for years. Deciding to leave them to it, Sam bade them both a curt goodnight, saying that the next day was set to be a damnably busy one. Palmerston didn't try to convince him to stay longer, but his farewell was warm; somewhat warmer, in fact, than their inconclusive meeting seemed to warrant. Sam strode back through the house in a state of whiskey-blasted irascibility, feeling as if he'd just been played for a fool, paraded like a chieftain from a savage land.

Footsteps trotted up behind him, and a hand was laid on his forearm on its backward swing. It was Street. 'A word, Colonel,' he said quickly.

Sam didn't stop. 'My time is *valuable*, Mr Street – I have told you that before, haven't I? What the devil was all that about? Kansas? *Slavery*, for God's sake? I don't like being manipulated. I won't damn well stand for it. There are plenty of other nations that want my arms. Why, the Emperor of France is –' *Steady now, Samuel*, warned a cool, sober voice from somewhere inside him; *watch your goddamn tongue.* 'The simple truth of it is that I don't have the leisure to stand about and be gulled by old Jeremy Diddler in there, with his curious hair and his ivory teeth and his miserable goddamn condescension! And so good night to you, Mr Street!'

Reaching the front door some seconds before the startled footman, Sam was forced to wait while his hat was fetched. Street seized the opportunity, delivering his argument with the speed and precision of a master chef slicing up an onion.

'He is using you, yes, but generous recompense will come. He was showing you – and Lord Russell there – that he is your *friend*. Lord Palmerston will not be in the Home Office forever, Colonel. He has greater things in mind. The government is desperately weak, and all this prevarication and delay over Russia is only making it look weaker. Our political opponents are too scattered and irresolute to mount any kind of challenge. It is a good time for a strong figure – a popular figure, who has shown nerve and decisiveness from the start.' The hat arrived; Street managed to meet Sam's eye as he pulled it on. 'And Colonel, it is an exceedingly good time to have such a figure as your friend.'

Sam scowled and stepped outside. 'We'll see about *that*, Mr Street, won't we,' he said, and raised his arm to summon to his coachman.

PART THREE

The Devil's Acre

1

The Exchequer on Bridge Street was the sort of inexpensive chop-house you could be done with in less than a quarter-hour. It was heaving with parliamentary types, aides, clerks and newspapermen for the most part. Circular tables were arranged across the main room like lilies on a pond, the parties dining upon them seated so closely together that they seemed in many places to overlap. Edward immediately felt rather out of his element, but was glad of the Exchequer's warmth after the chill fog that drifted about New Palace Yard. He removed his gloves and peered around in the low gaslight; spotting Saul Graff's stooped shoulders away in a corner booth, he signalled his intentions to the head waiter and started to edge over to his friend.

One word hung above the tables, shaping itself from the diners' cigar smoke in letters three feet high: *Sinope*. An Ottoman harbour on the Black Sea, it had been the site of the first major clash between Russia and Turkey, reported in the British press that morning. A Turkish flotilla carrying reinforcements and supplies had been sheltering there when a surprise attack was launched by a Russian squadron sailing out from Sebastopol. The Turkish ships had been blown to timber in under an hour, almost without resistance, and fires had spread to the shore; thousands of sailors and towns-people were believed to have perished. The mood in the Exchequer was one of condemnation, of outrage at a dastardly attack by the Tsar's men – and anticipation of

British action, especially as a fleet under Admiral Dundas was ready and waiting at Constantinople.

Opposite Graff sat the Honourable Simon Bannan, his friend's employer, hunched over a spread of newspapers with a monocle jammed in his right eye and a black beer bottle at his elbow. The radical MP was a solid block of a man with a short-cropped grey beard and an air of common sense affronted. The member for Limerick and a minor official on the Board of Trade, he'd been convinced to join Aberdeen's coalition by Sir William Molesworth, leader of the radicals aligned to the Prime Minister, on the promise of wide-ranging political reform. Although proudly Irish, Bannan took care to distance himself from the outspoken nationalism of the Commons' so-called 'Irish Brigade'. He took no open stance on the Home Rule question and seldom made an issue of his religion, even sitting stoically through Lord John Russell's frequent anti-Catholic statements in the House.

'The problem with radicals,' Graff had once said, 'and Irish radicals in particular, is that they are an army of captains. Any sense of a unified cause is soon sacrificed to personal glory. But not with Mr Bannan – he's prepared to put every other matter aside to bring about the betterment of the system at large. Dash it all, he even had no qualms about employing *me*, an Israelite not five years from his baptismal font, as his confidential aide.'

Edward sat himself next to Saul, who introduced him to Mr Bannan. The Honourable Member didn't so much as look up from his papers.

'They are calling it a massacre,' he declared in a clipped, educated brogue. 'Two nations are at war. Their navies fight a battle, one wins a decisive victory over the other – and they call it a massacre. People *die in war*. Did they honestly not realise that this was the case when they were calling for it so enthusiastically?'

'An easy enough thing to overlook, I suppose,' murmured Saul.

'It's all too clear what will happen now, Mr Graff. Pam and his supporters will call the affair a stain on British honour

284

or some other canting nonsense – urge that Dundas steam into the Black Sea straight away to protect poor Turkey from further attack. They have a sanguinary incident to cite, and they won't stop citing it. You just watch.' Bannan sighed, turning the page. His brow twitched in Edward's direction. 'So you are the Colt fellow. Mr Graff tells me that you have interesting news concerning your master.'

'Indeed I have, sir.' Edward took off his hat. 'Last week the Colonel was received at Carlton Gardens. He was granted a lengthy personal audience with the Home Secretary. Lawrence Street was present also, and there was talk of business – well, they were dancing around it, at any rate. Some manner of understanding is certainly in place.'

This got Bannan's attention. He shifted back on his bench, taking out his monocle, frowning in thought.

Saul's expression was quizzical. 'Seems a damned strange connection for Pam to be making at this point, don't it? I mean, he can certainly be of great help to Colt, but what's in it for him?'

'Oh, it's an arrangement of mutual benefit,' Bannan said. 'We can be quite sure of *that*. It is subtle, a small part of a larger plan – an eye-catching component of Lord Palmerston's continued machinations.' He nodded out at the customers of the Exchequer. 'Word will go around that the two of them have spoken, that they are on friendly terms. Pam'll make sure it seeps out somehow. It will add to the public's impression that he is the only one in the cabinet thinking about what the British Army will need if we go to war. The contrast between him and the Prime Minister will seem greater than ever. Pam is scoping out resources, they will say – trying to find ways to give our brave soldiers an edge over the Russian Bear.'

'But why on earth is Lord Palmerston so set on waging war?' Edward asked.

The Honourable Member began to fold away his newspapers. 'It plays well in the street, Mr Lowry – Christ Almighty, in this place too. Stout-hearted Britons all, rallying behind plucky Pam! Public opinion has a rare power, y'see, and our noble lord has become a dab hand at harnessing it.

285

This business at Sinope will have him positively jumping with joy – even as he prepares to deliver his denunciation and yet another call to arms.'

There was bitterness in his voice. Edward had heard of Bannan's own clashes with Palmerston in the House – his efforts to argue against war on economic grounds, in terms of the disruption to trade. Pam had rebuffed this scornfully, of course, with yet more discoursing on the obligations of British honour.

'He wishes to make the Aberdeen ministry, a government *he* serves in, look as ridiculous and ineffectual as he can. They call for reform, for an extension of the franchise backed by every other member of the cabinet – and Lord Palmerston alone blocks it. They want negotiation with Russia, and a peaceful end to the ructions in the East – and he calls at every opportunity for belligerent acts that will surely carry us to war.'

'Pam seeks the fall of the government, Edward,' Saul chimed in. 'He makes himself a faulty support, then deliberately gives the edifice a shake. He wants Aberdeen to undergo a humiliating collapse.'

'His ultimate aim,' Bannan continued, 'is to make himself the only option for Prime Minister. He wants the Queen, who has never tried to disguise her deep dislike for him, to be forced to ask that he form a government. He's engineering things so that she will have no other choice. That's where all this is heading, and it's quite typical of the man that he sees a war as a price worth paying to bring it about. He knows that a major conflict would soon finish off Aberdeen, and that there would be a great call for Pam, the mighty warrior-bulldog, to replace him.'

Bannan rubbed his eyes, squeezing thumb and forefinger in towards the bridge of his nose; Saul had told Edward that they were having a frantically busy week, with debates and divisions running on until three or four in the morning.

'To Lord Palmerston, y'see, as a childless aristocrat, war is an entirely abstract exercise. What difference to him if armies are sent to die in the East? Who does he know who might feasibly have to march before the Russian guns?'

The politician stared at his beer bottle. 'Whereas I have a son in the 18th Royal Irish, a captain. He will certainly go to war should Pam's play for the top office take us that far. For me, for the boy's mother and his wife, the prospect is very real.' He picked up the bottle and swigged straight from the neck.

'My cousin is a subaltern in the 44th East Essex,' Edward volunteered, reeling a little from all this worrying analysis. 'He too looks likely to be sent.'

A waiter arrived at the table with two plates of food – mutton chops with a slice of bread and a mound of steaming greens. Saul asked Edward if he would order; he declined, saying that he could not stay long. Bannan, meanwhile, was considering Colt's London secretary like a magistrate trying to get the measure of a suspect in the dock. Once the waiter had departed, he leaned forward to ask a question.

'Why exactly have you come to me, Mr Lowry? Why are you telling me about your employer's affairs?'

'Mr Graff is an old friend, sir. I owe him my position at Colt. We had an arrangement that I would inform him of the Colonel's activities in relation to the government – so that I could properly understand them myself, as much as anything.'

'And are you still comfortable with your position at this gun company now that the storm of war is drifting over us – and your employer is on such good terms with the minister doing everything he can to ensure that it breaks?'

Edward hesitated. 'It is business only,' he replied, reaching for the standard answer. 'Someone must supply arms, and the Colonel's are the best to be had.'

Bannan was unconvinced. 'You believe that, do you? All deliberation stops there?'

The secretary looked out into the busy chop-house, thinking of the doubts he had accrued over the past months; of Arthur preparing to go to war and the dreadful anxieties this had provoked within his family; of the serving girl's bloody slippers and the naked terror in her eyes; of the Navy revolver beneath his bed, hidden away like a black secret. It was difficult to answer with any conviction, so he did not try.

The Honourable Member took hold of his knife and fork and started sawing at his meat with sudden appetite. 'Mr Lowry, you must be aware that by coming to me you are effectively turning traitor. In my opposition to Lord Palmerston I might well use what you've told me about his preferential treatment of your Colonel – over, say, our own British gun-makers – to come at him. Colt might even end up losing the government custom he desires so much.' Bannan chewed and swallowed, then looked over at him. 'That factory of his could be forced to close. Mr Graff here might be obliged to find you a new position.'

'I understand this, Mr Bannan.'

Edward found that he could contemplate his act of betrayal with absolute equanimity. Besides, he didn't think it likely that the factory would shut down – the Colonel would never allow himself to be beaten with such ease. His hope was rather that any efforts made by Mr Bannan to investigate Colt's understanding with Lord Palmerston would create a valuable diversion. It might encourage further assaults from the likes of Adams, who would surely be alarmed by the connection between his American rival and the Home Secretary; it would certainly require Noone to make the safeguarding of the works his priority, ahead of his ongoing hunt for Caroline Knox, thus buying her some more time to locate her sister and make her escape from London.

He stood, putting on his hat, nodding to Saul as he prepared to leave. 'A good evening to you, sir,' he said to Bannan. 'You will hear from me again.'

Caroline left the crowd sheltering beneath the pediment of St Martin's and hurried down the steps towards him. They met on the pavement and without exchanging so much as a glance headed away from the tangled traffic of Trafalgar Square towards the Strand. She wore the clothes he'd bought for her a couple of weeks previously: smart yet plain, calculated to make her seem like a governess or a respectable young wife. Together they were utterly unexceptional, and they passed through the rainy streets without drawing any notice. She curled her hand around his upper arm, stroking the inside softly with her thumb. This small intimacy made him catch his breath; a foolish smile sprang onto his face and would not be removed.

The long, straight Strand was sunk in a smothering fog that reduced the light of its gas-lamps to a feeble glimmer. Vehicles and other pedestrians, moving slowly enough, seemed to charge from the murk; they stayed close to the shop windows, following the bright row of mullions and plate-glass as if it marked out the only pathway carved across a barren moor. Many of these windows were decorated for Christmas, displaying colourful placards conveying messages of festive cheer, garlands of holly, great pyramids of nuts or oranges and model nativity scenes. Walking past them on that wet winter's evening, Edward felt happier than he'd thought possible. The situation was absolutely insane, of course, crack-brained beyond belief. He was harbouring a criminal, someone who had stolen from his employer, the same employer he'd just betrayed all over again with Mr Bannan. There were people after her, dangerous men indeed. He was risking everything – his prospects, his liberty, even his safety. Yet how could any of this concern him? *She* was on his arm, Caroline Knox, pulling herself as close to him as she could. They would manage somehow.

Then she said, 'Amy's still here.'

Edward glanced down at her, his foolish smile fading; the silhouette of a wooden Gabriel was reflected in her wide, excited eyes. 'Is that so?'

Caroline nodded. 'I found someone who thinks they saw her up at the apple market, day before yesterday. She's still here, Edward, in London – and with Katie too.'

He didn't know how to react to this news. It was deeply pleasing to see her so hopeful, and he was glad that she might be reunited with the sister and niece for whom she plainly cared so much. Several weeks of searching had yielded nothing; both of them had started to think that it was futile, that Amy had left the city, never to be seen again. But this happiness was paired with a dull panic, a rising cramp in his chest and throat as something from which he had been deliberately averting his gaze was dragged unavoidably before him.

If she finds them, he thought, they will flee London together. She will leave me.

Back at his rooms on that first night, they'd shivered together in his dark, cluttered parlour, sharing a tea-cup of brandy as he tried to coax the fire to life. Sitting cross-legged on the hearth, Edward had watched the warmth break slowly across her tear-tracked skin. She'd sighed after her first sip of liquor, a sound full of gratitude and relief; and he'd felt a powerful urge to touch her face, to lay his fingers upon those two even moles on her cheek. He'd forced his attention back to the struggling fire. Only a low scoundrel would seek to take advantage of this circumstance. He was no such person.

Soon afterwards, he'd prepared a bed for her before the fire, the most comfortable spot in the apartment by his reckoning, and made to retire. She'd stepped forward, though, halting him, thanking him again for what he had done for her and taking his hands in hers. A sense of sweet inevitability settled upon them; they suddenly stumbled into an embrace, knocking aside a footstool and a pile of periodicals. For some minutes they stood very still, trembling again even though the coal fire was now hissing away steadily. Booted footsteps thudded up and down the staircase outside. Then her lips were tingling against his neck, softly tracing a line from his collar to his ear. He ran a hand down her spine to the small of her back; one of her thighs, smooth and supple, slipped between his. Their kiss felt long deferred, granted to them at last as everything grew so perilously strange, and it held all of their fear and yearning and hunger for solace. He did not reach his bedroom that night, and had not reached it since.

Early the next morning, they had shared their stories. He'd related the ordeal of the garrotting, which no longer seemed quite so serious. In turn, he'd learnt how she'd been drawn into the Irishmen's scheme and made to disregard him – and had been incredulous at how closely it matched his imaginings. The plot to kill Lord John was alarming, but it had surely been foiled; the conspirators were scattered and their access to the factory shut off. Despite his ardour, he'd only half-believed her account of the guns in the cellar. It was simply too unlikely. Privately, he theorised that they were in fact leftover weapons from the American works, brought to London at the start of the year. This would explain the missing Tower of London proof marks. As to their massive numbers, Caroline had last been down there in pitch darkness. She could easily have been mistaken.

It was difficult, however, to care very much about any of it. Every evening upon his return from the factory she was there, in his rooms, waiting; she would rise into his arms and kiss him; they would fall back down together on her makeshift bed and often stay there until morning, remembering to eat only when it was almost time for him to leave once more. He felt altered, as if he'd been opened up, liberated somehow; it was a sensation of such intoxicating freedom that he thought it might part him permanently from his senses. Yet despite all this, one worry was always present, huddled in a dark recess of his mind, tempering his joy just a little. And now, with this first solid piece of information on Amy's whereabouts, it had to be addressed.

Edward led her into the empty doorway of Coutts's Bank. 'Caroline, what is going to happen should you discover her?'

She turned her head away; she knew what he was asking. 'I have to find out if she's all right. I have to.'

'You mean that you'll convince her to leave town with you. That you will both go as soon as it can be arranged.'

'We ain't safe in London while that Yankee's here. You know that. Noone won't give up on us.'

He frowned, thinking how soon his modest savings could be withdrawn from his bank. 'Then I shall come with you.'

She looked back at him doubtfully. 'Edward –'

'Caroline, I would leave this instant if you asked it of me. I would go anywhere.' *I love you*, he thought, *more than anything else in the world.*

'You are a city creature,' she said, smiling tenderly, laying a gloved hand against his cheek, 'and don't you try to say otherwise. London is your place.'

Edward protested this passionately, desperately, knowing as he did so that he would never be able to convince her.

There was a terrible buoyancy to their exchange, as if it was all some sort of joke that no amount of earnestness on his part could convince her to take seriously. She leaned in to kiss him, to hush him it felt like, bringing her face from shadow into the weak gaslight – and at once he saw her meaning. Perfect as it was, this could not last.

The first sure sign that something was afoot came in the form of visits from the military. During the January of 1854 the Colonel conducted a veritable brigade of soldiers and sailors around his works. Their colourful uniforms became a common sight, threading their way through the lathes and drop-hammers and filing across the yard. Among them were some real high-ups; Lord Hardinge, commander-in-chief of the entire army, came to call one frozen Wednesday morning and chewed on a breakfast muffin as he studied the machines. Colt was entirely comfortable before these men, adopting a ringmaster's swagger, holding forth on the many stunning victories won in Texas and Mexico by the armies that had carried his guns and the general indispensability of the six-shooter to any modern military force. His guests were led through every department, shown pistol parts at each stage of manufacture and invited to fire off the finished article in the proving room. All were deeply impressed, directing their aides to take copious notes and subjecting the Colonel to some close questioning. He took this in good grace, by his standards at least, and anyone ranking above major was presented with a pair of engraved London-made Navys before they left.

On the surface of it, the reason for this rush of interest was obvious. Three days into the New Year, Admiral Dundas had been ordered to send a fleet into the Black Sea from Constantinople. Lord Palmerston, unsurprisingly, seemed to bear central responsibility for this development. Shortly after Edward's meeting with Bannan and Graff, the Home Secretary had suddenly resigned from his post. The explanation given was a fundamental disagreement over Lord John's latest reform proposals – but the widespread assumption was that it had been prompted by frustration over continued government inaction after the clash at Sinope. It did not last for much more than a week. After some frantic back-room appeasement, Palmerston was back in office; and a few days later Dundas had dispatched his warships to face down the Russian Navy.

Edward had received a note from Saul the next morning. 'Typically dramatic move from Pam,' it had read. 'He knows full well that Aberdeen would come to a total smash with him as an outsider – as a potential rival and agitator. So our conniving Home Secretary has forced a foreign policy decision! Our ships are on the front line in the Turkish war – peace is no longer possible! And a very happy New Year to you, my friend!!!'

Faced with the definite prospect of Britain at war, and with his factory being lauded in the most influential circles, Colonel Colt grew yet more hard-nosed in his protection of his interests. He'd been away over Christmas, God only knew where, and had returned to find discontent among his American staff. A delegation of about a dozen men, led by Gage Stickney, was demanding higher wages – a representative share, they said, of what the Colonel was producing. Edward had not been able to understand this demand. He'd seen the sales figures and the stock-room tally – the Colonel's wages were more than fair. Colt had been enraged by this piece of mutiny, as he'd termed it, but had appeared to consent, asking for ten days to calculate a fresh deal. Stickney, poor chump that he was, had agreed; and as soon as he'd left the room the Colonel instructed Edward to wire Connecticut for replacements, to set sail for London by the next Atlantic steamer. He then waited out the ten days, allowing the new workers to get as close as possible, before dismissing Stickney and all who'd stood with him.

It was a cold-blooded stratagem, in both conception and execution. Not only had these Yankees been cut loose from their jobs and cast out of their lodgings, they were also thousands of miles from home. But the Colonel had no pity for them whatsoever. All he would give his former employees was the address of the American consul in Liverpool, saying that this official would loan them the money for their passage if they didn't have it. There had been a fair bit of cursing and shouting, and the watchman had been called to see them off. The replacements from Hartford had arrived a few days later.

Among this party had been a new assistant for Mr Quill, an apprentice mechanic to take the place of Martin Rea. Lou Ballou had lapsed from his gastric upset into a deeper malady and was seldom seen about the works; Quill needed another pair of hands to keep the engine running smoothly. If he was glad of the help, though, he did not show it. Two months on, he was still in a state of wounded disbelief at Rea's treachery. His habitual good cheer entirely gone, he shuffled around the engine room like a man who had just seen a close relation put to death. Edward considered approaching him, consoling him, perhaps telling him what he knew about the details of Rea's plot; but he suspected that this might actually make matters worse and so kept his distance.

Besides, the secretary had his own burden to bear. Caroline's search for her sister continued. The sighting before Christmas had failed to yield results as yet, but she refused to be discouraged. Returning home to Red Lion Square, or arriving at any of the places they'd agreed to meet, became a daily trial for Edward. Each time he was convinced that she would not be there – that she'd have located her sister and be on a train rushing through the countryside, away from him forever. Her company brought him peace for an hour or two, and sometimes longer, as the prospect of disaster was delayed once again. But in the early dawn, while she lay sleeping by his side, the creeping ache of uncertainty would return.

It occurred to him that if Colonel Colt were to be bankrupted, if he left England and took Walter Noone with him, then she'd be safe. She wouldn't have to flee London. He'd never become a Colt manager, of course, but what the devil did that matter now? They would be together. With every bellicose development in the East, however, with every triumphant factory tour given to an army commander, the Colonel's future in Britain seemed more and more secure.

The situation Colt had been hoping for ever since he'd first decided to open a manufactory in Europe was coming to pass. He wasn't going anywhere.

Edward was brooding over this up in the factory office one afternoon when an unexpected visitor, a civilian, was shown in. He'd presented himself at the Bessborough Place gate and asked to see the Colonel. It was immediately obvious that this caller was American. Dressed in an approximation of Colt's own vivid style, he was a slight, vigorous-looking man of about fifty with a wry grin fixed permanently upon his face. The secretary rose from his chair and introduced himself, explaining that the Colonel was over in the proving room addressing a problem with a batch of ready-made cartridges. The visitor merely nodded in response, saying nothing, sauntering around the office with absolute self-assurance. He settled himself in front of the circular window, letting out a long sigh of contentment as he gazed over at the Thames. Edward was considering sitting down again and perhaps making a start on the day's correspondence when there was a thumping, creaking commotion out in the hallway, as if the factory block was being torn down from the inside.

'Here he comes,' chuckled the man by the window. 'Here's ol' Sam.'

The office door cracked open, whipping back against its frame, and the Colonel sprang through. At the sight of each other, the two burst into wild laughter, lunging forward into a back-slapping embrace.

'Why, Tommy boy,' Colt cried, 'when the hell did you get here?' Releasing his friend, he strode around the desk, elbowing Edward aside so that he could take a whiskey bottle and two short glasses from one of the lower drawers.

''Bout three hours ago,' Tommy replied. 'I came straight over. Quite an empire you've built for yourself, Samuel – even down to your little John Bull butler here.'

Colt laughed again, none too pleasantly, and ordered Edward from the room. The secretary made to retrieve the correspondence, so that he could work on it elsewhere, only to be shooed away. 'You can go. You're done for the day, Mr Lowry.'

'But Colonel, it's only four o'clock, and we have to –'

An impatient finger was pointed at the door. 'Just *go*, damn it!'

Edward walked from the factory into the winter dusk, smarting with humiliation. Somehow, despite his continued professionalism, Colt seemed to sense the change brought about in him by Caroline's plight – the change in his feelings towards the Colt Company – and was growing ever cooler towards him as a result. For a while, Edward had been worried that he actually suspected something. There had been that conversation in the carriage, just before the meeting with Lord Palmerston, when he'd brushed terrifyingly close to the truth; but it had never been pursued, convincing Edward that it had been simple chance, or perceptiveness even, rather than prior knowledge. Indeed, since the New Year and the escalation of business, Colt had shown little interest in his secretary at all.

Richards was over in the staff reading room, a dingy nook that was tucked around the back of the blueing department and shared its scorched, fishy smell. He was seated at a rectangular table in the centre of the room, working his way through a pile of newspapers and trade publications by the light of an old oil lamp, squinting through the smoke that curled from his crooked cigar.

'Our Mr Adams won't give in easily,' he remarked as Edward entered, jotting down a note on a piece of paper. 'The blighter's rumoured to be readying for another run at the Board of Ordnance. He wants to beat us to the government's business, Lowry! The old battle is waging once again, and I must take up my pen to retaliate.'

Edward sat opposite him, listening to this without interest. 'The Colonel has discharged me for the day, Richards,' he said. 'He has a visitor – a confidential visitor, it would seem.'

Richards lay down the newspaper and stretched back in his chair. 'Ah yes, Mr Hart Seymour.'

'You know of him.' Edward was not surprised.

The press agent angled his head and expelled a small exclamation point of smoke. 'My dear chap, Thomas Hart

Seymour is one of Sam Colt's tightest allies. They made a deal a few years back that became positively famous in certain circles. Sam's ready cash helped Hart Seymour to the governorship of Connecticut – and in return, mere days after taking office, he gave Colonel Colt his rank.'

'But surely it was a military appointment – a promotion?'

Richards wagged his finger chidingly. 'Now that's an *assumption*, Mr Lowry, ain't it? Has Sam ever said he was a soldier?'

'I suppose he has not.'

'You suppose right, my friend. No, it was that spry little cove up in the office who turned plain old Mr Colt into a colonel. They love their sinecures and special preferments over in America, y'know, as much as any of our City of London grandees. Some kind of militia act was used to pass it through, I think; Sam was made Hart Seymour's aide-de-camp, but it was a purely ceremonial position. He's never donned a uniform in his life. Never had so much as a single shot fired at him.' Richards tapped some ash on the floor. 'It's all just snake-oil, Mr Lowry, as our Yankee friends might say. A spot of gammon and spinnage to shift more guns – to make Sam stand out from his competitors. Masterful, if you think about it – brilliant in its sheer simplicity.'

Edward was in no mood to admire their employer. 'What is he doing here now then, this Mr Hart Seymour? Is he governor no longer?'

Richards shook his head. 'He threw his weight behind that hopeless booby Franklin Pierce in the presidential contest of fifty-two, and is en route to his reward. Mr Hart Seymour has been appointed the new American Minister to the Court of His Imperial Majesty Tsar Nicholas of Russia.' The press agent looked at Edward meaningfully. 'Should think there'll be a few fellows over in Whitehall who'll want a word with him before he carries on his way.'

'Indeed,' said Edward, climbing to his feet, thinking that he would head for Red Lion Square. Caroline usually gave up her search as it got dark and might already be back there – assuming that she hadn't found Amy and taken flight.

'You seem a little fraught, old boy,' Richards observed,

297

returning his attention to his newspapers. 'Is everything well?'

Edward gave a noncommittal reply, feeling a headache coming on, and walked out to the yard. As he buttoned up his winter coat, he noticed Noone and his men over by the Ponsonby Street gate, bunched around a match, lighting cigars and cursing the cold. They wore greatcoats over their uniforms; they were clearly about to resume their hunt for the Colonel's enemies. Edward's headache worsened at once; he ground his teeth so hard that they seemed to shift in his jaw. He considered marching over and demanding that they leave Caroline well alone – making them understand that she was a victim of Rea, not one of his accomplices. But of course he did nothing. He knew that if he were to talk to Noone, or make some amateurish attempt to follow him, it would direct the watchman straight to Red Lion Square and bring about the certain destruction of them both. The Americans were focusing their search on the Westminster rookery, as far as he could tell. Caroline, also, was looking out for them, and was disguised by the new clothes he had bought her. There was no reason for him to be unduly concerned; but he still felt a twist of panic as they went through the gate and made for the city.

Edward glared at the factory's gas-lit windows and the taut machine-belts whirring away within, slowly regaining his calm. He saw that he'd been granted an unforeseen opportunity. The works would be running for nearly three more hours; Noone's men were busy elsewhere. The yard was empty. After a couple of seconds' further reflection, he stepped back into the warehouse, removed a screwdriver from a shelf just inside the proving room and then walked around the side of the building until he came to the cellar door.

A new padlock had been fitted, a special reinforced kind that couldn't be removed in the manner Caroline had described. Undeterred, Edward put the screwdriver in his pocket and paced eastwards along the back wall. Turning the corner at its end, he came across a rusting iron grate, sunk into the cobbles to admit some natural light into the cellar. He removed his hat and set it on the ground, glancing about to check he wasn't being watched before crouching down and gripping the grate with both hands. It was about twenty inches long and heavy, but it lifted out easily enough, the old metal rasping against stone. Beneath was a black rectangle of complete darkness. Edward struck a match and lowered it in, craning his neck to see what he could. A few feet in front of the match's wavering flame was the wooden end of a pistol crate.

Laying down flat on the cold cobbles, he lit a second match and held it out at arm's length, stretching inside the cellar as far as possible. Now he could see a great number of these crates, more even than Caroline had estimated – and far, far too many to be the remainders of that initial American batch, as he'd suspected. Murmuring an apology to her, he tried to determine the number, but the match burned away before he'd counted half of them.

There was laughter outside the factory as a couple of foundry men came out on an errand. Edward replaced the grate and got to his feet, flipping his top hat back on so quickly that the inside edge rapped hard against his skull. He stood quite still for a minute until the voices went away, staring at the warehouse wall. It was easy enough to see how it was being done. The Colonel's unique system of production isolated the various manufacturing stages. Things could be arranged so that only a few key people in the finishing shops knew exactly how many guns were being made. The contents of the stock room, those guns that had been proved in the Tower of London and entered into the records of the British Government, didn't give anything close to a true account of the Pimlico factory's output – or its potential profits. This was what Stickney and his comrades had realised, and drawing notice to it, however indirectly, had earned them a swift and merciless dismissal.

There were hundreds upon hundreds of illicit guns down there, thousands of pounds' worth. What could the Colonel possibly have in mind for them? Caroline had suggested that he might be sending them back to America, but Edward wasn't convinced. There was a pistol works in Hartford, after all, every bit as advanced as this one, and with a more experienced staff. No, these guns were destined for another customer. Edward attempted to recall every meeting he had attended with the Colonel – every conversation he had overheard and every letter he had posted – but he could not think who on earth this might be.

He made for the Ponsonby Street gate at a brisk trot, wondering how soon he could arrange to see Mr Bannan. This was something he would want to hear about.

2

The child was screaming, a raw, gulping sound drawn up from the gut, made through angry displeasure rather than distress. Thrown against her mother's shoulder, facing backwards, she wailed dejectedly at the passing stalls, clawing at the heavy woollen scarf that had been wrapped around the lower part of her face – presumably as some sort of disguise. Caroline, watching the street from a doorway, could scarcely believe it. She stepped out into the crowds, weaving around an elderly man lugging a side of beef on his back, taking care to keep the infant's flushed little face in her sight.

In late January, Newgate meat market was just about bearable. The cold kept the smells down, and it was too early for the flies; come the spring they would thicken the air to the point where you almost had to fight your way through it. Caroline had deliberately left this market until last. The sheer quantity of dead flesh assembled in the alleys of West Smithfield had always made her green about the gills. She shivered to look upon the rows of sheep's heads, laid out like so many battered clogs; the flayed cat-like creatures that she supposed were hares (but which might easily have been cats), swinging from wire gibbets; the livers, kidneys and other unnameable things heaped onto tin trays, glazed with congealing blood. Walking through it all at some speed, she'd tried to move her gaze from person to person, avoiding what lay on the stalls as much as possible.

The child recognised Caroline as she drew near, her screwed-up eyes popping wide open. Sucking in a howl, she pointed with a grubby finger and blurted out a surprised half-word. Caroline stroked her cheek, wiping away a tear, and then loosened the scarf a little. The woman carrying her glanced back to see what had stopped the child's cries. Upon seeing Caroline she came to an abrupt halt.

'Caro?' she said disbelievingly.

Amy was as fatigued as ever, even thinner perhaps, and laden down like a pack-mule. There was a large basket on her arm and a knotted shawl slung over her shoulder. Both were full to bursting with food: strings of sausages, a cheese, several bottles and grocer's parcels, apples and onions.

'Good gracious, girl,' said Caroline, taking her sister's arm and pulling her into the narrow space between two of the meat stalls. 'Looks like you're buying for a bloomin' army.'

Amy set her basket on the frozen mud underfoot. 'We – we thought you'd fled, Caro, weeks ago. We thought you was long gone.'

It was a bright, breezy morning; a strong gust drove down the lane, making the dangling racks of knives and cleavers jangle together. 'Where you been, Amy?' Caroline asked. 'I searched for you all over. Every market in London.'

'Back in the Acre,' she replied, her voice little more than a mutter. Their eyes met as Amy lowered Katie to the ground; her daughter waddled straight for Caroline, hugging at her skirts. 'Mart thought it best to be where we knew. Jack's found us a place – an old dairy, close to that theatre of his.' She rubbed at her upper arms. 'Not that he goes in there no more.'

'Your Mart lied to me,' Caroline said as she heaved up the child, 'and to you too. There was no debt. He got me mixed up in something awful – in an Irish plot to shoot down a lord. A bloody *lord*, Amy. If it'd come out, if the peelers had linked me to it, they'd have seen me hang. Even now, Colt has his men hunting for me across the city. All 'cause of your bloody Mart.'

It was clear that Amy already knew about her husband's deceptions – that she'd known for some time, and any anger she'd felt had long since burned itself out. A change had come over her since they'd last met. Her crushing grief for Michael had been put away; not forgotten, but removed from the front of her mind. In its place was a dull composure, as if certain hard decisions had been made from which she would not waver. Caroline noticed the faint shadow of a bruise at the top of her jaw, just below the ear, and a new streak of grey in the single lock of hair that hung limply across her face.

'He's sorry about everything, Caro,' she said uncomfortably, 'truly he is. They – they just really need them guns.'

Caroline could hardly believe what she'd heard. 'What d'you mean? Surely they ain't still after this lord?'

'There's a new plan. Pat Slattery's come up with another way.'

'Oh no, Amy.' Caroline felt herself sag with dismay. 'Ain't you free from that villain yet?'

Katie wriggled impatiently, so Caroline started to jig her up and down; the child made a gurgling sound and patted at the light blue ribbon tied around her aunt's bonnet.

Amy caught her breath with a slight quiver, her head dipping. 'Something's happened between them and Mart. Only Jack seems to have any liking for him any more. But they still need him for this plan of theirs.' She wiped an eye with her shawl. 'I think they might hurt us if he don't do what they want. Hurt Katie.'

As she bounced the grinning infant on her hip, Caroline began to feel sick, a cold sweat breaking out across her body. This was far worse than she'd feared. She gestured towards the basket. 'That's for them, ain't it? You're all holed up in this dairy – and they've got you running out to buy their vittles.'

'They made us a deal. If we do everything they ask and they get all the guns they need, then they'll let us go. They won't try to follow us or nothing.'

Caroline leaned in close to her sister, lowering her voice to an exasperated hiss. 'Amy, who knows what might happen

303

before then! Colt's men are out hunting for us all. Walter Noone, their leader, is a *killer* – a butcher of the red men over in America, and more besides. Slattery can't be trusted not to do something foolish. He likes to think himself a cunning schemer, but you and I know the truth of it. We've got to get out *now*.' She adjusted her hold on the child and looked along the lane. 'I've a friend who'll help.'

Amy stayed quiet for a few seconds, considering this; then she touched the fabric of Caroline's shawl, seeming to notice her smart new clothes for the first time. 'This is a gentleman friend, I suppose,' she said. 'The fellow from the factory. The secretary.'

'That's him. Mr Lowry.'

Amy's fingers lingered on Caroline's elbow, cupping it; her brow furrowed with concern. 'What are you doing, Caro?'

Her meaning was plain enough. Caroline shook her head. 'It ain't like that. He's a decent man – a kind man. He cares for me.'

Amy tried to smile at this, but she was sceptical. Caroline coloured, ashamed, feeling as if she'd been caught out somehow. Her elder sister either thought that she'd sold herself, that she was little better than a whore; or that she was using an infatuated man like the lowest kind of fortune-seeker, tapping him for cash, letting him take the risk of hiding her and then skipping out through his door as soon as the right moment presented itself. It had to be admitted that there was some truth in both judgements. Caroline's affair with Edward Lowry was a sweet and cherished thing, but it had been brought about only by some very singular circumstances. She was determined that a change in these circumstances would cause it to end – that she'd leave him with sadness but no hesitation. It would be difficult but she'd do it.

'I only pray that you're taking care, girl,' Amy murmured. 'You know as well as I what can happen to those that don't.'

A barrow of pig carcasses was wheeled by where they stood, the rubbery snouts rocking in unison as it ran across a dip in the road. The sight caught Katie's attention, and she started to blab out a stream of high-pitched syllables, clapping her hands together excitedly.

'We must get away,' Caroline repeated. 'As quick as we can.'

Amy wouldn't have it. 'I won't leave without Mart. I can't. He's my husband, my daughter's father.'

'It makes no sense, Amy, us all being in danger. Surely if we got word to him, he'd see what –'

'They told me not to talk with no one. If I vanish they'll think Mart put me up to it, that we was trying to give them the slip, and then God only knows what they'd do to him.' Suddenly Amy put her arms around her sister's neck and kissed her hard on the cheek. 'Just *leave*,' she whispered. 'Go without us. Get yourself to safety.'

A hot tear gathered beneath Caroline's eye, running away around her nose. 'No,' she said. 'No, Amy, I won't.'

Amy let go of her and took back Katie. She was weeping as well now, her pale face crumpling. The child looked from her mother to her aunt; seeing their distress, her smile turned into a fearful whimper.

Shushing her, Amy bent down to retrieve the basket. 'Please, Caro, just let us be. I'm begging you.'

The hall of Edward's building on Red Lion Square was like a railway station or a post office – a dreary, public space with peeling yellow wallpaper and floorboards scuffed by the passage of many thousands of boots. It was around four o'clock when Caroline returned there, and she made it to the staircase without seeing a soul. The building was close to London's legal district; most of its residents were barrister's clerks, notaries or the like, still hard at work in the chambers of Lincoln's Inn or Temple.

Caroline shut the door behind her. The rooms were growing dark; the gas-lamps were already lit down in the square, casting dim orange rectangles across the ceiling, and fog was gathering in the tops of its trees. It was set to be another freezing night. She glanced around the small parlour, so familiar to her now that she could place its various objects with her eyes closed. There was the dining table before the window, large enough only for the two of them with knees pressed together; the dresser piled with unwashed cups and dishes; the bundles of journals and newspapers heaped around the tired settee; and the bed they'd made before the hearth, the disordered blankets thrown to one side, revealing a faint impression of their bodies on the cushions beneath. Edward would not be back for several hours at least. Caroline hugged herself beneath her shawl, shuddering in the cold, wishing that he was there.

She'd tried to follow them from the meat market but Amy had moved surprisingly fast, nipping around a couple of corners before climbing on a westbound omnibus – leaving Caroline standing helplessly on the pavement at Holborn Hill. For a minute or two she'd despaired, thinking that she'd lost them for good, but her reason soon returned. Things would actually be easier now. Amy had said that they were in the Devil's Acre, hiding in an old dairy. Surely such a place could be found without too much trouble. The only real problem was Slattery and his pals – and she even had a way of managing them.

The first time she'd found herself alone in Edward's rooms, Caroline had taken a close look around. Before very long she'd been pulling out the half-dozen cardboard boxes stowed underneath his narrow iron bedstead; and it was to one of these that she went now, setting a candle down on the floor beside her. In among a few dog-eared books lay a well-known shape, wrapped in an old shirt. Caroline lifted up the Navy, letting the grease-stained cloth fall away, bringing it close to her face. The candlelight flowed smoothly across the black metal of the gun, running into the tiny engraved leaves that wound along its barrel.

She would save her sister.

3

The first of Sam's two pieces of solid-gold luck arrived as unexpectedly and as beautifully as a balloon loaded with bullion just drifting on down into the factory yard. He'd been up in the office with Mr Lowry – by pure chance, really, as these days he was far more usually away giving chase to military men through the clubs of London – dictating letters to his sales agents in Liège, Brussels and Aix-la-Chapelle, and anyone else he could think of that might be of use to him on mainland Europe. The secretary was recording his words with prompt precision (his penmanship remained first-rate, it had to be admitted), but despite Sam's urgings this once-promising junior had no thoughts of his own to offer.

'Come on, Mr Lowry, where might be right for us? The Belgians are reluctant, damn 'em, but what about the Frenchies? They're sure to pile in to this bust-up with Russia, ain't they? I took tea with their emperor a couple of years back, y'know; funny little bastard he was, but he liked my guns well enough. Let's fire off a dispatch to him. Might as well start at the top! What d'you say?'

The Englishman merely shifted and nodded, not even looking up from the page before him. Sam grew seriously impatient, eventually asking straight out if he didn't see the importance of growing the company in Europe – of spinning out a web of international contacts and preferential trade channels. Still he got nothing more than a pat response.

The gun-maker began to wonder if the boy was about to attempt a back-stab like Stickney and those other traitorous Yankees, and would have to be slung out in the same manner.

Then one of the new men burst in, the acting foreman Sam thought it was, and in rather disbelieving tones reported the arrival of royalty. All three of them went directly to the circular window. A procession of the very grandest broughams, each one an oily black with an elaborate coat-of-arms emblazoned on its doors, was rolling in through the Ponsonby Street gate.

'Good Lord, Colonel,' said Mr Lowry, 'that's the Prince Consort.'

Sam stared back at him blankly.

'Prince Albert. The Queen's husband.'

A minute later Sam was down in the yard, raising his hat to this august personage as he stepped out into the rather miserable English afternoon. The prince was a fine enough specimen, tall and well-covered in Sam's own mould, albeit with rather sloping shoulders. Smartly attired in the solemn manner favoured by the British nobility, he had a high fore-head, a modest moustache and a lofty, slow, undemonstrative air. Sam perceived nothing in him of the divine mandate that was supposed to rest with these European monarchs; a Queen's consort he might be, but he certainly seemed to have no natural superiority over any freeborn citizen of America. He kept these thoughts well hidden.

They stood facing each other as the rest of Albert's party disembarked, the soldiers of the royal bodyguard exchanging appraising glares with Mr Noone and his men. Then, in a thick German accent, the prince apologised for making such a visit unannounced, and expressed an ardent wish for what he termed an 'ocular demonstration of the Colt manufac-turing process'. Sam assented at once, looking around for Alfie Richards and ordering the acting foreman to ready the works for inspection.

Thus began a rather stiff circuit of the factory. Sam's most humorous observations met only with polite, baffled smiles; but Albert wanted to see everything, every stage, scrutinising the machines in a manner that suggested more than a passing interest in engineering. On the machine floor he held a freshly bored barrel up to the light, marvelling at the perfect spiral of the rifle grooves as if he looked upon the most splendorous of God's orchids.

The tour ended in the testing range just off the proving room. Prince Albert was no marksman, it had to be said; he shot like an unlettered labourer trying to write down his name, great concentration leading only to a laughable result. The best possible noises were made afterwards, however, gratitude, admiration and so on. Biting back his fighting Yankee spirit, Sam even managed an awkward little bow as he handed over a boxed pair of presentation Navys, making himself think of the headlines. He was striding towards Richards before the royal carriage was out of the gates.

The press agent was smoking with the secretary, over by the warehouse. Richards had been kept busy of late, writing up the military visits for the armaments press and then monitoring the reaction to them. This suited him well; it kept him out of trouble, for the most part. Next to the secretary he still had something of a vagabond air, but his eyes were alert.

'Your friend Pam again,' he said as Sam approached, pointing towards the final carriage with his cigar as it pulled away towards Westminster. 'That was due to his influence, I'll wager, just like all those blessed soldiers.'

Sam frowned. 'How do you mean?'

'It is indirect, but he's surely the cause.' Richards smirked at Lowry; they'd been talking about this while the prince had been in the firing range. 'Word is that Albert was pressing for Lord Palmerston's removal from the cabinet, shortly before our dear Home Secretary decided to excuse himself at the end of last year. Some observers have asserted that Albert's distaste for Pam was due to the fact that the Consort, God save him, is a member of the House of Coburg – and a kinsman to Tsar Nicholas.'

The gun-maker considered this. 'So the prince wanted to be rid of the only member of this spineless government who'll stand up to the goddamn Russians.'

The press agent nodded. 'That's what was claimed. But it came to naught, of course. Pam has returned, more powerful and popular than ever, and poor, clumsy Albert is left trying to correct the impression that he is secretly on the side of our foes. Taking an interest in one of brave Lord Palmerston's pet causes – Colonel Colt's magnificent revolver factory – is surely a good way to do this, especially as he knows that we will do all we can to publicise his visit.' He blew gently on the tip of his cigar. 'Quite canny, really, for such a dull dog as the Consort.'

Sam reflected on this for a moment. It seemed that Lawrence Street had been right. His connection with that strange minister was bringing results. 'Write it up, Alfie,' he ordered. 'This'll hit the trade like a six-pound ball.'

The second piece of luck, the real stunner, arrived only a few days later, reaching Sam as he lounged against the marble counter of the sales office on Spring Gardens. He was being regaled by Mr Dennett, his London sales agent – a mostly redundant position, in truth, with Sam himself in the city. Mr Lowry stood over at the display cases, studying a fan of old Dragoons, while Dennett, a rather odious little reptile, told Sam at quite unnecessary length of the increase in individual sales that had been brought about by the prince's visit to the factory.

'Up five hundred per cent, Colonel, no word of a lie,' he said. 'Why, I can hardly refill my stock room fast enough!'

Then, thankfully, a liveried messenger had walked in and handed Sam a note on Board of Ordnance paper. It informed him in a smart clerical hand that he was wanted at his earliest convenience for a private discussion with Sir Thomas Hastings, Storekeeper of the Ordnance. The gun-maker set off immediately, instructing Mr Lowry to remain in Spring Gardens. Pall Mall was barely a hundred yards from the sales office, so he decided to chance the mud and make the journey on foot. Something told him that this was going to be good.

How very different was the Board of Ordnance from his last visit! The desk-clerk met him with respectful civility, waving over a footman to escort him to his destination; in the corridors people stepped aside humbly, as if in recognition of his importance; and upon arrival at the Storekeeper's door he was admitted at once, without a moment's shilly-shally or delay. Old Tom Hastings rose to greet him with a tumbler of spirits and a toothy smile, gesturing towards a pair of chairs set before his fire, ready for a two-man conference. After some brief pleasantries he got to the point.

'My dear Colonel Colt,' he began, drumming his fingers on the side of his glass, 'you must have realised that Great Britain is preparing for war.'

Sam's heart sang; it bellowed with animal glee; it jumped up on the table and beat its chest like a goddamn gorilla. His hopes for that factory by the river were to be realised. 'I have, Tom,' he replied gravely.

'And you must also know that the focus of this preparation, at this early stage, has been our navy. They are at the front line, as things currently stand – out patrolling in the Black Sea after that terrible massacre at Sinope. And a second naval front is expected to open up in the Baltic before very long.'

'Christ Almighty, Tom,' Sam said, nodding. 'I know this.'

'Tests have been conducted,' Hastings went on, 'comparing your revolvers with those of Mr Adams. I am delighted to tell you, Colonel, that they went in your favour. Yours have been deemed the pistols most suited to naval use.'

Sam couldn't help it; he laughed, driving his right fist hard into his left palm. '*Damn* you, Bob Adams!' he cried. 'How about that!'

Old Hastings permitted himself a small guffaw as well, and the gravity between them dissipated entirely. His party in the Ordnance Office had carried the day, it seemed, defeating Clarence Paget and the Adams faction. Sam's weapons, named in honour of a navy, would be used to outfit the fighting ships of the most powerful navy in the world. They drank down their drinks and negotiated the British government's first ever purchase of repeating arms: four thousand Colt Navy revolvers for the Baltic fleet, to be delivered inside a month. Hastings looked a little uncertain as he named these figures, as if he feared he might be asking the impossible.

Sam, however, was nonchalant. 'Get me my price, Tom,

and you shall have 'em. I told you my works was quick, didn't I? That number is nothing to us.'

They made a promise to set it all down in writing and shared an earnest handshake; and then Sam was on his way, heading back to the factory to deliver the news to his staff. He was sure that they would take the prospect of having to turn out four thousand pistols in a month with the professional coolness he demanded of them. There had already been some discussion about starting up a proper night shift. Perhaps the time had come to set this in motion.

The Colt carriage was waiting on the Mall, sent from the sales office by Mr Lowry. Sam told the driver to take him to Pimlico and climbed inside. Sitting down with a sigh, he put his boots up on the opposite seat and cut himself a generous plug of Old Red. Had Palmerston got him this contract as well as everything else? Was it due to the attention all those high-profile tours had won him? Or just the result of his weapons' undeniable superiority of design and manufacture? It really didn't matter. He chewed hard on the tobacco, lifted up high on a great fiery wave of exhilaration. It felt as if his beard was curling up into barbs; his fists were cast iron; his belly a great sea-barrel, steel-ribbed and strong.

'This is it, by thunder,' he said aloud, as the carriage started along Pall Mall. 'My rightful due has arrived at last.'

Yet it seemed that even the sweetest English apple had to have its bitter core; Christ, a goddamn hornet buried in its flesh. Less than a week afterwards, before the glow of triumph had faded, some kind of summons arrived at Sam's rooms on Piccadilly. He was being called as a witness by a Select Committee appointed by the House of Commons to investigate 'the efficacy and viability of the various small arms currently available in Great Britain'. The gun-maker realised at once that this had come about as a direct result of his contract to supply the Baltic fleet. He knew what was happening here. His opponents were panicking, and sought to slow his progress by whatever means they could.

'Damn it all,' he growled as he rode to Parliament, 'why

can't we just do business? Why does everything in this country have to be talked out so *endlessly*?'

Mr Lowry was with him, brought along to manage the factory papers and supply any necessary facts while Sam was giving his evidence. 'A Select Committee hearing proves that the Government are taking this matter seriously, at least,' he offered. 'It might be a prelude to more contracts.'

Sam shot him a contemptuous look. 'Horseshit. The sons of bitches want to hobble me, Mr Lowry. They want to stop me getting any more military money – to slam the door in my Yankee face. Just you watch.'

The unfinished Palace of Westminster was a daily sight for Sam, and he'd long ceased to pay it much attention. It had never particularly impressed him. Although massive, it was actually pretty uninteresting beneath the cathedral-style frosting, in his estimation – just a series of rectangular boxes arranged in a line along the riverbank. Stalking in through a looming, pointed archway, he was unsurprised to discover that the churchy theme continued inside, with patterned carvings, vaulted ceilings and unfathomable wall-paintings of fellows in suits of armour and ladies in odd pointy hats. What did it say about a country, he thought, when it chose to house its politicians – who were roguish dogs, like every politician the world over – in a building done up to resemble an ancient place of Christian worship? Were these scheming villains being equated with clergymen, or monks perhaps? Was it imagined that the practice of their dark arts somehow brought them closer to the Almighty? It almost made Sam laugh.

They were directed to a room at the back of the place, past the main chambers, overlooking the putrid Thames. The river's reek was just detectable through the thick smell of polish that hung about, giving a hint of something foul beneath all the newness. The committee room was decorated with emerald green paper, heavy crimson curtains and mahogany tables, a scheme of indigestible opulence. As Sam had suspected, he was to be the star turn, the centrepiece – the reason that the whole goddamn circus had been brought together. A couple of others spoke before him, but no one

313

took much notice; the forty-strong audience were soon whispering among themselves and a good number wandered out. When Sam Colt was called, however, every man was back in his chair, quiet and attentive.

He found that he recognised a couple of the dozen committee members who were sat before him. Neither were friends of the Colt Company. There was that mimsy clown Clarence Paget, looking rather pleased with himself; and to the right of him was George Muntz, the Member for Birmingham, the fellow widely believed to have called for this committee to be set up. Mr Muntz represented a gun-making town and was known to be fiercely opposed to the British growth of Colt. It was to be a pillorying. Sam nodded to them, signalling his readiness, vowing to fight with everything he had.

Their questions came thick and fast. How many arms could he make per week? Was he planning to start adapting his machines to manufacture muskets as well as pistols? What were the exact details of his government contract? Sam kept his answers vague, giving away little about his operations in Europe or America, or his future plans. What he did say, though, and say with gusto, was that his production rates were far higher, and his prices far lower, than any other gun-maker in Europe; that his machines were so easy to operate that he could build up an effective workforce from nothing, wherever he was; that his were the only weapons with fully interchangeable parts, enabling him and *him alone* to supply an army with effective spare parts for the guns he provided.

None of the committee members could challenge these points. They scribbled down notes and swapped glances, but they couldn't get at him. Sam perceived that there were several different agendas at play here. Some of these men were looking to pick his brains, to use his achievements as a template for a government gun works that would free them from the need to patronise private operators such as himself. Others, like Paget and Muntz, had some form of personal stake in the British weapons industry and wanted all foreign competition to be driven out. He also reckoned that there were one or two there who opposed him on broader political grounds – Aberdeen loyalists who knew of his friendly connection with the mutinous, grandstanding Palmerston. This division of purpose prevented any form of effective assault. The gun-maker started to think that the hearing was going rather well.

Then a stocky, grey-bearded fellow at the far end of the table sat forward in his chair and asked how many guns in total Sam had manufactured since his arrival in England. His accent was Irish, and his tone rather loaded. Sam frowned, requesting his name.

'Simon Bannan, sir,' he replied. 'I am a member of the Commons, but I also sit on the Board of Trade.'

Regarding this new interrogator suspiciously, Sam decided that he would remain as imprecise as possible. 'Well, Mr Bannan,' he said, 'I have not made so many. Some hundreds; some thousands, p'raps.'

'A very typical answer from you, Colonel Colt, if I may say. Which is it, sir – hundreds or thousands? And where on earth might *thousands* of London-made Colt pistols already have gone?'

Sam blustered through as before, saying that he had no figures with him, that the depths of the factory stock room held many secrets – and giving Mr Lowry a look of such ferocious authority that the secretary promptly put all the factory's papers back in his document case and slid it beneath the table. He was not obliged to make a full disclosure and the hearing eventually moved on. Bannan was plainly unsatisfied, but acted as if some kind of revelation had nonetheless been extracted from his unwilling witness. The Honourable Member asked that it be formally noted that Colonel Colt could not say how many weapons he had made or where they might all be, and that the true number might be in the thousands.

Sam's evidence was concluded shortly afterwards. Back in his seat, he felt oddly compromised, as if this Bannan bastard had won some kind of advantage over him – as if his close, pointed questioning had been based on prior know- ledge. But what could he possibly know? And from whom could he have heard it? These were not comfortable reflections, and the gun-maker sat rather ill-temperedly through a parade of other witnesses, all of whom were positively dying to gabble on about Sam Colt and his revolvers. He watched sails passing out on the river, hardly listening. What the devil did he care for the views of a handful of petty John Bull engineers and arms makers? They could dismiss him; they could laud him. He didn't care.

One witness brought out late in the proceedings won back his attention completely, however. The fellow was called from the back of the room, chairs scraping aside to allow the passage of an outsized form; Sam turned to see who it was and almost leapt from his chair. *Gage Stickney!* That lumbering, traitorous oaf! What in God's name was he doing there? Had he learnt about the hearing and volunteered? Or had one of Sam's foes tracked him down, knowing that his testimony would surely be a kick in the guts for the Colt Company? Sam tried to stay calm, but could feel himself purpling as the scheming son of a bitch went before the committee.

If Stickney had been summoned especially to do a number on Sam Colt he didn't disappoint. Keeping those brutish, unintelligent features directed very firmly towards his questioners, the lying rascal contradicted every one of Sam's proud assertions about the Pimlico works. The miraculous interchangeability of Colt pistol parts was a myth, he said; those revolutionary machines, also, were largely copied from pieces at the Springfield Armory, and took far more skill to operate and maintain than the Colonel had let on.

And then Bannan was there again, coming in with one of his killer queries. 'Mr Stickney, what would you say that the Colonel's overall aim was, back in America?'

'He wants to be the only maker of arms in the entire country,' the wretch answered at once. 'He shuts up everyone, and he keeps the whole of it himself. He has closed every establishment.'

Stickney's implication was clear: *this is what he seeks here as well*. A disapproving rumble went around the room. Unable to listen to any more, Sam got to his feet, departed the hearing without another word and charged back through the Palace's echoing vestibules towards the open air. A pontoon bridge of duck-boards stretched from the doors of Parliament to the gates of the bog-like construction site that encircled it. Sam kicked one up, sending it cartwheeling away across a puddle and spraying his coat with mud.

'Scheming mother*fucker*!' he shouted. 'After what I gave him – the chance I gave him that he damn well *squandered* – this is what he goes and does to me!'

Those nearby, a mixture of gentlemen, police, assorted lackeys and site labourers, were all studying the gun-maker carefully. He glowered back at them, laying down a challenge that he knew none would accept. Mr Lowry arrived at his elbow, flustered after a dash across the Palace. Sam rounded on him as if he were personally responsible for what had just happened.

'Who the devil was that Bannan character? What was he trying to do in there? One of Aberdeen's men, is he, opposing me because I'm linked with the fellow who's sure to take the old muddler's place?'

Lowry said nothing, opening his document case and rifling through the papers within – none of which Sam had so much as glanced at while giving his evidence to the committee. Losing patience, he snatched the case from the secretary's hands and cast it violently into the muck.

'God *damn* this island!' he barked. 'There are far too many crowded in here, d'you know that? Too many men squabbling over too goddamn little!'

Sam stomped away over the boards, out through the gates of the site to the square beyond. He raised a hand and the yellow carriage came into view a few seconds later. The time had definitely come for a trip to mainland Europe. He was damned if he was going to beg these people for their custom, or let his operations on this side of the Atlantic remain dependent on these blockheaded Bulls. It really made a fellow wonder if doing business in this godforsaken country was worth the effort. The pace of everything was so slow; the general attitude towards any kind of success or original thinking so goddamn grudging; the interests of those you had to deal with so tangled and corrupt. Sam started to map the journey out in his mind as he swung himself into his carriage: a train to Folkestone, a steamer to Boulogne, another train to Paris – and then onward to fresh opportunities.

4

The Mollys found a dark alley off Bessborough Place in which to prepare themselves. The sack that Jack had once used to carry his murphies was bulging with garments; the Irishmen started to root through it, dividing up the contents. Owen lit a match, ran it around the end of a cork and began marking up his face. They were dressing for battle.

Jack came to Martin's side and asked if he would join with them. 'I brought you a bonnet special,' he said, 'and your own bit o' cork.'

Martin shook his head. He didn't feel whatever it was he used to feel before they'd struck their blows back in Ireland. This wasn't Molly's work – or at least not the work of the Molly he'd known back then. The creature who visited him now was very different. It seemed that Martin had pleased her for the last time in the fight before the Parliament building. Since that fateful night she'd grown increasingly malign; there was no love in her any more, no guidance or protectiveness, only menace. He'd glimpsed her just a couple of hours earlier, back in the dairy, perched above the cattle stall where Amy was putting their child to bed, her long fingers working the air like the legs of insects. She had the look of a black witch, closer to the beasts than to man, ready to snatch Katie away to a lair beneath a hill so that she could feed on her innocent flesh. For a moment this vile apparition had left Martin too appalled to move; and when he made

319

to go over she'd leapt straight upwards, vanishing into the rafters.

The Mollys began to struggle into their outfits. This could be it, Martin thought – the end of my time with them. By morning he could be free, taking his wife and child away from London for good. It could not come fast enough. Amy had told him about her meeting with Caroline, whispering into his ear as they lay together in the straw of their stall. This was a complication that they really didn't need. His stubborn sister-in-law wouldn't ever give up on Amy and Katie. The longer they sat waiting in that mildewed shed, the greater the chance she'd try something – something that might queer Slattery's plan and bring down his ire upon them all. He'd instructed Amy not to tell anyone else. The Mollys thought that no one in London knew that they were still there, readying for action, and it had to stay that way. The best thing for the Rea family would be if the plan went off exactly as intended, enabling them to flee the city before Slattery went gunning for Lord John Russell.

Of the plan itself, all Martin had been told was that they were going to break into the Colt works, presumably with the aim of stealing as many revolvers as they could carry. He reckoned that his task would most probably be to lead them to the stock room and ensure that they took everything they'd need to mount their attack. Slattery had also made it clear that he still wanted vengeance against Colt for the setbacks he'd caused – for the sound thrashing Slattery himself had received at the hands of Walter Noone, from which he'd only just properly recovered. Martin's guess was that he'd be looking to start a fire, but burning this pile would be difficult. Colonel Colt had experience at laying out pistol works, and had taken care to arrange his premises so that any blaze would spread slowly, if at all. No gunpowder was stored on the site after hours either, so there was no chance of an explosion. Fire-carts would most probably be rattling into the yard before the flames had crept beyond a single department.

Up ahead, Slattery walked beneath a street lamp. Martin

hadn't seen a man done up in Molly's rags for some years now and the sight was a jarring one, bringing back memories of a truly desperate time. Amy had been made to fetch this apparel for them from the old clothes sellers on Petticoat Lane. The frocks must be black, they'd told her, and the bonnets ribboned in Irish green. Slattery's old dress was faded and patched, with chalky sweat-rings beneath each armpit; tight to bursting across his crooked shoulders, it hung in loose folds around the hips. He turned to look back along the alley, revealing a face scored with lines of burnt cork. Heavy circles had been drawn beneath his eyes and several strokes slashed across his cheeks, making his spare, pox-scarred features seem like an animated skull – a devilish spirit returned from limbo to wreak bloody havoc among the living.

A single wave of Slattery's hand brought the others over to him. Molly's rags made it hard to tell one from another, as was partly their purpose. A couple had pinned paper clover-leaves to their bonnets, and Jack stood an inch or two taller than the rest, but otherwise they were identical. Half a dozen Molly Maguires were about to be loosed upon Colonel Colt.

Slattery grabbed Martin's collar as he passed. 'Are you ready for what needs to be done?' he demanded.

Martin shook him off. 'What *is* to be done? You ain't told me yet.'

'Molly's work is all. You'll know soon enough.' Slattery fingered the frayed cuff of Martin's jacket with mocking tenderness. 'I'm glad you ain't in the rags, Martin. Wouldn't have been *right*, now would it?'

Hoisting their skirts up past their waists, the Mollys scaled the Bessborough Place gate, dropping down into the yard. Dawn was still three hours off; a single gas-lamp burned over by the warehouse. Martin climbed the gate last, and saw that Slattery was leading the way to the factory block. This was surely a mistake.

'Slattery, ye eejit,' he hissed at the gang of bobbing bonnets, making a wide gesture towards the warehouse, 'the pistols are over there!'

They ignored him. Jack slid a crowbar from his sleeve and cracked open the factory door. It shuddered back, the runner-wheel catching as if it knew who it was being forced to admit. Martin followed the Mollys inside, hurrying after them through the drop-hammers of the forging shop, into the engine room. As he entered that familiar place he realised their aim. They were going to cripple the Colt engine.

Slattery lit a candle, placed it on Mr Quill's work bench and then pulled a few old, misshapen tools out from under his dress. 'So, Martin,' he asked, nodding towards the still pistons, 'tell us how best to do in this bleedin' thing.'

'We should be over in the warehouse,' Martin spat. 'That's where your guns are. What about Lord John, Pat? This is a waste o' time.'

Jack spoke up, hefting his crowbar. 'We've got to punish him first, Mart, for what he done to Molly. It's the best way.'

'This here's what we want from you, Martin Rea.' Slattery was grinning like a madman. 'This is your debt to Molly Maguire – how you save what's left o' your bleedin' Saxon family.'

Martin stared at the low stone ceiling. Amy and Katie were back at the dairy, waiting for him to return. There was only one way that he had any chance of ever reaching them. 'Yous could split the boiler,' he answered at last. 'Bash in the drive axle.'

Slattery handed him a foot-long chisel. 'Off you go, then, pal,' he said, his voice straining with mirth.

Martin stood before the engine for a moment – the thing on which he'd expended the best of his life's energies, working alongside perhaps the truest friend he'd ever known. Then he lunged forward. The chisel's end punched straight through the copper flank of the boiler, releasing a blast of wet, metallic heat. Teeth gritted hard, Martin shifted his hold on the handle and tore downwards, as if gutting a hanging carcass; warm water poured across the brick floor. Through the corner of his eye he saw Jack swing his crowbar at the drive axle, knocking it out of shape with a resounding clang. The other Mollys had produced their own weapons and were soon attacking the rest of the engine in a range of spirited, noisy ways.

So caught up did Martin become in ripping open the boiler that he didn't notice everyone else had stopped until Jack tapped him sharply on the arm. He looked around; the Mollys were scattering, scurrying into the forging shop. On the far side of the factory, a lantern's light was reaching in through the open door. Someone was coming across the yard. They'd been discovered.

Martin was the last out of the engine room. Jack was running straight for the factory door. Slattery was already struggling to close it, to keep out those who approached, while the others pounded up the creaking staircase to the machine floor. As Jack arrived at Slattery's side, a shoulder was forced into the gap, the arm thrashing about, trying to grab hold of someone. The two Mollys pushed together as more hands fastened themselves around the edge of the door. Martin added his strength to the effort to force it shut, straining with all his might, but they were seriously out-numbered. After half a minute the door jumped back another few inches.

'Get your boot in there, Lee!' cried a Yankee voice – it was Walter Noone. 'Stick it right in, go on!'

'Ain't no use in this,' panted Slattery. 'Let go on three, aye?'

They counted down and hopped away; the door flew open, causing several of the Yankees to overbalance and topple through. Slattery darted for the staircase and Martin fell in behind him. They'd reached the machine floor landing before they realised that Jack wasn't with them.

They could hear fighting somewhere below.

'I got this cocksucker,' bellowed Noone. 'You go get the others!'

'This,' pronounced Slattery, drawing something from beneath his skirts, 'smells like a bleedin' trap to me.' He raised his voice, shouting down the stairs. 'We're a-coming, Jack! Don't you fret none, brother!'

He held a Colt Navy in his hand, the one remaining pistol from the three Caroline had got to them. Martin cursed under his breath; he'd forgotten that the Mollys still had it.

No mention had been made of it during the weeks in the dairy. Slattery leaned around the banister, cocking the revolver. There was a flash of white light and a loud, hollow bang as he squeezed off a single shot into the darkness of the stairway. Before he could fire again several reports sounded from the direction of the forging shop, and the beam next to his shoulder was blown to splinters. The Yankees were shooting back. Slattery scrambled for cover with a startled yelp, heading into the avenues of the machine floor. Martin went after him. Colonel Colt's contraptions stood in the darkness like the skeletons of strange, ancient monsters. The two Irishmen ducked down among them.

'The guns,' hissed Slattery, 'we've got to get to the bleedin' guns! We've got to get Molly's vengeance!'

Martin seized the grimy frill that drooped from the collar of Slattery's frock and twisted it up in his fist. 'You should've thought o' *that*,' he growled, 'when you was ordering me to do in the bleedin' engine!' He pushed Slattery away and pointed across the floor. A trail of abandoned tools, clubs and bonnets led to a knocked-out window – the route by which the other four Mollys had just made their escape. 'We've got to go, right now, or the bastards'll catch us as well.' The Yankees were coming up the stairs; Martin could even hear the hammers of their pistols drawing back. He climbed to his feet.

Slattery grabbed at his jacket. The bonnet was slipping around the side of his head, held on only by its length of green ribbon. 'It can still be done. We can still get to the warehouse – break in and take what we need.'

'That's just bleedin' madness, Slattery,' Martin replied, tugging the jacket from his grasp and rushing to the broken window.

There was no time for a careful exit. Martin hit the cobbles hard, the impact sending him stumbling to his hands and knees. As he picked himself up he heard the flapping of skirts, and then Slattery landed awkwardly beside him; he'd clearly accepted the obvious and was joining Martin's dash for safety. Together they ran for the outer wall, leaping towards it, clutching at its summit as their boots scrabbled for purchase between the bricks. Martin made it to the top and was about to jump down the other side when a glint of blued steel caught his eye, back over at the factory block's broken window. Something wrenched at his left arm, sending him tumbling over. He heard the pistol shot an instant later, echoing out across the Thames as he crashed into the gutter.

Martin rolled over onto his belly, trying to catch his breath. He felt Slattery's hands upon him, dragging him to his feet. There were cries from inside the gun works, boots thudding over the cobbles, and an order to unlock the gates. Slattery started for Westminster, lifting the front of his skirts so that he could break into a full sprint. Martin checked at his arm. There was a tear in the sleeve of his jacket, an inch or two above the elbow, and a heavy flow of blood was branching across the back of his hand. He loped after Slattery, wincing a little more with every step.

Twenty minutes later Martin was sat on a milking stool, leaning against the side of a cattle stall. His head was throbbing, his arm entirely numb and caked in black blood. The bullet had passed straight through, grazing the bone; Amy was trying to bandage it but her panicked sobbing was making this difficult. Katie watched from her bed, eyes round as buttons.

The Mollys, out of their rags now and with faces wiped clean of burned cork, stood in a miserable circle over by the boarded-up shop front at the dairy's far end, listening to Slattery recount the story of Jack's capture. His version told of a brave fight but narrowly lost. He was insisting that it had all been a trap; that there should have been only two men at most on duty at that time of night; that things would've played out very differently if he'd had the chance to fire off a couple more bullets. He was saying anything, in short, that shifted the blame away from him and his half-baked plan.

'But brothers,' he declared, 'we did succeed in one thing. We ruined that Colt bastard's engine. All o' them bleedin' Yankees will be out o' work come the morning. There's no way on God's earth that they'll meet that government contract now.'

This was more than Martin could stand. How could he claim any triumph at all when they hadn't gained a single revolver – when Jack Coffee had been run down like a coursed hare, and right that minute was in the hands of Walter Noone? 'Colt will repair that mess quick enough, Slattery,' he said. 'He has people who'll fix it in a matter o' hours. Even a split boiler is but a mornin's work for them. You cannot stop him that way. It was a waste o' bleedin' time, like I told you.'

Several unfriendly looks were directed at him, and he got a nasty sense of how changed things would be now that Jack was gone. The last tie connecting him to these men had been severed; the final trace of sympathy or fellow feeling had disappeared. They would turn on him in an instant, and gladly.

'You mean your precious Ben Quill, I suppose,' said Slattery, his voice curdling with contempt. 'Very well, Martin – you'll just have to bring him to us. We'll hold him as they're holding our Jack. I'm fairly certain that while the bugger's in our care we can convince him to leave off his duties wi' Colt.' The others let out a cruel chuckle. 'And then, when the place has been closed down, the workers dismissed and most o' the Yankees sent away, we'll have another run at it. We'll get us our guns, brothers. Molly will have her revenge. We just need to cleave to the bleedin' path.'

This was bad. With some effort, Martin rose from his stool. 'I won't let Quill be hurt, Slattery.'

Slattery took a couple of steps towards him. 'If you want to pay your debt to Molly Maguire you'll do what I bleedin' say and nothin' else,' he snapped. 'You see what's at stake here, don't you?'

A shape moved in the rafters. Martin glanced up, shivering with pain; she was hanging over his wife and child once more, a creeping, fanged thing horrible to behold, watching them both with a hunter's patience. He lowered his head.

'Aye,' he muttered. 'I do.'

5

Edward picked his way through the expectant crowd that packed the main concourse of Waterloo, treading on toes and having his toes trodden on, elbowing and being elbowed, trying to reach the arrivals platforms on the far side of the station. He was about halfway there when the steady beat of a drum over at the side gate sent those around him into a frenzy of patriotic enthusiasm. Policemen struggled to keep a channel clear as a sixty-strong square of infantry entered the building, marching in dress uniform with full field-packs on their backs. The iron and glass canopy overhead amplified the cheering to a deafening volume. *God save the Queen!* the people bawled; *God save her brave soldiers! Down with the Rooshin and his wicked Tsar!* They waved their caps, hats and handkerchiefs with furious passion, and many a cheek grew moist with sentimental tears. Edward stopped for a moment to take it in. The soldiers were an impressive sight, to be sure. Everything about them seemed sparkling and fresh, from the crisp whites and deep scarlets of their uniforms to the polished stocks of their rifles. It was more than some could bear; a number of young ladies were swooning from the sheer pitch of their admiration.

A sergeant yelled an order and the square wheeled to the left, towards a rank of specially commissioned military trains; a second formation was already coming in behind them, the trill of a fife now accompanying the drum. The infantry were travelling down to Southampton Water, where troop ships

327

would convey them first to Malta, and then on to Constantinople, in readiness for a move against Russia. It was happening at last; every newsboy in London was shouting it out at the top of his voice. Lord Seymour, British ambassador to the court of Tsar Nicholas, had left St Petersburg. A formal declaration of war was rumoured to be only days away.

Edward looked over at the military trains, their idling locomotives pumping up drifts of steam into the watery sunlight that shone in through the station's roof. Large boards hung at the end of each platform, painted with numerals: regimental designations, placed to direct soldiers to their carriages. The previous afternoon a '44' had hung prominently among them – and Edward had stood beneath it, bidding farewell to Cousin Arthur as he went off to fight. He'd been the only member of their family present; Aunt Ruth had suffered a nervous collapse at the news that her beloved son was to face the Russian cannon, and Edward's own mother was tending to her as best she could at her house in Sydenham Hill.

Arthur had not so much as mentioned any of this, however. He'd been with a group of other subalterns from his regiment, mere boys in red jackets, among whom he was clearly considered something of a buck. Edward had been introduced as 'the Colt man' rather than a relative; all of them had admired Arthur's revolvers, and several tried to convince Edward to send samples to them as well, once they were settled in their camp in Constantinople. Arthur discouraged this idea, seeming to take a childish pleasure in the distinction his six-shooters gave him. Puffing out his chest, he launched into another extravagant prediction of the many Russians he would kill with his Navys, likening the enemy on this occasion to rodents, who would be plugged with lead as they fled from his path. His comrades had obviously heard this routine before, and they met it with laughter and joking applause.

Edward had stayed quiet. He'd known that he should have been making the most of this chance to aid the Colt cause – to reveal that the Colonel was doing his utmost to win a contract with the Army, perhaps, and request that the young soldiers spread word of the pistols' excellence as widely as they could. Instead, he'd stood silently to one side, picturing Arthur standing on some Turkish battlefield in the months to come, surrounded by the dead like Walter Noone at Monterrey. He'd felt an urge to demand the revolvers back – to search through Arthur's luggage and seize them from him. In the end, though, he'd simply shaken his cousin's hand, begged him to take care of himself and left the station.

And now, unexpectedly, Edward was at Waterloo again, struggling through the second day of troop departures. Pushing past a final bank of well-wishers, he spotted Colonel Colt up ahead, dressed in his Yankee hat and a fawn travelling suit, talking with a senior officer while a porter dragged his steam-trunk onto a trolley. The secretary had no idea where his employer had been for the past fortnight. His suspicion was northern Europe, to the Colt sales offices in France and Belgium, but the gun-maker covered his tracks and threw down false trails as a matter of habit, making any hunch hard to verify. Indeed, Edward had penned several letters from the Colonel's own notes hinting that he was in fact headed back to America. The telegram announcing his imminent return, delivered that morning to a factory still reeling from the events of the night before, had thus come as a rather stunning surprise.

Seeing Edward approach, Colt bade the officer farewell, handed him a card and strode over at speed. 'Cotton, Mr Lowry,' he said by way of greeting. 'I want you to look into raw cotton, with all haste.'

Edward had been steeling himself to tell of the Irishmen's attack and the resultant halt in pistol production. This threw him completely. 'I beg your pardon, Colonel?'

'Have you gone deaf, boy? *Cotton.* Great Britain imports it in bulk, does she not? From India – from the southern states of my own country? For her mills and so forth, up in those northern towns?'

'I believe so, Colonel, but –'

'Well, find out the cost of a bale. Go to a few importers. Write some letters – don't be using my name, though. I've

329

an inkling that there's money to be made here, taking it from companies supplying your British mills and then selling back into Europe. Come on, write this down!'

Edward took out a notebook and pencil. 'May I ask what this has to do with gun-making – with our business?'

The Colonel glanced at him, amused by this query's impudent edge, but his reply was interrupted by a renewed riot of cheers from the concourse. 'Look at that,' he shouted a moment later, jerking a thumb at the soldiers, 'all these hundreds of men going off to fight without the benefit of the Colt revolver! That there's some woeful negligence on the part of your government, Mr Lowry!'

They walked from the station, advancing across the busy pavement. The gun-maker's wealth and importance hummed from him with a repelling energy, making the ordinary people part before him; and the instant they reached the pavement's edge the magnificent Colt carriage pulled up directly beside them, the shining yellow panels attracting the usual degree of covetous attention. The Colonel watched the porter load his trunk onto the back, flipped him a shilling and then told the coachman to take them to Piccadilly.

'Diversification is the thing,' he proclaimed as he opened the carriage door and climbed inside, 'for the true inventor and salesman. I've come to be known for my revolvers, but they're just one of many schemes to which I've given my time over the years. Undersea mines, for instance. Copper wires for the electric telegraph.' He settled in his seat, picking up the packet of letters his secretary had brought along with him and flicking through them.

Edward took a seat opposite. 'Colonel, I must tell you that last night –'

'And now,' Colt went on, ignoring him, tearing open one of the letters, 'as we try to get a bit of wider interest out in the continent beyond this little island, it has occurred to me that an international trade network might be useful for more than just pistols. I look to the future and I see a company that brokers deals over continents – that shifts all manner of cargo many thousands of miles. And I've decided to start with cotton. I've an old attachment to cloth trading,

Mr Lowry. It's how I made my first bit of cash, in fact, back in thirty-four – buying wholesale in Canada and then sneaking it across the border into Newport. The price of a roll of broadcloth almost doubled during that short journey.'

Edward considered this for a second. 'You mean you smuggled it in.'

Colt gave him a pitying look over the top of his letter. 'I saw an opportunity, Mr Lowry, and I took it. Didn't quite come off as well as I'd hoped, though, in the end.' He continued reading. 'Goddamn customs men.'

The news could wait no longer. 'Colonel,' Edward declared firmly, 'I'm afraid that there has been an attack upon the works.'

Colt listened to the details in silence, not lowering the letter before him. Pressure was building, though, his neck appearing to swell inside his collar; and as Edward related how the foreman had been forced to turn away the machine operatives, telling them there would be no work that day, the Colonel cast aside the letters, yanked down the carriage window and redirected them towards Bessborough Place in a furious shout. Slumping back on the seat, he drew a silver flask from his jacket and took a long gulp. 'Adams,' he rasped, wiping his mouth with the back of his hand. 'Has to be.'

Concentrating hard upon sustaining the correct professional air before his seething employer, Edward raised his voice over the street noise that was flooding in through the open window. 'No, Colonel, I'm told that this is something else. Mr Noone caught one of them. He's being held in the factory.'

The secretary's secret hope was that this assault would be Colt's undoing. With the engine disabled, there was no hope of them making the deadline for the Baltic Fleet contract, and the Colonel's reputation would certainly be damaged as a result. Not even Lord Palmerston would be able to protect him from this. The government would offer no further business to a man who had proved so unreliable in a time of national crisis. It could be a truly telling blow after the unsatisfactory one landed by the Select Committee.

Edward had seen Saul Graff a few days after that awkward afternoon in the Palace of Westminster. His friend had reported that Mr Bannan wasn't best pleased with how his public interrogation of the gun-maker had gone. Nothing significant had been elicited or revealed. Many were saying that despite his fractious behaviour the Yankee had got the better of the Honourable Member for Limerick; that Bannan had been beaten by Colt as soundly as Lady Cecilia Wardell, who since the previous winter had given up her protests and withdrawn from Pimlico, switching her efforts to campaigning against the coming war. The Colonel had shown himself to be a slippery customer indeed, a kindred spirit to the devious Pam – with whom he had no demonstrable connection of any kind. Just enough distance had been kept between them. Mutual amity was rumoured, but that was all. Legitimate channels had thus yielded no results. Edward's one ally of any influence had lost interest, for now at least. Perhaps a crude attack such as this would be more effective.

They clattered onwards, Colonel Colt swigging more liquor, cutting a plug of tobacco and sinking down into a brooding, masticatory silence. Edward looked at the open page of his notebook, where he'd written *prices of cotton bales* in a wobbling, hurried hand. He frowned at the words, pondering them again. This was an odd development.

The Irishman was hunched in a corner of the engine room, a forlorn and broken thing. His garb was absurd, cheap widow's weeds it looked like, made for a large woman but barely stretching across his labourer's shoulders; every seam was at the point of splitting open. It reminded Edward of a costume one might see on the stage, adorning a meddle-some great-aunt in a broad farce, but this was no comic actor caught mistakenly in Mr Noone's snare. Neither was he the sort glimpsed occasionally in the darker lanes around the Haymarket, dolled up in harlots' finery with faces painted, trying to pass for women; that tattered dress accentuated his masculinity rather than doing anything to disguise it. His intentions in wearing such a garment could only be guessed at. The prisoner's face was bruised beyond recognition, his red hair turned slick and black by his blood. Several of his fingers had been broken and he was hugging a chest of cracked ribs. Noone and his men had worked him hard. Looking upon this doomed wretch caused needle-points of perspiration to prickle across Edward's skin. As he lingered uneasily by the doorway he found himself imagining what further plans the Colonel's brute might have for his captive – what horrors he might be about to witness.

The factory around them was quiet, which seemed wrong indeed on a bright Wednesday afternoon. The American staff were fitting up parts that had already been made, or blueing and proving over in the warehouse block, but the engine was dead. Nothing could be cast, or cut, or drilled. They had been halted.

Colonel Colt stood in the middle of the engine room, hands on his hips in his old King Henry pose, glaring from the split boiler to the Irishman and back again. 'This son of a bitch used to work here, you say?'

Noone was leaning against the work-table with his arms crossed, one eye always on the prisoner. 'Just over there,' he answered with an almost imperceptible nod, 'in the forging shop. Got the boot for stealing, along with a few of his paddy pals – who I'll bet make up the rest of the gang.' He paused. 'Ben's assistant was one of 'em.'

Quill looked around with a scowl; he'd been leaning over the engine, prodding at its disordered innards with a long-handled spanner. 'You don't know that, Walt,' he snapped. 'None of us knows for sure what happened to Martin.'

'I saw 'em together, Ben,' Noone said. 'The cocksucker took you in. Played you for a goddamn fool. How d'you think they managed to do so much damage to your engine, and in so little time? He was there guiding 'em – telling 'em what to do.'

Quill shook his shaggy head, turning back to the engine. 'Mart wouldn't do this. He just wouldn't.'

Edward observed this exchange in silence, keeping his thoughts well hidden. Noone was right; he'd deduced only a fraction of it, in fact. It was painful to see Quill's loyalty

333

so misplaced, but the secretary was hardly about to add his voice to the watchman's efforts to disabuse him.

Noone's temper darkened. 'You soft bastard,' he said. 'That double-crossing mick had you eating from his palm like a pet sheep, and now you –'

Through his stupor, the Irishman suddenly realised that Colonel Colt was in the room with him. Gathering the last of his strength, he flopped out from his corner, reaching towards the gun-maker with his shattered, bloody hands. '*Damn* you, Sam Colt,' he croaked. 'Molly Maguire will see you in hell, so she will!'

Noone positioned himself over the poor fellow, drawing back a fist. There was a strange tenderness to his manner, like that of a knacker preparing to deliver the death-blow to a horse lying mortally wounded in the street. He planted a single, swift punch on the side of his prisoner's forehead, slamming him to the floor. Edward flinched, almost losing hold of his notebook.

The watchman glanced at Colt. 'The numbskull's been coming out with this nonsense all night,' he explained. 'Molly this and Molly that. I reckon it's some kind of paddy cult – hence the get-up.'

The Colonel wasn't interested. 'You've failed me here, Mr Noone, letting these bastards hurt me like this. I don't know what kind of a game you're playing out there in the rookery, but it's been distracting you from your rightful duties. Didn't you know something like this was coming? Lord Almighty, man, what the devil do I pay you for?'

Noone straightened up. His face was impassive – unrepentant. 'My thinking was that they were coming to steal guns. They wrong-footed me, Colonel, I'll confess it. Me and my boys were over in the warehouse. We came over quick as we could, but like I said, these motherfuckers weren't wasting no time. The mischief was done afore we could even push back the factory door.'

For all its candour, this account left Colt distinctly unimpressed. He fell to considering the mess of frantic footprints still smeared across the sooty floor. 'By thunder,' he said at last, 'this couldn't have happened at a worse moment. It'll surely take some superfine bluster to block this hole. How long to fix it, Mr Quill, would you say?'

The engineer was examining the boiler. 'A week,' he mumbled, his voice reverberating inside the split copper cylinder, 'if I can get the parts.'

'Too long,' Colt stated. 'Y'hear me? That's just *too goddamn long*.' He took out a letter from inside his fawn travelling jacket – the same one he'd been reading with such interest in the carriage – and brandished it at his employees like an arrest warrant. 'This here's a request from a big bravo of the London press, one of the great pens of this country. He wants to come and take a tour the day after tomorrow. This could be a prime spot of ballyhoo and I ain't going to tell him that it can't be done.' The Colonel put a hand to his brow for a second. 'All right then. We ain't finished yet. You get a new boiler in, Mr Quill. That's your first job right there. Spare no expense. Get it so the pistons move and it looks like everything is well. We'll see if we can't work this one through. Is Ballou still sick?'

'He made it in a few days back, Colonel,' Quill informed him. 'We ain't seen him since, though.'

Colt cursed, stuffing the letter into an outside pocket. A small part poked out; Edward squinted at it, wondering who this 'great pen' could possibly be. The handwriting was certainly elaborate, and the missive was several pages long – rather longer than one might expect for a simple request for a visit. The Colonel's latest admirer was evidently someone with a fondness for composition.

Noone was giving his employer a hard, dead-eyed stare. 'This ain't my fault,' he said slowly. 'You give me these tasks, finding your missing guns and the like, and then you tie my hands so I can barely do a goddamn thing. You take my –'

'Here's what I need from you, Mr Noone,' Colt interrupted. 'I need a *safe goddamn gun works*. You hear me? Everything else – *everything else* – is second to that.'

The Colonel started back towards the forging shop, ordering the insensible prisoner be taken to the police and handed over as a thief and vandal. Noone began to protest but Colt cut him off.

'You take him to the police this instant and you keep it quiet. The less people know about this the better. Discretion and safety, Mr Noone – those are your only concerns from now on.' The gun-maker strode from the engine room, rolling his shoulders as if trying to shake off his disgust with the whole affair. 'Up to the office, Mr Lowry,' he snarled as he passed. 'We got some letters to write.'

Caroline was sitting close to the fire, still in her bonnet and shawl, drying them before the flames. Rain was falling in the darkness outside; she'd clearly arrived back in Edward's rooms minutes before he had. He removed his hat and coat and walked over to her chair. She rose into his arms, kissed him softly, and laid her cold, smooth cheek against his. For several minutes they stood together, not moving, listening to the rain and the sounds of traffic in the street below. I shall remember this moment always, he told himself; yet even then she seemed to be slipping from him somehow, like a length of fine silk running away through his embrace, his efforts to hold onto it merely hastening its departure.

'The Irishmen have acted,' he said.

They sat down and he told her everything that had happened. She listened with calm acceptance, showing emotion only when he described the man who had been caught.

'Jack,' she murmured sadly. 'Oh, why'd it have to be him?'

Edward had some idea of what Caroline was doing out in the city. She'd told him about her conversation with Amy in Newgate market, and had revealed that she'd since come close to discovering the location of the Irish gang's den. He'd asked her what she intended to do if she found it. She'd grown vague, evasive even, saying that she'd watch them all for a while, learning their habits so that she could pick the best time to pull Amy and the child to safety. Edward had pleaded with her to reconsider. She wouldn't, of course, and rejected any offers of assistance that he made. His suggestion that the police might be alerted anonymously had been met with utter horror – the certain result of this, she'd claimed, would be both parents sent to gaol and their daughter locked up in a prison nursery or consigned to the workhouse. He'd come to believe that she didn't trust him to make the correct decisions. She wanted his affections and the shelter of his rooms, but little else. For the first time he'd started to wonder if he was being used.

'What are the Americans doing now?' Caroline asked. 'Are they out hunting for the others?'

Edward sighed and leaned back in his chair. 'The Colonel is not disposed to do anything like that,' he replied. 'His only concern at this point is safeguarding his interests. He wants it all kept as quiet as possible so the government don't lose confidence in him and he can make the right impression on this latest important visitor, whoever he might be.' He recalled the brusque conversation in the engine room. 'Noone is set to act, though. He's been made to look foolish and he wants to punish those responsible. Colt ordered him to leave it well alone, but I don't believe he'll obey.'

'I must do something soon, then,' she said.

Suddenly agitated by this show of resolve, Edward moved forward and took her hands in his. 'These are dangerous men, Caroline. This business is quite sure to end badly. Please, I beg you – you cannot let yourself get drawn in any further.'

She would not listen. Sitting there in the red lambency of the coals, blinking down at the hearth, she was so achingly beautiful that it almost hurt him to look at her. 'I – I just couldn't live with it if I left them to their fate. It would haunt me always, Edward, don't you see?'

They sat in silence, Edward's exasperation mounting until he could contain it no more. He turned away from her with a low groan and started to rise from his chair; but her hand snaked quickly up his forearm, fastening around his elbow, pulling him back. She edged closer, tilting her face to kiss his ear.

'I do care for you,' she whispered. 'Never think for a moment that I don't. You saved me.'

For a moment he considered resisting her, getting to his feet, perhaps storming out through the door and heading

into the rainy metropolis. It was impossible, though –
inconceivable. He simply couldn't do it. He felt her breath
on his neck, her fingers on his cheek, turning his head gently
towards hers; then their lips met, and for that night at least
his fears were forgotten.

6

Martin watched Rosie McGehan's theatre from the shadows of a crumbling doorway. The late bill had concluded some fifteen minutes earlier and a dozen of the most drunken patrons still milled beneath the row of gas jets that lit up the penny gaff's weather-warped frontage. An ale-fuelled dispute between a group of carters, Dublin lads from the sound of it, was turning ugly; some pallid whores hovered on the fringes, hoping to catch the victors while their blood was up.

As Martin looked on, a solitary figure approached from the direction of Millbank, a stout fellow with a familiar, rolling gait, dressed in rough seaman's clothes. He glanced at the 'McGehan's' sign before switching his attention towards the brawling carters, puffing a little irritably on a clay pipe. The moment had arrived. Martin prised himself from his alcove and limped across the broken paving stones. Every step was difficult. His arm remained excruciatingly sore and all but impossible to move. He still managed to get right up behind his man without being seen, though – close enough to catch a whiff of engine grease, and see the serpent's tongue curling across the back of his hand.

'Mr Quill,' he said.

The engineer started, turning with a curse. 'Mart,' he gasped, pushing his cap back on his head. 'Jesus Christ, you rattled me there.' Quill's first unthinking reaction upon seeing his assistant after three months of unexplained absence was one of relief. He breathed out hard, his shoulders relaxing, and he almost broke into a smile; then he remembered everything that had occurred and his round face creased with angry bafflement. 'What the blazing hell is this? What was your meaning, leaving me such a note? Dragging me all the way out into this wretched quarter?'

Martin made himself think of Amy and Katie, of escape from London and Pat Slattery's boys – to keep his mind away from the alleyway behind them where he'd been told to lead this harmless, unsuspecting man so that the Mollys could claim him as their hostage. 'This here's me home, Mr Quill, for better or worse. An old friend o' mine used to do a turn in that there theatre, in fact.'

Quill wasn't listening. 'What have you been playing at, Martin? Why the devil d'you leave me like you did?'

Facing the chief engineer again was proving far harder than Martin had imagined. 'It'd take a good while to explain.'

'You look awful. By God, I've seen corpses with more colour to 'em. Have you been ill – were you injured?' Quill noticed the stiff arm hanging uselessly at Martin's side; the inert fingers sticky with blood protruding from the end of his sleeve. 'Why, that's a serious wound right there. That's –' He stopped dead, his bushy eyebrows knitting together. 'Lord Almighty, you're the one they shot. I heard 'em boasting that they clipped one of the micks as he made his way over the wall. It was you.' The engineer lifted a wide hand to his mouth, laying the palm flat across his lips. He seemed close to tears. 'Sweet Jesus.'

There was no point in denying it. 'I'm sorry that it went the way it did, Mr Quill,' Martin said. 'Truly I am.'

Quill burst towards him with a choked bellow, shoving Martin back, striking near the injury he'd been so concerned for a few seconds earlier. 'You got any notion how goddamn *stupid* this makes me look?' he yelled. 'That son of a bitch Noone's been saying for months that you're rotten, that you're a spy for our enemies, that I've been royally chumped by my liking for you – and fuck it all if he weren't goddamn *right*!'

Bent almost double, his arm fizzing with pain, Martin felt

a sour lump of sick working itself into the passage of this throat. 'Holy Mary, Mr Quill,' he muttered, trying to gulp it down, 'I am *sorry*, d'ye hear? I didn't mean for things to go like this. How many times can I tell you?'

The stocky American stood over him; Martin wondered if he was to be given a beating. 'Colt is working me like a dog,' he said. 'He's charged me, Martin, *me alone*, with cleaning up what you and your friends did. Two days I got, to make it right. I just left the damn factory a quarter-hour ago, and I'll be back there before sun-up. There's some great celebrity paying us a visit, a book-writer or newspaperman or something, and it'll be my goddamn hide if the Colonel don't have a decent show for him.' He laughed bitterly. 'You've fucked me, Mart, good and proper!'

Trembling a little, Martin wiped his streaming eyes looked around. The quarrelling carters had departed. A couple of whores were patrolling slowly to and fro, watching them without much curiosity, but otherwise the street was empty. 'There was good reason behind what we did,' he retorted. 'We suffered in Ireland, Mr Quill – you cannot begin to imagine how we suffered. The British Government, all these lords in their fine coats and top hats, they doomed us to starvation. They did it on purpose, and our people died in their thousands. We was going to take revenge for this terrible crime. That was our goal.' He gripped his immobile left hand, rubbing the fingers. 'We had good bleedin' reason, d'ye hear?'

Quill had never heard Martin speak like this before, and there was nothing he could meet it with. It was completely beyond him. His fury petering out, he sat upon the theatre's step. 'I had such plans for us, Mart,' he said, his voice weighed down by disappointment. 'You and your family rescued from this miserable place. Us in business together, over in America. Seems ridiculous now, don't it? What a goddamn *fool* I am.'

Molly Maguire was lurking somewhere near the alley's mouth, mewling impatiently; she wanted Ben Quill delivered to her. *Get out of here*, he longed to say to the man sitting in front of him; *run to Pimlico, and don't look back*. 'You are a good man, Mr Quill. You showed me kindness that I won't soon forget.'

Quill's manner hardened. He angled his head, refusing to look at Martin directly. 'What exactly did you call me out here for?' he asked curtly. 'I got a load to do thanks to your little gang.'

Martin readied himself for the next lie. He thought of Amy's smile; her soft whispers as they lay entwined. 'I have the gun,' he said. 'The missing Navy – the one that was stolen last winter. Colt wants it back, don't he? I'm leaving London, going back to Ireland most likely. Thought I'd give it you afore I left.'

The engineer snorted, climbing to his feet. 'You ain't nothin' but a thief,' he growled, 'a base goddamn plotter.'

'D'ye want it or no?'

Quill spat in the gutter. 'Yesterday's news, that is, but I suppose it might redeem me some – in Walt Noone's eyes, anyways.' He glared at Martin. 'Let me have it then. After that we're done, you and me, y'hear? We're *done*.'

Martin nodded towards the alley. 'Down there.'

They set off, Quill following him around the corner of the ramshackle theatre, away from the glare of its gas-jets. It was like walking into a cave – into a demon's clammy lair. The lane was lined with dingy shops, all shut up for the night; the only light came from a scattering of lanterns and candles set in dirty front windows. An animal stench of fresh mess and raw flesh washed out from a skinner's yard just back from the alley's entrance. Someone was still inside, sharpening knives on a wheel. Martin could see cages stacked against a wall, cats and dogs crammed into containers barely large enough to hold them. A few whined or yowled, but most were past all protest. At the back hung the skins, stretched on racks; and out in the alley, piled in a glistening, hideous heap, were the day's flayed bodies, left to be claimed as meat by whichever soul was desperate enough to want it.

The Mollys appeared further along the lane, a row of dark shapes moving rapidly through the gloom. They fell into a line, walking rapidly. This would be quick and simple. No one around here would interfere. Martin doubted that a policeman came this way more than once a month, and certainly not after dusk. The dairy was only a short dash away, on the edge of the clearances. He might not even need to be worked over first.

'All right, Martin,' said Quill, 'where is it?'

'Up ahead. Not much further.'

The engineer was growing suspicious; all trust between them was gone. Martin looked at the approaching Mollys. One of them met his gaze, his face caught momentarily in a weak pool of light, and Martin saw not a man but a gruesome ghoul, a walking corpse with hollow eyes, the bones standing from its fleshless cheeks. They wore Molly's marks. This was to be a serious job. Her laughter gathered in the air like the rustling of dead leaves and they began to run, rushing past Martin and onto Mr Quill.

'*No*,' he shouted, reaching out with his good arm to push them away. 'No, this ain't what we – ' He was knocked aside, and told harshly to stay the hell out of it.

Quill was trying to give some account of himself, but against five Molly Maguires, all of them seasoned street-fighters, it was hopeless. 'Martin,' came his stifled cry as they broke him down, 'help me, for God's sake!'

Martin dived in again, ignoring his throbbing arm, making a grab for Slattery's collar. 'Leave off, damn you! We've got to get him to the bleedin' dairy!'

This earned him a blow to his bullet wound that pulled the earth from under his boots, tipping him into a black chasm. He landed squarely on the skinner's heap, the animals' limbs crunching beneath his weight. The bodies were slippery and warm; one of them, not yet dead, quivered horribly. With a grunt of revulsion, he twisted away into the middle of the lane. From there, on his front, he could see Ben Quill sprawled in the mud, utterly defeated. Slattery was at the engineer's side. He took out the Navy, the one Martin had promised Quill, checking the cylinder before slowly drawing back the hammer.

'For Ireland, brothers,' he said. 'For Molly Maguire.'

The shot filled the alley from end to end like a dazzling

flash of lightning, leaving no echo behind it. Quill's back arched as the ball punched through him, his fingers twitching in a final spasm before falling still. The dogs in the skinner's yard yelped madly; there were startled exclamations from within the shut-up shops, then the sounds of latches sliding back and windows swinging open. Amid this commotion Martin could hear Molly Maguire, cackling and clapping her hands in delight. He looked over his shoulder, his vision starting to blur as pain overwhelmed him. She was tucked up in the eaves of Rosie McGehan's, leering down at them like a giant, spindly bat. She'd got her first real taste of blood in a good long time, and she was happy indeed.

'Pa,' Katie declared firmly, patting her father's cheek with her tiny moist palm, and then giving his ear a tug. 'Pa-pa-pa.'

Martin opened his eyes. His head was lying in Amy's lap, across her thighs. She was fashioning a daisy from a piece of scrap paper, showing it to her daughter as she did so and talking to her softly. He felt as hollow and weightless as a corn-husk. Everything was edged with white light, a glowing trim like that given to the Holy Family in pictures. For a moment he was completely at peace; he could almost believe that they were away in a warm summer meadow, just the three of them, many hundreds of miles from the Devil's Acre.

'You have me heart, Amy Knox,' he murmured.

She smiled, folding over a petal. 'I know it.'

Martin tried to swallow. His throat was dry and there was a tart, cloying taste in his mouth. Someone had been pouring gin into him. Perhaps as a result, his wounded arm did not hurt at all; he had to glance down, in fact, to make sure that it was still attached to his body. Above him was a lattice of cobwebbed rafters and the high side of a cattle stall. Straw was tickling his ankles. They were in the dairy.

The night's events crashed back abruptly into his mind like a slide of rocks through a flimsy rooftop: the skinner's heap, the pistol's blast, poor Ben Quill's last convulsion. He groaned and tried to sit up but he seemed to be lashed in place.

'How did I get back here?' he asked.

Amy's expression grew dark. 'They brought you in about an hour ago,' she whispered, setting aside the paper flower. 'Said you was knocked down by one of Colt's men. Then they all went straight back out. Only Thady's here right now. I think he's been told to watch us – to make sure we don't leave.' She looked off to the right, out of the stall, checking that their guard wasn't listening. 'What happened tonight, Mart?'

Martin hesitated, sorrow and guilt flooding through him, scarcely able to believe what he was about to say. 'They killed Mr Quill. Shot him dead in front of me.'

Amy caught her breath, her legs tensing beneath his head. 'But – but why?'

'To do for Colt. To make sure that his engine won't get repaired, that he'll be embarrassed and forced to close his works. It won't work.' Martin put his right hand over his face. 'He has died because of me, Amy. Slattery fired the gun but I'm to blame. I used my friendship wi' him to bring about his murder, and Almighty God will surely see me burn in hell for it.'

'No!' Amy's anger overtook her shock. 'You weren't given no *choice*, Martin! How was you to know what was in that villain's mind?'

He lifted his forefinger to her cheek, placing it against the flushed skin. 'It were plain enough, though, weren't it? Any fool could have seen that they weren't just going to take the poor sod prisoner. I was a right idiot, girl, and Mr Quill paid the price.'

'You did it for us. You did it so we'd be safe – free from all this.'

Martin stayed quiet for a minute. Quill's killing had shown that they would never be permitted to put the Molly Maguires behind them. On top of everything else, Slattery had proved himself a hardened liar. He'd taken their righteous mission and turned it into something truly evil. Martin knew that he'd never be released from his debt – that he'd be forced to take part in ever more dangerous and bloody actions until one or both of them was destroyed. He was damned if he was going to wait around for that day to arrive.

Katie crouched down beside him, scared by her parents' desperate manner, burying her head in the crook of his neck and throwing her arm across his chest. Shifting a little in the straw, Martin put his hand on her back and began to rub it gently.

'And we will be free, girl,' he said. 'I promise.'

7

The famous guest arrived on foot, sauntering in through the Bessborough Place gate. This took Sam by surprise; he had everyone lined up outside the warehouse, ready for inspection after a grand private carriage had swept in through the main gates and made a stately circuit of the water trough. Instead, he found himself skipping around the factory block to head his visitor off, damning Walter Noone to the lowest, hottest shelves of hell as he did so. It was the watchman's job to make sure that confusions like this did not occur; he had so far failed to appear, however, joining Mr Quill on the roster of the Colt Company's missing. The whole occasion, in short, was shaping up to be an unqualified disaster. Two of his senior staff absent without explanation, his machines quite dead, his engine split open like a fig – all on the day that one of the most celebrated men in the entire city was coming to call with the declared intention of *studying the legendary Colt works in all their thundering glory!*

Sam caught sight of the guest and slowed his pace, twisting his head atop his neck until something clicked. This can still be done, he told himself; you can still pull it off. The resulting publicity, the article in the fellow's magazine that would be read by many thousands across Britain and beyond, was surely worth the effort of a few showmanlike contortions.

The famous author was a spry little critter, with an attitude of casual amusement better suited to the beach-side boulevard at Coney Island than a London gun works. His hair was a few inches longer than Sam thought necessary, and his beard, although confined to his mouth and chin, had been permitted to grow down to his collar in an affectedly artistic manner. Recognising Sam at once, he hailed him with actorly grandness and strolled over. Their handshake was a good deal firmer than the gun-maker had been expecting. His voice, too, was strong and rich, trained by performance it seemed, with the ghost of that stubborn cockney aitch manifesting before the odd word – smiling broadly, he declared that he was delighted to make Sam's 'hacquaintance'.

'Mr Dickens, it's an honour,' Sam replied, pumping the hand with a vigour to match the author's own, 'for me and all my people.'

This, he perceived, was an entirely self-made man – not an over-schooled literary gentleman born in the lap of privilege, but someone who possessed an almost American impulse for self-betterment, and had refused to let his station in life be defined by his birth. Of course, like most Americans Sam was also aware that Mr Dickens had visited his homeland a decade or so earlier and had painted a truly grotesque picture of it in the infamous novel *Chuzzlewit*. For many citizens of the Republic, Yankees and Southrons alike, the author was still considered a bitter enemy. Sam was as affronted by John Bull condescension as anyone, but the simple fact was that this fellow was currently at the very height of his popularity. Everything he'd published for at least the last five years had met with astounding success. Whatever he might have written in the past, he was plainly well disposed towards this particular outpost of American endeavour – and that, quite frankly, was enough for Sam Colt.

It was warm for an English March, but Mr Dickens wore a long cape over his clothes as if preparing for heavy rain. He removed it now, handing it to the single assistant who'd accompanied him, and Sam saw that it served as a disguise rather than a guard against the weather. The suit of clothes beneath was distinctive indeed, cut in the English style but in strong, assertive colours. His coat and trousers were the same rich russet as his hat, but shot through with a thin

348

check of yellow; his waistcoat a deep cerulean blue, the necktie an arresting shade of lavender. That, Sam thought approvingly, is the costume of a man of true character.

Lowry and Richards had followed Sam around to the Bessborough Place gate, and the famous author insisted on shaking their hands as well before proceeding any further. Both mumbled and beamed, impressed despite themselves. This brought Sam some amusement. Earlier on, Alfie Richards had been doing his best to seem perfectly bored by the prospect of meeting Mr Dickens, claiming rather imperiously that he was more of a 'Thack man' – whatever the hell that meant.

These introductions complete, Dickens turned his attention back to Sam. 'First of all, Colonel,' he began, 'I must apologise for the extremely short notice I gave you. I'm presently rather pressed for time, you understand, as I am engaged in preparations for my next literary hadventure – rallying myself, if you like, for my next charge against the reading public of our two great nations.'

Now this was interesting. Sam had never read a single word of Dickens himself but he understood that the stories first emerged in serial form. Were the author's article on the Colt works to appear in the same issue as an episode of this latest tale, sales were sure to be enormous. It would do more for the company than a hundred of Richards's pieces in the trade press.

'For your magazine, this is?' he asked. 'For *Household Virtues*?'

Dickens laughed lightly and patted his arm. '*Words*, my dear chap – *Household Words*. Yes, that's where I shall place it. I have not yet settled upon a title, but it is to be set in a northern mill-town. I came to feel that I should obtain a bit of first-hand knowledge of such a place before setting my pen to paper – so I betook myself to Preston and a couple of other sooty citadels, and achieved my end admirably.' He cocked his head thoughtfully. 'Wandering those dismal, uniform lanes, I came across many a hoary old soul, thirty years bent over a clattering loom; many a disillusioned radical spitting a sermon of fire upon a smoke-blackened street corner; many an impassioned union man electrifying his tavern audience with visions of solidarity, of a new –'

'Well, I ain't got time for no union here,' Sam broke in. 'You want to make common cause with the other hands against me, you find somewhere else to work. I pay well, Mr Dickens, I deal fairly, and I make my factory a decent enough place to be. What more could a reasonable man want?'

The author was regarding him with a wry, evaluating smile. 'Fascinating,' he murmured. 'I must confess that it did seem as though some of the more vituperative hagitators were sowing division with their employers that could only serve to worsen their situation in the long run. It is an error, I think, this tendency to unionise – but surely an understandable one.'

'You want to join a goddamn union,' Sam said emphatically, 'then you don't work for Sam Colt.'

'Quite so.' Mr Dickens cast a look around the plain brick blocks of the pistol works. 'At any rate, on my return to London I find that Colonel Colt of Connecticut is the toast of several really rather lofty circles. A large government contract, is that correct? A radical member routed in a Select Committee hearing?'

Sam glanced at Lowry; the boy was impassive. 'Something like that, yes.'

'I spent a good deal of time discussing your achievements with my friend Johnnie Russell – who says that he once hencountered you in the flesh in the garden of our dear Lord Palmerston. It was this conversation that convinced me to write to you. A wondrous revolver factory, marshalled by a brilliant American inventor, on the shores of old Father Thames? Why, sir, it sounded too amazing to miss!'

So there was the connection. It was yet another thing owed – indirectly perhaps, but still – to Palmerston. This Dickens, for all his interest in factory folk, liked to rub shoulders with some powerful people.

'A tour won't pose a problem.' Sam cleared his throat. 'At this point, though, I should tell you that the factory itself is closed at present.'

The author let out a gasp of disappointment. 'But my dear Colonel! Your famous machines!'

The Colt men, proprietor, secretary and press agent, delivered the cover story they'd prepared first thing that morning. The engine was being recalibrated, a lengthy and incomprehensibly technical process, in order to increase production speeds for the Baltic Fleet contract – and in anticipation of more government contracts in the future. Lowry presented the report he'd drawn up on the normal operation of the machinery, a tight, fastidious grid of figures that Mr Dickens looked at for a couple of seconds with eyebrows raised before passing it to his assistant. Sam then proposed that they go instead to the warehouse to see the famous Colt blue being applied, the parts fitted and assembled, and the finished weapons put through their paces in the proving room. The great author, appeased it seemed, indicated his assent.

They walked into the yard, over to where the skeleton workforce was arranged in front of the warehouse. There were perhaps forty souls in all: the American staff, the women from the packing room and a handful of others. Mr Dickens was recognised in moments, the women blushing and whispering excitedly behind their hands. The Americans were more guarded, no doubt remembering the row over *Chuzzlewit*. Sam crossed his arms and stared at them hard. They knew better than to try any impudence towards an important visitor. And besides, it wasn't as if any of them would have actually *read* the goddamn book.

Instead of halting by Sam's side and perhaps making an address of some kind, Mr Dickens kept on going, moving among the women of the packing room, receiving their praise with modest dips of the head and urging any who tried to drop a curtsey to stand back up and shake his hand. Within a minute he had them gathered around him in a circle and was asking them questions about their lives, appearing to take genuine interest in their replies. The gun-maker looked on, entirely mystified. What a man like that could hope to gain from conversation with girls on two shillings a day was utterly beyond him. Soon even the Americans were joining in, though, forgetting their reservations, laughing along at the dandy author's quick-witted remarks.

Eventually, Sam got the staff back to work and the tour underway. Mr Dickens was shown the blueing ovens, the fitters' benches and the many half-made cases and crates; he was taken around the washroom and the staff reading room (recent copies of *Household Words* had been piled there a couple of hours previously), and given a lengthy explanation of the ventilation system. He was impressed by it all.

'My word, Colonel Colt,' he announced at one point, 'this is truly the most modern-minded of henterprises. It seems to me, sir, that you are a new model of international employer – a man as benevolent as he is forward-thinking!'

After half an hour or so they came to the proving room, the usual concluding point of the tour. 'This is where the pistols are tested,' Sam informed his guest, 'or proved as we gun-makers term it, afore they're sent away for the regular government proof in the Tower of London.'

'*Prove all things,*' Mr Dickens recited as he entered. '*Hold fast to that which is good.*'

Sam sensed that this was from scripture, but knew no more than that. 'Indeed,' he said.

The celebrity surveyed the rows of finished revolvers laid out on tables; the heaps of tools; the tins of ammunition and powder; the wooden testing tubes and the small firing range. 'I must say that I'm surprised at its character,' he commented, moving to the middle of the room. 'I was rather expecting a mysterious iron-plated chamber – a dungeon devoted to arcane procedure and esoteric hexperiment – not this cheerful, workaday place. It brings to mind something of the shooting galleries of Leicester Square. D'you know them at all, Colonel?'

'My business has obliged me to visit a couple.'

'A good few scenes of *Bleak House*, my most recent tale, were set in such an hestablishment. One of my principal characters, the shooting master, of whom I grew very fond, was a former military man like yourself.'

Sam took up a position by the door, feeling a keen need for a chew. 'I ain't got too much time for books, in truth.'

Mr Dickens went quiet, lowering his chin with his eyes closed, a knuckle raised to his lips. His host was about to ask if anything was amiss when he jumped suddenly back to life.

'"Now what," says Mr George, "may this be? Is it a blank cartridge, or a ball? A flash in the pan, or a shot?"'

For a second or two Sam didn't know which way to look. The famous author was commencing some kind of impromptu performance, making the floor of the Colt proving room his stage. He took the parts both of this 'Mr George' – for whom he adopted a booming, drill-sergeant's voice and a flustered expression – and that of the narrator, in tones like a more excited version of his own. The smiths started to turn around, setting down the guns they were working on.

'An open letter is the subject of the trooper's speculations,' Mr Dickens continued, hand angled against his mouth as if delivering an aside, 'and it seems to perplex him mightily.'

He proceeded to embark upon an energetic mime of a man scrutinising an envelope, holding it at arm's length then bringing it close, screwing up his face and pacing back and forth, setting the thing down and then picking it up again – all the while supplying his own commentary to the fellow's confusion. It went on for several minutes before ending up where it had begun.

'"Is it," Mr George still muses, "blank cartridge or ball?"'

There were chortles and a smattering of applause. The gun-maker was wondering what exactly to do next when the door by his side opened just far enough to admit Walt Noone's scowling mug. Sam glared at him, ready to demand that he account for his absence that morning, but the watchman managed to speak first.

'This way, Colonel,' he muttered urgently. 'There's something you got to see.'

Sam didn't argue. He was glad of the excuse, to be honest; the exuberant Mr Dickens was starting to tire him. Nodding to Lowry and Richards, he followed Noone back out into the yard. The watchman led him wordlessly through the Ponsonby Street gate and straight on through the midday traffic – showing the palm of his hand to an approaching dray with such blunt violence that the driver drew it to an immediate halt. He was angry, madly angry, the lid rattling on a boiling kettle.

They strode onto the section of the quay given over to the Colt works. The wooden pier had been extended, and a coal barge was moored at its end. It had yet to be unloaded, the barrows standing empty on the shore; the labourers who would do the job stood off to the side in an apprehensive huddle, held back by Noone's men. Noone himself went to where the pier joined the quay, standing at the very edge, locking his hands behind his back and lifting up his chin. His meaning was plain enough. Sam went to his side and looked down at the river.

There was a band of black mud about six feet wide between the greenish water and the base of the embankment wall. Directly below the pier, amid the trash and debris of the metropolis, was a larger object, the shape of a packing case or small barrel; and laid across it, waxy white against the muck, was the lower half of a man's arm. Sam's first thought was that it was being devoured by eels, but he quickly realised that the serpentine forms swarming over it were not moving. They were tattooed on. This was the body of Mr Quill, his missing engineer.

'How long's he been in there?'

'Since last night at least. Tide keeps shifting him – he was lying on his back a minute ago.' Noone met his eye. 'You could see the great big goddamn bullet-hole in his chest.'

'Jesus Christ.' Sam reached into his pocket for the screw of Old Red. Fingers trembling, he sliced off a chunk with his clasp-knife and pushed it into his mouth.

'Colonel, I know where they are. I can go there right now and finish it. I can –'

'No, Mr Noone,' Sam interrupted, champing furiously, 'you will do no such goddamn thing. We do not need the fuss. If you draw notice to us in any way – if this business here gets out – then we're sunk. How many times are you going to make me say it? We can't be seen to be this vulnerable,

354

or this hated. The British Government will not touch us again if they think there's any kind of risk involved. D'you understand me?'

'We owe it to Ben Quill to see the motherfuckers what killed him get their rightful goddamn punishment.'

Sam shook his head. 'That ain't got a single thing to do with it. You hide that body, as soon as you can. Somewhere it won't ever be found.' He gestured towards the labourers. 'How much have they seen? Will they stay quiet?'

Noone looked away without answering. That kettle lid was rattling again.

'*Will they*, Mr Noone?'

'I can make them see our viewpoint, Colonel.'

'Very well then. Hide that body, and quietly. Get Lou Ballou in that goddamn engine room if you have to carry him over from the lodging house. Then we'll put our heads together and devise a new strategy.'

The watchman's frustration got the better of him. 'So again we do nothing,' he hissed. 'They kill one of our number and we do nothing. I'm loyal to you, Colonel, God knows I am, but this is starting to look like cowardice. We're losing right here – letting a bunch of ragtag Papist cocksuckers thumb their noses at us.'

Sam spat a long stream of juice onto the stones. 'No, Mr Noone, we are *winning*. We'll sell more guns, knock down our rivals and make a ton of money. Our company will become the unchallenged supplier of arms to the entire goddamn world. And if you want to keep your place in it, you'll do what I damn well tell you.'

Mr Lowry was approaching from the edge of Ponsonby Street. Sam broke off from the watchman and went to intercept him – but not before he'd come within sight of Mr Quill's arm. His eyes widened with disbelief; he knew what it was all right.

'What the devil are you doing out here, Mr Lowry? Shouldn't you be looking to our guest?'

The boy gathered himself with remarkable speed, managing a pretty good show of light-heartedness – pretending that he'd seen nothing. 'Never fear, Colonel,' he said. 'Mr Dickens is doing perfectly well without me. What has happened, may I ask? Can I be of any assistance?'

Sam studied Mr Lowry for a second. Why exactly had he left the warehouse? Had he been thinking to spy on them? The gun-maker remembered the suspicions Noone had voiced about the boy before Christmas. They no longer seemed quite so ludicrous. One thing was absolutely certain: there was rot here, deep inside his London works. It had led to theft, and sabotage, and now Ben Quill being dumped like garbage in the open sewer of the Thames. He couldn't say how the secretary might be connected to it all and he didn't much care. Steps would have to be taken. The system would have to be flushed.

'A delivery mix-up is all,' he replied gruffly. 'Sorted now.'

Back in the proving room the performance had resumed. The audience had swollen, the blueing smiths crowding in around the testing tubes and the women from the packing room lining up along the stairs, leaning eagerly over the banister. Everyone there was shaking with laughter; even Richards wore a grudging grin. Mr Dickens had removed his hat and coat and was throwing himself around with great enthusiasm. He was enacting a conversation between the booming-voiced character he'd been doing earlier and a more nasal but equally simple-minded lackey, each role requiring a complete change of posture and demeanour. They were discussing a dream of the lackey's – a dream of the countryside.

'"How did you know it was the country?"' inquired the booming voice, standing bolt upright, to the left. '"On account of the grass, I think. And the swans upon it,"' the nasal voice answered, crook-backed, to the right. '"What were the swans doing on the grass?"' The famous author paused, teasing out his audience's mirth. '"They was a-eating of it, I expect."'

Sam decided that this had all gone far enough. From the doorway, speaking tersely over the general hilarity, the gun-maker asked his guest's opinion of his pistols – now that he'd had a chance to cast an eye over the finished article. The workers scattered at once, hurrying back to their rightful labours. Mr Dickens turned towards his host, offering a laughing apology for getting so caught up in his capering. Sam repeated his question. Smoothing down his hair, the author looked again at the rows of newly proved Navys. He pronounced himself impressed, but seemed more interested in the gallery of promotional posters that had been pasted to the wall behind them. They featured illustrations of the revolver's gallant service across America; an Indian scene, Colonel Hays of the Texas Rangers seeing off a vastly superior force of Comanche, struck him particularly.

'I see that your revolver is a pacifying hinstrument of some potency, Colonel,' he said, holding out a hand for his coat and then pulling it on. 'An effective means indeed of keeping Christian families safe as your republic extends its borders across the wilderness.'

Sam nodded. 'It's the ideal weapon for combat against barbarian tribes, Mr Dickens. I made this case to your government, in fact, but I couldn't get 'em to send any to the army fighting at the Cape.'

'Give them time, sir, give them time. In his heart every savage is covetous, treacherous and cruel, and quite beyond reform. There will be further difficulties in the African colonies, mark my words. Those equipping the poor souls doomed to fight there will see sense soon enough.'

Sam picked up an unloaded Navy and passed it to him, stock first. 'That ain't piecework there, remember. Every part is fashioned by a machine.'

Mr Dickens worked the mechanism, admiring the smooth rotation of the cylinder and the hammer's precise snap. 'D'you know, Colonel,' he imparted confidentially, 'I believe that this hinvention of yours will have the most profound consequences for storytellers such as myself. The possibilities for a Bill Sykes or a Mademoiselle Hortense armed with such a device – why, the imagination positively reels!'

Sam admitted that this hadn't ever occurred to him. 'Want to try it out?'

A smith took the gun from the author's hand and set about loading it. Mr Dickens demurred, protesting that he wielded a pen, not a pistol; that he was but a frail, desk-bound creature not fitted to the robust pursuits of those from the

Colt mould. Predictably enough, however, the chance to perform again was more than he could resist. Half a minute later he'd accepted the loaded revolver and was being directed towards the range.

Stepping up to the firing line, Mr Dickens adopted the classic duellist's pose – dead straight, sideways, with his chest thrust out and his pistol arm raised at a right angle to his body. He then tilted back his head, shutting one eye and taking aim along the barrel. Despite this rather comical approach, his first shot was a good one, slamming straight into the black and earning some whistles and whoops from the smiths. Encouraged, grinning wide, he fired his second, and his third, filling the proving room with noise; and by his sixth he was sniggering like a lunatic.

'By my soul,' he panted through the powder-smoke, 'what deuced fun this is!'

Sam held out a fresh Navy. 'Will you shoot off another?'

'My dear Colonel,' the famous author declared, 'I don't mind if I do!'

8

Caroline was perched a few yards up the side of a dust-heap, dressed in her old, well-worn clothes so as not to draw attention to herself. Edward's Navy was hidden under her shawl. A further search of his rooms had uncovered a small supply of ready-made cartridges in the back of a drawer – small, papery tubes that had slotted easily into the gun's chambers. She had a nagging sense that something was still missing, something that might prevent it from firing properly, but she couldn't worry about this now. There simply wasn't time.

The dust-heap, a great accumulation of ancient ash, was about two storeys high, covered in coarse-leafed weeds with a cracked, tar-like crust that crunched beneath your boots. The yard it stood in had fallen out of use many years ago; the dustman's house was a mouldy ruin, stripped of its timbers and tiles. Like the dairy on the other side of its broken-down fence, it would not be safe from the mallets of the City Corporation's wrecking teams for very much longer. Evening was approaching, the sun sinking behind the treetops of Belgravia as church bells across the city chimed six o'clock. Lights winked along Victoria Street, tracing a path through the misty wasteland of the clearances. In the other direction, over the exhausted roofs of the Devil's Acre, jutted up the unfinished towers of the Parliament building, the engines at their summits puffing out final scudding clouds of steam.

Caroline made herself look at the dairy, a low shed of

mossy, discoloured brick. Three of the Irishmen had stepped outside a few minutes earlier, walking off towards the river, leaving only Slattery and two others inside with Amy and Martin. Almost immediately a vicious argument had begun. Even from her place up on the dust-heap, Caroline could tell that Slattery and Martin were really going for each other. Martin sounded weak, his voice thin and hoarse, but he was giving no quarter.

'Yous killed him, damn you,' she heard him cry. 'An innocent man and yous bleedin' *killed him*.'

'You helped kill enough on the Mother Isle, Martin Rea – Denis Mahon, remember him? And you was going to kill Lord John happy enough, wasn't you?'

'Never one that didn't warrant it, Slattery! *Never!*'

Their numbers were reduced, and they were distracted by their quarrel. Caroline had been watching them, waiting for such a chance, for the best part of three days. But now it had finally arrived she was glued in place, thinking only of Edward Lowry; of the comfort they'd found in each other's arms throughout that freezing winter. To rise from the dust-heap and go down into the dairy was to lose him absolutely. Caroline had thought that she'd accepted this. Seeing the continued distress that the prospect of their parting brought him had actually made her feel a little guilty, so much greater did it seem than her own. Yet at this critical moment she'd suddenly ground to a halt, like a horse refusing to venture out onto a frozen lake. As the shouts from within the dairy reached new peaks of fury, and Katie's wail was added to the clamour, she kept delaying her approach by another tiny portion of time, and then another. Just until that person over there reaches the end of the lane, she told herself; just until that crouching cat jumps up onto that wall.

Laying her hand on the hard curve of the pistol stock brought back some of her reason. Her sister was in there, and her niece: her family. They needed her. No one else was going to help them. She wiped her damp palms on her shawl, squeezed her eyes shut and whispered a short prayer.

When she opened them again there he was, in the dead centre of her vision, like a divine judgement upon her hesitancy – Walter Noone, Colonel Colt's watchman, striding along Old Pye Street. Despite his neat coat and shining boots, the Acre's inhabitants were leaving him well alone, warded off by a potent, unspoken threat. He stopped a short distance from the old dairy, studying the front entrance and the derelict premises on either side. As Caroline herself had done, he quickly decided that the dust-yard was the best way in and started for the gate.

She was almost overcome by panic. How had he found his way here? Had he been following her – and if so, for how long? Did he know that Edward had been giving her shelter? It didn't matter. She had to act at once. Skidding down the dust-heap, she met him as he entered the yard, pointing the pistol at his chest with both hands.

Noone wasn't surprised or alarmed to see her. If anything, his reaction was one of boredom. 'Well, if it ain't Lowry's whore,' he drawled. 'That preening bastard round here too, is he? All come to have a good chuckle with your Papist pals about the Yankee boy I've just had to sink in the Thames mud?'

'I don't know what you're talking about,' she replied, fighting to control her fear, 'but you ain't going in there.'

The watchman stared at her; it felt like violation. The Navy's long barrel started to wobble.

'You ain't with them no more,' he stated. 'You're here for someone else – the sister, that dark-haired bitch I seen hanging about with 'em before.' He nodded at her revolver. 'That ain't one of those you stole from us, is it?'

'I'll shoot you,' Caroline said, clicking back the hammer, 'so help me I will.'

This won her the slightest wince of scorn. 'It ain't loaded properly, you dozy cunt. Percussion caps are needed to fire a repeating pistol.'

Caroline glanced at the gun, lifting it a little, knowing that he was right; and he drove a fist straight into her in the eye, knocking her against the dust-heap. For a few seconds she was blinded, floundering dazedly in the black soil. A hot iron seemed to press down hard upon her cheek, stinging wickedly, making her curse aloud. Ignoring the pain as best she could, she rocked herself upright. A thick drip was crawling along her top lip. She touched her face; her nose was bleeding.

Noone was about ten yards away, pushing through the dust-yard's fence, heading for a side door in the dairy's wall. He'd drawn a pair of pistols from under his short coat. Rubbing her bloody nose with her sleeve, Caroline gave chase. The Irishmen were still arguing ferociously – actually fighting each other from the sound of it. They wouldn't hear the watchman coming.

'Amy!' she shouted. 'Amy, get *out*!'

It was too late. Noone had gone through the door. Tearing her skirts on the fence, slipping on a step and colliding with the outside wall, Caroline careened in after him.

Slattery and Martin were caught in mid-brawl, each screwing up a handful of his adversary's shirt, in the centre of the dairy's single rectangular room. Martin looked awful, pale and sunken-eyed, his left arm swathed in grubby bandages. The two other Irishmen were standing on either side of them, as if they'd been trying to pull them apart. All four now gaped at the intruder, their fight forgotten.

The dairy was a decayed place, its whitewash soured to a dirty yellow; the milk-urns that lined the walls had been eaten up completely by rust. There was a counter at the street end and a row of cattle stalls at the rear, in which its current residents had made their beds. From one of these, only a few yards from the side door, peeked Amy and Katie. They were clinging together, both struck dumb by fright. The sisters' eyes met; and if anything, Amy's confusion increased. Caroline remembered that, as well as being bloody and bruised, she still held Edward's useless Navy in her hand.

Noone was walking towards the counter, checking the dairy's boarded-up front – making sure that no one could escape through it.

'What the hell d'ye want?' Slattery shouted at him, letting go of Martin.

The watchman turned around. 'Did you think I wouldn't

362

come looking for you?' he demanded. 'Did you really think you could kill Ben Quill and nothing at all would happen?'

Slattery was defiant. 'Aye, so we killed him. What of it? We'd do it again, so we would, in a bleedin' heartbeat. Your precious Colonel is an enemy of Catholic Ireland – of our mistress Molly Maguire. She'll see him reduced to bleedin' nothing, d'ye hear?'

This didn't impress Noone one bit. 'You can talk whatever goddamn nonsense you like. The fact is you've stolen, you've cheated, and you've lured an innocent man, an unarmed man, to his death. I don't care what your reasons are – that there is rank cowardice in my book.'

'I ain't no coward, ye Orange bastard,' Slattery roared. 'Don't you be testing me now! Don't you dare do it!'

Noone's lip twitched. He said nothing.

Looks darted between Caroline, Amy and Martin. All three of them were thinking the same thing: this might be the moment to run for the side door. Martin took a small step towards his wife and child.

Noone noticed this at once and raised the pistol in his left hand, cocking it with his thumb. 'You stay put,' he said flatly. 'Don't think I ain't worked out the part you played, Martin Rea. You're the cocksucker that got Ben Quill to leave Pimlico in the middle of the goddamn night – to wander off into this stinking rookery. I knew right from the start that you was no goddamn good. Shame no fucker would heed me.'

Martin made no reply to this, but he continued to walk slowly towards his family, placing himself in front of them like a barricade. Caroline cast a sidelong glance at Noone. I shall throw myself upon him, she thought. Surely he wouldn't be able to get one of those guns on me in time.

Before she could act, there was a scuffle of movement on the other side of the dairy. Slattery was rushing for something in one of the far stalls, a pile of tattered black dresses it looked like, taking advantage of the watchman's distraction. A shot burst an instant later, pounding through the close air; Amy screamed, the sound strangely muted after the deafening bang. There was another shot. Slattery was firing at Noone. He still had one of the revolvers from the cellar.

Powder-smoke billowed and eddied, tinting the air like ink in water.

Coldly calm, Noone levelled his right-hand pistol and loosed four rounds in a couple of seconds. His aim was good, even through the smoke. One of the Irishmen dropped to the floor, struck in the neck; the other staggered, groaning, against the rusting urns; two fist-sized holes were smashed into the stall where Slattery had taken cover.

'Run!' cried Caroline, moving back to the doorway. 'Come on!'

Out came Amy, with Katie in her arms; Martin was but a few paces behind. Caroline pointed them towards the dust-yard. Several more shots sounded, from both Slattery and Noone, the muzzle-flashes projecting bright lines along the edge of the doorframe. Then Slattery threw himself through a window at the dairy's end, leaping back to his feet, kicking apart the dust-yard fence and lunging up the heap on its other side.

And so they all took flight from Walter Noone. Amy stayed in the lead, her howling daughter on her shoulder, dashing for the gate; her husband lumbered after her, his injured arm flapping uselessly, urging her onwards. Caroline brought up the rear, her muscles straining, dreadfully aware of the mortal danger that gathered at her heels. The watchman would not relent, that much was certain. Their only hope was that he might choose to pursue Slattery rather than them.

She heard the empty thud of the bullet striking Martin's back before the actual shot. He was panting heavily, saying 'That way, girl, over there' – but his voice was cut off abruptly, like a fiddle-string snipped with a pair of scissors. He collapsed face first into the dirt, not even lifting his good arm to break his fall.

Amy looked back in alarm. Seeing Martin lying there, she shrieked out his name and stumbled to the ground, letting go of Katie. On her hands and knees, she scrabbled to her husband's side and tugged at his shoulder, whispering frantically into his unhearing ear. Caroline made for the stunned, crimson-faced child, yelling to her sister that they had to keep moving but knowing in her heart that it was useless. Martin was dead. They would not get away now.

Noone was climbing through the broken fence, his pistol still raised. His eyes were on Slattery, who was struggling over the dust-heap in the direction of the clearances, a silhouette, framed by the evening sky.

'You stop right there!' the watchman barked. 'I ain't done with you neither!'

Slattery did not respond so Noone shot at him. A line of blood flicked out from the Irishman's thigh; cursing, clutching at the wound, he swivelled around to fire back, almost losing his footing as he emptied his last chamber into the yard.

An open hand seemed to clap hard against Caroline's midriff, sending a ripple shivering through her clothes. Her body snapped taut, then relaxed; a trapdoor opened beneath her, and down she went.

9

The ragged denizens of the Acre, startled by the quick sequence of shots, scuttled for cover like lice suddenly exposed under a log. A street-corner drunk shouted that it was the Russians, a detachment of the Tsar's finest who'd crept into London to mount a daring raid, and the air of panic increased. Edward, however, recognised the sound of a Colt Navy immediately. Moving from the path of a fleeing fruit-seller, he craned his neck, trying to find the source of the gunfire between the Acre's rotten buildings. There were two more shots, and screams; and he saw one of the Irishmen, limping down the side of a black hillock only one street away, leaving a drift of pistol-smoke hanging behind him. Picking a winding alley that seemed to lead in the right direction, he broke into a run.

In the space of a single day the situation had grown mortally serious. Benjamin Quill, the Colonel's blameless engineer, had been murdered. Edward had overheard enough of the conversation on the wharf to know that Walter Noone believed that Rea and his friends were responsible. He was certain that the watchman would now go after them at the very first opportunity, regardless of the Colonel's view on the matter. Caroline would probably still be close to the Irish hideout, waiting for an opportunity to free her sister. Edward could easily imagine her becoming entangled in the bloody show-down that Noone was sure to initiate. She had to be reached somehow, and warned, but he had no idea where she was.

The only course open to him was to follow Noone, do whatever he could – and pray that he was not too late.

Throughout the afternoon Edward had done his best to monitor Noone's movements. This had proved something of a challenge. The Colonel was determined to report Mr Dickens's visit as widely as he could, which meant a great stack of letters for the secretary to draft and pen. Deadened by worry, he'd barely considered the magnificent strangeness of having met Charles Dickens, shaken his hand and watched him perform in the Colt proving room; yet he was uncomfortably aware that the renowned author's evident delight in the Colt six-shooter would now be harnessed to the Colonel's cause. At the end of the day, by luck as much as vigilance, Edward had spotted Noone leaving the works by the Bessborough Place gate. He'd stuffed a couple of letters into his pocket, intending to tell anyone who asked that he was going to the post office, and started after him.

Keeping track of Noone as he went from Millbank to the Devil's Acre became increasingly difficult. The watchman had been marching along at quite a pace, and seemed to be acting on some very specific directions. He'd taken several tight turns, cut through a mob that had gathered around a reeking oyster stall – and then he was gone. Edward had searched about frantically for a minute or two before coming to a dismayed halt. A few seconds later the first shots had rung out through the rookery.

The alley he'd chosen led him to a misty, litter-strewn street, all but cleared of people by the gunfire. A lone child was wandering on the pavement, a girl of perhaps two years old with light chestnut curls and a paper flower pinned to the front of her grey-blue smock. She was lost in distress; sobbing, calling for her mother, she ambled to the gutter and sat down unsteadily. Could this be Katie, Caroline's sister's child? He walked towards her, saying the name softly. There was movement on the edge of his sight, through an open gate. He glanced over at it and everything was upturned forever.

Caroline was on her back, dark blood spreading fast across the front of her plain dress. Her face was ashen but for a ripe black eye; she was working her arms against the ground, paddling them in the dirt as if struggling to sit up. The bonnet had been knocked from her head, and her fair hair was clinging damply to her skin. He ran over, lifting her into his lap, cradling her shoulders. She gripped his hand and he found himself smiling, laughing almost, even as he was swamped with maddening helplessness.

What the devil was to happen now?

He looked around. They were in a dust-yard. Martin Rea lay a few feet away, clearly dead. A young woman who could only be Caroline's sister was clinging to his body, her face buried in his clothes. The black hillock, the dust-heap, rose at the yard's rear; and there was Colt's watchman, scaling it with quick agility, a smoking Navy in each hand.

'*Noone!*' Edward shouted, his voice cracking. 'Noone, what have you done?'

Noone turned, angling a pistol as if to shoot; seeing the secretary, he merely sneered a little, lowered the gun and carried on his way.

Caroline was attempting to speak, but gave up mid-word with an agonised gasp. There was a sharp trill somewhere past the dust-yard gate – the blast of a brass whistle. The police were coming, running over from the direction of the Abbey, alerted by the gunfire.

'Caroline,' Edward said gently, 'we must leave. We must get you to a – a doctor. To a hospital.' Where was the nearest one – Westminster, on Broad Sanctuary? Which side of the Acre were they on, even?

'Katie,' she managed to murmur. 'Please, Edward . . .'

'We won't leave her. We'll fetch her now.'

Edward eased Caroline to her feet, but they'd only walked a couple of steps before she went completely limp, losing all strength. As he lowered her to the ground again, he noticed that something heavy was dropping from her clothes and reached out to catch it. It was his revolver – Colonel Colt's gift. She'd taken it from under his bed, he realised, and had been planning to use it to save her family. He wondered if she'd so much as drawn it from her shawl before Walter Noone had shot her down.

Her eyes were rolling back now, the blue irises disappearing behind her flickering eyelids. This was impossible; it simply couldn't be real. How in God's name had it come to this? Edward leaned in close, fitting himself around her as he had so many times before, begging her to look at him and talk to him; but her fingers were slipping from his, and very slowly her head dipped down to meet the earth.

Hob-nailed police boots were hammering on the street outside. A constable stamped through the gate, going straight to Martin Rea, pulling his widow from the body and demanding that she provide him with an explanation. She could only wail in response, clawing at his hands and throwing herself back on her lifeless husband. The child, Katie, still sat in the gutter, staring over at her parents, desperate to approach them but too scared to move. Edward tucked the Navy revolver inside his jacket. More police would be arriving at any moment. He would surely face arrest; and when Colt discovered what had happened, some charge or other would be drummed up and he would be sent to prison. He took a last look at Caroline – at her corn-coloured hair and the two neat moles upon her white cheek. He tried to breathe but the air wouldn't enter his lungs. There was an ache in his chest as if his heart was being crushed, ground to paste beneath a rock. Wiping the hot tears from his face, he drew himself upright and walked out of the yard. He would do what she'd asked of him.

Shortly before dawn, Edward awoke fully clothed in the chair before his fireplace. He'd been dreaming with terrible vividness that Caroline's death had itself been only a dream; that he'd woken beside her in the sheets that now lay cold at his feet, where they had lain together only the previous morning; that he'd told her of the dreadful scene in the dust-yard and she'd called him a silly fool, kissing his nose and wrapping her warm, soft arms around his neck. He'd smiled, kissing her in return, feeling a pure and joyful relief.

Sitting there in the grey light of early morning, he was forced to remember the truth. She was gone – killed by a

Colt Navy in the Devil's Acre. All happiness had been taken from him. He was quite alone.

A weak whimper from his bedchamber, however, reminded him that this was not so. Leaning forward in his chair, he peered through the open doorway. Katie Rea was in his bed, a tiny lump beneath the coverlet. She was in the grip of a nightmare, sleep giving the exhausted child no refuge from the ordeals of the previous day.

Edward rose, stretching his stiff back. They could not stay in Red Lion Square. Noone had seen him in that dust-yard. He had no doubt that the watchman knew where he lived – where he had been sheltering Caroline Knox – and would be coming to call before very long. Katie's mother was certain to have been arrested and would face charges of some kind. If he was taken too, handed over to the police or worse, the child would enter the care of the parish. He well recalled Caroline's horror at this prospect. They had to flee, both of them.

Ready money was needed. Edward had just over fifteen shillings in cash – not an enormous sum. A visit would have to be paid to the pawn shop. The clothes he'd bought for Caroline before Christmas, a soft green dress, a black shawl and some snowy petticoats, were arranged on a stand in the corner. They would be worth at least two or three pounds to the second-hand clothes dealers over on the Strand. Hanging there, they seemed to hold a faint shadow of the woman who had worn them; his head grew light as he went over to the stand, lifting the hem of the dress in his hand. He could see her in it, clear as life, patting a crease from the fabric as she sat in front of the fire. It was no use. How could he possibly sell these garments? They were hers. He turned sharply, searching the cramped parlour for something else.

And there it was, resting on the table by the window: the presentation Navy. Edward looked at the perfect sheen of the blue; the crisp octagonal lines of the barrel; the delicate, interweaving forms of the decorative engraving that twisted around the frame. Any reputable pawnbroker would give ten pounds for such a rare and magnificent thing. That would take them well away from London and keep them for some weeks, if spent judiciously. He put on his coat and hat, packing Caroline's clothes into a carpet bag along with a couple of clean shirts and collars, laying the revolver carefully on the top. Then he scooped the slumbering infant from his bed and went out onto the stairs.

10

Sam hated policemen with a real passion. All they were good for, in his experience, was meddling and over-complication, and every man-jack of them was as bent as a goddamn coat-hook. Those he'd encountered in London were not a jot different from those back in the States. Indeed, the sheer mass of humanity over which they wielded such unreasonable power meant that their corruption tended to run deeper and blacker than that of their American counterparts, there being so many more opportunities to practise it.

The fellow sitting opposite him now – an Inspector Norris from the Westminster station – was a typical specimen, a pasty, overfed sort with an idler's skinny limbs. There was a studied ease to his movements, and a sly self-satisfaction in his features, that suggested he was used to having his interests accommodated. Norris had set his sturdy top hat down on the carpet beside his chair, crossed his blue-clad arms and was looking around Sam's Piccadilly apartment with an appreciative air. Next to him, standing at attention, was Walter Noone. On the watchman's wrists was a pair of iron manacles, their greased hinges glinting in the gaslight. From outside in the corridor came some lewd, muffled laughter; the two constables posted there, brutes in uniform from Sam's glimpse of them, were exchanging reminiscences of a recent jaunt in the Haymarket. The gun-maker cut himself a thick coin of Old Red and slotted it into his cheek. He had a feeling that this was going to cost him.

'So this is *normal procedure* right here, is it, Inspector?' Sam poured two glasses of bourbon. It was accepted without hesitation – a clear indication of what was to come. No righteous bleats about drinking on duty from Inspector Norris. 'Pulling a man from his dinner? Barging your way into his home?'

In fact, Sam had returned to Piccadilly gladly, despite the nature of the summons. It had removed him from a rather tedious dinner at the Garrick Club in Covent Garden, hosted (and dominated) by Mr Dickens. The famous author had invited him at the conclusion of the factory tour that afternoon, promising introductions to some important press-men. Yet instead of useful conversation the evening had been given over to endless speechifying and increasingly foolish recitations, culminating in Mr Dickens's performance of what was plainly a regular parlour-trick of his – an unbroken leapfrog along a dozen-strong line of his companions. Sam had declined to participate.

'There are four fresh bodies in the morgue at Westminster Hospital,' the Inspector stated blandly. 'Three vicious-looking Irishmen and a rather pretty girl. A domestic of some kind, I'd say.' Norris sipped his whiskey, taking his time. 'Rough hands, you see, from all the laundry.'

Sam knocked back his own drink. 'What's that to me?'

'They were shot to death with your pistols, Colonel Colt. My men tell me that a great many bullets were loosed very close together. I don't see how that can be anything but a repeating arm of some kind.' Norris angled his shoulder to include the stoic Noone in their discussion. 'And then there's this gentleman here, nabbed not twenty yards from the scene of the crime – an American gentlemen, Colonel, in your employ. He'd thrown away the weapons themselves by that time, o' course, but there was a plentiful quantity of powder on his fingers, and a few of your special-rolled cartridges in his pockets.' The Inspector shrugged, taking another sip of whiskey. 'We could make the case, if needs be.'

'I never shot the girl,' Noone said. 'I only wanted those what had –'

Sam glowered at him. 'Goddamn it, Mr Noone, you be

quiet and let the Inspector and me see if we can't come to an agreement on what happened here.'

He spelled it out clearly and carefully. The gun or guns in question were not Colts. He was a responsible arms manufacturer, and could account for each and every one of his weapons. There were other revolver makers in the city who were less rigorous, though – the Inspector might do well to direct his queries towards Mr Adams of Deane, Adams & Deane, whose workshop at London Bridge was open to whoever chose to stroll on in. As for Mr Noone there, the fellow was as dazzled by the majestic extent of London as any American. He'd developed a taste for wandering its limitless thoroughfares, often for hours on end; and this was what he'd been doing when he was apprehended by the Inspector's men.

Norris was regarding him shrewdly. 'So you expect me to believe that your man's presence in the Devil's Acre was merely a *coincidence*?'

The moment for the pay-off had arrived. Sam wrote out a banker's draft for two hundred pounds and slipped it inside one of the half-dozen cases of presentation Navys he kept beside his desk.

'Accept these,' he said, holding it out to Norris, 'as a token of my deep and abiding esteem for the London constabulary. And be aware that if I ever hear of this unfortunate event being in any way connected with me, I'll know at whose door to lay the blame. I appreciate you bringing this to me, Inspector, truly I do, but I ain't a man you want to cross.'

Norris raised his eyebrows, acting as if Sam's matter-of-fact bribe was an unforeseen and rather impertinent thing; but he took it all the same, and as he lifted the lid he could not hide his greedy pleasure. 'Well, Colonel,' he announced, picking up his hat and rising to his feet, 'it's plain enough what happened here. The Irish gangs around Old Pye Street have been feuding of late. These deaths'll be to do with that. It's a commonplace sort of event, in truth, and soon forgotten. Worse than rabid dogs, these blasted micks are.' Sliding the pistol case beneath his arm, he undid Noone's manacles and then hung them on his belt. 'I'll take up no more of your time.'

Once Norris had gone, taking his chortling underlings with him, Sam crossed the room, poured himself another bourbon and sat down upon his plush red divan. He looked coldly at Noone.

'What did you do with Ben Quill?'

The watchman was rubbing his wrists, sore from the policeman's bracelets. 'Colonel, we ain't done with –'

'An *answer*, Mr Noone, damn you.'

'Weighted him. Sunk him further out in the mud.' Noone stared at the floor – almost sadly, it seemed. 'He won't come up again.'

Sam considered this, chewing his tobacco mechanically. 'How the devil d'you know where those Irishmen were?'

'I been in that rookery a good deal, while you were busy with your lords and celebrities. I got people I can ask.'

The gun-maker caught the bitterness in his tone. 'Mr Noone, I ain't a goddamn gangster, seeking to rule through terror – and neither am I some kind of policeman serving out justice. I'm in this city to make guns and to sell 'em, you hear me, not to wage your little war.'

Noone met his gaze. 'It ain't over. One of them cock-suckers got away from me – the ringleader, it was. I clipped his leg but he got away. Two more days, Colonel, and I could –'

'You ain't listening,' Sam interrupted. 'You're done, Mr Noone. I'm sending you back to Hartford.'

The watchman hesitated. 'You *firing* me, Colonel?'

Sam shook his head; Christ, the fellow knew far too much Colt business ever to be fired. 'You'll be given a place at the works. Good pay. Light duties. Just two thousand goddamn miles from London.'

Noone lifted his chin, proud and angry, those fierce eyes sparking like a lit twist of fuse-paper. He was as unrepentant as ever; Sam supposed that a man who'd done the things he had couldn't have much room in his heart for regret. 'Your boy was there as well, y'know,' he snapped, trying to inflict a little vengeful discomfort, 'the English secretary. Taking the dead girl up in his arms. I was right about them, just like I was right about Ben Quill's assistant.'

'Well, many thanks,' snarled Sam sardonically, downing his whiskey, 'but that I'd already figured out for myself. Mr Lowry was heading for the door. He weren't the man I took him for at all. It's often the case for an employer of labour. A fellow can't be getting sentimental in such situations.'

'Ain't you going to do nothing, then?' Noone was incredulous. 'Goddamn it, I could go out and fetch him right now, bring that cocksucker back here for –'

Sam's patience ran out. 'By thunder, Mr Noone, I don't believe that you ever really grasped our purpose here. Your head's full of honour, ain't it, that soldier's pride of yours, but this is *business*. You'll take your leave, I'll get me another watchman, and we'll see if he can't keep my men and my machines safe – which you never quite managed to do, did you, despite all the goddamn Irishmen you killed.'

Noone's lips were pursed, and his lined forehead crumpling up like corrugated iron. Sam could tell that he was biting his tongue. 'Colonel, I –'

'Get out of here, go on. I'll wire Hartford, tell them to expect you.'

The watchman strode from the room without so much as glancing in Sam's direction, and slammed the door mightily behind him. He'll calm down sooner or later, the gun-maker thought – he'd damn well have to. There was no chance on earth of any other respectable employer giving him a position.

Rising from the divan, Sam strolled to a window, pulled back a pearl-grey curtain and looked out at the lamps of Piccadilly. A new chapter was beginning for the Colt Company. The difficult introduction to a fresh territory, after a long year of struggle and strife, was finally at an end. Some useful men had been lost along the way, it was true; Ben Quill's fate, in particular, was a goddamn shame. Edward Lowry prompted more conflicted feelings. Who could honestly say what had happened there? Given a fine opportunity for self-advancement, the boy had somehow fallen in with criminals and worked against the very man who'd sought to help him. It was truly inexplicable behaviour. That would teach him to put an unknown, a foreigner, in such a privileged post. Sam could only be thankful that he'd never let the boy in on the company's more sensitive operations.

Both, however, were easy enough to replace. Lou Ballou would get the engine running again, and there were a few promising juniors in Connecticut who could be tranfered to Pimlico to aid him. The workforce would be reinvigorated. It was a real chance to start over. Spitting his spent tobacco plug into an empty vase, Sam reflected upon his remaining London employees. There was definitely still some dead wood among them, and this was the time to chop it down. He went to his desk, reached for pen and paper and started to write a list.

EPILOGUE

1

Three weeks after the shootings, quite penniless, Edward returned to London. Climbing from the train at Fenchurch Street with Katie in his arms, he was convinced that he would be arrested at once. The constable they passed on their way out to the street, however, ignored them completely. Edward's intention was to leave the child with his mother and then go abroad, borrowing the money for his passage from Saul Graff; but when they arrived at her house at Sydenham Hill he was astonished to discover that there had been no mention at all of the dust-yard slaughter in the newspapers. No description of him had been circulated. Not a single policeman had called, asking his whereabouts. Neither had there been any sign of a grizzled, gimlet-eyed Yankee in a military-style cap. It was as if it hadn't happened.

They'd been hiding in Margate, in a small suite of rooms at the top of a deserted seaside boarding house. The proprietor was told that they were uncle and niece – that Katie had recently become Edward's ward after the untimely death of both her parents. The man had been happy to believe this, reassured by Edward's respectable appearance and the five pound note he'd produced before writing 'Mr Benjamin Quill' in the register.

At first the child would not talk or engage with him in any way; she just sat listlessly on the floor, staring at nothing. Next came the screaming fits, striking at all hours, when she would call out for her mother and father in the most piteous tones. Utterly out of his depth, Edward relied upon simple kindness and a steady supply of sweetmeats – and lemonade laced with a drop of gin to ease her off to sleep. He came to realise that she was not as scared of him as might have been expected. The only explanation for this he could think of was that she must have seen him with her aunt in those last awful moments in the Devil's Acre. By the time the money from the pawned gun had run out, the child was reaching for his hand as she tottered timidly along the wind-swept seafront; and meeting his eye when sharing her murmured, semi-intelligible confidences.

Edward's mother was glad to see her son safe and well, if rather drawn, but could not hide her shock at the sight of the two-year-old girl resting against his shoulder, her arms thrown around his neck. He told her only that he'd lost a close friend and suffered a dramatic rupture from his employer in the same dreadful afternoon; that the child had been entrusted to him by this friend before she died, and had no one but him to look after her. He was too tired to be able to tell precisely what his mother made of this half-story. She stepped back from the door readily enough, though, welcoming them both inside.

With the child out of his immediate care, the grief that had been held in suspension above Edward fell down upon him like a smothering shroud. He found that he could no longer bear to look out on the world, to dress himself and shave his face, to leave his room or even rise from his bed. As well as the constant pulse of sorrow, he was assailed by a terrible self-loathing, tormented by thoughts of everything he could have done but did not do. Lying on his back, he spent his days raking through the day of the Dickens visit, from beginning to bloody end, upbraiding himself severely at every juncture. *Why did you stay in the factory after you saw Ben Quill's corpse?* he would demand, striking his head with his palm. *Why did you not go straight into the rookery and hunt her down – run from street to street shouting out her name?*

His memories of Caroline were so clear that he felt he could almost summon her form before him, to the point of

382

being able to run his hand along the smooth undulation of her side; knowing all the while that she wasn't there, that she couldn't be there. At night, stirring from a fitful sleep, he'd swear that he could make her out in the darkness, watching him from over by the window. Sitting up, fumbling with a Lucifer match, he'd say her name out loud, his voice loaded with a strange, fearful hope. The flame would flare, revealing nothing; and he'd lie back among the sweat-dampened sheets, gazing numbly at the ceiling, listening to the frenetic thuds of his heart slowly subside.

Eventually, of course, Edward began to recover. He obtained a clerical position in a local architect's office, working on a string of new churches that were to be erected across the burgeoning villages to the south of London, and found sanctuary of a sort in the discipline and efficiency it required of him. Outside his working hours he set about discovering the fate of Katie's mother. Amy Rea had been convicted of robbery, he learnt, and sentenced to two and a half years in Brixton Prison – although what she had stolen and from whom was not specified. Edward wrote to her, reporting that her child was safe and being well looked after. He had no idea if the letter would be given to her, or even if she was capable of reading it, but he had to make the attempt.

As for Caroline and her brother-in-law, there was not a single earthly trace. No mention had been made anywhere of a shooting in the Devil's Acre. Edward couldn't even find a reference to their deaths. They had been erased.

Sitting in the reading room of a public library with a wealth of newspapers and periodicals at his disposal, Edward inevitably found himself investigating the continued fortunes of the Colt Company. Alfred Richards's regular postings in the armaments trade press revealed that most of the senior London staff had been replaced, Walter Noone among them. Edward dared to think that he might be safe.

The pistol works itself was flourishing, by the press agent's somewhat hyperbolic account at least. Over the summer of 1854, as the Army's expeditionary force camped out in Bulgaria and the Navy patrolled disputed waters in search of the enemy, the demand for Colt's revolvers underwent a steady rise. Orders in the thousands were placed for the Black Sea fleet, and dispatched with all haste to Constantinople. The Colonel, Richards claimed, had taken his rightful position as the armourer of the Empire; the formidable American eagle perched upon Britannia's shoulder, ready to lend its tearing talons to her cause. Robert Adams and his partners were still on the scene, expanding their works, insisting on fresh comparative trials and agitating at the Board of Ordnance, but Colt's remained the larger operation – and the significantly cheaper product. It was hinted that Army contracts, the really huge ones for which the Colonel had held out for so long, were sure to arrive soon.

Edward read all this with growing consternation. That the world was to become so filled with these firearms, these deadly devices that had already killed Caroline and countless others, now seemed to him like nothing short of insanity. He knew that this was not a rational reaction, and tried to remind himself that Samuel Colt was merely a businessman providing an effective tool – a model of highly successful entrepreneurship and self-promotion, in fact, to whose example he had once aspired. Yet Edward became increasingly convinced that this wasn't the complete picture. He recalled the numerous anomalies of his time as the Colonel's secretary, from the mysterious correspondence forwarded from Liège to that huge stockpile of unproved weapons Caroline had discovered down in the warehouse cellar, for which he'd never actually found an explanation. Something untoward was going on at the Pimlico pistol works. He resolved to keep up his watch on it.

With the end of summer came the commencement of the long-promised war. The nation looked on as that which they had cheered for so loudly stumbled to miserable disaster in the space of a few weeks. Reports from *The Times*, the *Courier* and a host of other papers left no doubt as to the chaos on the front lines, and the dire suffering of the troops. Cousin Arthur wrote Edward a rather peevish letter detailing how his Navys had rusted solid in the heavy Crimean rain, and now served him only as paperweights.

By the time winter arrived the campaign had ground to a complete standstill. The heavily fortified port of Sebastopol was under siege, and would not fall without a far greater assault than the Allied armies were able to muster. Certain quarters of Parliament became progressively more discontented, maintaining that the Army was failing because it was badly led and poorly equipped. There were calls for immediate and sweeping change at the very summit of the hierarchy. This, in Edward's estimation, all played directly into Colt's hands. Great Britain's patriotic fervour and lust for war could be made to work for the gun-maker – but so, surely, could her defeat. The beleaguered British troops needed to be given whatever advantages could be secured for them, as a matter of urgency. It would take only a little Colt ballyhoo to ensure that revolving pistols were added to such an inventory.

But the Colonel was nowhere to be seen. He gave no more well-publicised tours of the factory to prominent personages; there were no boastful announcements or grand claims in the press. The yellow carriage was absent from London's frozen, foggy streets. He was in America, it was rumoured, meeting with some of President Pierce's men in Washington – or in Egypt, seeking the custom of the new viceroy.

Then came the letter. Published in *The Times*, it had been written by an Englishman who had recently stopped in St Petersburg. There were a good many Americans in the city at present, he wrote, working on the Moscow railway; but also among them was a Colonel Samuel Colt, travelling with specimens of his machine-made repeating arms.

The newspaper's thin pages began to quiver in Edward's fingers as he thought it all through. The gun-maker was selling to Russia, Great Britain's enemy – aiming to provide revolvers to the very soldiers Cousin Arthur was being pitted against. Colt had been working towards this from the first sign of hostilities between the two countries. The defaced stamp on that letter forwarded from Liège had been the

385

imperial eagle of Tsar Nicholas I. Those crates piled up in the warehouse cellar had been put aside for the Russian market – which was why their existence had to be kept from the British Government and its official proving rooms. And here, Edward surmised, lay the reason behind the Colonel's unaccountable interest in raw cotton after that trip to mainland Europe. The bulky bales were to serve as the means of conveyance. Each one could hold a decent-sized crate of smuggled pistols; and the European trade routes he'd taken such care to develop could be used as an effective conduit to this clandestine customer. It suddenly seemed so damned obvious – shameless even. Edward snorted, drawing glances from those sitting around him in the library. So much for the *Anglo-Saxon bond*!

Word of Colt's visit to St Petersburg spread rapidly, the flames fanned by his gleeful rivals. We have nourished a *snake*, they cried, a venomous Yankee snake in the heart of our very own metropolis! This American, loyal only to his balance-sheet, is using English steel and English machine-hands to make guns that will be used to shoot down English soldiers on the field of battle! This is what happens when foreign entrepreneurs are permitted to operate unchecked on our soil, and given preference over our own craftsmen!

Yet just when things were looking impossibly bleak for Colonel Colt, sheer good fortune – or the hand of a powerful, unseen ally – came to his rescue. A fortnight after the publication of the damaging *Times* letter, the Board of Ordnance awarded him the largest revolver contract it had ever drawn up: five thousand pistols for the Army, for the officers and sergeants leading men across the battlefields of the Crimea, against the Russians with whom he was being accused of colluding. Colt could now claim to be the official supplier of repeating firearms to the entire British war machine. Emboldened, he decided to defend himself, penning a letter of his own to *The Times* from his stronghold in Hartford. Yes, he admitted, he had indeed been in St Petersburg, but only to visit the US ambassador, Mr Thomas Hart Seymour, an old friend of his. No weapons had been sold; no negotiations conducted. And as no one could prove otherwise, his opponents were forced to back down. He'd dodged it.

Edward went to see Simon Bannan as soon as he could, early in 1855. They met first thing in the morning, sitting down in the Honourable Member's office with their coats on, shivering as they waited for the heat of his freshly lit fire to build. Bannan was not particularly pleased to see him. The memory of that inconclusive Select Committee hearing and the spiteful gossip that had followed it was still a sore one. Edward had expected this – he'd counted on it, in fact, as he knew it could be worked in his favour. Mr Bannan, plainly a rather vindictive man by nature, bore a grudge against Colonel Colt.

He made his proposition, choosing his words carefully, but the gist was this: if Bannan would agree to employ him, he'd use certain facts that he'd learnt in the gun works at Bessborough Place to deal a heavy, even fatal blow to the Colt Company in London. Bannan's position on the Board of Trade, he hinted, and access to the books of the Customs House, would make this all the easier. The Honourable Member was immediately interested. He wanted Colt brought low, and still had hopes of exposing a connection to Palmerston that would cause the Home Secretary discomfort. The chance that Edward might be able to achieve something towards these ends was well worth a junior post in his office.

In the days after this meeting, at the start of Parliament's January session, Lord Aberdeen's administration finally collapsed under the weight of innumerable reports of Crimean misery and incompetence. Bannan was a vocal supporter of the motion for a full inquiry into the conduct of the war; and when it came to a division large numbers deserted the government, effectively bringing about its demise. Aberdeen's tenure as Prime Minister was over, but whatever triumph the radicals might have felt at this was tempered by the knowledge that only one candidate was available to replace him: Lord Palmerston.

For all his annoyance at this turn of events, Bannan also felt some grudging admiration. 'Palmerston planned it all from the first, damn him – from the very first. He egged feeble Aberdeen on to war, knowing full well that he'd fumble it and drop us in something like our current mess. It's a cunning, ruthless piece of work – there's no one else the Queen can turn to now, despite her reservations, and the public are crying out for his appointment. They want a speedy end to this accursed war, and they think their beloved Pam is the fellow to supply it.' He gave Edward a dry look. 'Good news for your former employer, eh? His protector is in the top seat.'

A change in government, however, especially during the confusion of a mismanaged war, meant interminable debates, unexplained delays and a marked lack of action, even as the popular press teemed with stories of British failure on the killing grounds before Sebastopol. Furthermore, the new administration's tardiness in following up that first Army order gave the battered Robert Adams a chance to regroup. His company took on a new lead designer, the former soldier Lieutenant Frederick Beaumont, and the new Beaumont-Adams pistol was born – the best ever made, Adams claimed to the Board of Ordnance, rectifying faults in both the Colt and Adams models. Edward could easily imagine Colt's frustration at all this. His factory, slick and streamlined under a new general manager, was said to be really belting along; the unsold weapons would be piling up in their thousands. He himself was back in Connecticut, far away from the Englishmen with whom he had feigned brotherhood on so many occasions. How could he not be tempted to make use of the covert system he'd painstakingly created?

The moment came one still afternoon early that summer. Edward was examining a ledger in the Customs House. As he slid a finger down a neat column of entries, a sharp, familiar word snagged his eye like a thorn catching on a woollen sleeve; and there was the signal he'd been waiting for. The Colt Company of Bessborough Place, London, was applying for a licence to export raw Indian cotton to its office in Liège, Belgium. He opened another volume, flicking quickly through the pages; a cotton importer, one of those he'd identified for

Colt shortly before leaving his employ, had supplied the Colonel with 145 bales a little over a week previously. This was it. He went to Bannan at once, and was heading for the telegraph office a minute later.

2

Sam strode into the factory, still dressed in his travelling clothes, gave a curt nod to an overseer and made for the staircase, with a chew of Old Red for each upward stride. As he ascended, he heard the hiss of chain and clang of hammer-heads in the forge; the high whine of drills and the searing scrape of lathes on the machine floor; the tapping of tools in the fitting room. The place was in fine fettle. This served only to increase his apprehension.

He threw back the door of the office to find a half-dozen people already inside, drawn from the ranks of his senior mechanics and overseers. Lou Ballou was there, and the foreman, whose name Sam had forgotten completely; and Luther Sargent, the Colt man of long standing who'd been brought over from Hartford at the end of 1854 to serve as general manager. Sargent was a level-headed soul who knew Sam's business inside out – the very definition of the steady hand upon the tiller. Tall with close-cropped hair and beard, he had an air of unflappable authority and stately competence, like the partner in a grand old bank. He knew how to dress too, unlike pretty much everyone else in Sam's employ; that afternoon he was clad in a berry-blue suit that Sam would have readily bought for himself.

Propped against the desk, halfway through some anecdote or other, was Alfred Richards, his cheeks rosy and his ruffed shirt dotted with what Sam hoped was a soup stain. His lean face lit up at the gun-maker's entrance, and he burst into a short, spirited round of applause. 'By the living jingo, Samuel Colt!' he cried, leaping from the desk and prancing over to wring Sam's hand between his. 'We weren't expecting you until tomorrow morning! You only arrived from Liverpool this afternoon, did you not?'

Sam nodded, looking over the office; a leather divan had been brought up there, he noticed, and set by the wall. 'Boat got in from New York just before dawn.'

'You could not wait to hear the details, I expect,' Richards continued sagely. 'The news has hit the trade like a bomb-shell – a bloody *bombshell*. Nine thousand weapons! This is what we dreamed of, eh, in the halls of the Great Exhibition? As we stood before this fine factory here when it was but a blasted hulk?'

Drawing back his top lip, Sam spat a bead of juice onto the floorboards. 'It's a good order, Alfie,' he said.

Richards stared at him as if this was the most absurd understatement he'd ever heard. 'I'll say it is! A *good order* – ha, yes indeed! It's said that poor Bob Adams had to be helped to a bloody chair when he learnt of it, and has been flopping about like the tragic muse ever since!' Laughing, he glanced at those around him, expecting them to join in. There were some chuckles; Sargent gave a silent half-smile, more at the press agent's liquor-flushed exuberance than at what he was actually saying. 'Your renown has never been higher, my friend,' Richards went on. 'Why, only the other day *The Times* – the bloody *Times*, that so delighted in trying to thwart you before Christmas – opined that had Cardigan's Light Brigade been armed with Colts they would have carried that frightful day at Balaclava!'

Sam made some response, his jaw working steadily, looking at Sargent. He'd known the fellow for more than eight years. The slight crook to his left eyebrow said that he was carrying something of real weight. Sam had made the journey to London to mount an inspection, to make sure that the Pimlico works was able to meet the staggering order that had so excited Richards. And it was staggering – that much was certainly true. Palmerston had come through at last. As always, no trace of the fellow's involvement could be found anywhere, but

391

there could be little doubt that he had played a critical role in directing the contract to the Colt Company. Sam had been pleased; a little annoyed still that they had been made to wait so long, left by this puffed-up John Bull politician to survive on mere scraps of custom, but pleased nonetheless. Then, waiting for him at the desk of Morely's Hotel, had been the note from Sargent, telling him to come to the works at once – and to brace himself for grave news. The vague nature of this warning had served as a pretty plain indication of what it pertained to.

There was a short, awkward silence. 'Forgive me, Sam,' Richards exclaimed with another laugh, 'but you don't seem particularly glad! Why, you're almost as damned phlegmatic as old Luther here. We should be *celebrating*, my friends! We should be back in that fine place in Piccadilly, that supper room, and –'

'Leave us, Alfie,' Sam interrupted, unable to take any more. 'Just for a minute. The rest of you as well.'

The Americans filed out at once. Richards lingered a second or two longer, looking probingly from proprietor to manager, trying to deduce what was going on; then he too walked into the corridor.

Sam shut the door behind him. 'Well, Luther?'

'They got the cotton, Colonel,' Sargent said simply.

An iron brace seemed to clamp shut around Sam's throat, blocking off his windpipe. He'd swallowed his Old Red. Putting a hand on his side, he bent over, gulping as hard as he could. The plug was shifting, but painfully and very, very slowly. *Men die like this*, he thought. Sargent was at his side, thumping his back with such vigour that he stuck out an arm to push the fellow away; and then the plug was clear, forced down inside him. Sam pulled fiercely at his collar, sending the ivory button pinging across the room, and reeled over to the desk. He leaned heavily against it, threw off his hat and drew in a few ragged, heaving breaths.

'All of it?' he croaked.

Sargent nodded. 'At Aix-la-Chapelle, en route to St Petersburg from the warehouse in Antwerp. A random customs search. Just damn bad luck.'

Sam made some fevered calculations. 'Lord Almighty, Luther, there was what, twenty-four in each bale? That's damn near three and a half thousand arms!' He coughed, feeling the lump of tobacco complete its journey into his guts. 'And they're proper lost, ain't they? Contraband goods in a time of war, caught passing through a neutral country – the sons of bitches ain't going to give 'em back any time soon.'

'There's also the fine.' Sargent paused. 'Eighty thousand francs is what I hear.'

A blistering torrent of energy coursed through Sam's limbs. Grabbing hold of the chair behind the desk – a sturdy mahogany piece with an iron pivot on its base – he lifted it clean off the floor and hurled it at the circular window. The chair stove straight through glass and frame, landing in the cobbled yard below with the bang of something being shattered into its component parts. There were shouts of alarm, and footfalls in the corridor; Sargent opened the office door a few inches and told whoever was outside to remain where they were.

'*Eighty thousand!*' Sam yelled. 'By thunder, Luther, that's going to fuck us good!' He paced back and forth, boots crunching over shards of the glass from the window, wiping a palm across his sweat-glazed forehead. 'And then there's the notoriety of the matter. If it gets out it'll surely finish me in England – Christ, in Europe! My rivals would leap on it. You saw the delight with which the bastards went after me last December. Nothing would give them greater satisfaction than to get this in the newspapers and hound us from the country. No one would help me this time. My British allies would run a goddamn mile.' He thought momentarily of Palmerston, of the lack of any kind of open link between them. The crafty old villain could deny all knowledge and leave Sam Colt to his fate.

Sargent remained entirely calm. 'I've done everything I can to keep your name out of it, Colonel. Sainthill, your man in Belgium, has been instructed to keep a low profile, and not make his interest in the seizure too plain. He tells me that for another ten thousand the officials involved can be convinced to keep the details quiet. They won't disclose that it was Colts or even revolving pistols that they found.'

Sam winced; yet more money. 'Would that work, though? Ain't it already too late?'

His manager shrugged. 'Nobody over here has heard a whisper about it yet, far as I can tell. They know what they're doing, these Belgian customs men. This one pay-off might cap the whole affair. Worth considering, Colonel, in my view.'

'Who did the packing? Men you can trust?'

Sargent nodded. 'All safe this end, I guarantee it.' He sighed. 'Like I said, it's just some damn bad luck.'

'What am I supposed to do, though, Luther, if these John Bull cocksuckers won't buy in a timely fashion?' Sam appealed to him. 'Tell me that! What the hell can I do but take my guns to those that are actually interested in 'em? I am an independent citizen of the United States of America. The British crown has no claim of loyalty over me. What do I care for their goddamn politics, or their wars?'

'The Russians will be disappointed, Colonel, for certain.'

Sam let out a bitter laugh, recalling long nights in Petersburg drinking vodka with moustachioed naval officers around the shipyards; and many dozens of hours spent trying to sleep under a fur coat in a rocking railway carriage with sheet-ice forming along its sides. This was what all that trouble had amounted to. 'Well, they're going to have to stay that way, ain't they, for now at any rate. We can't risk another hit like that. It'd sink us, Luther – take us to the bottom.'

His energy ebbing, Sam went to the divan, the upholstery creaking as he sat down. He looked out through the hole in the circular window at the thick grey of English summer cloud, absently reaching for the screw of Old Red in his pocket and cutting a fresh plug. Almost three and a half thousand guns were gone – a complete and irreparable loss. He'd have to pay eighty thousand francs in fines, and at least another ten in bribes, to keep the Colt name out of the newspapers. There was no upside to be found here. The Colt Company might survive, but it would be brought to its knees. The major contract with the British Army would only be paid on delivery. Before then he'd need to find money for enormous quantities of raw materials – coal, wood and steel – and many months of wages. His credit on both sides of the Atlantic would be stretched to its absolute limit. The busy factory beneath him suddenly seemed a doomed and fragile thing, made only of bamboo poles and blotting paper, ready to be blown to the ground.

Sam shook his head wearily as he folded up his clasp-knife. This London works had been an ill-advised project from the start, an unceasing parade of problems, delays and expense. The whole enterprise was the result of his one great flaw: his vaunting, over-reaching ambition. He'd extended too far, and attempted to establish himself in a foreign land that neither welcomed nor quite frankly deserved his endeavours. Sweeping change was called for here. This giant contract, now more burden than boon, would have to be honoured – which might take a little longer than usual, given the financial difficulties Sam had just acquired. Once this was done, though, and all nine thousand arms had been delivered, he would instruct Sargent to start winding down the works. Within a year the Colt Company's London outpost would be closed for good.

In the meantime he would direct his own attentions back to their rightful place. While over in America he'd heard a lot of saloon talk about the open strife in Kansas – clashes between slavers and free-staters which had quickly led to bloodshed. The two sides were bracing for further trouble, forming militias, mounting raids and arming themselves with all haste. The Colt Navy was sure to find a ready market among them both. Like many of his countrymen, Sam believed that President Pierce had lit a fire there that would spread to other states and burn for a generation. Considering this now, sitting in his London office, he felt a stirring of patriotism. If Europe was to break the Colt Company down, then the United States of America would sure as hell build it back up again.

Sam lifted his hand, as if ordering Sargent to halt. 'All right, Luther,' he said, slipping the plug of Old Red inside his cheek. 'I think I see a way out of this.'

3

'Saul Graves,' said Graff, one black eyebrow raised, as he pushed open the door of the Ship and Turtle.

Edward looked at his friend sceptically. 'And that is to be your name from now on – how I should address you?'

Saul nodded. 'Indeed yes, if I am to succeed – which I will, Edward, most assuredly. It is a sad but necessary step, this land being what it is.' He ran a hand before him in a shallow arc, tracing the letters of a banner or newspaper headline. '*Saul Graves, Liberal Member for Hampstead.* It has a pleasing sound to it, no?'

The tavern's high-ceilinged taproom was loud, crowded and misty with cigar smoke. Customers were still pouring in from nearby Green Park, where the fireworks had concluded only minutes previously; many of those around them were engaged in enthusiastic recollections of rockets, pearl streamers and tailed stars. This pyrotechnic display had been mounted, in part at least, to mark the rather inconclusive end to the Russian War. Neither side could rightfully be called the victor; the general sense was that the conflict had not been won or lost but simply stopped. Such was the disillusionment of the British public that nearly two months had been allowed to pass between the signing of the treaty in Paris and this celebration – from the March of 1856 to late May – so that it could be combined with the Queen's birthday festivities in order to ensure both a decent turnout and a suitably jubilant atmosphere.

Saul and Edward stood away from the main current of the tavern's patrons, beside a panelled partition.

'What does Bannan think of all this?'

'What the deuce does it matter what he thinks?' Graff retorted. 'With the advent of Pam our radical friend has been booted out into the bloody wilderness. The time has come for us to beat our own path. Now that the wretched war is finally over there's a chance for things to be done. A seat in the House is the first step. The next is an appointment to a ministry, and after that, who knows? It could lead to real power, my friend. Real progress.'

Saul looked towards the bar – towards the gleaming row of ale-pumps, the phalanx of bottles up on shelves, the team of barmen and pot-boys attempting to field many dozens of simultaneous orders – as if gazing off into his own glorious future. Then, suddenly, he grabbed hold of Edward's arm.

'You must run too. I'm sure we can find you a winnable seat before another election is called, and drum up the necessary support. Think of it, Edward! Us two, in bloody government! Imagine what we could accomplish!'

Edward's laughter ceased when he realised that Saul was entirely in earnest. Never had he seen his friend so animated; and although he suspected that the pint of whiskey they'd shared in the park might bear a measure of responsibility for this, he could also tell that there was genuine conviction beneath it all.

Graff released him. 'Give it some thought. You have the brains for it, the nerve, and the stamina as well. I shall endeavour to obtain us some refreshment, and will expect an answer upon my return.'

He began to work his way to the bar, soon vanishing among the hats clustered along it. Edward fumbled in his pockets, looking for a cigar, oddly flattered despite himself. What Graff proposed was absurd – wasn't it? Surely a man needed money, important friends and a whole raft of other advantages to aspire to political office. Yet his mind started to turn it over nonetheless. After eighteen months with Bannan he was not without connections. It would be an

398

extremely difficult and lengthy process, that much was certain; but perhaps there might just be a way.

A sharp pain in his side brought Edward's reflections to a halt. Someone had dug a knuckle between two of his ribs, as if trying to shove him aside. He twisted around to make a complaint – and was confronted with the equine features of Alfred Richards, fixing him with a savage glare. Before he could speak, Richards prodded him again.

'So it is over,' he spat. '*Pleased*, are you?'

Edward lifted his arm to ward off any further jabs, taken aback by the intensity of the press agent's loathing. 'What is this, Richards? What the devil d'you mean?'

The man glowered, saying nothing.

'If you refer to the war, then yes, I suppose I –'

'Colonel Colt is shutting up the London works,' broke in Richards contemptuously. 'He's making Hartford his sole site of manufacture. There's this infernal peace, of course. Guns are furthest from the government's mind, all of a sudden. The trade is flat as a bloody . . . a bloody . . .'

His thoughts seemed to wander off. Edward saw that he was deep in one of his liquor-filled troughs; he'd grown a thin, unhealthy-looking beard, his lower lip was split and he had a large scuff in the fabric of his hat. After a few seconds he returned to the present, poking an accusatory finger at Edward's chest.

'But we were finished long before that, oh yes indeed! That great loss last summer was the mortal blow – since then, we've just been bleeding away in the gutter. And you were behind it, weren't you, you damned turncoat? Leaving us to go to Bannan? Telling him all the secrets you'd learnt about Sam's business? Sam never said it – Christ, he never so much as spoke your damn name after you'd gone – but *I knew*, you blackguard. I bloody well knew.'

Edward wasn't about to deny it. 'He was smuggling guns to Russia, Richards,' he said. 'He was trying to supply revolvers to our enemy.'

For a moment he could see Cousin Arthur, sitting motion-lessly among the begonias in the garden of Aunt Ruth's cottage in Wandsworth. He'd been shot through the upper arm during the second assault on Sebastopol the previous September. The wound had become infected, leaving the surgeons at Scutari no option but to amputate the limb. His mother, so frail and enervated throughout the Russian campaign, was overjoyed to have him back alive, invalided out of the Army. The young veteran, however, was utterly disconsolate, reduced to a wasted, embittered husk.

Richards barely paused to take this in before waving it away. 'And what of it? Of course he was! They will get the things sooner or later – so they might as well get them from Sam Colt!'

'You cannot honestly believe that.'

The press agent's red eyes widened. 'Why, Mr Lowry, he's in bloody Russia right now! He travelled to St Petersburg the very instant that peace was declared. There was some surplus stock in the end, y'see, despite your treachery. He's shifting his peacemakers to the very chaps that were having the things shot at them not six months ago. The Russians love him, it seems, and he can operate without fear of what Bob Adams or Clarence Paget or your dear chum Simon bloody Bannan might make of it. And once all the guns are gone – which they will be, in a damned trice – he's vowed to go home for good.' Richards took a needy swig from a small brown bottle. 'He's getting married, or so he says.'

Edward began to shake his head. He remembered the last, desperate breaths that Caroline had drawn down on the floor of that Westminster dust-yard; the pressure with which she'd squeezed his hand, and its devastating release. 'I had to do it, Richards,' he said. 'It had to be done.'

Richards wasn't listening. 'A truly singular fellow was among us,' he fumed, a fleck of foaming spittle flying from his spilt lip, 'and you and your sanctimonious kind chased him off. And don't you be thinking for a second that you defeated him, Lowry. You defeated only *us*, you wretched ass – you and me and every other Englishman turned out of his works!'

With some relief, Edward heard Saul Graff call his name. His friend was struggling back across the tavern with two dark jugs of porter in his hands. Behind him someone climbed up onto the bar and proposed a birthday toast to the Queen. This met with a mighty cheer, and Saul was lost from view as several hundred glasses were raised aloft, their contents sloshing out over hats and coat-cuffs. Edward felt another vicious dig to his ribs; but when he looked back around, ready now to retaliate, Alfred Richards was already pushing his way towards the street.

The cab slowed to join the queue moving through the toll on Vauxhall Bridge. Almost anxiously, Edward peered out of a window at the mouth of the defunct pistol works. The buildings were devoid of life. No smoke came from the chimneys; the windows were the colour of day-old puddles. Up on the roof of the factory block the enormous white-washed letters of the Colonel's slogan were starting to show through the pitch that had been daubed over them, like a spectral reassertion of his departed authority.

It was a dreary mid-November afternoon. Fog lingered along the quays and hung in sallow drifts around the factory gates. Some manner of market appeared to be underway in the yard. Serious-looking gentlemen were stalking to and fro like crows, examining the pieces of Colt machinery that had been arranged for their inspection. Edward knew that this would be the last stage in the close-down of the works: the sale of the machines not deemed worth the cost of trans-portation back to America. Even the dead engine, the factory's stilled heart, had been torn from its cradle and dragged out into the cold.

The cab advanced a couple of places in the queue, revealing more of the yard. There against the wall of the warehouse was a rectangle of searing yellow so bright and strong that it cut through the day's dullness like the beam from a light-house. Realising that it was the Colt carriage. Edward sat upright and pulled away from the window, fully expecting to see that familiar, broad-chested form, dressed in its wide-brimmed hat and fur-lined Yankee coat, striding around its side. But no, the vehicle had merely been parked out there to be sold, like everything else. Colonel Colt was very many

401

miles from Pimlico. He cleared his throat, feeling a little foolish.

There was a giggle beside him. Katie was mimicking his alarmed, straight-backed posture. She was dressed in a new bonnet and mantle, both deep blue, bought for her that morning. As she'd moved from infancy to early childhood, the angles of her face slowly gaining more definition, her resemblance to her aunt had grown ever clearer. Her hair had become the same tone of light hazel; her smile contained the same unlikely mixture of affection, wilfulness and wicked mockery. A neat mole had even appeared high upon her left cheek. This likeness would sometimes cause Edward's grief to be suddenly revived, yet it brought with it a strange sweetness. To be reminded of Caroline by one so very much alive, at the outset of her years, gave him greater consolation than he would have imagined possible.

'Look over there,' he said, pointing at the yard as the cab started to move again, passing through the toll-gate and onto the bridge. 'What a smart carriage that is!'

The little girl, flattened her hands against the window pane. 'It is yellow, Mr Lowry.'

'Yes, Katie,' Edward agreed with a wise nod, 'it certainly is.'

'I rather prefer blue,' she declared, switching her attention to the barges crawling along the foggy river, their lanterns flashing in the murk.

They carried on through the corroded crust of factories and workshops that lined the southern bank, past the bare treetops of the boarded-up pleasure gardens and the handful of dejected-looking sheep that had been put out to graze upon the Oval. The cab turned right onto the Brixton Road. Outside the window now were the neat divisions of well-tended suburban gardens, with rows of identical houses standing at their ends – a grey parade broken only by the coaching inn, half-rustic in character, that served as the terminus for the Westminster and St James omnibus route. Heaps of decaying leaves were scattered across every common and clogged every drain. All the people they saw seemed to be hurrying home, coats and mantles buttoned up against the bone-chilling fog. It was only a quarter past three o'clock yet darkness already seemed to be drawing in.

After some minutes on the same straight avenue the cab swung into a lane with elm trees on one side and a tall wall on the other.

'We're almost there, I think,' Edward said.

Katie had been providing them with a chattering commentary throughout the journey, identifying particularly large horses or pretty bonnets; now, though, she fell completely silent, gazing down at her boots. A few moments later their vehicle stopped before an arched gateway, an ugly and enormous thing; the gate it contained was like that of an ancient stronghold, its massy planks studded with pyramidal nail-heads. Edward glanced at his mother. Sitting in the far corner of the cab, her hands folded in her lap, she was regarding Katie with concern. Together, they had done their best to prepare the child, but could not know how successful they had been. She was simply too young to understand fully what was about to happen.

'I will stay here, Edward,' she murmured. 'This is for you to do alone. I will come if I am needed.'

Edward climbed from the cab, lifting out the little girl and setting her upon the pavement, away from the mud of the lane. An ordinary crowd about a dozen strong had gathered for the release, all dressed in drab working clothes. Most had come on foot, although a single tradesman's cart had drawn up a little further down the road. Theirs was the only carriage, and a few curious stares were thrown their way. They were not the sort usually encountered waiting outside prison gates.

Somewhere in the depths of the prison a clock started to chime half past three. A small door opened in the gate and women started to emerge, all dressed in claret-brown gowns with grey shawls and bonnets. There was little jubilation among them as they regained their liberty; they looked to Edward like survivors picking their way from a wrecked train, dazed yet relieved, stumbling into the arms of friends and relatives. He glimpsed what appeared to be a familiar profile, careworn and pale with exhaustion but still so similar to Caroline's that it paralysed him completely. It was her sister – Katie's mother, Amy Rea. She soon spotted Edward standing there, frozen in place in his top hat and frock-coat, able only to blink back at her. Knowing who he must be, she started towards him; and as she left the crowd she saw the child hiding nervously behind his leg.

Amy cried out her daughter's name, her voice filled with longing and joy and a clear trace of apprehension. She made to run over, but came to an uncertain halt in the middle of the lane.

Katie turned to Edward. 'Mr Lowry . . .'

'Don't be scared,' he managed to say. 'It is your mother. We wrote her a letter, do you not remember?'

'But I – I do not –' Katie stammered, looking away, 'I do not know –'

Recovering herself, Amy took four quick paces to where they stood, her eyes never leaving her daughter. Saying Katie's name again, she crouched down on the pavement, placed her hands on the girl's shoulders and looked long into her face, searching for any sign of recognition.

'My angel,' she whispered, 'don't you remember me?'

Then she folded Katie in a close embrace, rocking them gently back and forth. After a few moments Katie's arm rose from her side. Finding a corner of the prison shawl, she gripped onto it tightly, bunching up the coarse cloth in her palm.

AUTHOR'S NOTE

The Devil's Acre is based around a series of historical events, from the factory visits of Lajos Kossuth and Charles Dickens to the seizure of the Russia-bound revolvers at Aix-la-Chapelle. Many of the details about Samuel Colt's time in London, however, remain unknown. The Colonel seldom left any more than accidental traces of his movements, for obvious reasons. What he did, where he went, who he spoke with and the understandings that were reached can often only be imagined – or deduced, perhaps, from the pattern of contracts he won from the British Government. Letters do survive between Colt and Lord Palmerston, who was the only senior British politician to take a serious interest in the American gun-maker and his Pimlico factory. Although rather vague, they are cordial in tone and contain clear suggestions that the two men intended to meet; and as Palmerston's power increased, so did the government's patronage of the Colt Company, despite a marked lack of consensus among British experts over the superiority of the Colonel's pistols.

Those who staffed the London works are similarly elusive. A few figures appear from minutes, press reports and scraps of correspondence, including the gigantic, peevish foreman Gage Stickney, who betrayed his employer at the Select Committee on Small Arms; Alfred Richards, failed barrister turned press agent, with his sweeping, gentlemanly language and troubled domestic circumstances; the disgruntled overseer Jabez Alvord, dismissing his charges in a letter to his brother as 'thick-headed Englishmen'. Many more are unaccounted for, though, and it is here that my own inventions – Benjamin Quill, Walter Noone, Edward Lowry – have been inserted, filling roles that would have existed within the gun factory's hierarchy.

Records of the men and women from the factory's lower reaches are even more scant, but Colt's well-known policy of employing cheap, unskilled workers and then training them up himself would have made the Devil's Acre his natural recruiting ground. A good number of those he took on would have been Irish – and where there were concentrations of poor Irish in the mid-nineteenth century there was a significant chance that Molly Maguires would be found among them. The Mollys emerged in the 1840s from a long tradition of secret societies in rural Ireland: of 'whiteboys' and 'ribbonmen' committed to the violent intimidation of their enemies, who were usually oppressive landlords or perceived symbols of English rule. Molly Maguire herself is a creature of myth. Neither her origins, nor her followers' bizarre tradition of cross-dressing and corking their faces before an attack, have ever received a definitive explanation.

Murderously active throughout the potato famine (a Major Denis Mahon was indeed killed by them in County Roscommon), many Mollys are believed to have scattered in its aftermath, settling in the cities of England and Scotland and emigrating to the new world. They would next come to prominence in the anthracite coal fields of Pennsylvania during the 1860s and 70s, when they waged a long and bloody campaign against mine-owners and their feared Pinkerton detectives. That they had a presence in London is beyond doubt, but there is no evidence that they ever planned a killing as ambitious as that conceived by Pat Slattery. The Irish hatred of Lord John Russell, however, was very real. John MacHale, firebrand Bishop of Tuam, expressed the views of many in a widely-circulated letter to the then-Prime Minister that told him bluntly: 'if you are ambitious for a monument, the bones of a people, slain with the sword of famine, and piled into cairns more numerous than the ancient

406

pyramids, will tell posterity of the triumph of your brief but disastrous administration.'

The novel's other significant characters are a mixture of fact and fiction. Lawrence Street, Lady Cecilia Wardell and Simon Bannan all fall into the latter category, although Bannan shares a few professional features with William Monsell, the actual MP for Limerick in the 1850s. Lord Clarence Paget and Sir Thomas Hastings, on the other hand, are historical figures who served in both the Royal Navy and the Board of Ordnance – and although their respective dispositions towards Samuel Colt are accurately portrayed in these pages, it should be stressed that the personalities given to them are entirely conjectural.

After the collapse of his London enterprise, freed from any pretence to an 'Anglo-Saxon bond', the Colonel sold openly to the Russians and anyone else with the money to buy from him, soon recouping his losses from the seizure at Aix-la-Chapelle. Returning to Connecticut in 1856, he finally married Elizabeth Jarvis, gave up the rigours of inter-continental travel and built a magnificent mansion overlooking his Hartford factory. Business boomed, Colt pistols selling in their hundreds of thousands as America drifted towards the Civil War – and the Colonel's weapons were to be widely used by both the Union and Confederate armies. Sam himself did not live to see the conflict's resolution. The gun-maker's dedication to both his business pursuits and his liquor eventually exacted its price and he died in 1861, aged forty-seven.

Although *The Devil's Acre* is a work of fiction containing numerous fabrications and distortions, many books and sources were consulted for the purposes of research. Perhaps the most important among these was Joseph Rosa's *Colonel Colt, London*, an engaging and detailed history of the short-lived factory at Bessborough Place. Also useful for getting a sense of Samuel Colt and his London venture were two entertaining biographies – Jack Rohan's *Yankee Arms Maker: The Story of Sam Colt and his Six-Shot Peacemaker* and William Edwards's *The Story of Colt's Revolvers: The Biography of Colonel Samuel Colt* – and the series of swaggering promotional pamphlets published by an anonymous English author (very probably Alfred Richards) in the early days of the pistol works' existence.

The novel's representation of the tangled political world of mid-nineteenth century London was crucially informed by the journalistic sketches of the Victorian parliamentary correspondent E. M. Whitty and several more recent histories, primarily *Parliament, Party and Politics in Victorian Britain* by T. A. Jenkins, *The Triumph of Lord Palmerston* by Kingsley Martin and the early chapters of Trevor Royle's *Crimea*. Valuable material for the Irish strand of the story was provided by *Exiles of Erin: Irish Migrants in Victorian London* by Lynn Lees, *Irish Nationalism and the British State: From Repeal to Revolutionary Nationalism* by Brian Jenkins and Kevin Kenny's definitive *Making Sense of the Molly Maguires*.

My depiction of London life in the 1850s is based on various Victorian publications, including the social commentary of Henry Mayhew, Adolphe Smith and Thomas Beames (especially Beames's gruelling *The Rookeries of London: Past, Present and Prospective*), Nathaniel Hawthorne's *English Notebooks*, which offer an amusingly acerbic American view of the metropolis and its people, Peter Cunningham's *Hand-Book of London, Past and Present*, Charles Manby Smith's *The Little World of London* and the anonymous and evocatively titled *London By Night, or the Bachelor's Facetious Guide to All the Ins and Outs and Nightly Doings of the Metropolis*. A number of modern histories also proved helpful; Jerry White's *London in the Nineteenth Century: A Human Awful Wonder of God*, Liza Picard's *Victorian London*, Lynda Nead's *Victorian Babylon*, Felix Barker and Peter Jackson's *The History of London in Maps* and Isobel Watson's *Westminster and Pimlico Past: A Visual History* were all regularly consulted.

Sincere thanks are due to my agent, Euan Thorneycroft, and my editor, Susan Watt; also Katie Espiner, Clare Hey, Alice Moss, James Annal and the team at HarperCollins; Jennifer Custer, Kate Munson and everyone at AM Heath; the family and friends who have given me help, encouragement or advice over the past couple of years; and most of all to my wife Sarah, who made it possible.

P.S.

Ideas,
interviews
& features …

About the book

About the author

'England's Foulest Graveyard'

The London of *The Devil's Acre*

ONE OF THE major attractions for me of Colonel Colt's Thames-side gun factory as the subject for a novel was the chance to write about Victorian London. I knew from the outset that each strand of the narrative would lead the story through some very different parts of the mid-nineteenth century metropolis. Sam Colt, in his efforts to win the custom of the government, would barge his way into the innermost sanctums of the British Empire; his conscience-stricken secretary Edward Lowry would inhabit a threadbare, overcrowded world of cheap lodgings and chop-houses; and the Irishmen from the factory floor, residents of the appalling slums that give the book its name, would drink and plot in the city's lowest taverns, and brawl in its most fetid lanes.

My research into the main locations of the novel held a number of surprises, by far the greatest of which was the character of Victorian Westminster. I'd already picked up a little about the Pimlico of the period, where stuccoed squares were gradually being laid out across reclaimed marshland under the direction of Thomas Cubitt. A speculator and master builder of keen social ambition, Cubitt wanted his nascent neighbourhood to rival aristocratic Belgravia to the north, and was immediately hostile towards any new commercial or industrial premises that tried to set up there – hence his insistence that the Colt Company remove the painted slogan from its roof. I was also aware that Millbank, the next district along the Thames, was home to the Victorians' largest inner-city prison, a vast panopticon that stood where Tate Britain does today. Westminster, however, was a complete shock. I'd expected it to be broadly similar to its modern incarnation, given over almost entirely to politics and affairs of state. This was not what I discovered.

In 1853, the year the novel opens, the building of the Palace of Westminster was at an advanced stage; although the towers at each end were still under construction, both the Commons and the Lords were already in use. Yet only a short distance from this imposing neo-Gothic edifice, literally just around the back of Westminster Abbey, lay the Devil's Acre, one of the most infamous slums in the whole of London. The Victorians called such areas 'rookeries', as their occupants were believed to arrange themselves as rooks fill their nests – by simply cramming into the available space until it could hold no more of them. To outsiders, even to other Londoners well used to dirt and horse-dung, the squalor of the rookeries was overpowering. Dotted with open cess-pits, heaped with all sorts of refuse including animal carcases, they hummed with disease and desperation.

The proximity of Parliament to such a place did not pass without comment at the time. Thomas Beames, journalist, street ▶

England's Foulest Graveyard (continued)

◀ preacher and city missionary, regularly ventured into London's grimmest corners to perform works of charity and evangelism. He had this to say in 1852 about the divided nature of Westminster: '*It is at once the seat of a palace and a plague spot; senators declaim, where sewers poison; theology holds her councils, where thieves learn their trade; and Europe's grandest hall is flanked by England's foulest grave-yard.*'

Along with others such as Henry Mayhew, Beames tried to mobilise opinion on this issue, but without success; rookeries would persist to the end of the century and beyond. Indeed, in the 1850s the only official response was to embark on a series of urban clearances, wide channels being carved through the dilapidated alleys and yards to make way for new roads. Tens of thousands were displaced, worsening conditions in the surviving slums as these refugees were added to their populations. The Devil's Acre was slowly compressed by the development of Victoria Street, a long avenue designed to provide a direct connection between Parliament and Belgravia, the address of many a lordly townhouse.

I knew that there would be a stark contrast between the horrors of the Devil's Acre and the other settings of the story, particularly the luxurious dining rooms, hotels and gentlemen's clubs toured by Colonel Colt in the course of his business, and felt that this would serve as a powerful illustration of one of the defining characteristics of Victorian London. However, I also wanted to show that some, like Amy Rea, did manage to scrape together a semblance of a respectable life in the rookery; and that others, such as her husband and his friends, had good reason to remain in its dank, maze-like streets. As was often noted by contemporaries, the rookeries offered an effective haven from the law, sheltering countless thieves and prostitutes. The police only ever made occasional forays within their precincts, and would usually face violent resistance when they did so. For those plotting to steal weapons from Colonel Colt – to use them to assassinate a prominent politician on the steps of the new Parliament – the Devil's Acre would be the perfect place to hide. ∎

Matthew Plampin,
London, May 2010

A Q & A with
Matthew Plampin

**How did you find writing the Difficult
Second Novel? How did it compare with the
experience of writing your debut?**

Like many writers, I'd spent a long time working
on my first book, *The Street Philosopher*, and it
was rather disconcerting to leave it behind and
move on to something new. I was also acutely
aware of how the two novels might compare
with one another and decided that I would
employ a more straightforward structure in *The
Devil's Acre*, with only one chronological strand
and fewer narrative points of view. I wanted
something tighter, set in a single city with the
fate of every main character bound closely to
Colonel Colt's progress.

Writing this book involved some steep
challenges, such as conveying the complex
history underpinning the story in an engaging
and readable way, and marshalling a large cast
of characters that included as many real
figures as fictional ones. It was an immersive,
all-consuming experience, and certainly not
easy – but I think I'd be worried if it had been.

What inspired you to write about Colt?

I first came across references to Colonel Colt's
English factory while I was researching the
Crimean War for *The Street Philosopher*. It
seemed incongruous that six-shooting Colt
revolvers, the quintessential guns of the Wild
West, were once manufactured by the
thousand in the heart of Dickensian London.
I decided to investigate a little further and was
soon hooked. There was a mystery here – why
had this enterprise, set up at great expense

and with such lofty ambitions, shut its gates after only three full years of operation? What had caused Sam Colt, a man not known for caution or defeatism, to retreat back to the United States? I found hints in the histories I was reading of unorthodox business practices, of calculated risks and barefaced deceptions, and saw the beginnings of a story.

From the start, much of the momentum behind this idea came from the arresting figure of Sam Colt himself. Bluntly spoken, barely literate and possessing a volcanic temper, Colt was an engineering and promotional genius who can be called the world's first truly international arms dealer, counting a number of governments among his customers. I was struck by his chillingly amoral attitude towards his trade; despite freely using images of slaughter in his advertisements, he maintained that he was merely a salesman providing a product, the application of which was simply not his responsibility. His potential as a character was clear.

I also started to consider the London pistol factory itself, planted by the side of the Thames, producing state-of-the-art weapons only a short distance from one of the worst slums in the city. I imagined it must have attracted all kinds of malign attention; and before long plotlines involving thieves and saboteurs were developing in my mind.

How do you begin to turn a figure from history into a character from fiction?
I tend to start with the words of the historical figures themselves, taken from letters, ▶

A Q & A with
Matthew Plampin *(continued)*

◀ lectures or publications, which I find invaluable when trying to create a 'voice' for them. I'll then work my way through any biographies that might have been written and also see if I can locate a photograph or painted portrait. When this information has been gathered, I set about integrating them into the structure of the story and planning their relationships with the other major characters.

With Sam Colt, who has by far the biggest role of any actual person I've used in my work, this process was remarkably smooth. Colt's brash personality emerges sharply from the few histories devoted to him; the letters that survive crackle with impatience and irascibility; a studio photograph taken in 1857 shows a massive bearded man in a fine suit, a 'Yankee Henry VIII' radiating aggressive pride. I had a vivid sense very early on of how the novel would follow his adventures through London, and the changing relationship he would have with Edward Lowry, his ambitious, slightly callow (and entirely fictional) English secretary.

For more minor characters, where considerably less historical material is available, creative license has to be relied upon more heavily. Most of the real people who appear in *The Devil's Acre* left few traces of their lives behind them. The traitorous Colt foreman Gage Stickney is a good example: he now only exists in a couple of brief mentions in factory documents and the minutes of the Select Committee on Small Arms.

The truly famous figures I've used posed some different problems. An enormous amount has been written about someone like Lord Palmerston; the important thing about his appearance in *The Devil's Acre*, however, is that it is filtered through Colt's point of view, which gave my research on the then-Home Secretary a distinct slant. I had to get a sense not only of what Palmerston might have been like, but what the Colonel might have made of him – of how the two men might have interacted.

Generally, I'll try to be as truthful as I can, but in the end the historical figures in my books have been drafted into a work of fiction – they are versions of a person serving a story rather than attempts at definitive portraits. I have also, on occasion, added the odd unverifiable detail to amuse myself and enliven the character. There is no evidence, for instance, to suggest that Sam Colt ever chewed tobacco.

Are you tempted to revisit any of the characters from your two novels?

Yes, most definitely. I like the idea of the books existing in their own universe, and in fact put a passing reference to the Crimean War coverage of the *London Courier* (the newspaper I invented for *The Street Philosopher*) in *The Devil's Acre*. There is one particular character from the first novel who I suspect might have another tale in him; Sam Colt's early life, also, is rife with hilarious and horrifying escapades.

Do you have any more historical figures on your hit list for future novels?

I'm currently working on a story that might well involve a couple of Impressionist painters, and some of the more colourful ▶

A Q & A with
Matthew Plampin *(continued)*

◄ figures from French radical politics of the late 1860s. I also have a long-standing ambition to write something about the magnificently strange artist Augustus John, who scandalised polite society in Edwardian England by living as a polygamous Romany-style gypsy, trailing around the countryside in a painted caravan.

What have you read and loved since the publication of *The Devil's Acre*?

In common with many others I greatly admired Hilary Mantel's *Wolf Hall*; I felt she reinvigorated a somewhat over-familiar story, making it fresh, compelling and profound. For the past few months I've been working my way through Emile Zola's Rougon-Macquart series, partly in preparation for a Paris-set story of my own, and have been captivated by the novels' unflinching confrontation with the realities and tragedies of mid-nineteenth century life. Also, as a committed *Moby-Dick* fan I was hugely impressed by Philip Hoare's *Leviathan*.

What are you working on at the moment?

As mentioned above, I'm a good way into a story set during the four-month siege of Paris that came at the end of the Franco-Prussian War of 1870-1, when the city was starved, bombarded and brought to the brink of ruin. At its centre is Hannah Pardy, an English-woman who comes to Paris on the eve of the siege in search of her twin brother Clement, a painter long resident in the city who has recently gone missing. Her intention is to collect her brother and escape back to England before the Prussian Army arrives; but when she tracks him down in the drinking dens of Montmartre, her plans undergo an abrupt change . . . ■

Not
The End

Go to channel4.com/tvbookclub for more great reads,
brought to you by Specsavers.

Enjoy a good read with